F●REIGN AFFAIRS

Wide open spaces...

Men of the land...

The world's most eligible men!

Dreaming of a foreign affair? Then, look no further!
We've brought together the best and sexiest men the
world has to offer, the most exciting, exotic locations
and the most powerful, passionate stories.

This month, in *Western Weddings*, we bring back two
best-selling novels by Day Leclaire and Susan Fox.
Whether they like it or not, these rugged ranchers
are about to find themselves tamed! And from now
on, every month in **Foreign Affairs** you can be
swept away to a new location – and indulge in a little
passion in the sun!

Next month there's sizzling seduction in:
ISLAND PLEASURES
by Susan Napier & Caroline Anderson
Don't miss it!

DAY LECLAIRE

Day Leclaire and her family live in the midst of a maritime forest on a small island off the coast of North Carolina. Despite the yearly storms that batter them, and the frequent power outages, they find the beautiful climate, superb fishing and unbeatable seascape more than adequate compensation. One of their first acquisitions upon moving to Hatteras Island was a cat named Fuzzy. He has recently discovered that laps are wonderful places to curl up and nap – and that Day's son really was kidding when he named the hamster Cat Food.

Don't miss Day's captivating new book *The Bride Price* in Tender Romance™ – available April 2002!

SUSAN FOX

Susan Fox lives with her youngest son, Patrick, in Des Moines, Iowa, USA. A lifelong fan of westerns and cowboys, she tends to think of romantic heroes in terms of stetsons and boots! In what spare time she has, Susan is an unabashed couch potato and movie fan. She particularly enjoys romantic movies, with lots of meaningful eye contact between hero and heroine! She also reads a variety of romance novels – with guaranteed happy endings – and plans to write many more of her own.

Susan Fox loves to hear from readers! You can write to her at: PO Box 35681, Des Moines, Iowa, 50315, USA.

Look out for *Her Forbidden Bridegroom* by Susan Fox, in Tender Romance™, available July 2002.

western weddings

DAY LECLAIRE & SUSAN FOX

UNTAMED PASSIONS, WAY OUT WEST!

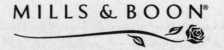
MILLS & BOON®

MILLS & BOON and MILLS & BOON with the Rose Device are registered trademarks of the publisher.
Harlequin Mills & Boon Limited,
Eton House, 18-24 Paradise Road, Richmond, Surrey, TW9 1SR

Western Weddings © Harlequin Enterprises II B.V., 2002

The Nine-Dollar Daddy and *Wild at Heart*
were first published in Great Britain by
Harlequin Mills & Boon Limited in separate, single volumes.

The Nine-Dollar Daddy © Day Totton Smith 1999
Wild at Heart © Susan Fox 1997

ISBN 0 263 83185 X

126-0302

Printed and bound in Spain
by Litografia Rosés S.A., Barcelona

western weddings

THE NINE-DOLLAR DADDY

WILD AT HEART

THE NINE-DOLLAR DADDY

DAY LECLAIRE

To Gillian Green, editor extraordinaire, who came up with the concept for this series and was generous enough to include me.
Thanks Gillian!

PROLOGUE

"CLASS is dismissed," the teacher announced. "Have a good spring vacation. Oh, and Hutch Lonigan? I'd like to see you before you leave."

Uh-oh. He could tell from her tone that she wasn't happy. A stream of hulking seventh-graders filed out, flicking him quick, amused glances. Of course, they always looked at him that way. As a ten-year-old daring to invade their territory, he was often treated with a mixture of scorn, suspicion and occasionally open dislike.

Stacking his books in a neat pile on his desk, he slipped from his seat and approached Mrs. Roon. "Yes, ma'am?" The teacher shuffled some papers. *She's nervous*, he realized. Okay. Maybe that would work to his advantage. Settling his glasses more firmly on his nose, he fixed her with a cool, direct gaze. That particular look always seemed to bother people. "I hope there isn't anything wrong." He didn't phrase it as a question.

She glanced at him quickly, then away. Flipping open a folder, she thumped her index finger against a neatly printed set of papers. "It's about your proposed science experiment."

Uh-oh. He'd been afraid of that. "Yes?"

"It's... You must admit, it's a bit unorthodox."

Nothing wrong with that. He waited, allowing his silence to weigh on her.

Mrs. Roon cleared her throat, leafing through the papers in his file as though they held the words she so desperately sought. "I'd like you to consider choosing a different subject."

"No."

"Hutch…"

Her voice had softened, grown motherly. He thrust out his chin another inch. He already had one mother. And she *never* used that pitying tone on him. Not ever. "No," he repeated.

"I understand why you want to conduct this experiment. But it's not acceptable. You must see that?"

"It's a logical approach to resolve a problem that no one else has been able to correct."

"Meaning your mother."

"She's not logical." He ticked his points off on his stubby fingers. "She doesn't see the problem. Therefore she's unlikely to attempt a solution. This experiment will remedy that."

"I'm sorry, Hutch. But I can't authorize your project. At least, not without her agreement."

He balled his hands into fists, then realizing how much they gave away, shoved them into his pockets. "*No!* If she knows about it, the results will be compromised."

Mrs. Roon sighed. "I'm afraid my decision's final. Without your mother's written permission, you'll have to choose another project. Even with her permission, I'm not certain I'd approve. It's too…too…" She gave a helpless shrug. "You're an intelligent boy. And it's a sweet, noble thought. But you must see that it's not appropriate?"

She was using that tone again. He pressed his lips tightly together and continued to glare. "Is that your final word?"

"Yes, Hutch. I'm afraid it is." She closed the folder and slid it across her desk toward him. "We're off these next two weeks for spring break. Take that time to choose another project."

"And if I refuse?"

"Then I'll speak to your mother about it."

"You realize you're not giving me any choice."

"I'm sorry," she repeated.

"Me, too," he muttered beneath his breath. "It's been nice working with you, Mrs. Roon."

Picking up the folder, he returned to his desk. He stood and stared at the tidy stack of books, his brain working at a furious rate.

Mrs. Roon wouldn't change her mind and he couldn't risk his mother's finding out about his experiment. With those two premises a given, he analyzed his predicament. In his mind, the problem formed the trunk of a massive tree, the various solutions growing from it into a huge network of crisscrossing branches. It took only a moment to settle on one of the more intriguing choices.

A tiny smile played around his mouth. It was a thin branch, one way off by itself. A very shaky limb indeed. Risky to climb. But the potential results... They far outweighed that risk.

Turning, he took one final look at his teacher. "Thank you, Mrs. Roon. I'll take care of it." Picking up his empty backpack, he settled it over his shoulders.

"I'm glad, Hutch," she said with a huge, relieved smile. "Aren't you taking your books home with you?"

"No need."

She laughed at that, the sound a little too high-pitched. He made most people nervous, though he'd never understood why. Smart must scare some adults—at least when it was a kid being smart.

"I guess not," she said. "You probably have them all memorized anyway."

"Most of them," he agreed, heading for the door. "Goodbye, Mrs. Roon," he added as an afterthought. He didn't look at her again, his mind already busy listing what he'd have to accomplish over the next sixteen days to achieve his goal. It was a daunting agenda. But then, he always did love a good challenge. He closed the school-room door with a decisive click.

And finding his mom a husband would undoubtedly be the greatest challenge of all.

CHAPTER ONE

Equipment/Items Required For Experiment:
1. Find perfect man—see ad and check Mom's schedule.
2. Obtain contract/agreement for services.
3. Prepare list for "love" experiments.

HUTCH stopped in the middle of the sidewalk in front of the bright yellow house and stared up at it. Glancing at the newspaper ad, he double-checked the address. Unfortunately, it was correct. The numbers matched. Carefully refolding the ad, he returned it to his back pocket. Jeez. Yellow Rose Matchmakers on Bluebonnet Drive. How corny could you get? Even the picket-fenced house looked silly, all yellow and white with a girly mailbox covered in painted roses. His mother would love it. He hated it. It left him feeling even more out of place than the first time he'd walked into the seventh grade and had everyone eye him as if he was some sort of freak.

Unlatching the white gate, he followed the walkway to the porch steps, stomping up the six wooden risers. Stomping eased his tension. It was a guy thing and doing guy things always helped when you were stuck in a "girl" kind of place. A door barred his entrance, frosted glass preventing him from seeing inside.

Taking a deep breath, he shoved open the door and stepped across the threshold. To his surprise, it didn't seem much like an office at all, but like a real house. The overwhelming scent of flowers made him wrinkle his nose and he grimaced at the cause—a huge floral arrangement perched on a nearby table. Man, how did they stand it? They needed to get some dogs and cats in here to help cut

8

the odor. He peered around, his attention snagged by a desk that occupied a room off the entranceway. Relief surged through him. Desks meant business.

He didn't look left or right, just focused on his goal— the expanse of wood with a nameplate on it that read Receptionist. An old lady stood behind the desk, frowning at a computer printout. Not a good sign. Beside her hovered a man and woman, whispering to each other. The man held a camera while the woman clutched a notepad. They gave him a cursory, dismissive glance. That was okay. He'd gotten used to that sort of reaction.

Setting his jaw, he reached into his pocket and yanked out a fistful of crumpled bills, along with a handful of change. He slapped the money onto the glass-covered top. A quarter rolled toward the old lady, stopping shy of the edge of the desk. It was a whole nine dollars and eighty-four cents. A pitiful amount, but it was his life's savings and he'd worked darned hard to get even that much.

"I want to buy as many dates as I can with this," he announced loudly.

That got everyone's attention. The man and woman stopped whispering and stared at him in sudden, predatory interest. The receptionist put down her computer printout to study him. Eyes as piercing blue as his own fixed on him and one fine white brow arched upward. "Kind of young, aren't you, sonny?"

Warmth bled into his cheeks and he scowled. He didn't like people making fun of him. He got enough of that at school. "It's for my mom. She needs a man and I want the best one you got."

Just like that, her eyes changed. The blue grew as warm and sunny as a hot San Antonio sky. "Do you now?" she murmured. Beside her, a flashbulb went off.

Poking a hand into his back pocket, he came up with the carefully folded ad. He spread it next to his money. He saw the Yellow Rose Matchmakers logo. As always, it cheered him. Yellow roses. It was a good sign. As good an omen as the huge bouquet of yellow roses decorating the old lady's desk. It even made him more tolerant of the stink. "I'd like the San Antonio Fiesta Special. Please," he added as an afterthought.

"Does your mom know you're here?" the woman with the notepad questioned.

"No. It's a birthday present. A *surprise* birthday present."

The receptionist inclined her head. "Oh, I don't doubt it'll be that." For a long moment, she continued to fix him with her intense blue gaze, weighing, examining, scrutinizing. He returned her look boldly. At long last, satisfaction eased her expression and a broad smile slipped across her mouth. She checked the hallway leading to the back of the agency. "Ty?" she called. "I could use your help."

Hutch didn't hear the man approach. One minute the doorway was empty and the next it was overflowing with a huge, broad male. "What's up?" he asked in a voice that rumbled like a distant storm.

"He's my grandson," the old lady explained in an undertone. "He'll take good care of you and your mom."

It required every ounce of determination for Hutch to keep his sneakers planted on the oak floorboards instead of plowing at light speed in the direction of the nearest exit. He hadn't anticipated this!

"I'd appreciate it if you'd do me a favor," she said to Ty, casting a meaningful glance toward the woman with the notepad and the man with the camera. "Maria and Wanda are out to lunch and I'm conducting business. I need you to get this young man started on our San Antonio Fiesta special."

The man's pale green gaze switched from the receptionist to pierce Hutch. "Come again?" he asked softly.

"Help him fill out an application for his mother." Another flashbulb lit up the room. "Please."

"Willie—"

"It's not that hard, Ty." She slapped a multipaged form

onto the desk. "Use my office. Have him answer these questions as best he can. Once you're done, we'll run his mother through the computer and see who we get for a match."

"I need a good one," Hutch inserted determinedly. "The best one in there."

Willie smiled. "I'll make sure of it personally. Go with Ty and he'll help with the forms."

Hutch slid a longing glance toward the door leading to freedom. He could either make a break for it and run on home or he could go with the human mountain. He weighed his choices for an endless nanosecond. Then, settling his glasses more firmly on the bridge of his nose, he nodded at the man. "Let's go," he said.

Ty took the application from Willie and enclosed it in the biggest hand Hutch had ever seen. He checked out the man's feet. Jeez. They were every bit as huge. He'd better be careful where he stood. One misstep and he'd be flatter than an amoeba squashed between glass slides. Without another word of acknowledgment, the man started down the hallway. Hutch trotted cautiously behind.

Opening a door, The Mountain waved the application toward a pair of cushioned chairs set at angles in front of a desk. "Have a seat."

A computer overwhelmed half the broad wooden surface, putting Hutch at his ease. Sidling into the office, he chose the chair closest to the door. His feet dangled ridiculously and he folded them cross-legged beneath him, not caring if his shoes dusted up the cushions. He shot a hard look at the man, daring him to comment. Silence reigned for a full two minutes.

"Why don't you want to help me?" Hutch finally asked.

"I don't work here. I guess you could call me a silent partner."

"Oh." He hadn't offered the expected answer and Hutch took a moment to digest it. "Why did the old lady—"

"Her name's Willie Eden. She's the owner."

"Why'd Miss Willie ask you to help me, then?"

"Like she said, I'm her grandson. I check over the business every so often to make sure it's running smoothly. Today was my checkup day."

"Bummer."

A slow smile built across the man's lean face. "My thoughts exactly."

"What was with the pictures that guy took of me?"

"More bad timing. They're reporters here to do a follow-up story on the agency. I suspect they found you perfect copy."

Hutch couldn't conceal his alarm. "Are they gonna put me in the paper? They can't! This is supposed to be a surprise."

"I'll take care of it."

To his astonishment, Hutch realized he believed the guy. There was something solid and dependable about him. Trustworthy. "So what now?"

"Now we do what Willie said." He frowned down at the application. "We fill out this questionnaire. It might be a bit tricky. A lot of these questions are personal."

"No problem. I know what I—my mom. I know what *my mom* wants." The man's pale green gaze latched onto Hutch again, as cutting and direct as a laser. He'd be a tough man to fool. In fact, Hutch suspected he'd be near impossible to fool. Best to play this part straight. "Okay... To be honest, I wouldn't mind if there was stuff about him I liked, too. I'll need to get along with him, same as Mom."

"Not an easy prospect, I suspect."

The Mountain's gaze continued to cut, burrowing in uncomfortably deep. How much could he see with those odd, piercing eyes? Hutch stirred nervously. "I won't be too picky, if that's what's worrying you. I can't afford to be." To his relief, the gaze eased enough for him to breathe a little better.

"What's your name, boy?"

"Hutch Lonigan. And before you bother asking, I'm ten."

"Ty Merrick. I'm thirty-one. Now that we're clear where we stand, why don't we get down to business." He picked up a pen. "What's your mother's name?"

"Cassidy Lonigan."

"Address and phone."

Hutch reluctantly supplied it. "But you're not gonna call her, are you?"

"That's up to Willie." That slow smile appeared again. "I'm just following orders today, remember?"

"Okay, I guess."

"What's your mom's age?"

"Old. That's why we have to get this taken care of fast." Ty's smile grew. "Don't suppose she's told you how old?"

"She's gonna be twenty-nine tomorrow. That means she doesn't have much time left. Jeez! She's already got her first couple of wrinkles." He gestured toward the corner of his eyes. "Before you know it, she's gonna be a total prune."

"Going downhill fast. Got it."

"Don't write that down!" Hutch considered a way around the problem. "Maybe if they go somewhere dark, her date won't notice. Write down that she likes romantic settings. They're dark, right? Movies and candlelight and stuff?"

Ty disappeared behind the form. "Good suggestion, kid. I'll make a note of it." His rumbling voice sounded oddly choked and the papers rustled. But a moment later, he lowered the form, looking as mountainlike as ever. "Next. Height and weight. Do you have a clue about those?"

"She's not fat. I guess she's okay in that department. And she's pretty tall for a girl. Bigger'n me," he added beneath his breath.

Of course, Ty heard. "Give yourself a chance, kid. Male

hormones tend to kick in later than women's. And she's got a whole passel of years on you.''

"I know. It's straight genetics." His chin inched out and he tried to tuck it back in. By Ty's expression, his attempt hadn't met with much success. "Either I got the height gene or I didn't. Since tall is a dominant trait, chances are in my favor that I'll shoot up one of these days.''

"Then there's not much point in worrying about it, is there?'' came the cool response. "Hair and eye color?''

"Brown and gray.''

"I assume it's her hair that's brown and her eyes that are gray?''

For the first time, Hutch felt the urge to laugh. It escaped as a tiny snort. "Yeah.''

"What a relief.'' An answering grin flickered across Ty's face.

"Wanna see a picture?''

"Sure.''

Hutch dug the photo from his pocket and handed it over, hiding a smirk at the mountain man's reaction. Ty's expression was sorta the way Hutch's got over a big bowl of ice cream. Course, his mom was a lot better than ice cream. Even the kids at school thought so. If they had a contest for best-looking mom, he'd win hands down.

Without a word, Ty returned the photo and picked up the application form again. "Occupation?''

Hutch frowned in thought. "I think she's a waitress this week.''

"This week?''

"She takes what she can get, okay? She works really hard. It's not like she has a husband or anything to help pay the bills.''

Ty held up his hands—long-fingered, hard-worn hands. Hands like his mom's, only a lot bigger. It helped ease Hutch's distress to see the evidence of a man branded by work. "Easy, buster. I'm just asking the questions on the application. I'm not judging. Got it?''

Hutch nodded, aware he'd revealed too much of himself to this man. He'd have to watch that. "What else do you need to know?"

"Marital status. Children. Type of residence."

Hutch took a deep breath. "We live in an apartment. She's single. Lonnie—he was my dad—took off five years ago." He shrugged. "I guess I shoulda said divorced. The papers came through a while after he left. As for children…I'm it. So the guy won't have to worry about having any sniveling brats around. It's just the two of us and I won't give him any trouble."

Ty lowered his gaze at the telling comments. "I'm sure you won't." Poor kid. Calling his father by his given name. Did he realize how desperate he sounded to find a replacement? Doubtful. The boy had it all figured out…or thought he did.

"Okay. What's the next question?" Hutch demanded.

Ty flipped to the second page. "What would her ideal partner be like? Any idea?"

"A cowboy."

"Come again?"

"Or a rancher."

"You're kidding."

"Well, it's the only kind she hasn't tried yet."

Uh-oh. "Tried?"

"Yeah. Places we've lived and stuff."

Ty tapped his pen against the application form. It was the "and stuff" that bothered him. Did Hutch mean that the way it sounded? Had his mother tried out various types of men, seeking the perfect partner? Ty's mouth tightened. For some reason, it bothered him to consider that possibility, especially after seeing Cassidy Lonigan's wide, generous smile and the hint of vulnerability peeking from big gray eyes. "You move around a lot?"

"Have to. At first we were keeping up with Lonnie. Now Mom's trying to find us the perfect home."

To go with her perfect man? "I gather she hasn't found it yet?"

"Nope. That's why I decided to help. Her way isn't working."

"And you think this will?"

"You use that computer sittin' there, don't you?" At Ty's agreement, Hutch nodded in satisfaction. "Then it'll work. Now, what else do you need to know?"

Deciding a change of subject was in order, Ty asked, "Does she have any pet peeves?"

"April Mae."

"Excuse me?"

"That's the girl my dad ran off with. April Mae. Lonnie had to wait until she graduated from high school before leaving us and that peeved Mom a whole lot. I don't think the guy you pick oughta mention her cuz Mom'll have a thing or two to say on the subject. And none of it'll be good."

"I imagine."

"Is that it? Are we finished?"

"Not quite." Ty frowned, running a hand across his jaw-line. He didn't like having the boy answer these questions. They'd already discussed some pretty intimate issues. Unfortunately, it was about to get a whole hell of a lot more intimate. "Now for the tough part."

Hutch practically shot off the chair. "You're kidding! You mean all those other questions were supposed to be easy?"

Ty offered a sympathetic smile. "'Fraid so. It gets a little more personal from here."

"*More* personal? What else can they want to know? You mean like…like…" An expression of abject horror crept across Hutch's face. "No way! That's disgusting. My mom doesn't *do* that sorta stuff."

Ty buried his amusement. She had to have done it at one point or another since the evidence sat glaring straight at him. Not that he'd mention that small detail to Hutch. He was a smart kid. It would occur to him in time. "You know…this would be easier if we could get her input. You sure you can't bring her here for her birthday? We could ask all these questions and get a better sense—"

"No! She won't do it if—" Hutch broke off, his face reddening.

Ty's amusement faded. "Please. Don't stop there. You don't think she'd agree if she knew what you were up to?" Great. Just what his grandmother needed. More trouble. He leaned across the desk, shoving a bud vase aside. The single yellow rose it contained trembled at the rough treatment. "Look, kid. If it's not something she wants, why give it to her?"

The boy's youthful chin jutted out again and Ty released his breath in a slow sigh. If the kid wasn't careful, someone would take that jaw as a challenge and peg it with a fist. Not that Hutch would give up. He was a scrapper. Too bad he didn't have the size to back his attitude. It would save him a few hard knocks.

"She may not want it," Hutch announced, "but she's gonna get it anyway."

"I'm sure she'll appreciate that." The boy flushed at Ty's dry tone. "Face facts, kid. If you aren't able to answer the questions, I can't run her profile. So either you answer or she does. Which is it going to be?"

Hutch's face screwed up in distaste. "Oh, man. This is *not* good. What other questions are there?"

Ty glanced at the form. "Strengths, weaknesses, general interests and hobbies. Personality type. Goals and ambitions. And then she's supposed to describe herself." The boy appeared nonplussed. A first, Ty was willing to bet.

"Well, shoot…" Hutch released a gusty breath, his bewilderment rapidly dissipating. "Okay. Does your phone have a hold or mute button?"

Ty checked. "Both."

"And does it have a speaker button?"

"Yes."

"Perfect. May I use it for a sec?"

Ty shoved the phone across the desk. "Be my guest."

Picking up the receiver, Hutch rapidly punched in a se-ries of numbers. "Hey, Mom? It's me. You on your way to work?" He waited a moment, listening. "Oh, good. I'm putting you on speaker, okay?"

Hutch stabbed a button and a voice sweeter than a honey-coated Georgia peach filled the room. "…sweetpea, I don't mind."

"You're not supposed to call me that, remember?"

"Sorry, sweet—Hutch. So what's up? Where are you?"

"I'm at a friend's house and need some help. I'm work-ing on a science project for school and—"

"A friend?" The excitement in her voice was painfully apparent, lacing the words with a warmer, heavier note of maternal concern. "Have I met him? Or is it a her?"

"Him. No, you haven't met. About this project—"

"What's his name?"

Hutch exhaled noisily. "His name is Ty Merrick. Mom. Pay attention. This is important."

"I'm sorry, sweet—Hutch. How can I help?"

"We're doing a personality survey for this science ex-periment and I need to ask you a bunch of questions."

"Oh…" There was a momentary pause. "Will anyone realize it's me?"

"It's confidential," Ty murmured to Hutch.

"Is that you, Ty? Gracious. You sound all grown up."

Hutch started. "The kids in my class are a lot older than me, Mom. You know that. Ty's…really big."

"Oh, dear. Was I being rude? Sorry about that, Ty. I hope I didn't embarrass you."

His name came across the phone line as warm and gentle as a sigh. The way she said "Tah" wrapped around him. It wasn't a Texas accent. Perhaps he'd been more accurate about that Georgia peach than he realized. Suddenly, he had the urge to meet a leggy twenty-nine-year-old with brown hair just a shade shy of black and gray eyes that

shone like silver. To see if up close and personal the eyes—
with the tiny wrinkles in the corners that Hutch found so
disturbing—were as intensely appealing as her voice.

Apparently, he'd waited too long to respond. Her breath
caught and she said, "I did embarrass you. I'm *so* sorry,
Ty. I didn't mean—"

"You didn't embarrass me." It took an instant for the
soft reassurance to reach her—soft, so she wouldn't realize
he was a man, not a child. "I was trying to figure out where
your accent was from."

"Oh." Sunshine filled her voice, breaking through the
clouds of uncertainty. "I'm from the good ol' goober state
of Georgia."

"Goober?" he questioned, intrigued.

She chuckled, and a picture of her generous smile filled
his mind. Darn that photo! One look and he'd been a goner.
"That's what they call peanuts back there. We might be
the Empire State, but we're really a bunch of goobers."

Hutch stirred. "Mom. Can we ask you questions? Do
you mind?"

"Not at all. Fire away, sugar."

"Okay. I'm gonna put you on hold for a sec so me and
Ty can pick the questions."

She laughed. "You don't want to discuss them in front
of me?"

"Can't. It might corrupt the results."

Her laughter blossomed, as rich and smooth as her voice.
Ty clenched his jaw against the sound, not quite believing
the effect it was having on him. "We can't allow that, now
can we? Go ahead and talk. I'll wait."

"Thanks, Mom." Hutch stabbed the hold button and
frowned at Ty. "You almost gave it away."

"I don't like deceiving people. Next time don't rope me
in to your lie. I won't tolerate it. Are we clear about that?"

Abashed, Hutch nodded. "Yes, sir. Sorry."

Ty gave him a stern look. "Okay. Let's get this done."
He tossed a list of character traits across the desk toward

the boy. "I need some idea of what she considers her personality type. Read your mom the list and have her choose the ones that best describe her."

Hutch frowned at the sheet. "I could probably figure these out."

"It's better if she did it."

Apparently, Hutch agreed because he leaned forward and punched the hold button. "You there, Mom?"

"Right here."

"Okay. I'm going to read off a list of personality traits and you pick the ones that fit you best. Got it?"

"I think I can handle that." By the subtle amusement coloring her words, Ty suspected she was well accustomed to Hutch's high-handedness. As soon as her son finished rattling off the list, she said, "You can definitely mark me down as sentimental and affectionate. I tend to be huggy," she confessed, probably for his sake, Ty realized.

"*Real* huggy," Hutch inserted.

"I also consider myself extroverted. I like jobs that bring me in contact with people. And I'm pretty self-assured. I'm going to do what I think best, regardless of anyone else's opinion." She hesitated. "What else hits home? I guess you could call me adventurous, since we move around so much. But romantic is definitely out."

"Aw, come on, Mom. What about all those smelly bubble baths and candles? Those are romantic."

"Those, my poor misguided son, are feminine, not romantic. I can enjoy 'girl stuff', as you like to call it, without having it involve a man or romance. It's for my own pleasure, not to entice a husband."

Ty shot Hutch a disgruntled look. Obviously the woman had been badly burned by her ex. Chances were excellent that she wasn't the least interested in the services the Yellow Rose had to offer. Just his luck. And just Willie's luck, too. What the hell were they going to tell the reporters if Cassidy refused to cooperate? "Remind me to wring your neck when we're done here,'' he told the boy in an under-tone.

A hint of red crept into Hutch's cheeks, but other than that one telling sign, he acted as though he hadn't heard. ''Go on, Mom. Any others?''

''Let's see.... I'm tolerant, practical—''

''No way.''

''Sure I am, Hutch.'' Utter bewilderment laced her voice. ''Why would you think I'm not practical?''

Hutch snorted. ''If you were practical, you wouldn't keep givin' stuff away. You wouldn't let our landlady help herself to clippings off your rosebushes any time the mood took her. And you woulda sued Lonnie when he stole all our money and ran off with April Mae in your new pickup. She's not practical,'' Hutch repeated to Ty. Otherwise he wouldn't be sitting here finding her a date, his tone added.

''I sure wish your daddy hadn't done that,'' she admitted in a low voice. ''I'm afraid it set a bad example. And it left hard feelings between the two of you.''

Cassidy's simple observation threatened to rip through Ty's callused hide. It came across as unbearably painful. He had to get this show on the road and this kid on his way. Fast. Before he formed an attachment to a honey-warm voice and a prickly ten-year-old brainiac. He punched the hold button before Hutch could get to it. ''Let's move this along, kid. And stop coloring the results. Just ask the questions, let her answer them and move on to the next. Got it?''

''Yeah. I got it.'' Hutch sounded as subdued as his mother. ''And so's you know... It wasn't Lonnie's running off that left hard feelings. It was what he said on his way out the door. He hasn't called since he took off and...'' The chin wobbled for a telling instant. ''And he made Mom cry. The next guy she marries isn't gonna do that. He's gonna make her laugh.''

Ty stirred, suffering from a nasty case of empathy. The kid just wanted his mother to be happy. Too bad he thought a man could do that for her. "Look, boy," he said gently, "you don't find happiness by getting married. You find it inside yourself first and then share it with others. Sometimes through marriage. And sometimes through friendship."

Hutch folded his arms tight across his narrow chest. "You sound like my mom."

That didn't surprise him. Cassidy sounded like a level-headed woman—unlike her stubborn son. "Maybe you ought to listen to her."

"Maybe," the boy muttered. "What's the next question?"

Ty scanned the page. Damn. "I'll read off this particular bunch, if you don't mind."

"Okay."

"And you're not going to interrupt?"

Hutch shrugged. "Not unless she gets it wrong."

Ty bit back his response and punched the hold button. "Ms. Lonigan?"

"Still here, Ty." To his relief, she sounded a lot more chipper.

"These next few are going to be a bit personal. Just answer them the best you're able."

"Go ahead."

"What's your favorite way to spend an evening?" He found himself unexpectedly curious to hear the answer.

"That's an easy one," Cassidy replied. "I'd spend it in a hot, scented bubble bath with a bunch of those stinky candles Hutch hates so much. Oh! And a good book."

Ty blinked at the image his mind created, the fantasy made easy thanks to one slightly creased photo. He pictured mounds of frothy bubbles clinging to white silky skin and dark hair piled on top of her head, with damp strands surrounding a piquant face. Huge, somber gray eyes with a hint of mischief sparkling in their depths would peek at him from the middle of the tub. And candlelight would catch in the bubbles and play across her shoulders, emphasizing the purity of her skin. He'd swipe a speck of foam from the tip of her upturned nose before leaning down to—

"Is that all your questions?" Cassidy interrupted.

Ty snatched up the application. *Keep your mind on business, son*! "Sorry. I have a few more. What are your strengths and weaknesses?"

"Boy, those are tough ones. I guess I'd say I'm a hard worker." She'd probably had to be, Ty acknowledged. "As for weaknesses…"

"You're too generous," Hutch spoke up.

"That's not a weakness, sugar." There was a brief pause and then she sighed. "To be perfectly honest, I guess I'm too darn proud. I want to take care of myself and Hutch so I don't have to depend on anyone ever again. Whatever I need, I plan to get for myself."

Ty considered her comment. No doubt her ex had a lot to do with her attitude. He could understand that. Cassidy Lonigan reminded him of Willie—a strong, determined woman, chock-full of passion and energy. He smiled. Hell, she should have been a Texan born and bred. She'd fit right in. "Next question. What's your idea of a perfect date?"

"Goodness, that's an odd one," she said with a trace of uncertainty. "You said this is for a science project?"

"Yes," Hutch injected hastily. "I'll explain it to you after it's done."

"Well…I guess a perfect date would be yellow roses and food." Her laugh eased across the line, stirring an odd sensation deep in Ty's gut. He could almost see her face light up, her expression filled with humor and spirit and character. "So long as you feed me, I'm happy."

"And the yellow roses?"

"I like them. They're…hopeful."

"She's got a thing for them," Hutch whispered. "That's why I picked this place."

"Makes sense," Ty muttered. At least, as much sense as any of this made.

"Listen, boys, I have to get ready for work. Are we almost finished here?"

"Just one more question," Ty said. "What are your goals and ambitions?"

"To raise my son the best I can," Cassidy answered promptly. "I'm saving to buy a house of our very own. A small place with a yard and a garden where I can plant yellow roses. A home where we can set down roots nice and deep. The permanent kind."

Ty understood all about roots. His family had lived in the San Antonio area for generations. The homestead he owned had been his father's and his father's before him—a long line of Merricks stretching into the past, their history and heritage planted so deep in Texas soil, they could never be yanked free. "Roots are good," he agreed.

"I'm glad you think so, Ty. That's my goal. To have a home, my roses, and most important of all, my family close by. I don't want or need another blessed thing beside that."

"Not even a husband?" he suggested.

"Gracious, no! *Especially* not a husband. What put that crazy idea in your head?"

Her vehement response exploded in the room. For a long moment, Ty sat quietly in his chair, struggling to control his temper. "I haven't a clue," he answered through gritted teeth. Heaven help him, he was going to kill the kid. Maybe he could step on him and claim he'd squashed the boy by mistake. "Thanks, Ms. Lonigan. I appreciate your taking the time to talk to us."

"You're certainly welcome. Hutch? When will you be home?"

"I'll be back in time for dinner, Mom." His voice held a nervous squeak that, fortunately, his mother didn't hear.

"Call if you're going to be late. And feel free to invite Ty if you'd like."

The instant the connection was broken, Ty leaned across the desk toward the boy. "Definitely not a husband?" he questioned softly. "*Definitely not?*"

Hutch waved a dismissive hand. "It's a temporary fix-ation. She has this thing about being independent right now. I'll take care of it." A nervous bravado crept into his ex-pression. "How come you stopped the interview? That wasn't all the questions."

"Aside from the fact that it's an exercise in futility?"

Hutch cleared his throat. "Yeah. Aside from that."

"The last one would have tipped our hand, which might be for the best, all things considered."

"No! I—"

"So, you'll have to answer it," Ty cut in. "Assuming we're continuing with this nonsense."

"I'm still sittin' here, aren't I?" Before Ty could argue that particular assertion, Hutch asked, "Okay, what's the last one?"

As pointless as the final question seemed, it would com-plete the damned form and get this mule-headed kid on his way. "What do you think your mother is seeking in a re-lationship?"

"What do you mean?"

"What does she want from the guy she dates?"

"Oh. That's easy." Hutch offered an endearing grin. "You can tell she doesn't know it yet. But she wants mar-riage."

OPERATION HUSBAND
by Hutch Lonigan
Progress Report

The Mountain wasn't very happy with me. Said I was keeping secrets and better cut it out. Well...yeah, I'm keep-ing secrets! How else am I going to get a dad? Anyway, he promised to have a man available for Mom by tomorrow for her birthday. Once that happens I can get the experi-ment going. The computer better pick a good one. I might not get another shot at this. I still have to set things up at school and may have to put Plan B into action. Hope not. But Mom comes first! And since she won't take care of this herself...somebody's got to take charge.

Looks like I'm it.

CHAPTER TWO

Equipment and Procedures to Organize:
*1. Take Mom to Yellow Rose Matchmakers without her
catching on.*
2. Have the computer do its magic.
*3. Check the stats on the match. (Note: Make sure this
guy's not a loser.)*
*4. Convince Mom to go along with it. (Sure wish wishes
were scientific!)*

CASSIDY calculated the figures for the fourth time. Not that
it changed anything. The bottom line on her checking-
account register still added up to the same pitiful amount
as before—an amount too small to meet all her current
financial demands. She clenched her fingers around the tiny
nub of a pencil her boss, Freddie, had been wasteful enough
to trash, her knuckles turning white from the strain. What
the heck was she going to do?

A lock of thick, dark brown hair drifted into her eyes
and she pushed it away with hands that trembled. Darn it
all! Why couldn't she have curls instead of hair so painfully
straight not even a rubber band would hold it? At least curls
could be confined or cropped short. At least curls would—
Stop it, she ordered herself briskly. *Stop wasting time on
foolishness and focus on the serious problems.* There were
certainly enough of them to keep her occupied.

She scowled at the check register again. Okay. The final
payment on Hutch's computer would come first, she decided. It had to. That computer was his future. She tapped
the pencil on the scarred kitchen table. And maybe if she
spoke to Mrs. Walters, explained that she'd pick up an extra

27

shift or two and get the money together by the end of the week, the landlady would let the rent slide a few more days. She might…especially if Cassidy bribed her with another clipping from her poor rosebushes.

Okay, what next? The utilities. She'd dole out a few precious dollars on her electric bill. That way, the computer would have a place to live and the juice to run it. Let's see…next on the list would have to be food. She perked up a bit. Perhaps Freddie would have some leftovers from the restaurant she could take home. That might help stretch their pennies. And she could give up all the extras. No more instant coffee. Skip the odd lunch. Tape up the hole in her sneaker. Not get sick or twist any more ankles. She could get by. Sure she—

"Everything okay, Mom?"

She glued a bright smile on her face. "Just fine, sweetie. Why?"

Hutch perched on the edge of the chair across from her. "Your eyes are that funny color again."

She stared at him in bewilderment. "What funny color?"

"Like pencil lead." He glanced at the open check register. "What's wrong?"

"Nothing. Everything's great." He didn't believe her, not that his skepticism surprised her. He often saw things no one else noticed. "Really," she insisted, "we're fine."

"I can tell if there's something wrong," he explained patiently. "When you laugh, your eyes are a pretty silver. But when you're upset, they look like lead. So, what's wrong?"

"Oh." Crud. "I hadn't realized."

Smile! she ordered herself sternly. *Think of something happy*. She forcibly summoned a picture of Hutch right after she'd given birth to him. Even then, he'd displayed an intense curiosity that was such an innate part of his character. He'd peered up at her with huge blue eyes and she'd known in that instant that she'd do anything for him…sacrifice anything. He'd been the one bright spot in months of fear and desperation. He'd made everything worthwhile and just thinking about him eased her tension.

Cassidy smiled. "How's that?"

"Hey! They're silver again."

"It must have been the light," she teased.

"I guess." He kicked the table leg. "You won't forget about tomorrow, right? You need to get off work for a couple of hours so I can take you for your birthday surprise."

She frowned, fingering the checkbook. "I don't know, Hutch...."

"You promised, Mom. Please."

"And a promise is a promise," she conceded with a sigh. "Okay, sweetpea. I'll talk to Freddie." And to Mrs. Walters. And to the electric company. They'd all understand. She drew an anxious breath. There wasn't any choice. They had to.

"He wants a father."

Willie nodded. "Most boys do, Ty. Is that so bad?"

Ty unhitched his shoulder from the support pillar he'd been leaning against and turned to face his grandmother. She sat at the far end of the porch in a large wooden swing, her favorite spot at the Yellow Rose to "ruminate" as she called it. "Not for Hutch. But I doubt Cassidy feels the same way. She sounded as though she'd had her fill of men." An understatement if ever he'd uttered one. "What if she kicks up a fuss because we've encouraged this kid's scheme?"

"Is that the impression she gave when you spoke? Did she seem like a troublemaker?"

Ty frowned. No. He'd sensed Cassidy Lonigan was a warmhearted woman devoted to her son—a woman thrilled to her tippytoes that Hutch had a friend. A friend she'd immediately invited over for dinner. "She'll date whomever the computer picks. She won't like it, but she'll do it for the boy."

"There you are, then. Problem solved."

"It's not solved, Willie." He frowned, not quite sure why he was involving himself in the Lonigan match. He had more than enough work waiting at the ranch. Nice, strenuous, mind-numbing jobs. The sort that didn't leave room for thoughts of Georgia peaches and porcupine boys. But Willie had raised him from the time he was a snot-nosed whelp. He owed her more than he could ever hope to repay. Investing in her company and checking up on her business interests periodically was a small way of showing his appreciation. "Is it wise to encourage this kid's scheme when it's clear his mother isn't interested?"

"Perhaps she'll discover the man of her dreams," Willie replied complacently, setting the porch swing in motion. "That *is* what we do, Ty."

He released his breath in a gusty sigh. "You've been borrowing Wanda's rose-tinted glasses, haven't you? I hate when you do that."

Willie chuckled. "Don't pick on Wanda. She's the best employee I have."

"That's open to debate."

"Just because she's a romantic—"

"That's not the objection I have to her and you darn well know it."

Willie brushed that aside. "It's not like we don't have a few romantic legends in our own family."

"Don't start that again," he warned.

"You're the most hardheaded man I know." Her snowy brows drew together, signaling her annoyance. "Do you really think I'd have told you about The Kiss if I didn't believe in it myself? What do you take me for? Some doddering old half-witted fool?"

"Yup." He joined his grandmother on the swing and slung an arm around her shoulders, plying her with the sense of humor he'd inherited from the Eden branch of the family. "I suspect you're one step away from a padded room with a beefy guard named Louie."

Willie clicked her tongue in exasperation. "Oh, go on with you. I'm serious. Because you haven't kissed the right woman yet doesn't mean she isn't out there wondering what the heckfire's keeping you."

"You've been feeding me this story since I was a baby," he objected. "When are you going to give it up?"

"Never! It was as true for your parents as it was for your grandfather and me. Just as it was true for his parents before him, and his before that. Mark my words. It'll happen to you, too."

Ty bit off a laugh. "One kiss and I'll know."

"Whether it's true love." She gave an adamant nod. "Yes, sir, you will. It's taking you a bit longer than it did the rest of us is all."

"I believe we were discussing Cassidy Lonigan's love life. Why don't we focus on that and keep me out of it?" He didn't wait for her to agree—which was probably just as well since it looked as though agreeing with him was the last thing likely to escape the sharp edge of her tongue. "That reporter's still sniffing around, isn't she?"

"She was…intrigued by young Hutch. She was particularly intrigued by the fact that we let him buy a date for only nine dollars."

Ty didn't like the sound of that. "She didn't think you were doing it as a publicity stunt, did she? I'd be happy to clarify the matter for her."

Willie waved off his concern. "Yes, the question was raised. And I believe Maria set the woman straight in short order."

Somewhat appeased, Ty asked, "So this reporter's going to follow up on the dates the Yellow Rose arranges?"

Willie shrugged. "Probably."

"And when nothing good comes from it? What if Cassidy rejects the candidates the computer chooses?"

"Why don't we worry about that if it happens?"

Something in his grandmother's tone had him fixing her with a sharp-eyed gaze. She sounded almost…complacent.

That had to mean trouble. "Why don't we worry about it now. Perhaps we can come up with some alternate ideas if the worst happens."

"You're such a pessimist, Ty."

"I'm realistic. Cassidy Lonigan had one bad marriage. From what the boy said, she's tried various other relationships without any success. So he's decided to take a hand in matters. That's not a formula guaranteed to yield positive results."

"Stop being so logical," Willie groused. "You're thinking with your head—"

"I certainly hope so."

"Yes, well, it's her heart we're concerned with, isn't it? That's what we've been hired to engage. Why don't you give the agency a chance before deciding it won't work?"

"Maybe I'd be more willing to go along if it wasn't for last month's foul-up. Does that ring a bell? When your dear employee kept matching everyone all by her lonesome? Wanda didn't even have the computer—" He broke off with a frown. "What did she call it?"

"George."

"She didn't even have *George* plugged in."

"Her success rate was phenomenal. You can't argue with that."

"Great, except for one small problem. Yellow Rose Matchmakers is billed as a *computerized* dating agency, remember?"

Willie dismissed that with another wave of her hand. "Minor details. The bottom line is…the agency made the matches and they all ended in matrimony. What makes you think this one won't?"

Ty's memory replayed a slow, husky Georgia drawl, the kind that slid all over a man before seeping deep inside. The kind that went with sultry nights, a large bed and hours of hot, sweet loving. "I gather the lady is running scared."

"Then we'll have to be certain we pick someone who'll break her in gently, won't we?"

Ty's mouth twitched. "You make her sound like a horse."

Willie nodded. "In a way, I suspect she's a lot like a mare who's had a rough first ride. It's our job to make sure her next experience is more satisfactory."

"Wrong."

"Wrong?" Her eyebrows winged upward. "How's that, boy?"

He leaned forward and planted a kiss on her tanned cheek. "Making sure her next dating experience is satisfactory is *your* job, not *ours*."

Willie simply smiled. "We'll see."

"Careful, Mom. Don't peek."

"Oh, Hutch. I'm going to trip. Is this blindfold *really* necessary?"

"I want it to be a surprise. And it won't be if you peek."

Cassidy chuckled. "I won't look, I promise. But you'll have to steer me. If I fall and break a leg, I won't be much good as a waitress." The words had barely escaped when her size ten sneakers tangled. "Dagnab it!"

Hutch helped prop her up. "Easy does it. I won't let you fall. Now stand here for a minute while I open the gate."

"There's a gate?"

She tried to catch a glimpse of where they were headed from beneath the voluminous bandanna that served as a blindfold. Not that she wanted to spoil Hutch's surprise. But she'd been wearing the darned thing ever since they'd gotten off the bus a few blocks back. It seemed a wise precaution to make sure she wasn't about to stumble over her own two feet again. With her luck, she'd end up having all five feet eight inches sprawled in a jumbled heap of arms and legs across a painfully hard sidewalk.

She wrinkled her nose a couple of times hoping it might edge the bandanna up a bit, but it remained stubbornly in place. Her son had tied the blindfold with the same thoroughness he gave most of his endeavors.

"Don't bother. I made it tight."

"Come on, sweetpea," she said with a sigh. "Stop teasing. Where are we?"

"At your birthday present. Okay. Now, here come some steps. Put your hand on the banister. That's it. And hold on to me with your other hand. One more step and we'll be on the porch."

An atypical nervousness assailed her. If she'd considered herself the least bit psychic, she'd have thought something momentous was about to occur. Of course, she no longer indulged in such foolish fantasies. She'd learned that painful lesson years ago. "Whose house is this?"

"Not telling. Just stand there while I open the door."

"We can walk right in?" Her concern increased.

"Yup. They know me here." He helped her inside, then released her arm. "You wait by the flowers while I go get Miss Willie."

Cassidy heard the squeak of the door closing behind her, followed by a familiar, rumbly voice addressing Hutch. Where had she heard that distinctive intonation before? she wondered. A customer? A fellow tenant? A teacher? Instead of waiting for her son's return, she took a hesitant step forward and promptly tripped again. Strong arms closed around her—definitely not Hutch's arms. He swept her upward and the bandanna caught on his shirt button, slipping downward a fraction of an inch. The narrow gap afforded her a tantalizing glimpse of the man who held her.

He was impressively large, formed along the same lines as Texas—broad, bold and built to last. Taut sinew and lean, powerful muscles rippled along the ridged biceps beneath her palms as well as across the chest she was practically nuzzling. She dug her nose out of its resting place, but not before a clean, earthy scent filled her nostrils. Heavens to Betsy, but as they'd say back home…the man had a nice stink hanging on him.

He wasn't as handsome as Hutch's dad, Cassidy conceded. But then, Lonnie's good looks had only served to disguise the shallow person beneath. This man's features were blunt and distinctive, drawn with strong, sweeping lines. No question. He was all man, while Lonnie had been a boy when they'd first met and a boy when they'd last parted.

Easing her gaze upward, she found herself staring into the most intriguing pale green eyes she'd ever seen. They gathered her up, impaling her as they dug down deep— searching for a clue to the self she kept tucked safely away. *Slipping clear to her soul*, came the disconcerting thought.

Not safe, a warning voice rang in her head.

She instantly overreacted, a regrettable personality failing she'd yet to correct. She wriggled from the man's arms with more speed than grace, flailing for a brief instant as she fought to keep her limbs from tangling again. "Oops! Don't tell Hutch I saw!" she whispered hastily, yanking her blindfold into place.

She took another quick step backward, filled with an odd urgency to put as much distance between them as possible. She stumbled once more, still not quite secure in her footing. Instantly, his hand closed around her arm and she sensed the latent strength behind his hold.

"Are you okay?" he asked.

Not safe, the warning voice shrieked—louder, in case she hadn't heard clearly the first time.

"Oh, hush up," she muttered in exasperation.

She never listened to those smart-alecky inner voices anymore. They always got it wrong, starting with the time they told her going to bed with Lonnie was a good idea and ending on the day they urged her to fight April Mae for the "honor" of keeping her selfish jerk of a husband. After that disastrous occasion, she realized these were *dumb* inner voices instead of the clever, instinctive ones most people got, so she'd refused to listen further. Not that *they'd* stopped handing out bad advice.

"Excuse me?" Mr. Rumbly Voice said.

Oops. "Sorry. I wasn't talking to you. I was having a small personal argument."

"Uh-huh. You do that a lot?"

"No," she lied cautiously. "I was just arguing with myself. *Everybody* does it." She swept her arm through the air to indicate a whole horde of everybodies. The back of her hand connected with a resounding crack. Carefully, she lowered her arm and grabbed a gulp of air. When would she learn to keep her various body parts under control? "That was you, huh?"

"Yeah. That was me."

She swallowed at the tight tone. "Sorry about that. Sometimes I forget that I'm longer than I feel." She lowered a corner of the blindfold an inch, wincing at the bright red mark on Rumbly Voice's cheek. "You see, I always wanted to be small and dainty. So in my head, my reach is only about twenty-two or -three inches instead of—" She broke off at his incredulous expression.

"Oh, please," he insisted, "don't stop there."

Cassidy sighed. Why did people always look at her like she was crazy when she explained this? False body images were very common. They also caused a person to be a bit of a klutz, a fact she went out of her way to demonstrate with disgusting regularity. She cleared her throat. "I forget my reach is twenty-six inches instead of twenty-three. It's those extra three inches that hit you."

"I see. In that case, I'll make sure I stay clear of them."

And stay clear of you, he might as well have said. Like she hadn't already realized that. "Don't worry. I'll save you the trouble." She yanked the blindfold back into place. "Hutch?" she called. "Where are you, sweetpea?"

"Right here, Mom. Bring her in," Hutch added, apparently addressing ol' Rumbly Voice. "Willie's ready to run the form."

"What's going on?" she demanded.

"Relax, Ms. Lonigan."

Probably afraid if she tensed up, she'd haul off and slug

him again. A distinct possibility, she wanted to warn. All her life she'd struggled to project the image of a graceful Southern belle, like her Aunt Esther. To be small, dainty and gardenia sweet. To her dismay, she'd ended up tall and klutzy, with an unfortunate tendency to speak her mind, forgetting more often than not to lace it with the prerequisite honey. No steel magnolia was she. But, oh, how she longed to be.

"I'm relaxed," she assured him. "But I wouldn't object if you explained what's going on around here."

"Hutch has gone to a lot of trouble to set up this little surprise. I'm sure you don't want to spoil it."

She caught the subtle warning at the exact same instant she recalled where she'd heard those deep, earthy tones before. Lord, she hoped she was wrong. "Ty?" she murmured apprehensively.

"At your service."

Oh, crud. "I...I thought you were a friend of Hutch's."

"I am."

Double crud. "But he told me... I thought—"

"That I was a kid. Sorry about that."

He slid his hands behind her head and she kept carefully still. More than anything, she wanted to bolt. Instead, she held her ground, refusing to give in to ridiculous fears—not to mention a totally unwarranted attraction. She sniffed. It had to be his scent she found enticing because there sure wasn't much else she found attractive. Well...other than his size and interesting eye color. Oh! And his voice. She had a weak spot for deep, rich voices. "What are you doing, if you don't mind my asking?"

"I think we can dispense with this now," he replied, sweeping the blindfold from her face.

Now that she knew his identity, she couldn't resist staring at Ty. He was supposed to be a boy. He was supposed to be a friend of Hutch's. Instead, he was blatantly male. Uncomfortably male. Thoroughly male. And he knew more about the intimate details of her life than any man of recent acquaintance.

"Surprise, Mom," Hutch announced, drawing her attention. "Happy birthday!"

Relieved, she edged closer to her son. "What's up?" she questioned lightly.

For the first time, she realized there were others in the room besides her son and Ty. Next to Hutch stood a handsome, white-haired woman. Something about her bearing and looks suggesting a familial relationship with Ty. And off to one side hovered a man and woman, both watching her with uncomfortable intensity.

The older woman stepped forward and offered her hand. "Welcome, Ms. Lonigan. I'm Willie Eden, owner of Yellow Rose Matchmakers. Your son has purchased our services for your birthday present."

Uh-oh. "What services?" Cassidy asked, fighting to conceal her apprehension.

"We're a dating agency."

Damn. She pasted a delighted smile on her mouth, praying Hutch couldn't tell how horrified she was. "What...what a lovely surprise."

Beside her, Ty snorted softly. "Good save."

A flashbulb went off nearby and she blinked to clear her vision.

"Keep smiling," Ty warned beneath his breath. "They're reporters."

"Whose idea was this?" she questioned between gritted teeth.

"Your son's."

That changed everything. A more natural smile crept across her mouth and she enveloped Hutch in a hug. "Thank you, sugar."

"You don't mind, do you, Mom?"

She ruffled his pale blond hair. "Of course not," she lied gamely. "What a sweet idea. How in the world did you come up with it?"

"I saw their ad in the newspaper. It's the *Yellow Rose* agency, Mom. Get it? *Yellow roses*. And they use computers."

That explained Hutch's interest—if not what prompted this little venture. "You don't say. Computers, huh? I see why that would appeal. Very scientific."

"You can't lose. Miss Willie's gonna run your application now, and then we'll find out who your date is."

The older woman lifted an eyebrow. "Are you ready?"

Cassidy caught a hint of sympathy in Willie's voice. Apparently, the owner had sensed her lack of enthusiasm. Had she fooled anyone other than Hutch? She slid a quick glance in Ty's direction. Nope. Not likely she'd fool ol' Rumbly Voice. "I'm as ready as I'll ever be," she said with a wry smile.

Willie walked to the computer and punched a series of buttons. A minute later, the laser printer began humming, spitting out an initial page. "Well, my goodness. Will you look at this. It's found a ninety-nine percent match. I don't think I've ever seen that happen on a first try before."

"Who is it?" Hutch demanded. "Is he your best one?"

"A ninety-nine percent match suggests he's an excellent candidate. Can't get much better than that," she confirmed.

Hutch frowned. "I don't know. There's still that bad one percent. Could be a problem."

The next sheet scrolled out of the printer. "Okay. Here come the results. And the winner is..." Her eyes widened in dismay. "Oh, dear."

The reporter and photographer crowded closer, leaning over Willie's shoulder. "What's it say?" The reporter snatched the printout from Willie's hands and frowned. "Ty Merrick. Wait a minute. I know that name...." Like a hound dog tripping over a hot scent, her nose twitched. She pivoted toward Ty, and Cassidy half expected her to start baying as she honed in on her prey. "Hey! That's you."

"Willie! What the *hell* have you done?" Ty snatched

the paper from the reporter's grasp. "This can't be. There must be a mistake."

Cassidy pinched the sheet from between his two fingers to give it a quick look-see. No doubt Ty was right and there'd been an error. These things happened, especially with mechanical oddities like computers. It probably didn't say Ty Merrick at all. No doubt it listed a similar name like Rye Belleck or Sy Serrick or Tom Selleck. Hey! A girl could dream. Or maybe it wasn't her profile they'd run. Sure as shootin'. That's what must have…

She read through the paper three full times before conceding defeat. Texan rancher Ty Merrick was a ninety-nine percent ideal match for waitress Cassidy Lonigan. How that was possible, she couldn't quite figure. But there it sat, topping a full page of bewildering statistics, glaring at her in huge, bold, underscored black print.

Crud.

"There must be a mistake," Ty repeated. "I'm not even in the damn computer."

Willie cleared her throat. "Actually, that's not true. You see, we put you in there as a test case and I guess we forgot to take you out."

"Well, match her with the runner-up."

"There *is* no runner-up. Usually we have three or four close matches. But in this case, there's only one. You."

Hutch grinned. "Happy birthday, Mom. I bought you him." He pointed at Ty. "He's your present."

Oh, joy. "Gosh darn it! That's wonderful. I couldn't be happier." Not bad, she congratulated herself. Got that out without choking or being struck down by lightning. Amazing.

Ty cut through the people separating him from his grandmother and wrapped an arm around her shoulders. "Excuse us for a minute. Willie? We need to talk."

"Can't this wait?" she asked.

Ty regarded her through narrowed eyes. For a woman who never got flustered, his darling grandmother sure as hell looked flustered. "I'm afraid it can't." Cupping her elbow, he marched her across the room. The instant they were out of the reporter's hearing, he demanded, "What the *hell* do you mean, the computer chose me?"

"Now, Ty, don't get your knickers in a knot." Her nervousness had dissipated, replaced with a more typical aggression.

Ty folded his arms across his chest and fixed his grandmother with a cool gaze. "I don't wear knickers, Willie. I never have." The look she returned was every bit as cool as his. A genetic trait, he decided dryly. And an amazing recovery, in view of her earlier agitation. "Now explain how my profile showed up in your computer."

"You were a test case." A thread of defensiveness shot through her voice. "We entered your data when we were first setting up the computer so we could do some trial runs. I thought you'd been deleted."

"But I wasn't."

"No."

"Fine. Delete me now." For the first time in his entire life, he saw Willie blush. It was quite a riveting sight considering her brash personality. Flustered... And now blushing. Something was going on. And come hell or high water, he'd get to the bottom of it. "Willie—"

"I can't delete you," she stated bluntly.

"I'm sure there's a computer expert out there somewhere you can hire to remove the pertinent—"

She waved his remark aside. "It just takes a push of a button."

"Then push it."

"I would except..." She sighed. "Ty, the reporter saw. She knows you're Cassidy's match. I can't delete you now."

"Well, use one of the other names the computer gave you. There's always three or four matches."

"Like I said. Not this time. You were the only one. A ninety-nine percent match at that."

He could practically hear the bone-fracturing sound of a steel-jawed trap snapping closed around him. "Mind explaining how this happened?" he questioned with admirable restraint.

"I can't say. But it did and there isn't anything I can do to change it now." She planted her hands on her hips and stared him down, her clear blue eyes oddly reminiscent of Hutch Lonigan's. "I need you to date this woman."

"And if I say no?"

"That's your choice, of course. I can't force you."

Hah! Why use force when a little grand-maternal guilt would work, as well? "What will happen to the business if I refuse?"

She strove for a stiff-upper-lip sort of look. "Frankly, I'm not sure we could take the adverse publicity, especially after the incident with Wanda."

She didn't pull her punches, and several blistering invectives burned the inside of Ty's mouth, desperate to purple the air. He managed to bite them back. When he'd been a brash, unruly kid, pinched ears and soap mouthwashes had cured him of that youthful indulgence. Now that he was old enough to say what he pleased regardless of the consequences, he had too much respect for the woman who'd raised him to offend her with the salty edge of his tongue. "What would I have to do?"

"Take her out on a few dates."

"How many?"

"As many as it'll take to satisfy her kid."

"That's a tall order, Willie. I don't think he's someone easily satisfied."

His grandmother shrugged. "Maybe she won't like you. Then you'll be off the hook."

He shot her a sharp glance. "But you won't. What happens if she doesn't want me?"

For the first time, a smile slid across Willie's face. "You think that's likely, boy?"

"Anything's possible."

"Right. And maybe the sun will rise in the west and set in the east."

"This isn't going to work, old gal," he said compassionately. "I'm not in the market for someone like Cassidy Lonigan. So either she'll get hurt, the boy'll be hurt or your business will take the hit. I just don't see this ending well, no matter how we handle it."

"There's one possibility you haven't considered."

"What's that?"

She peeped at him from the corner of her eye. "You might actually take a shine to this woman. She might be the one you've been waiting for all these years."

Ty shook his head. "You have a better chance of getting that western sunrise, sweetheart."

"All you have to do is kiss her. Then you'll know for certain."

"Sure, Willie. Whatever you say."

He struggled to ignore the image of wary eyes—large gray eyes that darkened to pewter when outraged and lightened to silver whenever she looked at her son. To ignore the way a halo of hair so dark a brown it bordered on black, surrounded the prettiest face he'd seen in ages. To ignore long, trim arms and legs perfectly made to wrap around a man. What would it be like to kiss Cassidy Lonigan...assuming she didn't kill him in the process? Would her kiss be as sweet as her voice? Or as painful as the back of her hand?

"Will you do it?" his grandmother demanded in an undertone. "Will you take her out?"

There wasn't a single doubt in his mind. He'd do anything for Willie. "I'll date her. But you have to run her profile again and see if there aren't a few alternate candidates you can line up. This kid wants a dad. I'd like to see him get one." He scrutinized Cassidy. "Although I suspect it's going to be one hell of a tough sale."

"Mr. Merrick?" the reporter called. "Could we get a shot of you and Ms. Lonigan?"

"I'd really rather not," Cassidy began.

"We won't print the picture without your permission," the reporter hastened to say. "But we were so intrigued by your son's request, we thought it would make a great story for our readers."

"Don't you like my present?" Hutch piped up, a trace of uncertainty edging his voice. "I bought him just for you."

It was the first hint of vulnerability Ty had ever seen the boy reveal. Striding across the room, he dropped an arm around Cassidy's shoulders and drew her close. "I'm sure your mom is thrilled. She's surprised is all."

Cassidy stiffened within his hold. "Very."

"Relax," he ordered beneath his breath. "The poor kid spent every dime he had for this. You don't want to disappoint him, do you?"

That got through to her. Her eyes widened and he caught a quick glimpse of worried Confederate gray before thick, dark lashes swept downward to conceal her expression. "Thank you, sweetpea. You couldn't have picked a better present."

A flashbulb lit the room again. Then the photographer frowned at them. "How about giving her a kiss?" he suggested. "It would make fantastic copy."

Ty glanced down at Cassidy. Her pink lips were parted in dismay and he suppressed a sudden urge to sample them, to see if they were as sweet as they looked—to see if the honey in her voice flavored her mouth, as well. She went rigid within the circle of his arms. Kissing her probably wasn't a good idea. In fact, if her expression was anything to go by, it was an incredibly bad idea. But for some reason, that tempted him all the more.

"Oh, what the hell," he muttered.

Lowering his head, he captured her tiny gasp of distress. For the space of a heartbeat, his mouth connected with hers in a quick slide of soft, moist lips. He cupped her cheek, determined to taste more of her, to drink in the most delicious sensation he'd ever experienced. Before he could, she jerked free, a hand covering the lower half of her face, stealing from him the promise of paradise.

A growl of annoyance reverberated deep in his chest and he reached for her, prepared to drag her back into his arms. If it hadn't been for the angry defiance flaming to life in her eyes, he'd have done it. He took a deep breath, then another, gathering up his control. What the *hell* had just happened? He'd never lost it like that before. Never forced himself on a woman. Nor had he ever been so affected by a simple—

Kiss.

He sucked air. Damn. Was it possible? Was there something to that ridiculous legend of Willie's? There was only one way to be certain. "We'll definitely have to try that again," he said for her ears alone.

Her annoyance turned to rock-solid determination. "Not a chance."

"We seem to have a match," Willie interrupted with undisguised satisfaction.

"Except for that one percent," Cassidy replied, her full attention focused on Ty. No doubt she'd decided to keep the enemy in sight and at arm's length—all twenty-six inches this time. Smart move. "I'm a bit worried about that."

Ty smiled, outwardly relaxed while inwardly, hunting instincts as old as mankind stirred to life. *Run, sweetheart. Run as fast as you can—while you still can.* It wouldn't stop him, not until they'd shared another kiss. Depending on the result, he'd either let her escape, if that's what she preferred...or bind her tight. "That one percent won't bother me," he warned gently.

"Oh, really?" Her answering smile bit like sugarcoated poison. "What a shame. It bothers the heck out of me."

As Cassidy headed for home on the bus with Hutch, she stared glumly through the dust-grimed window at the bustling San Antonio traffic. Today was sure one for her scrapbook. What in the world was she going to do? Her sweet, wonderful son had played a truly rotten trick. He'd bought her the one thing she wanted least in the world—a man. And he'd done it in a way that prevented her from refusing his little surprise without hurting him. Nor, apparently, could she return the impossible ''gift'' or trade him in for a different model. Not as long as the computer matched them at ninety-nine percent.

Perhaps it wouldn't have been so bad if Hutch had purchased someone different. Someone safe. Someone she could control. But instead, he'd gone to buy the equivalent of a harmless kitten and come back with a half-starved mountain lion.

Cassidy frowned. Now that she thought about it, that was precisely what Ty reminded her of. The mix of tawny blond and brown strands of hair coupled with those odd green eyes and powerful musculature all added up to one thing. Good ol' Leo the Lion. He even moved with the same sleek assurance, all controlled power and relentless strength. And that kiss!

Her mouth tingled at the memory and she lifted a hand to her lips.

She couldn't remember the last time she'd been kissed. Of course, whenever it'd been, she hadn't panicked like a frightened schoolgirl. Come to think of it, she'd never *been* a frightened schoolgirl. Maybe if she had... Her gaze slid to Hutch. *Don't go there*, she ordered herself. If she'd lived her life differently, she wouldn't have her son. And she loved Hutch with all her heart and soul. Heck, she'd do anything for him.

Cassidy shut her eyes, surrendering to the inevitable. Anything. Including dating a hungry mountain lion.

Ty stood on the porch of Yellow Rose Matchmakers and stared blindly out at the quiet residential street. This wasn't going to be easy. Not even a little. Assuring himself that what he'd shared with Cassidy Lonigan hadn't been a fluke would be a snap compared to what would inevitably follow. It was the next part that would take every ounce of determination and patience he possessed. How did he convince a woman who didn't believe in love that not only did it exist, but that it could be found in a first kiss?

Willie joined him on the porch. "It's happened, hasn't it, boy?"

"I'm not a boy," he retorted mildly.

"You're avoiding the question. Is she the one? Was I right?"

He noticed his grandmother hadn't taken her usual place on the porch swing but stood in the shade, her posture as ramrod straight as always. Only the slight clenching of her arthritic fingers gave away her tension and confirmed his suspicions. "Did the computer really match us?"

"Yes."

"But you knew ahead of time what the results would be." Her silence was all the confirmation he needed and he sighed. "Did you fudge the data, old gal?"

"No."

"Was I really a test case?"

Again there was a long, pregnant pause. "Let's just say Wanda suggested I undelete your profile," she admitted reluctantly.

Ty couldn't help it. He laughed, the sound tinged with irony. "She always was better at matching people than that damned computer."

"Actually, she disagrees with it this time."

He turned and looked at his grandmother, arching his brow in question. "How's that?"

"She says the computer's wrong. It's not a ninety-nine percent match." Willie smiled complacently. "It's a full one hundred percent fer-sure fire perfect fit."

Progress Report
The results aren't quite what I expected. Seems I'm stuck

with *The Mountain* for my experiment. Don't know if that's going to work out because Mom doesn't like Ty. *(He sure likes her, though!)* But since I don't have any other choice, I'm going ahead with my plan. I'll see what happens after their first date. If it doesn't go well, I'll have to set Plan B into motion.

CHAPTER THREE

Final Countdown to First Experiment
   *Ty called. He promised to stop by today. Something
about Mom's application form. I'm not happy about this
part. I think he's going to have her look it over and
rerun it if it's not right. But if they do that, I may be
dealing with somebody different and... Well, to be honest, I sorta like Ty. I don't think he'd be the type to leave
Mom when the going gets tough. So, if I choose him to
be my dad, I might have to find a way to manipulate the
results if they rerun the form. Perhaps a quick phone
call's in order....*

TY SAW Cassidy the instant he stepped into the small café.
She stood beside a table, a huge, overloaded tray in one
hand, a folding stand in the other. With a practiced maneu-
ver, she snapped the stand open and started to lower the
tray onto it. Halfway there, she froze. Her head jerked up
ward and her gaze swept the room before landing on him.
She'd sensed his presence, he realized with satisfaction.
Good. Her awareness of him was as intense as his for her.

As it turned out, it wasn't good. Her eyes widened, sweet
vulnerability betraying her before she could veil her reaction. The tray wobbled ominously and he caught the subtle
hitch of her breath as a load of plates slid to one side.
Damn. He should have remembered she was a tad on the
uncoordinated side and not surprised her—at least not at
such a critical juncture.

"Cassidy!" His voice cut through the hum of conversation. "Watch it, sweetheart!"

With a gasp, she tried to right the tray, but it was too

49

late. With almost poetic grace, first one plate, then another somersaulted off her tray. A greasy Tex-Mex burger, fries, a plastic glass brimming with tea and heaps of creamy cole-slaw competed with each other to be the first to land on her customer. A particularly aggressive burger won, splatting dead center in his lap. The upper half of the bun spun through the air before lighting on the patty, perching there like a cocked hat.

"Oh, good gravy!" Cassidy dropped the now empty tray onto the stand. She started to reach for the gently steaming burger, then hesitated, apparently thinking better of it. "I'm *so* sorry."

The customer stared in disbelief at his grease-soaked lap for a split second, than leaped to his feet with a yelp of pain. "It's burning!" he shouted, slapping at the front of his trousers. Clumps of food tumbled to the floor, including the offending burger. He glared at her from beneath a cap of dripping coleslaw. "Didn't you hear me? It's burning. Do something!"

Springing into action, Cassidy snatched a pitcher of ice water out of the hands of a nearby waitress and tossed the contents toward the circle of grease. Ice cubes ricocheted off the man from chin to knees.

Ty winced. That had to hurt.

"Is that better?" she asked. "Is it still burning?"

"Better? *Better*!" With an enraged shriek, he erupted from his booth. Tripping over the tray stand, his loafers shot out from under him and he added himself to the debris of dishes and silverware littering the floor.

Shouldn't have worn loafers, Ty decided judiciously, tipping his Stetson to the back of his head. They were ridiculous footwear. Any sane individual would have known that. He folded his arms across his chest and waited to see what further entertainment Cassidy's customer would offer. It wasn't long in coming. The man flailed around on the floor some, making sure his backside was as thoroughly soaked with food and grease as his front side. He also struggled hard to talk. His jaw ground away like he'd bit down on a particularly tough piece of jerky.

"Spit it out," an old-timer encouraged cheerfully from a nearby table.

The man flopped around some more, his face turning an interesting shade of purplish red. Finally, his voice kicked in, blasting out at full volume. "I'm going to *kill* you, you stupid…"

Oops. Entertainment over. Ty didn't wait to hear any more.

While the man tossed dishes aside in an attempt to regain his footing, Ty loped over to Cassidy. Sweeping her safely behind him, he leaned down and hauled the man to his feet. "Easy does it, friend. It was an accident. The lady apologized, so I suggest you let it go."

"Get the hell out of my way, *friend*. My beef is with her, not you."

The customer kicked a plate out of his way, sending it smashing into a nearby chair. His petty act caused his heel to slip on a lemon wedge and sent him tumbling to the floor again. Ty shook his head. Dumb move. Real dumb— not to mention messy. Any puddles of food the fella had missed last time, he took the opportunity to visit on this occasion. Of course, the man's nasal accent betrayed him as being from one of those states decidedly north of the Mason-Dixon line and well east of the Mississippi. Quite likely that explained his less-than-gentlemanly behavior. The poor Yank had grown up disadvantaged.

"Your beef isn't with the lady any longer," Ty explained gently. "Now it's with me." Cassidy stirred against his back and he knew she was going to do something incredibly foolish—like interfere.

Sure enough, she tugged on his shirt. "This isn't your concern, Ty. I can handle it. I have experience with this sort of thing."

He stifled a groan. Of course she had. No doubt legions of customers had been on the receiving end of her special brand of service. If they'd been anywhere else, he'd have laughed at the absurdity. As it was, he didn't dare take his gaze off the irate customer. "You're not helping any, sweetheart. If you'd just let me—"

She tugged at his shirt some more, putting a severe strain on the seams. An ominous popping sound came from the threads in the vicinity of his shoulders. "Please, Ty!" The soft way she continued to pronounce his name tied his guts in a knot, destroying his focus. "You're going to lose me my job."

"I don't think you need my help with that," he advised after due consideration. "You seemed to be accomplishing that quite well on your own."

"How can you say such a thing?" She yanked at his poor, abused shirt again, snapping a few more vital threads.

"Perhaps it has something to do with him." Ty jerked his thumb toward her former customer who'd just managed to slip-slide to his feet.

"Move aside," the man unwisely ordered. "I have a small matter to discuss with that little bit—"

Ty cut him off before he could finish spitting out the word. "Watch your mouth, son, or I might have to watch it for you," he warned, crushing his Stetson more firmly on his head. It wouldn't do for it to hit the floor should a scuffle ensue—not considering the tile's current condition.

"What did he call me?" Cassidy interjected, outraged. Her arm forgot it was twenty-six inches and clipped Ty's left ear. She shook her finger in the general direction of her customer. "You watch your mouth, mister."

"I believe I just said that," Ty thought to mention.

Her arm shot past his ear again. This time, he was quick enough to duck. The finger got another thorough workout as she continued scolding. "There are ladies and children present, in case you hadn't noticed."

And every one of them was watching with openmouthed fascination.

"So? I don't give a sh—" Ty carefully gathered up the

man's collar, cutting off the flow of air to his lungs. Whatever the man had been about to say ended in a high-pitched squeak.

"Now then," Ty said, taking charge. Or at least trying to. "Let me explain a few things to you, friend. What happened was a real shame. And as much as it rankles for me to admit it, Cassidy does have a small organizational problem with her arms and legs." He loosened his grip on the man's collar a tad. The poor fella was looking a bit blue around the gills. "But if you try to hurt this woman or offend these customers with more unmannerly language, I'll be forced to do something about it."

For the first time, the man seemed to notice the size of the obstacle between him and his goal. He sucked air into his lungs. "Like what?" he asked a trifle less belligerently.

Ty removed one callused hand from the man's collar and held it up for inspection. He'd always considered his hands absurdly large. Evidently, the customer thought so, too. Ty folded his fingers into a ham-size fist. "Does this answer your question?"

"Ty?" Cassidy tried to peek around his shoulders. Fortunately, they were bulky enough to make that a near impossible feat. A few more shirt threads split. By the sudden loosening of his right sleeve, he suspected she'd eliminated at least one seam. "What are you doing? I can't see."

"I'm just being neighborly."

Bewilderment edged her honeyed voice. "Neighborly?"

It was hard to maintain an intimidating facade with a sleeve drooping around one wrist, swallowing the fist he might need to plant on her customer's nose. But he persevered. "I'm explaining to our newfound friend that he was trespassing on private property. He's agreed not to do it again." He gave the customer a gentle shake to encourage his cooperation. "Right?"

The man gawked at Ty's exposed biceps and swallowed. "Yeah. Yeah, right."

"What private property?" Cassidy piped up. "Whatever are you talking about?"

A few of the surrounding customers chuckled. One was even stupid enough to clue her in by waving a clenched fist in the air. Damn.

"You didn't threaten him?" she demanded in outrage. His back received the punishing impact of an elbow, a thumping index finger and possibly her knee. It was hard to tell. Maybe he should have left this guy to her mercy after all. Probably would have served him right. "Ty, you have to leave. Now. Go wait in your car and I'll be with you in a few minutes."

Nothing like having his authority undercut. He felt all of five years old. "I can't do that, Cassidy. The only thing between you and certain death is me," he explained patiently.

"I'm sure you're exaggerating."

Ty contemplated her customer's hopeful expression. "I'm equally sure I'm not."

The owner chose that moment to approach from wherever he'd been hiding. "What's going on here? What's happened?" he questioned as though he hadn't seen a blessed thing.

The customer gestured toward Ty and Cassidy, a malicious light entering his now less-than-intimidated gaze. "Your waitress dumped her tray on me. She's ruined my clothes. And she probably caused a severe burn to my...to my..."

"Peter, Paul and Mary?" Ty offered helpfully.

"Never mind where! I'm going to the doctor right away. You'll have my bill in the morning. If she's still here when I come again..." He started to point at Cassidy, ran up against Ty's chest and thought better of it. "I'm going to sue!"

"Totally unnecessary," the owner said. "Cassidy? I'm sorry, dear. But you're fired."

"*Again*? Gosh darn it, Freddie. How long this time?"

Her boss slid a quick glance at his irate customer. "Permanently, I'm afraid. I won't dock your wages for the cost of the dishes or this gentleman's expenses, but it might be best if you left now."

Ty wrapped an arm around her shoulders. "Come on, sweetheart. You don't need this sort of hassle."

"No, I don't. But I *do* need to eat and pay my rent," she argued. "Come on, Freddie. Be a darlin'. I can't afford to lose my job. How about if I went back to washing up?"

Her boss shuddered. "You about bankrupted me with all the dishes you broke. That's why I made you a waitress."

"I could bus tables."

"Please, Cassidy. Don't say stuff like that. You know I'm on heart medication. Look…I'll provide you with a good recommendation. Heck, I'll even lie." Freddie shrugged. "Best I can do, under the circumstances."

"There's not a chance you're going to save this job," Ty informed her in an undertone. "The best thing you can do is walk away. I'll help you find another one. With the Fiesta coming up, it shouldn't be too tough." At least, not until she'd worked her new job for a few hours and her employer saw her in action. "If push comes to shove, I'll hire you myself." He'd have to find a nice, safe occupation for her—like stuffing pillows or something.

"But—"

"Please, Cassidy," Freddie whispered, "I can't afford the trouble."

That stopped her. With a dignity that impressed the hell out of Ty, she whipped off her apron and handed it to the owner. "I'll be back tomorrow for my paycheck. Thanks for hiring me in the first place."

Without another word, she headed for the exit, words of encouragement following her the entire way. Clearly, she was well liked here. Ty grimaced. With one annoying exception. It was a darned shame.

She turned on him the instant they hit the sidewalk in

front of the café. "Do you have any idea what you've done?" she demanded.

"Saved your hide?"

"You got me fired!"

He corralled her toward his pickup. "The way I see it, I saved you from a customer bent on rearranging that pretty face of yours."

"I—you…" He'd actually managed to distract her. Amazing. "You think I'm pretty?"

A smile tugged at the corner of his mouth. Drop-dead gorgeous would be more accurate. Hadn't anyone told her that before? At a guess…no. Well, that would change. Right now. "I think you're beautiful."

Rose-soft color highlighted her sweeping cheekbones. "Why…thanks. But that still doesn't let you off the hook." She worked on rekindling her anger with a regrettable amount of success. So she wasn't one to have her head turned with flattery, he noted. Good for her. "I needed that job. If you'd have just let me handle it—"

"You'd have been a shade wiser and a hell of a lot sorer."

She hesitated, her vulnerability peeking out again, turning her eyes to charcoal. "Do you really think he'd have hurt me?"

"If he'd ever gotten his footing, he'd have decked you." While she chewed that over, he opened the door to his pickup and loaded her in. With any luck, by the time she awoke to her surroundings, they'd be under way. "I'm sorry I lost you that job. I'll put out a couple of feelers tomorrow."

"No, thanks," came her immediate response. "I can manage on my own."

"I'm sure you could," he agreed, stripping off his ruined shirt. He reached into the back seat of the extended cab and grabbed the spare tee he kept there. He couldn't help but notice that her eyes tried to swallow up her face and her mouth went fishing for flies. Apparently, there was something about him she liked. She turned her head away so fast her braid did the Texas two-step and he buried a grin. *Too late, sweetheart. I already caught you staring.* He climbed behind the wheel and started the engine. "You'll let me help you find a job anyway."

"Why's that?" she questioned, a hint of strain threading her voice.

"Because, as you pointed out, I was partially responsible for getting you fired." He pulled into traffic, pleased that she hadn't insisted he off-load her at the nearest bus stop. Seeing him bare-chested must have thrown her good and proper. He'd have to remember that. "This way, I have a chance to redeem myself."

"Oh. Okay, then. You can help."

He half expected her agreement to sound grudging. It didn't. It came across as... Generous. As though *she* was helping *him*. The sheer illogic of it amused him no end. She didn't want his assistance finding a job because it ran counter to her independent nature. But if her compliance would make him feel better, she was happy to go along. Crazy woman. He slid her a quick look. Crazy, kissable woman.

"You never did say what you were doing at the café," she prompted, the beginning of a frown puckering her brow.

"I came to talk to you about the Yellow Rose." That much was true enough. He wouldn't mention his other reason. With luck, he'd just *do* it, assuming the opportunity presented itself.

Her frown deepened. "I was afraid of that."

"I know you're not happy about these dates, so I thought we'd go over your application privately and rerun it. That way, we can make sure you're matched with the best possible candidate."

"I don't want to date anyone."

"I understand that. But for Hutch's sake, you're going to have to. I figured you should at least have a decent selection of men.'' Damned magnanimous of him, all things considered. Not that Cassidy saw it that way.

She set her chin in a manner identical to Hutch. So that's where the little squirt had learned it. ''I don't want even one man, let alone a whole slew of them.''

''I wasn't exactly offering a slew,'' he retorted, vaguely insulted. ''Just a couple of alternatives.''

With a little sigh, she leaned back against the seat. Her careworn hands bunched the skirt of her dress, pleating the light blue folds before smoothing out the creases. ''Hutch thinks he's being helpful.''

''I know.'' He waited.

''I'm...I'm not interested in a relationship.''

''I know that, too.''

''So why are you doing this? Why agree to date me?''

For a brief instant, he was tempted to explain about the kiss. Considering how skittish she was about this dating business, he thought better of it. Instead, he decided to show her. He pulled the pickup to the curb outside her apartment complex and switched off the engine.

Unbuckling his seat belt, he leaned across the space separating them and unfastened hers, as well. ''What happened last time made me curious.''

She stilled, freezing up so fast it felt like a blue norther had lost its way and come screaming down on San Antonio, bringing with it a blast of icy arctic air. ''What are you talking about?'' She knew. Knew, but refused to admit it aloud.

''I'm talking about that kiss.''

Her misty gray eyes widened in alarm. But he caught the momentary glimmer of another reaction, as well. A hint of answering curiosity. ''Nothing happened,'' she protested. ''We barely even touched lips.''

Ever so cautiously, he cradled her face in his palms. Her skin was soft. So soft he worried about scraping her with the roughness of his hands. ''Then there's nothing to be concerned about.''

"I'm not," she fibbed.

The lie was so blatantly transparent, he didn't bother calling her on it. "Good. So this time when I kiss you, you won't get angry, right?"

While she took a few precious seconds to weigh the pros and cons of her response to that one, he eased her deeper into his embrace. She didn't resist, didn't protest, so he did what came naturally. He kissed her. Fully. Like he'd wanted to ever since that last aborted encounter. Their lips met as though they'd practiced a thousand times before. Joined easily, melded completely. She tasted incredible, like a brand new flavor he sensed would be his permanent favorite.

His reaction was as instantaneous as last time and far more intense—perhaps because it was a real kiss rather than a fleeting touch of lips. So much for needing further proof. *One kiss and he'd know.* And he did. Knew with every fiber of his being. Cassidy Lonigan was his future—a sweet, hot, delicious, permanent sort of future.

He didn't rush. The woman in his arms wasn't a treat he intended to hurry. Hell, she wasn't a treat at all. More like…destiny. And one didn't fight destiny any more than one galloped headlong through it. One worked toward it, fulfilled it, explored it. And enjoyed the hell out of it. He sank into her, intensifying the kiss. Yeah. One enjoyed every destined moment.

She made a small sound deep in her throat, an intriguing combination of surrender and rebellion. Her hands flattened on his shoulders even as her tongue crept into his mouth, slipping home like a thief in the night. It surprised him. He'd never thought Cassidy a woman of half measures. She struck him as the all-or-nothing type. And she proved it the next instant.

Rolling onto one hip, she wrapped her arms in a stranglehold around his neck and slanted her mouth more fully over his. And then she consumed him as if he was an ice-cold dessert served up on a scorching hot afternoon. She wriggled closer and her knee plowed onto his lap, damn near emasculating him. Sheer instinct had him catching her leg just in the nick of time, his palm rasping across her bare skin.

Her gasp burst into his mouth and he absorbed the slight shudder that shot through her. Curious to confirm the cause, he stroked his hand upward from her knee. Her pulse jolted in response and a soft moan of longing reverberated against his chest. How long had it been since she'd last been touched, he wondered, since a man had slipped a hand beneath her dress and given her pleasure? Had anyone ever caressed the sensitive skin along her thighs or massaged the taut muscles of her legs until she relaxed so deeply she couldn't move? Did anyone ever see to her needs, or was she the one who always gave? It struck him as past time that she be on the receiving end of a little TLC.

She broke off the kiss with a groan and buried her face in the crook of his neck. "I'm so sorry. I can't believe I did that."

"Nothing to apologize for. I'm sure as hell not offended," he soothed with a tender smile. "But next time, I think we'll pick someplace a little more private."

Cassidy peered around in surprise, as though just realizing their location. Her eyes grew wide again. "How do you know where I live?"

"Hutch supplied your address when he filled out the application."

"Oh." She didn't look pleased. "You mean we've been sitting outside my apartment—"

"Necking," he offered helpfully.

"I can't believe this happened." She ripped free of his arms and glared at him. "This is all your fault."

"You're right. And I take full responsibility for your forcing yourself on me." He nudged the conversation in a slightly different direction before she gathered her wits enough to verbalize her indignation. "Can you arrange for someone to stay with Hutch for the next few hours while we review your application? I thought we could go somewhere private and decide how to handle it. Maybe have dinner together.''

''After what just happened?''

He wasn't quite certain what one had to do with the other. But she'd seen a connection, which was the important part. ''All the more reason, don't you think?''

She stewed for a moment. ''I—I don't know. I guess we could.''

If that was an agreement, it was one of the most reluctant he'd ever heard. ''Is that a yes?'' he asked.

She hesitated for a split second more, then nodded. ''It's a yes. We might as well get it over with.''

''Gee, thanks.''

She had the grace to blush, not that she retracted anything. Stubborn woman. ''I was scheduled to work tonight anyway,'' she said. ''So I've already arranged for a neighbor to keep an eye on Hutch. If you'd give me a minute to change, I'd appreciate it.''

''Sure thing.''

He'd hoped she'd ask him up to her apartment. He didn't want to push, but the more he learned about her, the more comfortable he'd feel about that kiss they'd shared. He still had a tough time believing she was the woman he'd spend the rest of his life with. Two days ago, he'd have sworn that people couldn't fall in love at first kiss—until he'd locked lips with Cassidy.

''Care to invite me up?'' he prompted, well aware she had no intention of doing any such thing.

''I wasn't planning to,'' she confirmed with devastating honesty.

''I realize that.'' He gestured toward the apartment building. ''But since Hutch has his nose pressed to the window, you might want to change your plans.''

''There's not much to see,'' she informed him casually. Too casually.

He reached out and tugged on the end of her French

braid, wondering why she didn't want him to join her. It was almost as though she had something to hide. "It's going to happen at some point. You might as well get it over with."

Her breath escaped in a gusty sigh. "I'm being ungracious, aren't I? My Aunt Esther always told me it was one of the worst sins I could commit."

"Oh, I'd have thought there were a few worse ones."

"You're right," Cassidy confessed. "And I even came up with one or two of them to prove it." She offered a charmingly crooked smile. "Okay. I'll be polite. Would you care to come in for a cup of coffee, Mr. Merrick?"

He inclined his head. "Thank you, Ms. Lonigan. I'd like that very much."

It didn't take long to troop up the two flights of stairs to her front door. Hutch stood there waiting for them. "Hiya, Ty."

"Hey there, kid." He started to ruffle the thatch of blond hair, but at the last instant thought better of it. No doubt Hutch considered himself too old for that. Instead, Ty fisted his hand and held it out, carefully bumping knuckles with the boy. It wouldn't do to accidently bruise him. He suspected Cassidy wouldn't take it well.

"Mrs. Welch just left," Hutch said as they walked inside the apartment. "We're supposed to let her know if you want me to stay with her this evening. So..." He cocked his head to one side. "What are you doing home?"

"I..." A blush licked at her cheekbones as she closed the door. "I was fired."

Hutch's mouth dropped open. "*Again*? What happened this time?"

She darted a quick glance in Ty's direction, then looked hastily away. "I was distracted and dropped a tray on a customer," she muttered.

Hutch whistled. "Wow. That's a new one."

She scowled at Ty, letting him know where she placed

the blame for the incident. "With any luck, it won't happen again."

"Man, I'd be really ticked if someone dropped a tray on me. Was he hurt? Did he yell? Did he kick up a ruckus? Is that why you got fired?"

She suffered her son's questions with amazing good humor. "Fortunately, Ty kept the customer from getting too upset."

Hutch stilled. "Ty was there, huh? When you dropped the tray?" A knowing gleam sparked in his bright blue eyes. Damn, but the kid was smart. "*In*teresting."

Cassidy's color deepened, raging across her face like an out-of-control brushfire. "Yes, he was there. Now, if you don't mind, I have to change. Mr. Merrick and I are going…are going…" She trailed off in confusion.

"On your first date?" Hutch offered helpfully.

"I guess you could call it that," she admitted. *If it gets one of their dates out of the way,* Ty read between the lines. "We're going to review my application form. Why don't you entertain Mr. Merrick while I get ready. See if he'd like a drink."

"Okay."

Head held high, Cassidy swept from view, the door to her bedroom shutting behind her just shy of a slam. Through the hollow-core panel, Ty heard an odd scuffling noise and Cassidy's muffled voice saying something he couldn't quite catch. But before he could ask about it, Hutch spoke up.

"She's never done that before, you know," he commented.

"Slammed the door?"

"No. Dropped a tray on somebody."

"I'm relieved to hear it. Though I suppose it was only a matter of time."

Hutch snickered. "She does trip a lot. She keeps saying it's because she's shorter in her head than in real life."

Ty grinned ruefully. "Trust me. I know all about those extra three inches."

"Yeah." Hutch matched his grin—a purely masculine moment. "They sometimes get me, too. Especially when she gets excited and starts waving her arms around. Gotta be a fast ducker. You wanna sit?"

Ty eyed the two ancient chairs the living area had to offer. A scrapbook stuffed with papers rested on one. He could just read what had been scrawled across one of the loose bits of paper: *Great new apartment. Very roomy.* He glanced around. She considered this roomy? His closet had more space. He examined the chair again. It probably couldn't handle much more weight than the scrapbook, he decided. The other wasn't much better. Neither looked capable of containing him for longer than two seconds flat before splintering. "I'll stand, thanks."

"Okay. You wanna drink?"

"Sure."

He followed Hutch into the kitchen. There wasn't much furniture in here, either, though the place had been scrubbed spotless, as if to make up for the vast expanse of emptiness. A table had been pushed against the far wall, one leg shored up with a phone book. Two mismatched chairs were tucked neatly underneath each end. Squashed next to the counter was a refrigerator older than Willie. As far as he could see, they didn't own any small appliances—no toaster or coffeemaker, let alone a microwave.

Hutch rummaged in one of the cupboards and Ty caught a glimpse of the contents. Two plates, two bowls and two glasses. That was it. It told a grim story. The boy removed one of the glasses, opened a nearly empty refrigerator and grabbed a quart of milk. He poured Ty a glass and handed it to him.

"I didn't think the computer was gonna pick you," the kid commented as he returned the carton to the refrigerator.

Ty took a swallow of milk, guilt souring the taste. It wasn't bad enough he'd helped Cassidy out of a job. Now he was as good as snatching the last drop of milk from their mouths. *You don't need this sort of hassle*, he'd blithely told her. *The best thing you can do is walk away.* Hah! Did she have any financial reserves to get by on until she found another job? He suddenly realized that Hutch was waiting for an answer and shrugged. "I didn't know the computer would pick me, either. But I'm glad it did."

"You like my mom?"

"Yes." He forced himself to finish the milk and wondered if there was any tactful way of restocking her fridge. Knowing Cassidy and her independent streak, he rather doubted it.

"You want to marry her?" Hutch asked, catching Ty off guard.

Damn, the kid was direct. "It's a bit early to tell, don't you think?"

Hutch didn't reply. He simply waited.

Aw, hell. If it hadn't been for that damned kiss... "I'm giving it serious consideration."

The chin jutted out an inch. "I'm part of the package, too, you know."

"I knew that going in," Ty reassured him gently.

Gradually, Hutch relaxed. "Okay. Do you want to see my room?"

"Sure." Carefully washing the empty glass, Ty upended it on the drain board.

Hutch's room proved to be a revelation. Shoved in one corner was a mattress, minus a box spring or frame. Instead of a dresser, cartons lined one wall, with clothes neatly folded in each. The rest of the room was dominated by a huge desk—and a very expensive state-of-the-art computer. That simple fact told him more clearly than anything else where Cassidy's priorities lay.

"Nice setup."

Hutch glanced uncertainly at him. "The school told her to get me one. I'm..." He snatched a quick breath and then said in a rush, "You better know right off. I'm smart."

Ty nodded. "I figured as much."

"No. I mean I'm *really* smart," Hutch emphasized. "Scary smart. So if that's gonna bother you, maybe you should say so now before…" Resolutely, he turned his face toward the computer. "Before anybody gets their feelings hurt."

"Hutch." The boy ignored him, busying himself with the machine. "Look at me, please."

Reluctantly, Hutch lifted his gaze to Ty's. Settling his glasses more firmly on the bridge of his upturned nose, he braced himself. "Yeah?"

"It doesn't bother me."

"Okay."

"Look at me and listen to what I'm saying to you, kid." Brilliant blue eyes fastened on Ty's face again, a desperate kind of hope burning in the apprehensive gaze. "Smart's okay with me. Even scary smart. I don't have a problem with it and I won't. Got that?"

The chin wobbled. "Yeah. I got it."

"Good. Now, why don't you show me how this thing works."

The next few minutes passed with Hutch chattering away a mile a minute. Ty could see why the school had recommended a computer for the boy. Did they have any idea, though, what a financial sacrifice it had been? He doubted it. He suspected Cassidy Lonigan's pride came in as abundant a helping as her generosity.

"Hutch? Where…?" She appeared in the doorway then and smiled uncertainly. "Oh. There you two are. Everything all right?"

"Great! Ty knows almost as much about computers as I do."

She lifted her eyebrows, impressed. "Wow. That's quite a compliment."

She'd brushed out her braid so her hair fell in a straight dark curtain to cup her shoulders. She'd also changed from her uniform into a light gray, short-sleeved blouse and matching slacks. Looked like he wouldn't be slipping his hand under her skirt again today, Ty realized regretfully. A damn shame.

"You look great," he said. And she did. Fantastic, in fact, despite the lack of a skirt. The slacks emphasized her endless legs and narrow hips, while the soft color made her eyes more intense than usual. "Ready to go?"

"I guess."

Her enthusiasm underwhelmed him, but he simply grinned. "Good."

She avoided his gaze, fixing her attention on her son. "I'll call you from the restaurant and give you the phone number. And I'll send Mrs. Welch over, although I think she wants to watch you at her place tonight."

"Okay."

She dropped a kiss on the top of his head. "Don't open the door without looking to see who it is."

Hutch glanced at Ty and grimaced. *Women*, his expression said. "I know."

Still she hovered and Ty suspected that if she wasn't wringing her hands, he and Hutch would be doing some fast maneuvering to get clear of those twenty-six inches. "I won't be late."

"Have fun and goodbye," Hutch said meaningfully.

She'd run out of things to say and knew it. Surrendering to the inevitable, she walked to the door. Turning, she announced, "I'll see you *soon*." Apparently, that pointed declaration satisfied her, for she allowed Ty to tow her from the apartment without too much of a struggle.

The instant they left, Hutch frowned. Part of his plan was working. The computer had picked the perfect man for a father. But his mom was proving to be a bit of a problem. Calling up a certain file, he keyed in his password to open it and began typing.

Progress Report

Bad news. Mom hasn't changed her mind about Ty even though they kissed. They don't know I saw, but I did. Course, his losing her job for her didn't help. You'd think he'd have thought of that! For sure that smacker he planted on her should have made her want him for a husband. But, noooo!

Conclusion

Maybe those things take time. Maybe you have to be exposed to a bunch of kisses before they take effect, like germs or something. She hasn't caught a love cold yet, cuz they haven't been around each other long enough. Or maybe he's catchier than she is. If that's the case, we'll have to be where he can infect her more often.

Proposed Response

I talked to Miss Willie about the changes Ty's gonna make to the application form and she promised to make sure it didn't reject him. So I have that front covered. As for further infecting Mom... Looks like Plan B will have to be put in motion after all.

Finished, Hutch printed up his latest entries, folded the pages carefully and slipped them into a preaddressed envelope. Tomorrow he'd mail it.

Just as he'd promised.

CHAPTER FOUR

Experiment #1: Protective Instincts
Goal: To bring out the protective instincts in Ty.
According to the documentary I watched at school last
month, the male in the animal kingdom will protect his
mate from harm. So let's see whether or not he's capable
of that. Because if he's not, he isn't the right man for
Mom.
Procedure: I hate to do this to my own mother, but she's
gonna have a bit of bad luck....

"SO, WHERE are we going?" Cassidy demanded the instant
they left her apartment building.

She probably should have asked instead of demanded.
Aunt Esther had done her best to drum graciousness and
tact into Cassidy's stubborn psyche. Unfortunately for all
concerned, the lessons hadn't taken.

She shot Ty a disgruntled look. He'd had the upper hand
in what passed as their relationship for far too long and
she'd had a *really* bad day, thanks to him. Asserting herself
would clue him in to that fact. At least, that was the plan.
"Well?" she prompted impatiently.

To her frustration, he waited until they were both settled
in his oversize truck again and buckled into their seat
belts before replying. "We're going someplace private.
Someplace where we can get to know each other and talk
without interruption."

No wonder he'd trapped her in his pickup before answering. A knot formed in the pit of her stomach—or was
it a hangman's noose that threatened to choke her? Maybe
both. "How private?" This time she asked. Nicely.

"Very."

"Like a private restaurant, right?"

"Not exactly."

Uh-oh. Panic set in. He was a man; she was a woman. He'd kissed her. She'd dissolved into a pathetic puddle. And now it was vital she find the means to slip away before he touched her again and started the process all over. "I'll need to let Hutch know where I am," she babbled. "He has to be able to reach me in case there's a problem. I can't just—"

"Easy, sweetheart. Relax. My jacket's on the back seat. There's a phone in the pocket. Call Hutch and I'll give him my private number. That way, he can reach us no matter where we are." He glanced at her, his green eyes calm yet implacable. "On this, or any of our future dates."

Her alarm intensified. "You're assuming there's going to be more than one."

"It isn't an assumption." He braked for a red light and turned to look at her, resting his arms along the top of the steering wheel. He filled his side of the truck, his shoulders impossibly broad, the power of his arms straining the fabric of his shirt. "It's a fact."

"Stop doing that," she groused. "It's not fair."

He lifted a tawny brow. "Doing what?"

"Looking like…" Gesturing toward all the deliciously male parts that kept distracting her every time he flexed, she accidently clipped his shoulder. To her relief, he hardly flinched at all. "*That*. It doesn't give me a fair chance when we argue."

For a brief instant, something hot and primitive flared to life in his gaze. If the light hadn't turned green then, she knew he would have kissed her. Again. "All *that* bothers you?"

Would she ever learn to keep her mouth shut? "Only when you tense it up so the ripply stuff shows through your clothes," she muttered.

"And if I wasn't wearing any clothes?"

So she'd actually *see* the ripples in all their naked glory, like when he'd changed his shirt earlier? No way would she answer that one! She might think about it for a spell or two or drool a bit, but he wouldn't drag a single blessed word out of her on the subject.

Her silence must have blabbed because his chuckle rumbled over to her side of the pickup and eased into her pores. She could feel an ache building—an ache for something she'd spent years burying beneath a hard-won control. Did he know what that laugh did to her? He must. Somehow he'd discovered how long it had been since she'd last been with a man and— He interrupted before she could finish her thought, thank heaven.

"Next time we argue, I'll strip down to guarantee an easy win."

Cassidy stifled a groan at the image. Why couldn't he be sensible? More importantly, why couldn't she? "If you'd just do things my way, that wouldn't be necessary," she explained.

His dark voice reached for her again, wrapping her in warmth. "Do you really think that's going to happen?"

No. "Absolutely."

To her intense relief, he didn't laugh outright. "Face it, sweetheart. You're stuck with me. Your son purchased the San Antonio Fiesta Special from Yellow Rose Matchmakers. That means you date me or one of the other candidates the computer picks until the Fiesta's over. Since the computer only coughed up one match so far, it looks like I'm all yours for the next month."

Did that also mean she was all his? Oh, no. Not a chance. "Hutch couldn't possibly have had the money for something like that," Cassidy protested.

Ty grinned. "Willie gave him a bargain. You'll be pleased to know that I came at the rock bottom price of nine dollars plus change. He'd have made it ten, but he needed bus fare to get back home."

Her pride did a quick jump start and she struggled to

keep it under control—without notable success. "How much does it really cost?"

"That's not important."

"It is to me. If he didn't pay enough—"

"Don't bother finishing the thought. There's no point."

"I can't take advantage of your grandmother's generosity. It wouldn't be right. Besides, I don't like being obligated."

"Too bad. It would offend her if you refused the discount. The deal she made was with the boy, not you. And since she runs the Yellow Rose, she's allowed to strike any deal she wants."

Cassidy gave up. She wasn't going to win this particular fight and she knew it. She slid Ty an assessing glance. Considering his earlier threat, if she pushed, he'd start whipping off his clothing. And as interesting a sight as that would be, surrendering to his stronger will seemed the best option for her mental health. For now, at any rate. "Thank you. That's very kind of Miss Willie."

"See? That didn't choke you too badly."

A smile teased her lips. "It darn near killed me," she retorted.

"Hardly showed at all."

She settled against the bench seat and forced herself to relax. "So where are we going that's so private?"

"My place."

She jerked back upright. Crud. "I don't think—"

Ty released a sigh of exasperation. "Do you argue over everything?"

"Just about," she answered with painful honesty. "But I have a point this time. It's not appropriate to go to a man's place on the first date." Good grief. If she didn't know better, she'd have sworn she'd opened her mouth and Aunt Esther had voiced one of her "rules".

"Old-fashioned girl, huh?"

"Not really. Let's just say I learned common sense the hard way." Maybe the hardest way possible.

"I'll behave." He gave her another of those cool green glances—the sort that warned he was always in control and she'd do well to remember it. "Willie'd have my hide if I didn't."

"Hah." Cassidy folded her arms across her chest. "Don't tell me she could slow you down once you'd made up your mind about something."

"She's been known to put a damper on my enthusiasm from time to time."

"But she hasn't stopped you," Cassidy guessed shrewdly.

"Not when I want something bad enough."

She doubted he meant it as a warning. Still, she intended to take it that way. The sensation of being hunted returned full bore. Ty exuded an innate patience and determination that matched the sheer size and power of the man. Instinct told her that once he'd fixed his sights on a quarry, he'd track it relentlessly. Capturing his prey would only be a matter of time, his success a given. More and more she'd begun to suspect he'd fixed his sights on her. Whether he'd done it at the request of his grandmother or to help Hutch, she couldn't guess. But unless she found a way to dissuade him, he'd have her in the end—something she preferred to avoid at all costs.

For the hour it took to reach his place, she worried endlessly about how to extricate herself from her latest predicament. Finally, she gave it up as pointless. Why fuss about what she couldn't fix? She'd had that particular lesson drummed into her more than once. Too bad she was such a slow learner. Ty turned into a gated entranceway just then, which succeeded in distracting her. As they bumped along the gravel road, she focused on their destination—a large homestead that topped a bluff and overlooked an endless spread of cattle country.

"Is all this yours?" she asked in astonishment.

"Yes."

She studied the impressive building as they approached.

The main part of the house had been roughly hewn from logs, with succeeding generations expanding from there, combining wood with stone as the house sprawled outward from its well-aged core. "It looks old. Has your family owned it for long?"

"It's been in Merrick hands for a while now."

"How long's a while?"

He shrugged. "Think Alamo and add a handful of years."

"Your roots go deep."

She couldn't help voicing the wistful observation. What would it be like to have the land of your forebears beneath your feet? To know that generation after generation had lived and died, loved and cried, laughed and grieved on the same spot. She'd give almost anything to be connected to that long a lineage, to help continue it.

To belong.

Yearning turned to determination. Okay. So she didn't have a heritage to match Ty's, nor could she offer one to Hutch. That didn't mean she couldn't make a home for them. As soon as she'd saved enough, they'd have their own house. It might not be like this, but it would be a start. She'd learned long ago that thirsty roots dug deep. Soon she'd belong somewhere, too.

"What's wrong?"

She'd been so preoccupied with her thoughts and plans, she hadn't realized they'd stopped. Ty's all too observant gaze was fixed on her face. How much had she given away? she wondered uneasily.

"I was thinking about what it must be like to have a family history like yours." She waved a hand toward his home. "A connection to the past."

"Proud. Comfortable. And frustrating," he answered promptly.

"Frustrating?" She swiveled to look at him. "Why?"

"It comes with a lot of responsibility."

Her eyes narrowed. "You have a problem with that?"

"No. But my father did. He felt trapped by his legacy."

"Did he run?" The question escaped before she'd considered the wisdom of asking it.

"Yes." It was his turn to level a narrowed gaze on her. "Familiar with that response, are you?"

Cassidy escaped the car as though sprung from a trap, nearly hanging herself before she remembered to unclasp her seat belt. Ty exited, as well, only he did it without incident. He reached into the back seat of the extended cab and recovered the cell phone from his jacket.

"Why don't we get this over with?" she suggested uncomfortably, as he dropped the compact phone into the pocket of his jeans. Anything to end their conversation.

"I assume you mean our first date."

She had the grace to blush at his dry tone. "I'm sorry. I didn't…" Setting her jaw, she turned to confront him over the width of the truck's hood. "Actually, that's precisely what I meant. I apologize for being rude about it. But to be honest, I'm not interested in dating anyone."

"You haven't told Hutch you feel that way."

She shrugged. "It hasn't come up."

"Hutch isn't waiting for your ex to sweep back into your lives?"

"No."

"Then I gather I won't have to worry about that, either." There was no mistaking his satisfaction.

Cassidy studied the taut planes and angles of Ty's tanned face, wishing she could read his expression as easily as she used to read her ex-husband's. Unfortunately, Ty was more self-contained, which unnerved her no end. The need to escape intensified, growing in direct proportion to the aggressive gleam in his eyes.

She tumbled into speech. "You're doing this for your grandmother's sake, right? I know from what you said at the Yellow Rose that you weren't supposed to be in the computer. It was all an…an accident. These dates…they're just for show. Aren't they?"

He circled the pickup, his movements slow and measured and deliberate. Even so simple an act spoke of tightly caged power. "Yes, I agreed to date you for my grandmother's sake. No, I wasn't supposed to be in the computer. As to whether or not it was all an accident, only my grandmother and Wanda know the answer to that." He stopped directly in front of her. "And finally, if imagining our dates are for show makes you more comfortable, then go right ahead and believe it. As far as I'm concerned, they're to test whether or not a ninety-nine percent match is good enough."

She forced herself to stand her ground, refusing to scurry from his approach. It was tough, especially considering how her feet itched to do some fast backpedaling. But she managed. "Good enough for what?"

"To go from dating to something more."

That's what she'd been afraid of. From the start, she'd run scared. Now it turned out she'd been justified. "Maybe we could give this one date a try and not worry about the rest. In fact, if it's a really lousy date, you might not want another," she suggested hopefully.

"I agree." He swallowed her elbow with one huge hand and escorted her to the front door of his home.

"You do?" Relief washed through her, as revitalizing as a cool spring shower.

"Yup. You don't need to worry about a thing. I'll take care of all that, particularly the worrying."

"That's not what I meant," she began. Stepping across the threshold, she lost track of what she'd been saying. "Oh, my."

"Like it?"

"What's not to like?"

Cassidy looked around with hungry eyes. Now here was a home, well loved and well-worn. In the entranceway, wide, pegged-oak planks gleamed like mellowed gold in the late-afternoon sunlight. The wood was slightly trenched in places, giving evidence of generations of traffic. In front of her extended a long hallway. Off to one side she glimpsed a parlor, while off the other was a spacious living room. Above her, attached to a heavy iron chain, hung a wagon-wheel chandelier.

Ty noticed the direction of her gaze. "It came off the wagon the first Merrick bride rode in on."

"I'll bet everything around here has a history."

"Just about."

"I don't."

Ty cocked his head to one side. "You don't what?"

Cassidy indicated the pioneer antiques that dotted the parts of the house she could see. "Have a history like this."

"Everyone has a history. Some know it and some don't."

"Well, I don't." She didn't understand why she was making such an issue of it.

"Does it bother you?"

Truth vied with the need to protect herself. As usual, honesty won out. "Yes."

"Progenitor envy? I never would have thought you capable of it," he mocked lightly.

Her mouth twitched. Unable to help herself, she turned to smile at him, realizing her mistake an instant too late. He stood lounging against one of the rough-cut support pillars, looking for all the world like a gunslinger from the old West—tall, broad, lean and deadly. And resolute. Very resolute. His eyes glinted in the dusky foyer, reflecting endless patience and determination, as well as a heat more scorching than El Paso in August.

"Damn," she whispered.

He inclined his head, his comprehension instantaneous. "My thoughts exactly."

Escape became imperative, the urge driven by sheer, unadulterated panic. *Not safe, not safe, not safe*! shrieked the voices. She backed toward the door, untangling her feet as she went. "I can't do this. I thought I could, but I can't."

"You can't have dinner with me?" he asked gently.

"You know what I mean. I can't do..." Her hand darted through the air, just missing an heirloom hat rack. "This."

"Ah. Much clearer."

She glared at him. "Stop it, Ty. I don't know what you want from me. But whatever it is, I can't give it to you. Please take me home."

He hadn't moved from his position against the support post. But she noticed that all his many impressive ripples tensed. "What will you tell Hutch?"

Oh, no. Hutch. How could she have forgotten? "I'll...I'll tell him it didn't work out between us."

"You'd lie?"

That stopped her. She released her breath in a long sigh, her shoulders slumping in defeat. So much for escaping unscathed. "No."

"I didn't think so." He uncoiled from his position. "Come around back. We'll have dinner by the pool. I hope you don't mind if it's casual tonight."

She tucked a strand of hair behind her ear and smiled airily. Not that she fooled him. Oh, no. Not this guy. Not for one little minute. "Sounds great."

The pool area was dazzling and looked slightly out of place—too much for such a basic, stark environment. Slabs of various sized and hued rocks were cemented into a free-flowing patio with flowers dotting the area, some in halved whiskey barrels and others in stone planters. Mexican petunias were on the verge of blooming, while the verbena lobelia and portulaca had already flowered in a stampede of color. Off to one side was a trellised area with tables and chairs beneath. Overhead, the broad leaves of a hearty mustang grapevine provided shade. One of the tables had a gorgeous floral arrangement made up of yellow roses and baby's breath. Had he known how much she loved yellow roses, or was it in honor of his grandmother's business? Unwilling to consider the possibility they were for her, she turned her attention to the pool.

It was an amazing sight. Constructed of some sort of dark

rock, it had three levels with waterfalls flowing from one section to the other. Jagged stone slabs provided platforms for lounging on each of the levels. Thrift spilled from some of the rock ledges, the hot pink, blue and white flowers providing a brilliant floral cascade.

Overwhelmed, Cassidy didn't know what to say. "Wow" struck her as the safest comment.

"It was my father's contribution to the homestead," Ty explained dryly as they crossed to the table decorated with the roses. "The top pool is a hot tub. Useful during the summer, wouldn't you agree?"

Oh, dear. "I gather you don't use it much."

"Sure I do. I just turn off the heat and dump in a block of ice."

"Try squeezing in a bucket of lemons and adding a bag or two of sugar," she suggested brightly, taking a seat at the table. "You'll have it made."

He chuckled. "Sounds like a plan." A short, rawboned woman appeared then, carrying a tray with drinks. "Cassidy, this is Edith, my housekeeper."

Edith set a brimming glass of iced tea in front of Cassidy and a long-necked bottle of Shiner Bock beer in front of Ty. Drying her hands on her apron, she subjected Cassidy to an intent examination. An instant later, her expression relaxed and she smiled. "Willie was right. You'll do fine. Anything I can get for you, just holler. Hear?"

Cassidy couldn't decide how to answer the first part of the housekeeper's comments. As for the rest... "Thanks. I will," she finally said, deeming it the most appropriate reply.

"She doesn't mean any harm," Ty explained as soon as Edith left. "She's lived and worked here for so many years, she's become family. Unfortunately, that means she speaks her mind whether we want to hear it or not." Her expression must have been more revealing than Cassidy had intended because he sighed. "Okay, so it's a strange first date."

She let him off the hook with a laugh. "It's a relief to hear you say so. I was beginning to think the past twenty-four hours were normal for you."

He grimaced. "Yeah, right. I'm always inundated by ten-year-old brainiacs who want me to date their mothers. My grandmother is constantly computer-generating my women while my housekeeper gives them her personal stamp of approval." His mouth twisted to one side. "All they leave me to do is convince my date that she wouldn't rather be anywhere *except* with me."

If only that was true. "Well...not *anywhere*," she allowed. "There've been one or two side benefits to dating you." Including one brief instance when she'd been all too happy to curl up in his lap and let the world drift by while they shared some of the most exquisite kisses she'd ever experienced in her life. She forcibly buried the memory as deep as she could.

Apparently, it wasn't deep enough. Ty easily read her mind. Ignoring the glass Edith had provided, he hefted the beer and saluted her. "Thank heaven for ripples," he muttered, taking a long swallow directly from the bottle.

She gave him a cheeky grin. "You can say that again."

His gaze took fire, though he answered prosaically enough. "Since this isn't a normal first date, I thought we'd go over the application Hutch filled out and make sure it's right. Willie said she'd run it through the computer and see if there aren't more matches."

Cassidy choked on her tea. "More?"

"Three to half a dozen is typical. But for some reason the computer only came up with one for you."

Gazing across the flower-dotted patio, she strove for a nonchalant shrug. "Guess I'm not an easy match."

"Good."

Startled, she glanced at him. "Why is that good?"

"I don't feel like sharing."

She straightened in her chair. Uh-oh. "Look...I thought I made myself clear about this. Your kisses might knock

my socks off, but I'm not interested in any sort of relationship. Not ever. Got it?''

"Not even for Hutch?"

Ice clinked as she returned her glass to the table with
more haste than care. "That isn't fair."

"He wants a father."

"He has one. He doesn't need another."

"Then why did he turn up on Willie's doorstep?" Ty
didn't give her a chance to concoct an answer to that one.
He shoved his chair away from the table. "If you'll excuse
me, I'll get your application form and let Edith know we're
ready to eat."

Cassidy scowled at his back as he strode across the patio.
He must be aware that his leaving forced her to stew over
his parting shot. *Then why did he turn up on Willie's doorstep?* It was an excellent question. Did Hutch really want
a father so badly? He'd never said so. Of course, buying
those dates didn't leave a lot of room for misinterpretation.

She nibbled on her lower lip. Why was he suddenly so
anxious for a father? Was it something she'd done?
Something she hadn't done? She thought they were managing well enough. Sure, they had to watch their pennies.
But she'd always assumed they shared the same goals.
They both were after a home of their very own and a place
to put down roots. She reached for the floral arrangement
and fingered a velvety rose petal. Not to mention a place
to grow her yellow roses.

But apparently her son wanted more. A lot more.

The instant Ty returned, she asked, "Since you have all
the answers, tell me why Hutch wants a father." Her voice
had a husky, defenseless quality she hated. Had he heard
it? She couldn't afford to betray any weaknesses. Not to
him. Not when she was already so susceptible to him.

"Most boys want a dad," he replied, dropping a folder
on a vacant chair. "Is that unreasonable?"

"Yes." The word sounded whisper soft and gut-
wrenchingly painful. Cassidy could sense him absorbing

her reply. She expected a pitying expression to creep into his eyes. To her surprise, he shrugged matter-of-factly.

"Not all men are like your ex. You should know that by now."

She shivered. Not really. After Lonnie, she hadn't allowed a man close enough to risk getting hurt again. Nor would she. She'd barely survived the five years of hell she'd called married life. If she gave her heart into another man's keeping and he walked out on her...

"I won't marry again," she stated implacably.

Ty's mouth tightened. "I know you want me to accept that as your final word on the subject." He leaned across the table toward her, spearing her with those clear, soul-deep eyes. "But I won't."

It was that kiss. That damned kiss. She'd always been brutally honest with herself and this time was no different. She preferred facing facts squarely on, and the fact was...she and Ty made for a combustive combination. From the minute he'd pulled her into his arms, she'd been lost to everything but his touch. In fact, she'd been so lost in a sexual haze, she'd even allowed him to slip his hand beneath her skirt, something she hadn't done since... Just remembering brought a hot flush to her cheeks. Of course, he noticed.

To her eternal relief, Edith's arrival prevented him from commenting. The housekeeper placed steaming hot plates piled high with green hickory-smoked ribs and pinto beans in front of them. How odd to be on the receiving end of a meal instead of the one serving it.

"Real meat," she said appreciatively, not realizing until a second too late how her comment would sound.

Ty stilled. "Is that a treat for you?"

Crud and double crud. "Yes," she admitted, scrambling for an explanation that fell somewhere between the truth and a salve for her pride. "We try to limit our consumption of red meat." Although in her case it was because of cost rather than for health reasons. "Nice weather, isn't it?" Great. That was about as subtle as a train wreck.

Edith let her off the hook by slapping a small plate on one side of the table. "Thought you might also appreciate some damp towels," she said. "So I brought those along with the napkins."

"You thought right," Ty agreed. He glanced at Cassidy, his expression more tractable than earlier. "Ribs might be messy, but they're a guaranteed icebreaker. It's hard to be formal when you're covered in barbecue sauce."

To her amazement, his comment enabled her to relax. She couldn't remember the last time a man had gone out of his way to put her at her ease. And though she might not be happy about the situation she'd been forced into, she could certainly be gracious about it. "Aren't you upset that you've been caught up in this dating mess?" Kisses aside, that was.

"If the circumstances had been different, I would've been." He gave her a level look. "If the circumstances had been different, I would've put a stop to it."

What circumstances? she wondered uneasily. Perhaps she wouldn't risk asking. "So why didn't you stop it?" she demanded instead.

"Simple. I wanted to date you."

Her breath caught. Well, that was sure frank. It also gave the exact answer she least wanted to hear. "But I saw you arguing with your grandmother about it."

He shrugged. "That was before we kissed."

Damn! Why in the world did she have to give him such an enthusiastic come-on? "It was a simple kiss, Ty. Get over it."

He actually had the nerve to laugh. "It was more than that and you know it."

Maybe. All right, definitely. That still didn't change how she felt. "I told you. I'm not interested in dating." She shoved her plate aside. "I'm through with that."

"At twenty-nine?"

Her gaze darted away again. "What does age have to do with anything?"

"You're far too young to allow one bad experience—"

"You know nothing about it!" she snapped.

"I know what Hutch told me. And if I didn't think we'd suit, I'd have told Willie to run the application again."

"Aren't you doing that anyway?"

"I'm having her rerun the form for your sake, not mine."

That brought her up short. "Oh."

"It's the truth, Cassidy."

She released her breath in a gusty sigh. "I believe you." And she did. Ty hadn't made any bones about his attraction to her. She was the one running scared, not him.

"But trust comes hard, doesn't it?"

There was no point in denying it. "Sure does."

"Then why don't we make an agreement? No shading the truth. I think it's important we be honest with one another."

She wouldn't have too much trouble with that. The truth had a way of tumbling out of her mouth whether she wanted it to or not. "Okay."

He nudged her plate back in front of her. "When we're done eating, why don't we go over that application and make sure Hutch got it right."

"Okay." Her mouth pulled to one side in a half grin and her hunger returned with a vengeance. Good gravy, had she really been about to waste all these great ribs? "Worried about that one percent?"

"Terrified."

The minute they were finished and had cleaned off the excess barbecue sauce with the damp towels Edith had supplied, Ty picked up the folder and removed a stapled packet.

"Let's take a walk while we go over the application."

"Fine." Did she sound as nervous as she felt? It had been one thing to answer Ty's questions believing he was a kid working on a science project. But to let down her guard with the man striding beside her was another matter altogether.

He handed her the papers. "Here. Start with the first page. It's just the basic statistics. Age, height, weight, educational background, hair and eye color. That sort of thing. Does it look right to you?"

She glanced over the information, slipping swiftly past the line with her age. She always winced seeing it in black and white. "How did Hutch know my weight?"

"He didn't. I guessed after meeting you."

"You're two pounds off."

He reached into his shirt pocket. "Here's a pen. Feel free to change it."

"Not much point," she admitted ruefully. "After that meal we just ate, it's probably right on the mark. Oh, and you'll have to change my occupation. I'm not a waitress anymore."

"Leave it until you see what sort of job you pick up next week."

She could hear an undercurrent of determination in his voice and sighed. "You're still resolved to help me, aren't you?"

"Yup."

"Any point in my refusing?"

"Nope. Since I'm partially responsible for your losing your job, I should help you find another."

"Partially?"

"Well...I didn't drop lunch on the guy, but I suspect I was the cause." He leaned down so his mouth came dangerously close to the side of her face. "If you hadn't been busy looking at me, you might have paid more attention to that tray."

"I—"

"Now don't go forgetting our agreement."

She frowned in confusion. "What agreement?"

"To be truthful with each other."

Her mouth snapped shut. Darn it all! How did he know

she'd been about to fib? "All right, fine. You distracted me."

"The feeling's mutual, sweetheart."

Rattled, she buried her nose in the application. "Where were we?"

"Running away?"

"Yes."

"Go right ahead. I'll catch up soon enough."

That's what she was afraid of. She scanned the next page, her attention snagging on one of the answers. "Now where did he come up with this one?"

"Which?"

She pointed. "Ideal partner. Why would he think I'd want to date a cowboy?"

"I believe Hutch said that was the only type you hadn't tried before," Ty replied in neutral tones.

"*What*?"

He lifted an eyebrow. "A small misunderstanding?"

"To put it mildly. Oh!" She began to laugh. "Oh, dear. I think I see."

"Care to clue me in?"

"It's Hutch's dad. Lonnie was something of an expert at trying out different fields of endeavor. I believe at the time of our divorce the only type of employment he *hadn't* tried was wrangling."

Ty's mouth curved upward—a most attractive sight. "Got it."

She glanced at the sheet again and promptly choked. "Pet peeves...April Mae. I swear I'm going to kill that kid."

"Would you care to change it?"

"Yes! Where'd that pen go?" He recovered it from his shirt pocket and handed it over. "Turn around." Using his broad back as a table, she took perverse pleasure in scratching out April Mae's name and scribbling in "liars".

"Hey, easy. You already ruined one shirt today."

"Oh, sorry."

"Done?"

She forced herself to step away, fighting the temptation to linger over the broad, sweeping planes of his back and all those lovely, irresistible ripples. Yum. "Okay. I'm through."

He twisted around. "I think the rest of the questions were ones you answered on the phone. But you might want to give them a quick check, just to be sure."

She scanned the last few pages. "Looks fine to me."

"In that case, I'll give Willie the changes and let her run it again."

"Is that it, then?"

"Not quite. There's one more detail we still need to check out."

"What?"

"This."

She should have seen the kiss coming. Or perhaps she had and pretended otherwise. So much for absolute honesty. Just as before, she dove into the kiss with an enthusiasm he couldn't mistake. With a soft groan, he responded with equal zeal. Why did this keep happening? Cassidy wondered helplessly. She should be shoving him away, not clinging like moss to a rock.

The image seemed appropriate, though—soft on hard, flourishing in a place no life should be possible. Ty offered her heat where for so long she'd only known cold. He gave freely of himself rather than doling out affection in grudging nuggets. He'd never shown annoyance with her clumsiness or accused her of gracelessness. He hadn't even thought it. If he had, she'd have heard it rumble through his dark voice or seen it slip across his expression. She'd have sensed his impatience or distaste.

Instead, all he'd ever betrayed had been a stark desire, followed by an immutable determination to put his stamp on her, to claim her as his. She'd never experienced that before. And despite herself, she found it all too compelling.

She wanted to be loved to the exclusion of every other woman, just as she wanted to love as completely in return.

Love.

She ripped her mouth from Ty's, fighting for breath. Where the heck had that word come from? "I can't do this," she whispered, escaping from his arms in a whirlwind of hands, elbows and knees.

For a large man, he moved with amazing agility, escaping serious injury thanks to hair-trigger reflexes. "Easy, sweetheart, easy," he soothed. "It was just a kiss."

"If that's all it was, I wouldn't be overreacting like this," she argued, despising the small quiver fluttering through her voice. It made her sound unbearably vulnerable.

Gentle laughter glittered in his pale eyes. "Then you admit it was more than a simple kiss?"

She scowled. Somehow he'd tricked her. She wasn't quite sure how, but retreat seemed the best option. "I'd like to go home now, if you don't mind."

"Fine," he readily agreed, which only ticked her off all the more. No doubt he felt he'd won a major victory in their dating war. She wished he didn't appear so smug about it. Or so incredibly enticing.

Put a damper on it, girl!

And she tried. She sincerely tried the entire way home. But she fast came to the conclusion that the only thing guaranteed to ease her hunger would be to leave the feast. And that meant leaving Ty. The instant they reached her apartment complex, Cassidy jumped from the pickup, only to be brought up short at the steps to her building. Hutch sat on the stoop, a scruffy mop resting in a tangled heap beside him.

"I blew it, Mom," he began.

With a muffled groan, she turned to face Ty, not in the least surprised to find he'd followed her. "Looks like we're going to have to change that application form again," she warned.

"Really?" His calm reaction washed over her like a balm. "Why's that?"

She pressed her lips together to keep them from trembling. "We've just been evicted."

Progress Report

I told Mrs. Welch she didn't have to watch me after all. I wanted to get everything done without her figuring out what I was up to. I have to shut the computer down for a day or two, so I'm making a few last notes until I'm on-line again. Plan B has been set in motion and everything's proceeding right on schedule. Mom's due home any minute, so I have to get going. Want to be downstairs when she arrives. I wrote up my plan for Experiment #2, just in case this all works out. I know it's a bit premature, but—

Oops. The landlady's banging on the door. Gotta go.

CHAPTER FIVE

Experiment #2: Relocation
Goal: Okay, this is gonna be tricky. If Ty's protective instincts check out, he'll take care of Mom when she loses the apartment. I'm hoping he'll take us home with him. Of course, Mom is gonna say no. So I'll just have to find a way of making her agree without her realizing I'm behind it.
Procedure: Limit Mom's options so she has to let Ty help whether she likes it or not!

EVICTED. Cassidy didn't wrap it up in pretty words, Ty noted. Although how pretty she could have wrapped an eviction notice he couldn't quite imagine. His brows drew together as he considered her situation. What sort of sorry SOB would toss a helpless woman and child out on the streets in the middle of the night?

"You've been evicted?" Ty demanded of Hutch. "You sure?"

At the boy's confirming nod, Cassidy's shoulders slumped for a fraction of a second. Then she stiffened her spine and set her jaw. "Okay. We can deal with this."

"So that's where he gets it," Ty murmured.

She turned dark eyes in his direction. "Pardon me?"

He made a fist and lightly tapped her rounded chin. "Hutch always sticks his out, too. I gather it's a family trait." He'd knocked her off balance with his comment, which gave him a chance to address Hutch. "What happened?"

"Our landlady, Mrs. Walters, saw me with Miz Mopsey."

"Who?"

At the sound of her name, the mop beside Hutch shifted ever so slightly so that the tangle of off-white strings poofed out as if they'd been zapped with an electric charge. The dog offered a halfhearted, guilty-sounding bark. Hutch patted what might have been the head. "Animals aren't allowed here, so we've been keeping her secret."

Ty lifted an eyebrow. "Jeez, it's a dog. Who'd have guessed."

Hutch scuffed his toe. "I'm sorry, Mom. Mrs. Walters caught me sneaking the mop out for a walk and made me pack everything up. We have to leave *now*."

"She can't do that. It's illegal," Ty stated. "Why don't I talk to her?"

"*No!*" Hutch erupted off the step. "She…she was mean. I don't want to live here anymore. She wouldn't let Miz Mopsey stay inside even for one night. So we don't have any choice. We have to leave. Right away."

Right away, huh? Interesting. Ty folded his arms across his chest and did some jaw-setting of his own. "Trust me. I can change her mind."

Beside him, Cassidy stirred. "Thanks all the same, but this isn't your problem. It's mine. And it isn't just Miz Mopsey. We're also behind on the rent."

"I suspect that's my fault, too," he retorted, all the while keeping his gaze fixed on a red-faced Hutch. "You couldn't have earned much tip money today, thanks to me."

"No, I didn't," she conceded. "But it wouldn't have made that much difference. I had some unexpected car expenses this month, too. It put us behind."

"Still… The woman shouldn't have made Hutch sit out here on the stoop."

"To be honest," Hutch began—a first since they'd arrived, Ty was willing to bet, "it's Miz Mopsey who has to stay on the stoop. Not me. I was afraid to leave her alone, so I decided to sit with her until you got back."

"What about Mrs. Welch? Why isn't she still watching you?" Cassidy asked.

"I...uh...told her you'd just pulled up."

"You know better than that," she scolded, though clearly, her heart wasn't in the reprimand. "I'll go in and start packing."

"No need. I took care of everything." Hutch smiled angelically. "I didn't want you to have any more hassles after what you've been through today. So I packed everything up and stashed it right inside the door."

She leaned down and ruffled his hair, offering a tremulous smile. "Thanks, sweetpea. I don't know what I'd do without you."

"I could make a wild guess," Ty muttered.

She swiveled to frown at him. "What did you say?"

He attempted to match Hutch's innocent smile. "I said, I'd like to have you as my guests." He wasn't the least surprised when she shook her head.

"Thanks, but that's not necessary." Her tone was adamant. "We'll stay in a motel for a night or two while I look for a new place."

He could press the issue but suspected it wouldn't get him anywhere. Cassidy Lonigan might have a voice like sweet syrup, but it covered an indomitable will. Backing her in a corner would only force her to fight all the harder for her freedom. She didn't wait for his reply but opened the door to the apartment building and picked up the first of the boxes stacked inside. Clumping down the steps, she tripped along the sidewalk toward a rusted-out rattletrap. Watching her, Ty didn't know whether to laugh or pack the woman up in one of her own boxes and dump her in his truck. Following her example seemed the smartest choice for now. He climbed the steps and selected the largest of the cartons stacked by the door. Passing Hutch, he surprised a scowl on the boy's face.

"What's with you, kid?"

"Nothin'."

Yeah, right. It didn't take more than half a brain cell to figure out what was bothering the boy. "You don't know your mother real well, do you?"

That got a reaction. "Course I do! She's my mom."

"Then you ought to know what would happen if I insisted the two of you come home with me. Now get your butt off that stoop and grab a box."

By the time he and Hutch had reached Cassidy's bucket of bolts, she was on her way back for a second load. "She'd keep sayin' no," the boy said as they stowed the boxes in the car.

Ty suppressed a grin. So the kid had been paying attention. "And if I kept pushing her?"

"She'd tell you no, come hell or high water."

"Watch your mouth, boy."

"Yes, sir. Sorry."

Seeing that at least Hutch's contrition was sincere—if little else—Ty relented. "If there's one thing I've learned about your mother, it's that she's prideful and as self-sufficient as they come. I might not like the decisions those traits cause her to make, but I respect your mother too much to try to impose my will on her. It's her choice or no choice. So until we find a way to coax her down our pathway while keeping her pride and independence intact, we back off. Let her check out all the other available trails first. With luck, she'll eventually see things our way."

Hutch beamed. "No problem. I think I can get her on the right path."

"Now why doesn't that surprise me?" Ty muttered.

"Because you know I'm smart. Scary smart." The boy adjusted his glasses and fixed Ty with serious blue eyes. "And that doesn't bother you, right?"

Ty snorted. "Not hardly."

Something akin to relief crept into the boy's gaze. "Just checking. You could have changed your mind since earlier."

"I haven't and I won't. Now, do we have that settled once and for all?"

"Yeah."

Ty jerked his head toward Cassidy, who was lugging two scraggly potted rosebushes—nary a leaf or bud in sight—down the sidewalk. "Then shake a leg. We can't let your mom do all the work."

It didn't take long to load the boxes that contained the sum total of the Lonigans' meager possessions. With the exception of the computer, which had been carefully stashed by Hutch on the back seat, it was a pitiful collection. Even so, one large box didn't fit, no matter how many times Cassidy tried to force it.

"It's the books," she said to Hutch. "Maybe we should leave them for Mrs. Walters to donate to the library."

Ty folded his arms across his chest. "Or you could ask me to hold on to them until you're settled into your new place."

"I really don't want to impose..." she began, then ground to a halt. Something in his expression must have given a hint to the anger smoldering inside. With a quiet word of thanks, she turned the carton over to him. "I'll let you know where we end up."

"No need. I'll follow you to the motel."

"That's not necessary..." She released a gusty sigh. "You're going to pull the man thing, aren't you?"

"If you mean, am I going to make sure you get to a motel safely, then yes, I'm pulling the man thing." He eyed her vehicle in disgust. "Considering your car—and I use that term loosely—is held together by rust and sheer faith, it's the least I can do. And, no doubt, the least you'll allow me to do."

To his intense satisfaction, her expression revealed a hint of consternation. "Thank you," she murmured again. "I owe you. Come on, Hutch. Climb in."

To Ty's amusement, the boy didn't utter a single word of protest. Nor did he offer any words of farewell.

Interesting. Sudden suspicion held Ty in place. Sure enough, when Cassidy turned the key in the ignition, nothing happened. Not a cough. Not a whimper. Not even a bellow of smoke and gasping death rattle.

"Gosh, Mom," he heard Hutch exclaim. "What's wrong?"

"I…I don't know."

"Well, pop the hood and let me take a look."

Burying his amusement, Ty braced his shoulder against a convenient tree trunk and waited. Hutch climbed out, Miz Mopsey in tow. Cassidy joined them at the front of the car. She opened the hood and locked it in place while her son climbed onto the fender and peered into the greasy mass of wires and steel. Ty bit back a shout of laughter as the dog wriggled her way up beside the boy, snuffling beneath the hood as though offering her opinion on the matter.

"Need help?" he called, knowing before he even spoke what the answer would be.

"No, thanks," Hutch hastened to reply. "I see what it is." He glanced over his shoulder at his mother. "It's the caliper switch. Burned clean out."

She sighed. "Crud. Can it be fixed?"

"Not tonight."

Ty strolled over for a peek. Never having heard of a caliper switch, he was curious to see what the kid had done to the car. It only took a second to discover that the battery had been disconnected. He slanted a glance at Cassidy. She was totally oblivious. No question, mechanics weren't one of her strong points. Fortunately, mind-blowing kisses were.

"Sure you don't want some help?" he offered casually.

"Oh, no. Hutch can deal with it," Cassidy insisted.

Ty shrugged. "Okay by me." Hell if he'd argue. If she'd asked, he'd have told her the truth about the battery. But since she chose to be stubborn, she could suffer the consequences—especially since those consequences worked to his advantage.

"Well, darn." She ran a hand through her hair, turning the straight, dark sheet into an attractive tumble. "I wonder how expensive caliper switches are?"

That brought him up short. "I don't expect the repairs will cost you much at all," he hastened to reassure her. He'd be damned if he'd let the kid add to her financial worries.

"Really?" Relief surged through her voice.

"At the risk of stepping on your independent nature, could I offer you a place to stay tonight?" He strove for humble and came within spitting distance of it. "I have a cabin between the main house and the bunkhouse that's not in use."

"Oh." She brightened at that little tidbit. "That would be lovely. How much is the rent?"

White hot anger shot through him. He managed to control it through sheer dint of will. Barely. "Maybe you better take Miz Mopsey and go wait in the pickup," he advised softly. "Hutch and I will move everything over."

"But—"

"Now."

Her eyes widened in alarm and he knew it was just dawning on her that he was a hairbreadth away from thoroughly losing his temper. "Are you upset about something?"

"I'd be happy to discuss it with you another time."

She planted her hands on her hips, compelling him to jump clear of her elbows. "Is it because I wouldn't go home with you initially?"

Since Cassidy was intent on discussing this out on the sidewalk, he'd empty the pasture. No point in innocent bystanders getting injured in the ruckus when they locked horns. Ty caught Hutch's eye and jerked his thumb toward the pickup. "Hutch, you wait in the truck with Miz Mopsey."

Hutch looked from one to the other with interest. "You and Mom gonna fight?"

"Discuss, boy. We're discussin' the situation."

"You might want to discuss, but I've seen Mom like this before. She wants to fight."

"*Hutch*!" Cassidy and Ty rapped out in unison.

"Fine. But you're not fooling me." Hutch stared pointedly at Ty. "I warned you I was smart. It doesn't take a mental giant to see you two are ready to rumble." With that astute observation, he gathered up his dog and trotted toward the pickup.

"There. See what you've done?"

Ty drew a deep breath. Patience. If he could just manage to hang on to his patience, he'd have the future Mrs. Merrick safely almost-tucked in his house. The cabin was just a few short steps away. No doubt an excuse would arise that would bounce the stubborn woman from there into his arms—and into his bed.

"Apparently, my eyesight isn't that great," he allowed, hustling Cassidy to the far side of the tree he'd been leaning against—and more importantly, out from under Hutch's watchful eye. "What have I done?"

"You've upset my son."

"Your son is not upset."

"You made me yell at him."

"He handled it amazingly well."

"I *never* yell at him."

"He'll live. Now, are you going to help load these boxes, or would you rather wait in the truck with Hutch?"

Her chin made a reappearance, poking in his direction. "I think it would be best if you drop us off at a motel."

He'd had all he could take. Striking with a speed that would have done a rattler proud, he snagged her around the waist and yanked her up against him. He avoided her pinwheeling arms and a wayward knee with practiced ease. Her size ten sandals were another matter. Why the hell did the heels on women's shoes have to be so damned pointy? Fortunately, his boots were tough and her accidently tromping on him didn't hurt much more than when he'd broken his leg. He decided to ignore the crunching pain, especially since kissing her made it well worthwhile.

Their mouths collided, then joined in complete accord. Her lips were soft and moist beneath his, eagerly parting at the touch of his tongue. She wrapped around him with all the warmth of lamb's wool on a frigid night and he returned the favor by easing into her with the same sigh he used slipping into a steaming hot tub after a hard day of wrangling.

His reaction to her touch was stronger than before. The closest he'd come to the sensation was when he'd slammed back a double shot of whiskey. The liquor-driven wildfire had shot from his throat straight to his gut and left him feeling both powerful and sucker punched, all at the same time.

Cassidy hit harder still. She also brought out every primitive instinct he possessed and every protective one, as well. He needed her in his life with a desperation he couldn't mistake. Now all he had to do was convince her that she burned just as fiercely for him.

He pressed her against the tree trunk, leaning into her. Hell, he fell into her. His mouth moved more forcefully on hers and he filled his hands with her soft, plump breasts, thumbing the kerneled tips. She must have liked it. With a low groan, her nails climbed his back, carving deep, loving half-moons into his flesh. She even stopped grinding into his toe long enough to clip his ankle, wrapping a long leg around his. He only prayed he lived long enough for her to love him to death in bed.

The honking of a nearby truck horn forced him to release her.

She stared up at him, her gray eyes silver in the moonlight. "Are you trying to kiss me into submission?"

"Is it working?"

She hesitated. The instant he started to lower his head again, she broke into speech. "I think that was Hutch honking. Maybe we'd better load those boxes."

"And where am I taking you?"

She cleared her throat, offering a tentative smile. "Would you be willing to put us up for a day or two?"

"And how much is the rent?"

"I believe…" She moistened her lips—plump, damp, delicious lips. Lips still carrying his taste, he was willing to bet. "I believe you offered to have us as your guests."

"Now was that so hard?"

"I'm not used to having someone else in control. I'm usually the one who manages everything."

"You think I'm trying to take over, is that it?"

"It sure feels that way."

"Well, I'm not. I admire strong women. Hell, Willie's about as tough as they come. The only time you'll get a fight from me is when you're choosing the most difficult path just to be ornery."

"Going to a motel was not—" One look in his direction and she broke off what she'd been about to say and closed her mouth. Skirting the tree, she grabbed her precious rosebushes from the trunk of the car and trotted toward his pickup.

"At least life will never be dull," he muttered to himself.

Depositing the potted bushes in the bed of Ty's truck, Cassidy glanced at him over her shoulder, offering a dazzling smile. Uh-oh. "I have an idea. I can help around the ranch in exchange for room and board. How about that?"

He restrained himself from responding. It was tough, but he did it. "Nope," he said beneath his breath. "It'll play hell with my self-restraint, but it won't be the least dull."

Ty stood at the door of the cabin, his arms folded across his chest. "How did this happen?"

"I'm sorry, Ty," Hutch said with a big show of contrition. "I musta left the door open when I took our clothes over to your laundry room. I guess the stupid critter snuck right in. Thank goodness we hadn't unpacked your pickup yet."

Cassidy sniffed, her expression clearly one of disgust. "A skunk!"

"Don't scrunch up your face like that, Mom," Hutch whispered. "It'll give you wrinkles."

Ty's foreman, Lorenzo, stuck his head in the doorway, then swiftly withdrew. "Damnedest thing I ever heard of, boss."

"Isn't it though." Ty pinned his gaze on the shuffling ten-year-old beside him.

"There are six different types of skunks indigenous to Texas, you know," Hutch volunteered, a hint of anxiety creeping into his voice. He fingered his glasses, nudging them higher on the bridge of his nose. "It coulda been a western spotted skunk. They favor rocky bluffs like this area around here."

"Think so?" Ty asked very, very softly.

"Maybe." The boy blinked rapidly. "I know it wouldn't be the eastern spotted. We're too far west for them. Or the hooded skunk. They're pretty darned rare. And they tend to be farther south, as I recall."

"You seem to recall quite a bit."

"Well, I do remember a few facts from the books I've read. Like…" He swallowed, darting Ty a nervous glance before doggedly continuing. "Like it could also have been a striped skunk. 'Cept they'd rather be in the woods."

"You read some weird books, kid," Lorenzo offered. "Ever tried comics?"

"No, sir. Not since I was three. As for the skunk…it could also be the common hog-nosed."

"Don't have any rooter skunks around here," the foreman explained kindly. "Wonder what made him spray?"

Ty fixed his gaze on his soon-to-be son. "Or why he'd be out exploring during the day. Most skunks are nocturnal."

Hutch swallowed visibly. "Gosh. Who knows? Maybe he has insomnia. That might have made him upset enough to spray."

Ty glanced at Cassidy, his mouth tightening into a grim line. She looked like hell. No doubt she felt like it, too. Right now, she carried the weight of the world on her shoulders and this latest incident was one more crisis she didn't need.

"Did it ruin anything?" she asked, tension vibrating through her voice.

"We were real lucky, Mom. None of our clothes got it since we had all that wash to do. And I hadn't unpacked my computer yet."

"Or much of the truck, by the look of things." Ty stepped through the doorway of the cabin and inhaled deeply. The pungent aroma had already started to dissipate. Interesting. He'd never known skunk stink to be quite so accommodating. "Guess that only leaves us with one op tion."

Cassidy nodded stoically. "Sure does. If you wouldn't mind driving us to a motel, I'd be grateful."

"No! We can't! I mean—" Hutch broke off and shrugged awkwardly. "I was hoping we could move into the bunkhouse instead. I've never stayed in one before. It sure would be educational."

Ty shook his head. "No way. That's a men-only bunkhouse. And your mom doesn't come close to qualifying."

"Oh," Hutch said with a return of last night's angelic innocence. "Where could *she* stay? Hey! I know. How about in the main house?"

"I don't think—" Cassidy began.

"Great idea." Ty gave Hutch a hearty slap on the back. To his credit, the boy only staggered a little. "Cassidy, you can stay up at the main house, and Hutch can sleep in the bunkhouse with the wranglers. Hope you like getting up early, kid. My men roll out around five-thirty."

"Five," Lorenzo corrected with a wicked grin. "And since you're off for spring break, *chico*, you can lend us a hand. See what wrangling's really about. What do you say?"

Ty didn't wait for the little genius to come up with an excuse. "Glad we have that settled. Lorenzo, get some of the men to move these boxes up to the main house. Hutch, you lend a hand."

"I'm not sure about this," Cassidy tried again.

"What could be better?" Ty wrapped an arm around her shoulders. "You'll have a place to stay while you look for an apartment and a new job. And we can get all those pesky dates out of the way. It's a win-win situation."

"I guess...."

"Would you mind helping Edith direct traffic? She'll show you the rooms you can use and you can tell the men which boxes go where."

She brightened right up, just as he'd hoped. Figured. No doubt she found the idea of telling people where to put things too appealing to resist. Oh, yeah. It was going to be a very interesting marriage. He slanted Hutch a quick look. Once he explained who was in charge of this little party. He caught the boy by the scruff of his neck before he could scamper off, ignoring his desperate little wiggles to break free.

"While you help Edith, I'll get Hutch settled," he informed Cassidy with a winning smile, praying she wouldn't notice her son squirming beneath his hold. She didn't, and the minute she'd escaped hearing range, he addressed her son. "Give it up, boy. You might be able to talk rings around half of Texas, but you don't have a prayer of talking your way from under my hand."

Hutch scuffed a well-worn sneaker in the dirt, the fight draining clean out of him. "Okay. I won't run."

"You have something to tell me, boy?"

"Yes, sir."

"Get to it."

"It wasn't a skunk that made that smell. I did it with some chemicals."

"You mean you lied. Again."

Hutch gulped. "Yes, sir."

"What did I tell you about lying?"

"You don't abide it."

"No, I don't. You have something more to tell me?"

Hutch attempted a smile, the angelic devil back for an encore. "I don't understand. What do you mean?"

"Don't bother shoveling that line of bull with me. Unlike your mother, I know a cowpatty when I'm about to tromp through it. I'm talking about the apartment and the car."

Hutch's face collapsed into lines of defeat. "We were evicted. Honest. That much is true. But…" His chin wobbled briefly before he brought it under rigid control. "But only after I walked Miz Mopsey past Mrs. Walters's door once or twice. Or maybe a bit more."

Ty bit down on his tongue. Hard. "What about your mom's car?"

"I disconnected the battery cables," Hutch whispered.

"Why?"

"So you'd take us home with you. That way, you and Mom could…you know."

"Oh, I know all right. But you sure as hell shouldn't."

Ty thumbed his Stetson to the back of his head as he mulled over his options. He had half a mind to clue Cassidy in on the whole sad story. But the stress he'd seen lining her face gave him pause. If he told, pride would force her into a motel. Not only would it add to her financial burden, but…damn it all. He'd only just gotten her here. He didn't want her leaving. So, what the hell should he do?

Hutch echoed Ty's thoughts. "What are you going to do?"

"If I was smart, I'd tell your mother about all the stunts you've pulled."

"Hey, Ty? Since you don't mind that I'm smart, I don't mind if you aren't," Hutch offered generously.

Ty suppressed a laugh. Fixing a fierce scowl on his face, he said, "Don't get cocky, kid. That's three times you've hung me up with your lie. There better not be a fourth incident or you'll live to regret it."

"No, sir. There won't be." Hutch peeked up at him, for the first time looking far younger than his ten years. "Are you going to punish me?"

"There'll be consequences, that's for sure." Maybe if he kept the boy busy, he wouldn't have time for mischief. Doubtful, but it wouldn't hurt to try. "First, get that cabin aired out. Then clean it from top to bottom. Edith will tell you where to find the supplies."

"I'll take care of it right away. Anything else?"

"Yeah. Just to make certain you don't have the energy to come up with any more clever ideas, the next two weeks you're going to learn all about wrangling. Lorenzo will be happy to teach you."

Hutch grinned. "I can? Really?"

"Don't get too excited. It's hard work and long hours."

The boy shrugged. "I'm used to that," he said with heart-tugging sincerity. "I don't mind."

"Tell me that at the end of the two weeks and I might believe you. And finally, I want your word of honor that you're through lying."

"I am. I promise."

"Not so fast." Ty propped his size fifteen boot on the first step of the cabin and leaned down so he and Hutch were at eye level. "You take a minute to think about what I'm asking. A man's word might be all he has to offer someone. You don't give it lightly. And once given, you stick to it, no matter how tough it might prove to be."

Hutch stared solemnly through the glinting lenses of his glasses. "No fudging, huh?"

"None."

"Okay. I give you my word. I won't tell any more lies."

"Fair enough." Ty held out his hand, engulfing the boy's in a man-to-man shake. To his surprise, Hutch didn't rush off but stood shuffling his feet some more. "All right, kid, spill it," he prompted with a sigh.

"Well..." The boy adjusted his glasses for a moment

before continuing. "Since we're being so honest, I think there's something you should know."

Just great. One more lie to keep from Cassidy. "What's that?" he asked warily.

"It's about the reason I bought Mom those dates...."

Ty waited, not quite sure where this latest confession was headed.

"You see...I went to Miss Willie's because I wanted to get myself a dad," Hutch revealed in a rush.

Okay, that wasn't so bad. It merely confirmed what Ty had long suspected. "Yeah, I guessed as much. I wouldn't consider that a lie, so don't sweat it."

"Thanks, but there's another reason I bought Mom all those dates."

That figured. "Go on."

It took three more minutes of foot scuffing and throat clearing before Hutch managed to spit it out. "Mom's planning on moving back to Georgia."

Damn. "I hope you're joking, kid."

"I wish I was. You see, Mom's aunt and uncle live there. They're the ones who raised her. When she got married, they weren't real happy about what she'd done. But now she wants to move back there so she can mend fences and put down roots. At least that's what she said."

Ty swore beneath his breath. He'd hoped to have time to slowly court Cassidy, to break down the barriers she'd spent so many years erecting. But it looked like their leisurely courtship was about to turn into a whirlwind romance. And unfortunately, it would take a hell of a lot more than sweet talk and kisses to persuade a certain wary divorcée to walk down the aisle with him. She wouldn't be easily wooed back into the marriage bed, no doubt about that.

"When's she planning to move?" he demanded.

"As soon as she's saved enough money to make the drive and completed one last goal she set for herself."

"Goal? What goal?"

Hutch shrugged. "Never said. But I know it's important."

"Okay. Thanks for warning me. I'll take care of it."

"What are you going to do?"

Ty glanced toward the main house and sighed. "Why don't you let me worry about that particular problem? Maybe I can offer her some incentive to stay put for a while."

"Sure you don't need my help?"

Ty managed to contain his response to a simple, unequivocal, "Positive."

"I don't know," Hutch said morosely. "Once Mom's made up her mind, it's real tough to get her to change it. She can be pretty darned stubborn."

"Yeah, well, I can be pretty darned persuasive. In case you weren't aware, gentle persuasion has moved many a stubborn mule."

Hutch's pale brows drew together. "What if that doesn't work?"

"Then I'll hog-tie her to a fence rail until she sees reason."

And chances were good he'd have to do precisely that.

Progress Report

I'm back on-line now and the experiments were a success. Ty did just what I hoped. You know…he's okay. He's kinda tough, but fair. Even when he found out what I'd done, he didn't yell or anything. And he didn't treat me like a kid, even though he keeps calling me that. He's punishing me for lying, but that's okay. Except for having to clean the cabin, the punishment is gonna be fun. I always wanted to be a cowboy, even if it's only for a couple of weeks.

Oh! And I told him about Georgia. Boy, was he mad. But at least he knows. Maybe now he can stop her.

I don't want to move to Georgia. I want to stay in Texas. I want to stay with Ty.

The truth is…I want Ty to be my dad.

CHAPTER SIX

Experiment #3: Living at Ty's + Romantic Situations = Love
Goal: I think people fall in love faster when they hang around together a lot. Now, Mom won't go for that. She's really good at saying no! And Ty seems to want to take it slow for some stupid reason. So I'll have to find ways to hurry them along if I'm gonna have a dad before I turn fifty!
Procedure: Get them in places where they'll want to kiss. (Yuck!)

TY CONFRONTED Cassidy across the generous expanse of his office. "The hell with gentle persuasion! I should have known it would never work with you," he bellowed. So much for broaching this subject with delicacy and tact. "Now, what do you mean you're moving to Georgia?"

The hell with gentle persuasion? Where had that come from and what did it have to do with her impending move? "What's wrong with Georgia?" Cassidy bellowed right back, grateful for the solid door separating Ty's office from the rest of the house. With luck, it would limit the number of people overhearing their "discussion". Well...with a *lot* of luck.

He glared at her for an endless moment before muttering, "I don't live there and neither should you."

Her lips twitched and her anger faded as swiftly as it had risen. "Do you realize how ridiculous that sounds?"

Unfortunately, while her annoyance had ebbed, his had intensified. He booted a leather ottoman out of his path and came to loom over her. Not that she let him get away with it. Heck, no! She shoved her nose to within inches of his and glared back.

"I'm ridiculous?" he demanded. "Why? Because I want you to stay here? Because I'm willing to admit there might be something happening between us, while you're intent on running away?"

He knew just which buttons to push to ignite her temper. "I'm not running away." She fought to lower her voice. "I'm going home."

"Home?" That stopped him. "Why didn't you mention this before?"

"I…" Good question. Why hadn't she? Maybe she hadn't said anything because she suspected he'd react precisely like this. Or maybe she'd kept quiet because she'd taken one too many pages from Lonnie's book on how to sneak away without anyone knowing. "It didn't come up," she said, airing the excuse with a hint of bravado.

Not that he swallowed it. "Bull. We agreed to be honest with each other, remember? Now give it to me straight. Why are you moving to Georgia? I thought you'd told me you didn't have a heritage or roots or a home like mine."

"I don't. Not really. I guess you could say Georgia is as close to a home as I've ever had."

Home. How odd that sounded. She'd never thought she'd call her old neighborhood by that name again. Not in this lifetime. But if she reconciled with Aunt Esther and Uncle Ben, she and Hutch would have family and roots. They'd finally belong instead of being tossed to and fro across Texas like hapless tumbleweeds. She could stop running.

"You still consider Georgia in those terms—as home—even after a ten-year absence?"

Not really. "Of course."

"You have family there?"

"An aunt and uncle," she admitted. "We've exchanged a number of letters recently and they've indicated that they'd like me to come back. They want to get to know Hutch and put our problems behind us. They're not as young as they used to be and I'm not sure how much longer they can manage on their own." She gave a helpless shrug. "It seems right somehow."

"To mend fences and put down roots."

"I see you've been talking to Hutch."

Ty ran a hand across the back of his neck. "A bit. I can tell you he's not anxious to leave Texas." His eyes glittered with undisguised frustration. "I'm not anxious for you to leave, either."

Why did she have the uncontrollable urge to throw herself into his arms and confess her desire to remain right where she was? Why did the idea of returning to Georgia suddenly feel so very wrong? And why did a part of her continue to fight so darned hard to deny those urges?

"That decision was made long before we met."

"And now that we *have* met?" He dropped his hands to her shoulders, enclosing her in warmth. It was a warmth she wanted to inhale clear down to her soul, a revitalizing warmth like a fragrant summer breeze on a starlit night. It carried the whisper of promises kept and hope renewed and a fathomless, endless love. "Now that we've touched each other, now that we've kissed?"

She shivered, caught by those dueling urges. The one continued its strident demand that she find a home in his arms and never leave, while the other replayed the history of her last botched love affair. Her only love affair. The voices of fear won and she pulled free of his grasp, surrendering ground in order to distance herself from him. She tripped over the poor abused leather ottoman in her haste and it rolled drunkenly on its side.

"Look..." She lifted her chin, attempting to project a calm control she didn't feel. "I left home under unfortunate circumstances—"

"You got married. Sure, it didn't work out, but at least you—"

"I was pregnant." The truth escaped in a rush.

That brought him up short. "A shotgun marriage?"

"Not really. My aunt and uncle didn't want me to marry at all. They thought I should have the baby and put him up for adoption. Instead, I took off and married Lonnie."

"Does Hutch know?"

She shook her head. "I haven't mentioned it. If he'd ever asked, I'd have been frank with him." She gave a self-conscious shrug. "There's not much point in lying. All he has to do is check the date on my marriage certificate against his birthday. Since there's only seven months between the two, it doesn't take a lot of brain power to figure out what happened."

Compassion turned his eyes to jade. "No. I can't see Hutch being easily fooled."

"Nor would I want to fool him." She wrapped her arms around her waist, aware of how telling the defensive gesture must appear. "For all Lonnie's faults, he did the honorable thing by me back then. It wasn't easy for him. He's a runner by nature and it must have taken a lot of guts to marry me when every instinct urged him to grab the first bus out of town."

"So why did he run after five years? Why hang in there so long?"

Cassidy firmed her lips, praying Ty wouldn't notice how they trembled. But to this day, the memories skulked in the far recesses of her mind like shadowy nightmares. "He didn't hang in there. He ran at the first opportunity—one short month before Hutch's birth, to be exact."

"The month *before*..." Comprehension dawned, along with a deep, burning anger, an anger directed squarely at Lonnie. "And you spent the next five years chasing after him."

Hearing it stated out loud made her decision seem downright pathetic. But she'd been so young and so scared. And so desperately broke. Pride had come last in a long list of needs—a list Hutch had topped, just as he topped it now. "Something like that."

"What stopped you from following him? April Mae?"

"No. I could have dealt with that. But he hurt Hutch, said unforgivable things. And that made me realize that no father was better than a bad one." By that time, she'd also discovered that she could scrape by on her own.

"I'm sorry, Cassidy. You must know that not all men are like Lonnie. Some of us have staying power."

A knock at the door saved her from answering. Edith poked her head into the room and glowered at them. "Dinner's on," she announced. "Miss Willie arrived while you two were having your little discussion. When she heard the set-to goin' on in here, she decided to wait in the dining room with young Hutch. She asked for a drink. A strong one. And the boy asked for one, too. Gave him the most powerful lemonade I had on hand. If we don't eat soon, the sugar rush is like to knock him loopy."

Ty nodded. "Go ahead and serve the meal. We'll be right there." The second the door slammed behind her, he turned to Cassidy. "This discussion isn't over yet."

"It is as far as I'm concerned." She kicked the upended ottoman back into position. To her surprise, Ty leaped out of the way. Jeez. No need to overreact. It wasn't as if she was aiming at him or anything. "Now that Hutch has told you about Georgia, you can understand that a relationship between us would be impossible."

"We'll see," was all he said. "Shall we eat?"

"I could use the fortification," she muttered.

A quick grin slashed across his face. "Stoking up for our next battle?"

"Something like that."

"Oh, don't worry. I'll keep you well fed." He waited until she swept past before adding, "Not that it'll do you any good. This is one war I intend to win."

To Cassidy's relief, dinner turned out to be a delight. Willie entertained them with stories of her dating agency and the various matches they'd made, particularly her most recent ones. "Autumn and Clay were already crazy about each other," she explained. "They were just too stubborn to realize it."

Cassidy cupped her chin in her palm and smiled wistfully. "But you got them to see the light?"

"Not me," Willie denied. "I have to give Maria credit for that one. She knew how to handle those two. And don't forget Cody and Emily."

"Not to mention that damned magazine article," Ty inserted in annoyed tones.

"What article?" Cassidy questioned, thoroughly confused.

"Now, Ty, don't fuss. Emily didn't know they were going to do a hatchet job on us. That was the magazine editor's fault. Fortunately, Wanda saw through all the lies and ended up making the perfect match, without even using the—" Willie broke off with a laugh and inclined her head toward Hutch. "Good gracious. I think it's time a certain young man turned in."

Startled, Cassidy glanced at her son. He'd nodded off at some point, his cheek pillowed by an uneaten pile of mashed potatoes. His glasses sat cockeyed on his face, making him appear far younger than ten and infinitely more vulnerable than when he was awake and busily manipulating the world around him and the hapless mortals peopling it. Beneath his chair, Miz Mopsey snored delicately, apparently as exhausted as her master.

"I'll carry him to one of the spare bedrooms," Ty offered. "I think the bunkhouse better wait one more night."

Cassidy pushed back her chair. "Thanks. I don't know what's wrong with him. I've never seen him so worn out. You'd think he'd spent the whole day working instead of exploring the ranch."

Inexplicably, Ty chuckled. "Oh, I suspect he found a chore or two to keep him busy. Get used to it, Cassidy. Ranch life might be a bit more physically strenuous than he's used to, but it won't hurt him."

Her maternal concern faded. "I'm sure you're right. In

fact, it'll probably be good for him." She watched as Ty levered her son onto his shoulder. Scrawny arms crept around his neck and clung. For some reason, the sight brought tears to her eyes. She cleared her throat, hoping no one would notice how husky her voice had grown. "He doesn't get out in the fresh air as much as I'd like."

"Don't tell me we're in agreement about something?" Ty demanded. "You're willing to admit that ranch life is good for the boy?"

She wrinkled her nose at his teasing. "I suppose that ninety-nine percent had to kick in sometime."

"Ninety-nine point four," Willie corrected, her tone reflecting intense satisfaction.

Cassidy turned, surprising a smug expression on the older woman's face. "Excuse me?"

"I reran your form with the alterations Ty gave me and it came up ninety-nine point four percent this time. It seems the changes improved your odds."

Oh, great! "Well, maybe…" she conceded. "But there's still that one percent difference."

"Point six," Ty corrected, gently digging potatoes out of Hutch's ear and wiping gravy off his cheek. "And closing all the time."

"According to the computer," Cassidy pointed out before addressing Willie again. "I don't suppose your machine made any additional matches?"

"Nope. Looks like you're still stuck with my grandson." She lifted her glass and winked. "Better the devil you know, I always say."

"Hey! Whose side are you on?" Ty protested.

No question about that. Clearly, Miss Willie approved the match as much as Ty and Hutch. Which left her standing all alone and defenseless—not to mention tempted beyond endurance to buckle beneath their not-so-subtle pressure. "What would you have done if there'd been other matches?" Cassidy asked.

A lazy grin crept across his mouth as he started to leave

the dining room. She gave chase, curious to hear his answer. "I'd have invited them up to the ranch," he explained as he headed down a long hallway. "That way, I could have checked them out before they dated you."

Yeah, right. "Don't you mean scared them off?"

He shoved open the bedroom door next to hers. "That, too."

"I don't get it. Why are you so certain we'd make a good match?" She turned down the bed and stepped out of the way so Ty could lower her son to the crisp cotton sheets. "I mean, it can't really be because the computer said so."

He tugged off Hutch's sneakers and jeans and then removed his glasses, gently setting the wire rims on the nightstand. "It isn't."

She moistened her lips, steeling herself to ask the question that had been plaguing her since yesterday. "It's that kiss, isn't it?"

"Yes." With infinite care—more care than she'd ever seen Lonnie display—Ty pulled the sheet over Hutch and tucked it around the boy's sleeping form. "Didn't you feel it, too?"

She preceded him across the room and switched out the lights. "That's just a physical response," she replied in an undertone. "Hardly enough to base a serious relationship on." She should know. She'd fallen into that trap once before.

He pulled Hutch's door closed. "It's a start."

She shied away from the eventual outcome that predicted. Why couldn't she get across that she wasn't interested in a long-term affair? Heck. She wasn't even interested in a short-term one. "But there's more, isn't there? More than just a kiss."

He hesitated in the darkened hallway. "I guess you'd call it a family tradition."

"Kissing?" she asked in disbelief.

A broad smile slid across his bronzed face. "That's right."

"Interesting tradition."

"Oh, it gets even more interesting." He propped his shoulder against the wall and captured her hand, drawing her to a halt. "You see, according to legend, the Merricks always know their soul mates when they finally meet."

Not safe! In a replay of their first meeting, the words shrieked in her head, threatening to deafen her. But she was helpless to resist his comment or the inexorable pull on her hand. "How do you know?" she demanded.

"The same way you knew. It only took one kiss."

Panic darkened her eyes to slate. "No. Don't say that."

"It's only fair that I tell you the truth."

Fair? What was fair about any of this? Her response to his kisses wasn't fair. Hutch's desperation to have a father wasn't, either. But least fair of all was her uncontrollable reaction to Ty, a reaction that echoed his and that grew more intense with each hour in his company. "You don't understand. I'm not interested in dating."

"You got that part across loud and clear. The question that remains is…why?" He tilted his head to one side. "I've heard Hutch's opinion on the matter. What I haven't heard is yours." He paused a beat. "But not tonight, I don't think. You look exhausted."

He'd let her off the hook and ironically enough he did it at the very moment she was tempted to crawl into his arms and tell him everything. She really must be exhausted. "I think I should turn in now." *Ask me to stay.*

He feathered a hand along her cheek. "Anytime you want to talk, I'll be here for you."

"Thanks. Please say good-night to your grandmother for me." She took a deep breath, almost drowning in the scent of him. Using every scrap of strength she possessed, she turned away. After all, her independence was more important than anything.

Right?

* * *

Cassidy glanced around the room Ty had assigned her and released a sigh that was half beatific and half sorrowful. This one room was larger than her entire apartment—and that didn't even include the attached bathroom. The tub alone could hold the navy's Pacific fleet with room to spare for a yacht or two.

Clipping her ankles as she attempted to skirt the haphazardly stacked boxes, she dug through the smallest of the cartons for her scrapbook. Next to her rosebushes, it was her most prized possession.

She managed to unearth the overstuffed book and carried it to the huge four-poster bed, dropping it onto the mattress. It did a lovely little bounce before scattering a few odd mementos across the spread. To her amusement, one of them was a note she'd written, praising her last apartment for being so roomy. Of course, without furniture to clutter up the place, a shoe box would seem spacious.

Stripping off her clothes, she dug through another box for her nightgown. Pulling on the slip of cotton, she returned to the bed and plopped down beside her scrapbook. "Plopping" proved to be her undoing. For some inexplicable reason, landing so solidly on the bed was one more mistake in the multitude that comprised her life.

The bed collapsed at one end and the mattress tilted against the wall, sending her and the scrapbook cartwheeling toward the headboard. She banged against the heavy oak frame and was instantly buried beneath an endless cascade of downy pillows and soft cotton bedding. With a muffled shriek, she kicked her legs to try to free herself from her cocoon. Not that it did much good, since her feet were sticking straight up in the air.

The next thing she knew, the door ricocheted open. There was an instant of absolute silence, broken by a half-smothered chuckle.

"Don't you dare laugh!" she ordered crossly.

"Sorry." She heard Ty's leisurely tread as he approached. A second later, he peered down at her with an expression of careful inquiry. "Need help?"

With all her heart, she wished she could refuse. Considering she was practically standing on her head, her dignity spared only by the fortuitous drape of a sheet, she didn't dare brush him off. She glared at her toes for several long seconds as she weighed wisdom against pride. Too bad she hadn't been able to spare the extra couple bucks to purchase an eye-catching red polish for her toenails, she thought irritably. Maybe it would have distracted him just a tad. But, no. They were as naked and exposed as the rest of her and he wasn't the least bit distracted. Her dilemma held his full attention.

Crud.

"Yes, I could use your help," she said, surrendering with a sigh. "If you wouldn't mind."

"My pleasure." He reached down and slipped his hands beneath her arms, carefully lifting her free of her predicament. To her relief, he also snagged the sheet, so her assets remained well protected. "Should I bother asking what happened?"

She grimaced, carefully draping herself in crisp cream-colored cotton, her scandalously naked toes peeking out from beneath the improvised robe. "It's your bed. You tell me."

"Give me a minute." He stripped away the rest of the bedding, including the pillows. Her poor scrapbook had scattered across the floor and he worked cautiously around it. "Looks like the rails have been disconnected from the headboard. You're lucky the whole thing didn't collapse on top of you."

She eyed the heavy piece of carved oak and winced. That would have hurt. "How did the rails get disconnected?"

He gathered up the small pile of bolts he'd unearthed beneath the bed. "I assume with a wrench."

She stared in bewilderment. "But...why?"

"When I find out, so will you. In the meantime, I'll get the tools I need to reassemble the bed."

Before he could act, the door flew open and Hutch stood there, Miz Mopsey at his heels. "Something woke me up," he said, making a big production of rubbing his eyes. The dog barked her annoyance, too.

"Sorry about that, sweetpea," Cassidy said. "My bed collapsed."

"Oh." His attention switched to Ty. "What are you doing here?"

"I came to help your mom."

"Oh," Hutch said again. "You were rescuing her, huh? That's really cool. Isn't that cool, Mom? You have somebody to rescue you now. You've never had someone do that before, have you?"

Ty folded his arms across his chest and fixed a certain young troublemaker with a piercing gaze. "Why do I have the impression we need to have another discussion, boy? I don't suppose you know how this bed got derailed."

To Cassidy's surprise, Hutch began scuffing his toe against the carpet and hemming and hawing. She groaned. "Oh, Hutch! You didn't."

Hutch swallowed. "I think I'm really sleepy now." He gave an exaggerated yawn. "I better get back to bed. Come on, Mops."

"Good idea," Ty inserted smoothly. "Good night."

The instant Hutch and his dog disappeared, Cassidy turned on Ty. "You don't really believe he unbolted the rails?"

"Sure do."

"But...*why*?"

"You heard him. He wants to turn me into some sort of knight in shining armor. I'm supposed to rescue you."

"Not a chance..." She stumbled to a halt. Was it possible? A week ago, she'd have sworn the idea of Hutch's buying her a date was ludicrous. But he had. Perhaps he'd taken this dating nonsense one step further. Perhaps now he was angling for a— "Oh, no."

Ty cocked an eyebrow. "Change your mind?"

"It's…it's possible," she conceded.

"I believe the word is 'probable'. Give me a minute to find a wrench and pliers and we'll have your bed back together in no time."

He returned so quickly she'd only had a chance to pull on a robe and start gathering up the various papers that had come loose from her scrapbook. He immediately stooped to help. She wished he hadn't. He knelt too close and smelled too good. And those ripples were bothering her again, too. They strained against his shirt each time he reached for a piece of paper. Ignoring him didn't help. Nor did closing her eyes. Unable to see, she couldn't get her scrapbook collected with a speed that was fast becoming a necessity. Even worse, with her eyes closed, she shut all the delicious sights and sounds inside where her mind could play them over and over in every delectable detail.

"So what's all this?" he rumbled at her.

She risked a quick peek at what he held. "Just stuff I've kept over the years." She strove to sound casual. But with him hanging all over the top of her, it was difficult. "You know. Feel-good stuff. Like a gratitude journal."

He frowned at the slip of paper. "'The rose clipping I gave Mrs. Walters bloomed today,'" he read. "'It's great that someone is getting flowers from my bushes.' That made you feel good?"

"Well, sure…" Her brows drew together. "I wouldn't have had any roses if I hadn't let Mrs. Walters take a clipping."

"But you didn't get the flowers. She did."

Cassidy hated when he used logic on her. Did he have any idea how difficult it was some weeks to find the positives in her life? That particular day, the roses were the one bright spot in twenty-four hours of unbearable darkness. "I got to share in the pleasure of them," she argued.

Sort of. At least Mrs. Walters had let her see the pretty yellow bloom when she'd knocked on the door to brag about it.

Ty picked up another scrap of paper. "'We had meat today. Not the kind you have to stew for hours, either. But real, honest-to-goodness'..." His voice trailed off. "Aw, honey..."

"Don't." She moistened her lips. "Don't pity me. It's okay to be poor, you know." She gave him a crooked smile. "It makes you appreciate the small things."

"Like having ribs at lunch the other day."

"Yeah. Like that."

His mouth compressed. "And like this? 'Freddie canned me today, but I sure am grateful that he let me work for so many months.' You're grateful to him? He fired you!"

"But he hired me in the first place," she pointed out. "He didn't have to do that. He was very tolerant, especially considering how many dishes I broke. It's a wonder I didn't put him out of business through breakage alone."

"Uh-huh. And for today I suppose you'll put in there about how grateful you are that Hutch unbolted your bed rails."

Her chin crept out. "Maybe." Then she released her breath in a sigh. "No. I don't think that's going to make it into my scrapbook. I'm really sorry about this, Ty. I'll speak to him in the morning."

"Don't worry about it." He retrieved the final piece of paper and handed it to her before turning his attention to the bed. "Why don't you let me talk to him?"

"Don't bother. He's my son. I can handle it."

"I'm sure you can. But I suspect this is one of those occasions when a man's touch is called for. Will you let me discuss it with him?"

Cassidy hesitated. Boy, oh boy, did she want to refuse. He glanced up at her from his reclining position on the floor. Good gravy, he was big! Big, male and sexy as the dickens—with a wrench in one hand, a collection of bolts in the other and a smile that promised a sinfully delicious night. She couldn't remember the last time that particular combination had been in her bedroom. Now that she thought about it, she'd never had anything like Ty anywhere close to her bed.

''You can talk to him,'' she reluctantly agreed.

''Why the hesitation? Am I stepping on toes?''

At the reminder, she frowned at her unvarnished toenails, wiggling them as she considered. Was he treading where he didn't belong? Did that explain her reluctance? Or was it because with each day that passed, he became more and more intricately locked into their lives? Soon she'd be leaving Texas. The minute she accomplished the one final goal she'd set for herself, she and Hutch would gas up the car Ty disparagingly referred to as a rattletrap, load it with all their belongings and limp eastward toward Georgia. Once there, they'd mend fences with Aunt Esther and Uncle Ben and sink their parched roots into rich, red Georgia clay. There wasn't room in her plan for a six-foot-four-inch Texas rancher with enticing green eyes and a come-to-bed smile.

Ty climbed to his feet and approached. His huge, steel-tipped boots stopped scant inches from the end of the bare toes she'd been contemplating. ''You haven't answered.''

''I'm thinking.''

He stooped so she was staring at the top of his head. Streaks of sun-kissed gold threaded through his light brown hair, tempting her to slip her fingers through the richness. ''Okay,'' he demanded. ''Which toe was I stepping on?''

''Excuse me?''

He pointed to her big toe, grazing the unpainted tip. ''The 'this is my problem and I'll handle it' toe?''

She shivered at his touch. ''Nope. Not that one.''

His finger tickled the next in line. ''Maybe it's the 'I don't want to be obligated' toe. No, wait. How about this little fella? The one I affectionately call 'Remember the Alamo'. The toe of death before surrender.''

A smile slipped across her mouth. "Not that one, either."

"Hmm. That only leaves two more." He tapped the next in line. "It can't be the prideful toe. No need in this case. Which leaves this teeny one at the end. The 'he's getting too involved and we're leaving for Georgia soon' toe. Right?"

"Bingo," she whispered.

"So that's the little troublemaker." He reached into his back pocket and pulled out the pliers he'd been using on the bed. "I can take care of that problem easily enough. Now hold reeeeal still."

"Oh, no, you don't!" With a shriek of laughter, she danced around him and leaped toward the bed.

"No, wait," he exclaimed an instant too late. "I only fixed the one—"

She was in midair when the warning reached her. She hit the mattress solidly. As she bounced up, the mattress and box spring collapsed in one corner. Her second bounce sent her rolling in a tangled ball of arms and legs toward the corner of the headboard again, her skull cracking on the solid oak. Her backside wedged into the tiny cubbyhole formed between the dipping mattress and the headboard.

"Rail," Ty finished with a sigh.

"Now you tell me. Gosh. What pretty stars."

Ty was on top of her in an instant. "Hang in there, sweetheart. I'll have you out in a sec." Behind them the door banged open.

"You're rescuing her again," Hutch announced in delighted tones. Miz Mopsey barked her delight, too. "I'll bet you've never been rescued twice in one day, have you, Mom? I'll bet you like it a bunch, don't you?"

"*Hutch!*" Ty and Cassidy shouted in unison.

The only response was the scamper of feet and pitter-patter of paws rapidly retreating down the hallway.

"I know you're partial to that kid," Ty said, popping her free. "But I'm afraid I'm gonna have to kill him."

She yanked her nightgown back into position and retied her robe. "No problem," she said, shoving hair from her eyes. "I'll help you." They glanced at each other, sharing a moment of perfect accord, their annoyance giving way to laughter.

"He's a challenge, that's for damned sure. Fortunately for you, I love a good challenge." Ty shifted the headboard and slipped the last rail into place. "Give me a second to bolt this together and you should be safe enough."

She frowned. "I have to tell you. The floor is looking better and better."

He resumed his position beneath the bed and went to work with his wrench. "Or you can join me in my room."

Say what? Where had that come from? "Sure," she scoffed, trying to sound offhand. "That's just the sort of complication we need now."

"You're right. It is." The wrench hit the floor with a clatter. "In fact, I've got an even better complication. How about marriage?"

"Marriage!" She blanched. "Who said anything about that?"

"I did." Slowly, he climbed to his feet. "And just so you know…I'm gonna keep saying it until you agree. So. Will you marry me, Cassidy?"

"That's impossible," she whispered.

"Is that your answer?"

"Please don't do this."

"Is that your answer?"

"Yes!"

He grinned. "Yes?"

"No! Yes, my answer is no." She folded her arms across her chest and scowled at him. "I can't marry you."

"Okay." He collected his wrench. "Today's answer is no. We'll see what it is tomorrow."

Hadn't he been listening? "It'll be no tomorrow, too."

"That's one possibility. Of course, there's another."

"What's that?" she asked apprehensively.

He paused at the door. "I could get lucky. Tomorrow you could tumble into my arms like a hot jalapeño, ripe for the plucking, and beg to be mine."

"Yeah, right. In your dreams."

His green eyes seemed to catch fire, burning her with their intensity. "There, too," he said. And then he was gone.

Progress Report

Well, it's not going quite as smoothly as I'd hoped. I thought maybe Mom would like having Ty come to her rescue. Instead, they were just mad that I disconnected the rails. But I'm not giving up yet. I still have another idea how to get Mom married off. I'll just make sure Ty gives her all the things she likes best. All the things a dad should remember to give a mom. The kind of stuff that makes her cry cuz she's happy, not cry cuz she's sad.

CHAPTER SEVEN

Experiments #4–7: The Great Mom and Ty Experiments
Goal: To set up situations where Mom and Ty will be
alone so they can get to know each other better and get
the 99.4% part of their match working instead of wor-
rying so much about that stupid .6% difference. (Mom
sure does fuss about that a lot!)
Procedure: Have Ty give Mom all the nice stuff and
good times Lonnie never did.

"GRAB a shovel and start digging a hole right over there
by the porch steps," Ty said, pointing. "And I'll dig one
on this side."

A very subdued Hutch nodded his compliance. "Yes,
sir."

Ty let him work his hole for a while before speaking
again. "So what happened last night?"

"You mean with Mom's bed?"

Cute. "Yeah, that's what I mean."

"I…uh…unbolted it."

"You want to tell me why?"

"So you could rescue her." Hutch wiped the sweat from
his brow, his expression earnest. "Nobody's ever saved her
before. Not until you came along."

"I appreciate that, but—"

"This way, Mom can be like a fairy-tale princess." He
beamed. "Girls like that kind of stuff, don't they? I don't
think she's ever been a princess before."

No, she hadn't. At least, not judging by the bits and
pieces he'd gleaned from her scrapbook. Still… The kid
better stick a sock in it, or the princess was going to load

her glass slippers into her rusty pumpkin carriage and high-
tail it to Georgia. And the good ol' prince would be minus
a wife, minus a son and living unhappily ever after.

"I appreciate your help, Hutch. But it's time for me to
take over now. Your mom could've been hurt last night.
You wouldn't have liked that, would you?"

Hutch shook his head. "No way! I didn't mean to hurt
her."

"I think you should tell her that, not me." Ty dumped
fertilizer and topsoil into his hole. "Okay, bring me one of
those rosebushes."

"How come we're planting them?"

"Because otherwise they're going to die. And I don't
want to see your mom's expression if that should happen."

"Heck, no." Hanging over the hole, Hutch watched Ty
carefully smooth dirt around the roots. "You're hoping
they'll grow some flowers, aren't you?"

"Yup. I'm hoping once she sees how well her roses grow
in Texas soil, she'll decide to plant her own roots here,
too."

Hutch nodded his approval. "Good idea."

"I thought so." Ty rocked back on his heels and tipped
his Stetson off his forehead. "But these roses are going to
need time to grow. You can't rush 'em. Do you read me?
Do you understand what I'm saying?"

Hutch released a long, drawn-out sigh. "You want me
to stop helping you and Mom?"

Ty suppressed a grin. "You're quick, kid. I always did
like that about you." He removed his gloves and shoved
them into his back pocket. "I don't mind your helping, so
long as I ask for it first. Okay?"

"I guess." Hutch adjusted his glasses. "You sure I can't
help just a *little*?"

"Now that you mention it, I could use some." Ty nodded toward the side of the house. "Why don't you grab the
hose and give these bushes a drink?"

*   *   *

Ty caught Cassidy going through her wallet a few days later, counting out the piddling stack of bills that were undoubtedly all she had left to her name. From his vantage point, the few there were carried good ol' George Washington's enigmatic smile. Not pleasant to be down to a handful of one dollar bills. Desperation would undoubtedly follow close behind and Cassidy desperate wasn't a sight he cared to witness, any more than her reaction should her precious roses die now that he'd planted them.

Then he thought of something and roundly cursed himself for a fool. They were supposed to have picked up her paycheck from the café. With all the craziness of the past several days, he'd forgotten about it—although he'd remembered to retrieve her car and reconnect the battery cables. He'd also taken a few minutes to have an intriguing discussion with Cassidy's former landlady. What he'd do with the information he'd gleaned, he hadn't quite decided.

His mouth slanted in a wry smile. No question about it. Once he convinced the love of his life to join him in holy matrimony, he'd have his hands full with their ingenious— not to mention devious—son. At least their conversation a few days ago had helped. Ever since they'd planted the rosebushes, Hutch had been on his best behavior.

"Ty?" Cassidy caught up with him on the porch, a worried frown lining her brow. He longed to smooth it away, to ease her fears and concerns and allow her to concentrate on the pleasures life offered instead of fighting for sheer survival. Unfortunately, she wouldn't let him. Not yet, at any rate.

"What can I do for you, sweetheart?"

She'd stopped protesting his use of endearments, although they were almost guaranteed to bring a flush to her cheeks. "I need to go into San Antonio for the day."

"Would you like a lift? I'd be happy to drive you there."

She avoided his eyes. "That's not necessary. I'll take my car. I have…things to do."

"Things." What sort of things? he couldn't help but

wonder. Not that he couldn't guess. No doubt they were independent things. Things guaranteed to put as much distance between them and raise as many barriers as she could manage.

This time, she did glance at him, her gaze direct and forthright. "I have to get a job and find a new place to live, as you're well aware."

Uh-oh. "You agreed to stay here as my guest until after our Fiesta date," he reminded in his mildest tone of voice. It was one of the few concessions he'd wrangled out of her.

She looked like she wanted to argue. Being a smart woman, she thought better of it. "You're right, I did. But in the meantime, I have an appointment I can't miss."

His relief was tempered by concern. "You feeling okay?"

A smile eased the strain he read in her eyes. "It's not that sort of appointment. It's a project I've been working on. A long-standing one. And if I don't make it there today, I might not get around to it again any time soon." She took a deep breath. "So it's now or never."

She didn't explain further and he knew better than to push, though her determination intensified his curiosity. He might want to insist she share every aspect of her life with him, to trust him with all the intimate details. But that would have to wait until she was ready. "Sounds like it's important to you," he limited himself to observing.

"Very. It's a project I've been working on for some time now." She glanced toward the bunkhouse. "The thing is…I'm going to be back late and I wondered if you'd mind keeping an eye on Hutch."

"You know that's not a problem. Sure I can't give you a lift?"

Her chin came into play, settling along lines that warned he'd lose this particular argument should he choose to turn it into one. "Thanks, but this is something I have to take care of myself."

He inclined his head. "Think you'll be home for dinner?"

She didn't call him on his use of the word "home". Instead, she checked her watch. "I should be. If not, I'll phone."

With that, she trotted over to her car, spent a good three minutes wrestling the door open, climbed in, banged her head on the frame and spent another three minutes tugging it closed. The car started with a sputtering grumble and she disappeared down his driveway in a plume of dust and exhaust. Well, at least he'd filled her gas tank—filled it nice and full so she could drive long and far.

He shook his head in disgust. How damned charitable of him.

It was late when Cassidy returned to the ranch and she was starving. Her appointment had taken nearly eight hours and her mind—what little remained of it—was numb. She'd called to warn she'd miss dinner and Ty had promised to save her some. She stood just inside the front door and absorbed the ageless silence of the hallway, comforted by the sheer solidness of her surroundings, welcomed by the whispers of the past that filled every nook and cranny of the homestead. And she relaxed for the first time in weeks.

She'd come home.

"Ty?" she called.

"In here."

His voice came from the direction of his office and she crossed the hallway to hesitate outside the half-closed door. Pushing it open, she stared in disbelief. Everywhere she looked were baskets and vases overflowing with yellow roses. In the middle of the room, he'd set a table for two. Silver glistened in the subdued lighting, while crystal and wafer-thin porcelain gleamed. Best of all, the wineglasses were brimming with a rich red Cabernet Sauvignon. Next to the table stood a cart with the most delectable aromas she'd ever inhaled wafting from beneath covered dishes.

It took a moment to find her voice. "What's all this?" she asked, although it seemed obvious enough.

Ty offered a lopsided grin, one as irresistible as it was endearing. "It's for you. Edith and I figured you'd be wiped by the time you got in. And since moving to the ranch has forced an extra couple hours' drive on you whenever you have to go into San Antonio..." He trailed off with a shrug. "Besides, it gets us started on those dates."

Tears pricked her eyes. They had to be from exhaustion since she wasn't one to cry when someone acted this incredibly sweet. Although, if she was honest, she'd admit that she couldn't remember the last time someone had taken care of her like this. Cosseted her. Made her feel special.

He crossed to her side, standing so close his woodsy scent became a part of her. "Are you crying?" he asked.

She shook her head in instant denial. "I can't be. I never cry."

His laugh slipped around her, as warm as an embrace, and he reached out to catch a tear with his knuckle. "Well then, you've sprung a leak. You've got all this wet stuff spurting out of your eyes."

Reluctant amusement fought with the tears she'd denied. "This is the end of March. I'm sure it's just a spring shower."

"No doubt," he said gently. "Hungry?"

"Famished."

"Sit down and we'll eat."

"You waited for me?"

"I didn't want you to eat alone."

"Thanks," she whispered, unbearably moved. She hesitated by the table and her hand crept out to finger the white damask tablecloth. "I could get used to this."

"I'm counting on it."

The urge to flee overwhelmed her, just as it infuriated her. Where did these feelings come from? She wasn't Lonnie, to run at the first hint of commitment, was she? And though she valued her independence, Ty hadn't tried to steal that from her. Anyhow, not so far. He might propose once a day, but he took her refusals in stride and with good humor. In fact, he teased her unmercifully, promising to get even when she finally broke down and accepted his marriage proposal.

"Give me a second to wash up," she requested. And to get herself under control.

"Take your time. I'll have the salad and appetizer ready to go as soon as you get back."

"An appetizer? I'm impressed." Her tears slowed and she even managed to achieve a light tone. Not that she fooled him. But at least he didn't say anything her pride could take exception to. "I'll be right back."

She used the powder room at the end of the hall. Standing in front of the mirror that hung over the washbasin, she scolded herself for a good five minutes. What the heck was she so afraid of? Why couldn't she accept the small kindnesses Ty offered with a modicum of the grace Aunt Esther had drummed into her? It didn't mean she owed him or had to pay him back for his generosity. Her mouth twisted. Nor did she have to marry him, no matter how much she might—

Oh, no. Her eyes widened in disbelief. That wasn't possible. She couldn't have fallen for Ty. Not so soon, and not after all she'd been through with Lonnie. Hadn't she learned her lesson the hard way? Hadn't she learned that men loved women until it became inconvenient or until the responsibilities became too much? Or until someone better came along?

But Ty isn't Lonnie, the voices inside her head insisted. Darn those nasty, illogical *wrong-thinking* voices. Sure, Ty seemed a different type than her ex-husband. But she had Hutch to worry about. She couldn't risk the heartache that would follow if her relationship with Ty didn't work out. Because if it didn't, she wouldn't just lose a husband this time.

Tears burned her eyes again. This was Merrick land. Any

roots she put down would have to be yanked up and re-planted elsewhere. Considering how fragile those roots had become—as fragile as her poor rosebushes—she doubted she could survive another transplant.

Besides, she'd come so close to achieving the goals she'd set for herself five long years ago. She'd proven that she could be a good mother to Hutch, that she could support and raise him on her own. She'd learned to stand on her own two feet, to depend on no one but herself. She'd even contacted her aunt and uncle and discovered that they were as heartsick at the manner in which they'd parted as she was. And she'd taken the final step toward her most important goal, getting her—

A soft knock sounded on the door. "Honey? You fall asleep in there?"

She sniffed. "No."

"Everything okay?"

"No." She rested her forehead against the oak panel and splayed her hand across the cool wood. As a substitute for Ty's warm arms, it lacked a great deal. "Not really."

"Anything I can do?" So understanding. So gentle. So loving.

So tempting.

"Those voices are talking to me again."

There was a long silence. "The ones you told to shut up when we first met?" he asked cautiously.

"Yeah. Those ones."

"What are they telling you?" Apprehension grated his voice.

"That you're not Lonnie."

That perked him up. "Hey! I'm beginning to like those voices."

"Oh, really? They're also the ones that told me to sleep with my ex before we got married."

"Ah. I see the problem."

She swiped the tears from her cheeks. That darned spring

shower had turned into a summer torrent. "So now I don't know what to do."

"How about opening the door and having some dinner? We can decide whether the voices have me pegged right another time."

She opened the door a crack. "You don't understand. That's the problem."

He stood just outside the doorway, smiling down at her, his eyes so full of love it hurt to look at him. "What's the problem, sweetheart?"

"How can I possibly trust them when they were so wrong before?"

He cupped her damp cheekbone. "Maybe they've gotten older and wiser since then. It can happen to the best of us."

She hadn't thought of that and it cheered her immensely. "I think I'm hungry now."

"Great. Let's eat. I'll light the candles so I don't see all the wrinkles Hutch claims you have and we'll stuff ourselves until we can't move."

A laugh broke from her. "He told you about the wrinkles, huh?"

"He's even the one who suggested the candlelight."

"Lovely." She joined Ty in the hallway. "One of these days that kid's going to go too far."

"I suspect that day's right around the bend."

They entered his office and he gestured toward the table. "Have a seat. There's salad and homemade tortilla chips to go with Lorenzo's personal salsa. Then for the main course we have—"

The lights winked off just as Ty pulled out her chair. She took a stumbling step forward, tangled with the chair leg and plunged full force against him. He hadn't anticipated the blow. He went over liked a felled tree, carrying her with him. He also managed to snag the tablecloth on the way down. Dishes and silverware, flowers and food pelted them as they hit the floor with Ty flat on his back and Cassidy riding on top.

"Are you hurt?" he questioned urgently, running his hands over her, checking for damage.

She lifted her head and looked around. Not that it helped. The room was pitch-black. "I...I don't think so. What happened?"

"The power must have gone out." He groaned, shifting beneath her.

"What about you? Are you okay?" Alarm filled her and it was her turn to check him for damage. As far as she could tell, everything seemed intact. At least, all his ripples were where they belonged. "What's wrong?"

"There's salsa and chips sliding down my neck."

"Really?" Her stomach growled. "I could probably help with that," she offered diffidently.

"What the hell are you doing? Damn it, Cassidy! Are you *eating* off me?"

"I'm hungry." She held a broken chip to his mouth. "Want some?"

"Oh, I want some all right."

Tossing the chip aside, he thrust his hands into her hair and found her mouth with amazing accuracy. Salsa mingled with a flavor so inviting, so delectable, that she could easily spend a lifetime savoring it. Her lips parted and she practically inhaled him. His tongue swept inward, a welcome invasion. He groaned again, but she suspected that this time it had nothing whatsoever to do with the salsa dripping down his neck.

She reached up and cupped his face. Blind, she could only trace the hard, sculpted lines. His brow was broad, his cheekbones high and taut. And his lips... She skimmed them with her callused fingers, only then realizing how abrasive her touch must feel. "Am I being too rough?" she asked in concern, whipping her hands away from his face.

His laugh was smothered against her mouth. "Not hardly. Why?"

"My hands. They're..." She shrugged, the movement scraping her breasts across his chest. "You know."

"You've worked hard, sweetheart." His hands covered hers and he returned them to his face. "But we're a matched set in that department. Haven't you noticed?"

For some reason, his observation filled her with delight. "You're right. We are."

"We match in other ways, too."

Her sigh filled the air. "What ways?"

"Let me show you." His legs parted slightly so she slipped into the angled notch they formed, his hips cradling the most feminine part of her. He eased his hands up the length of her spine, pressing her so close she could feel each lovely ripple of the muscles supporting her. "See how well we fit together?"

"You can't be comfortable with me draped all over you," she protested.

"You don't get it, do you? You're perfect. You fit me better than any woman I've ever known." He held her close, made love to her with his mouth and his hands and his gentle, rumbly voice. "As far as I'm concerned, you can drape yourself over me any day of the week. You can drape yourself over me when the snow flies, or when it's hotter than Hades, or when the day's been tough or life's been unfair. If you need someplace to go, my arms are waiting. They're always open for you, sweetheart. When we're old and gray and I'm not as strong as I used to be, my arms will still have one purpose. And that'll be to hold you."

Tears mingled with the salsa dripping on his neck. "Oh, Ty."

He released a rough laugh. "Why I want to marry a woman who does so damned much leaking, I'll never know. Except that I do." He gathered her up, kissing her senseless and then kissing her some more. "Get ready for today's marriage proposal, love. If you can resist a man flat on his back covered in salsa and chips, you're the stubbornest woman I ever have met. But here goes—"

Somewhere behind them, a door banged open and a

flashlight beam played across the devastation of the room. Eventually, it landed on them and wobbled violently. "Oh, golly," came a breathless voice.

Cassidy tried to squirm out of Ty's arms, but he held her fast. "Hutch? Is that you?"

"Whatcha doin' down there, Mom?"

"The power went out and I couldn't see where I was going, so I tripped."

She could actually hear his gulp. "But...where's your candles? You were supposed to have candles."

Ty shifted beneath her. "Boy, if I discover you had something to do with the power cutting out, there'll be hell to pay! You got that?"

"Uh-huh." The door banged shut and ten-year old feet scampered down the hallway. Two minutes later, the lights flickered back on.

Ty helped Cassidy stand. Lettuce, salsa, roses and wine spattered his formerly cream-colored carpet. "Damnation," he muttered. "Watch the broken dishes. I guess we should be glad we weren't cut."

Cassidy eyed the wrecked room in undisguised horror. This was all her fault. Why had she ever agreed to stay here? It had been a mistake from start to finish. "I'll pay to replace everything that shattered and arrange to have your carpet cleaned."

He shot her an infuriated glance. "If you value your life, don't go there. I don't expect you to pay for a damned thing. Clear?"

She studied the glittering shards of their wineglasses dotting the carpet. "Clear as Waterford crystal."

"I'll have a little chat with Hutch in the morning and get this nonsense straightened out. In the meantime, I think there's a dish or two on the cart that hasn't been dumped. Why don't we shower and meet back down here in ten minutes?"

Sensing it was wiser to agree than argue, she acquiesced

with a nod. "Though I would like to suggest we try paper plates."

There was a moment of absolute silence and then a reluctant laugh from Ty. "With plastic knives and forks?"

She grinned. "And foam cups for the wine."

He gave her a gentle push toward the door. "Go on and get cleaned up. And don't worry about the mess, okay?"

"I'll try not to worry *too* much." She hesitated in the doorway. "By the way…thanks for filling up the gas tank. It was sweet of you."

"I didn't want you to run out," he said with more than a touch of irony. It only took a second for her to catch the double meaning.

The instant she had, she did precisely that. She ran.

"What do you mean, we've run out?" Cassidy coasted her car to the side of the road in the nick of time. The engine gave a final coughing sputter and died. "How can we be out of gas? I topped off the tank on my way back from San Antonio three days ago."

"Let's see, three days ago…" Ty frowned in mock concentration. "Oh, right. That would've been the day you went into town to do…*things*, as I recall."

She folded her arms across her chest and locked gazes with him. "Exactly. *Things*."

"Well, one of the *things* you might have considered doing was filling up the tank." Ty pointed at the gauge, flicking it with his finger. "When that needle points to the big *E*, it means you're sucking fumes. Or didn't Hutch ever explain that to you?"

"Oh! I'm telling you I topped off the tank on my way back to the ranch," she argued. "I should have a full tank. See that *F* at the top of the dial? Hutch told me that means full and that's what the damn tank should be."

He grinned at her sarcasm. "Why, I do believe my sweet Southern belle just said a naughty word."

"Damn it all, see what you made me do? I never swear."

"It's all my fault, right?"

"Hey, you're the one who insisted we take my car into town."

"With good reason, if memory serves. I wanted my mechanic to check it out while we picked up groceries for Edith. If you're still bent on driving this thing all the way to Georgia, I'd feel a lot better if it had a chance of actually getting you there."

"Thanks a lot. Instead we're out of gas in the middle of nowhere like a couple of teenagers on their first date." She glared at him, her gray eyes as stormy as a weather front. "Why did you have to live in the middle of nowhere? What's wrong with civilization anyway?"

He shrugged, planting a booted foot against the inside of the door. "I like some space between me and my neighbor," he said, giving the door a good hard kick. It reluctantly creaked open, allowing him to escape. He reached into the back and plucked out the plastic bags of groceries. "You coming?"

She wasted several seconds shoving at the door on her side before giving it up as a lost cause. Wiggling out from behind the steering wheel, she tumbled headfirst through the open window. "How far is it to the ranch?"

"Not far. Fifteen, twenty miles. If we hustle, we'll be there by dinnertime." He tried not to chuckle at her expression. "I'm kidding, honey."

Relief blossomed across her expressive face. "It's not fifteen or twenty miles?"

"Oh, it's that far all right. But I expect we'll get a lift before we've hiked too many hours."

"Thank heaven."

He pointed his boots toward home and kicked them into gear. "And when we get there, I'm going to have to kill your son again."

"Hutch? What does he have to do with...?" She slowed to a stop, then turned around to glare at her car. "Oh, he didn't!"

"Odds on he did. Like teenagers on a first date, remember? Running out of gas is a classic."

With an exclamation of fury, she caught up with Ty, relieving him of some of the grocery bags. "You're not killing him," she announced in no uncertain terms.

"I'm not?"

"No. Because I'm gonna do it first."

"You know why he's pulling all these stunts, don't you?"

Cassidy blew out a sigh. "I know. But that doesn't mean he can keep setting us up like this. The bedroom incident was bad enough."

"Actually, I liked the power outage best." To his delight, a blush licked across her cheekbones. "That one came closest to working, don't you think? Of course, if we'd gone much further, one of us would have ended up with glass in our—"

"Talking to him hasn't helped," she hastened to cut in. "Perhaps if we simply ignored him? Once he sees it's not working, maybe he'll stop."

"And is it?"

"Is it what?"

"Is it not working?"

Cassidy quickened her pace. "No," she said emphatically. "It's not."

"Okay. Is it working now?"

Cassidy sagged to the floor of the saddle house, anger warring with her sense of the absurd. It had been close to a week since the incident with the car and they'd both hoped Hutch had given up on his little attempts to throw them together. Apparently, they were wrong. "I'm not so easily won over. You should know that."

"You'd think I'd have bought a clue by now," he muttered. He tried the knob to the small wooden building for the fiftieth time. It remained as solidly locked as the last time he'd attacked it. "Just what the hell did that kid think we were going to do in here anyway?"

"Talk?" she suggested. "Settle our differences?" Kiss? She played with the leather reins of a bridle dangling from a peg on the wall. The metal bit clunked overhead and she hastened to let go of the reins so the whole darn thing didn't fall on top of her. "Who can say with him? I haven't been able to follow his thought processes since he was four. I'm not likely to figure it out now that he's ten."

"What about Lonnie?" He skirted a pile of saddle blankets and ropes and joined her on the floor, dropping his Stetson onto his bent knee. "How did he handle Hutch?"

Her mouth thinned. "He handled his son the same way he handled everything."

"He ran."

"As fast and as far as his wallet would allow. Which was rarely too far since we were always broke."

"Did Hutch's brilliance intimidate him?"

"You might say that." She looked up at him. "Does it intimidate you?"

Ty tipped his head back against the wall, exposing the long, tanned line of his throat. "Hutch asked me that a number of times. Asked if it bothered me that he's so smart."

"And does it?"

"Not a lick. The only thing that bothers me is that he won't stop this nonsense. I thought you said ignoring it would help."

"I guess it's going to take a bit more ignoring."

"Or a few more chores to keep the boy too busy for mischief."

She gave a ladylike snort. "How long does it take to send me out here on a fool's errand and lock the door as soon as I step inside?"

"Wily little brat."

"He's certainly determined. Which makes me think…" She pulled her legs tight against her chest and rested her chin on her knees. Ty wouldn't like this next part. Heck, she didn't much like it herself. But she had to do something to put an end to this nonsense. "This is getting out of hand. It's time I made a serious effort to find a job and a new place to live."

"I thought you were going to stay here until after the Fiesta." His voice rumbled like a threatening volcano. "Staying here saves your having to pay rent and—"

"And gets Hutch's hopes up. It can't be good for him to spend so much time and energy throwing us together. Eventually, he's going to get frustrated. And angry."

Ty thrust a hand through his hair. "I think we were better off when we were ignoring the kid," he muttered. "Where the hell did all this talk of leaving come from?"

"You know it's always been in the works."

"Look...as long as we're here, we might as well put the time to good use. You keep saying you don't want to get involved again, but we already are."

"No—"

"The real question," he said, cutting her off, "is why you're so afraid to admit it. What harm will it do to confess having feelings for me?"

What harm? It would destroy her, that's what harm it'd do. When the passion died, as it was bound to, it would leave two strangers sitting in a room staring at each other. Perhaps there'd be other children by then, in addition to Hutch. More children to be made miserable when Ty got itchy feet or grew tired of seeing her face across the breakfast table each morning.

"It would cause too much pain when the relationship ended. And it would cause Hutch irreparable harm."

"Who says it's going to end?"

She leaped to her feet. "I do. And it will. It always does."

"That's the biggest load of bull—"

The door swung open and Lorenzo walked in. He took

one look at Ty and Cassidy and the expressions on their faces, did a quick one-eighty and hustled back outside.

"No, wait!"

Cassidy erupted toward the door. Along the way, she somehow managed to snarl her feet around a coil of rope and did a header straight for the floor. Ty caught her at the last possible instant. With a sigh, he tossed her over one shoulder and thrust the door open with the other.

"Sorry to be so clumsy," she told his back in a tiny, subdued voice.

"Clumsy? You?" Ty scooped his Stetson up off the floor and crushed it down on top of his head. "Hadn't noticed."

Ty stood on the porch and gazed out over his property with intense satisfaction. The past two and a half weeks had been the most interesting, frustrating and pleasurable he'd ever experienced. He'd become accustomed to having Cassidy nearby and—despite Hutch's antics—found the boy's inquisitive nature and undisguised enjoyment of their time together more fulfilling than he could have imagined. It fueled his soul.

Cassidy joined him on the porch, carrying a pair of steaming mugs. "It's chilly this morning. I thought you could use this to take the edge off."

"Thanks," he said, accepting the coffee. "But don't let this April cold snap fool you. It'll warm up soon enough. By this afternoon, it'll be on the high side of eighty-five."

"Wish I owned a swimsuit."

He grinned. "Not necessary for my benefit. I can make sure you have the pool area all to yourself and you can enjoy the fine art of skinny-dipping. I'll even give you a few pointers if you want."

"Gee, thanks."

He sidestepped her elbow and even salvaged most of his coffee. Sheer self-protection had taught him to stay fast on his feet these past weeks. With a few years under his belt or a decade or four, he'd have a black belt in Cassidydodging. He looked forward to it. "Don't forget about our Fiesta date," he thought to remind her. "We'll be leaving after lunch today and staying at the Menger for a couple of nights."

"I *had* forgotten," she admitted. He could tell something was bothering her by the way she gnawed on her lower lip. She finally turned the poor thing loose, leaving it plump and red and tempting as hell. "Is this really necessary? Can't we have our dates here instead of going to the expense of a hotel?"

"*Here* everyone's watching. *There* I'd have some privacy with you and wouldn't have to spend all day checking over my shoulder to see what stunt your son's about to pull." He didn't give her a chance to argue the point. "Give it up, Cassidy. Hutch bought the Fiesta special and that's what he's getting. The reservations are already made and Willie agreed to stay with the boy while we're gone. She'll arrive in time for lunch."

A frown formed between her brows warning that she hadn't given up the argument quite yet. "I don't know, Ty. I think we should talk about th—" She broke off, shading her eyes against the early morning sun. "Speaking of Hutch…what's he doing?"

Ty squinted. No question, the kid was up to no good. He was busily passing something from hand to hand as he slipped across the yard. As focused as he was on whatever he held, he hadn't noticed them yet. The boy stepped into a patch of sunlight and Ty caught a flash of yellow and red.

"Oh, sh—" He vaulted over the porch rail and loped toward Hutch, fighting for calm so he wouldn't frighten the boy.

Progress Report
Everything's proceeding right on schedule. Well…maybe

a little slower than on schedule. But I have high hopes. Just a few more experiments and I should have Mom and Ty right where I want them. Married and living happily ever after.

CHAPTER EIGHT

Experiment #8: Writing this one up ahead of time.
Haven't finished with experiment seven yet, but this is
it! Time is running out.
Goal: Mom needs to tell Ty everything. I don't think he
knows she has a secret. Heck, she didn't even squeal to
me about it. Not that she had to. I figured it out a long
time ago. But I think she's afraid to tell Ty. Afraid he
won't love her.
Procedure: Slip the letter that came for her today into
her suitcase without her seeing.

"HEY, boy," Ty said quietly. "Nice snake."

Startled, Hutch looked up, a guilty expression creeping
across his face. "I found it," he said, moving to hide the
reptile behind him.

"Whoa there! Don't do that." Ty spoke more sharply
than he'd intended and fought to moderate his voice.
"Hutch, listen to me. I want you to put the snake down.
Nice and easy."

"It's just a longnose." He held out his hands, allowing
the snake to wriggle from one palm to the other. "I found
it on a rock. I think it was after some sun cuz it's so cold
this morning. Did you know that a longnose ——"

"You can tell me all about it after you put it down," Ty
interrupted with an edge of desperation.

Cassidy joined them, flinching back when she saw what
Hutch was holding. "Oh, yuck! Why did you pick that up?
You know how much I hate snakes."

Hutch's gaze skittered away. "Longnoses are really in-

145

teresting, Mom. And pretty. I wanted to study him for a bit before letting him go.''

Ty glanced at the barn and saw a few of his wranglers headed toward them. If he couldn't convince the boy to get rid of the snake fast, all hell would break loose and someone would end up on the wrong side of a set of fangs. ''Hutch, listen carefully. If you don't put the snake down right this second, I'm going to start talking to your mom about caliper switches and eviction notices.''

It worked like a charm. Hutch tossed the snake aside. The closest wrangler saw it, let out a holler and began stomping his 13D Justin mulehides all over the fleeing reptile. With loud shouts, the others followed suit. Ty grabbed Cassidy and her son and hustled them from the scene of the massacre.

''Did you see what they did?'' Hutch demanded indignantly. ''Why didn't you make them stop?''

''Because if they hadn't killed it, I would have. That was no longnose, boy.''

''Not a—'' Hutch skittered to a halt, his face paling. ''That was a *coral* snake? I thought they were nocturnal.''

''They're poisonous, aren't they?'' Cassidy asked uneasily.

Hutch nodded vigorously. ''They're a member of the cobra family. And I actually picked one up. Cool! Heck, if it had bitten me, I'd probably be—''

Ty caught the boy in a bear hug, effectively muffling what he'd been about to say. ''*Sorry*. You'd have been real sorry. No harm done, Cassidy.'' She didn't look terribly convinced. He strove to sound casual and came close enough to pass muster if no one was listening too carefully. ''Hey, would you mind rustling up some more coffee? I'm afraid I spilled mine.''

''But the snake…?''

He risked a quick glance over his shoulder. ''Not likely to bother anyone any time soon.'' He made a mental note to make sure the few grisly pieces the wranglers had left behind were cleaned up before Cassidy returned. Fortunately, she didn't realize how bad the situation might have been if corals weren't so docile or if this particular one hadn't been fresh out of hibernation and too cold to kick up a fuss at being handled. If she'd known, she and the boy would undoubtedly be packed and gone within the hour. "Er...the coffee?"

"Okay," Cassidy said with a shrug. "I'll get it."

"Thanks." The instant she disappeared inside, Ty confronted Hutch. "You've really done it this time, boy. I'd talk fast, if I were you."

"I didn't know it was a coral. Honest."

"Kid, you know everything. How could you not know that? You must have heard the expression, 'Red and yellow, kill a fellow. Red and black, can't hurt Jack.' If the red and yellow bands are together, keep away from it. Got it?"

Hutch nodded. "Sorry, Ty. I didn't mean to scare you."

"Well, you did. If anything had happened to you..." Ty's jaw worked for a moment. "I would've had a hell of a time getting your mom to lay off the waterworks," he finished gruffly.

"Yeah. She would've been upset." Hutch hesitated. "Lonnie wouldn't have been, though."

Ty frowned. Where the hell had that come from? "Now why would you say such a thing?"

The boy made a face. "He didn't like me much. That's why he and Mom broke up, you know. Because of me."

"I thought it was over June July."

"April Mae." A brief grin flashed. "Naw. She wasn't the real reason. It was my fault."

What had prompted this? Something was sticking in the boy's craw and it had been there since they'd first met. Perhaps the time had come to get it sorted out. "Why do you think you're responsible for their breakup?" Ty asked conversationally.

Hutch kicked at a rock. It ricocheted across the yard and dinged the hubcap of Cassidy's rattletrap. "I heard him. It was the day Mom got my test scores back. The ones that told her how smart I was. I was only five, but I have a really good memory." He slanted Ty a quick look from beneath his lashes. "That's one of the things the tests discovered. About my memory. Well, anyway, I remember what Lonnie said and…"

"And?" Ty prompted.

Hutch lifted his shoulder in a casual sort of shrug. "I did tell you I was smart, didn't I?"

"Yeah, kid. You did."

"Scary smart. I told you that, right?"

Ty's gaze sharpened. "I believe you may have mentioned it."

"And it doesn't bother you? Not even a little?"

"Nope. In fact, it's one of the things I like best about you."

A flush crept into Hutch's cheeks. "You do? Really?"

"I wouldn't lie to you about something like that." He waited a beat, but the boy remained stubbornly silent. "Five years is a long time to have something eating at you. Might as well get it out into the open where we can have a look-see. What happened when the test results came in?"

"Oh, you know. Nothing much." Light, breezy, unconcerned…and lying through his teeth. "Mom put together this big party. She used some of her meat money to buy balloons and bake a cake, and hung up decorations and everything. I think she knew people would treat me differently when they found out I was a brainiac and this was her way of making me feel good about myself." Hutch made a production of adjusting his glasses. "When Da— Lonnie came home, I was in my room getting ready for our party. But I heard him. Mom told him all about how smart I was and he said…he said…"

"I gather he didn't like it," Ty offered gently.

Hutch gathered himself, his jaw clenched so tight it was a wonder his teeth didn't shatter. "He said I was a freak and he didn't want no part of me."

"Aw, Hutch…"

The story came tumbling out. "That's when Mom took his plate and glass from the cabinet and told him to get out and never come back. That stupid ol' April Mae was welcome to him since between the two of 'em they might come up with half a brain, which was all either of them were ever likely to need."

Go Cassidy, Ty thought fiercely. Damn, he wished he'd been there to cheer her on. With any luck at all, she'd have had all twenty-six inches swinging fast and furious. And her bastard of an ex would have tumbled out of there sorer, if not wiser. But that still left one small kid nursing a world of hurt. Slowly, Ty stooped until they met eye to eye. It took every ounce of self-possession to answer calmly. "Good thing you inherited your smarts from your mom's side of the family. Otherwise I suspect you'd have been as dumb as a rock."

Hutch blinked rapidly and offered a watery grin. "Guess so."

Ty nudged his Stetson to the back of his head and chose his words with care. "Hutch, this world is peopled by all sorts of folks. Some don't like anything that strikes them as different, and when they come across it they take fright and run. Or they say stupid things even if they don't mean them. I suspect your father is one of those types. Maybe someday he'll grow out of it and you'll be man enough then to let bygones be bygones."

"Maybe."

"But, kid, you can't color your world with Lonnie's crayons, if you know what I mean. Especially when he's only using one color. You can't allow his views of you to determine your views of yourself. Try not to let one mean, thoughtless remark scar you. It's not worth it. We're what we make of ourselves, not what others tell us we are."

"Then…" Hutch's chin trembled for an instant before he brought it under rigid control. "Then it's okay with you that I'm smart? It won't make you leave?"

"Not a chance," Ty said emphatically. "Your mom won't ever have to hand me my plate and glass because of you. Know why that is?"

Hutch's blue eyes clung, afraid and wary and desperate. "Not 'zactly."

Ty dropped heavy hands on the boy's skinny shoulders. "Because I love you as much as I would my own son. And I'm proud of you, kid. Proud and honored to have you as my friend."

Hutch's head dipped in acknowledgment. "Okay. That's good." He peeked shyly up at Ty. "You're not going to hug me or anything?"

Ty fought a grin. "I might."

"Well, okay." Hutch scuffed his feet in the dirt. "But just a quick one. And you better pound me on the back in case anybody's lookin'. That way, it's a guy thing and not like I'm a little kid and need a hug or anything."

Ty swept him up and held him as tightly as he dared. He didn't pound. Hospitalizing the kid probably wouldn't be wise. But he did tap a bit. Gently.

Very gently.

Tears filled Cassidy's eyes and she slipped silently off the porch, praying they didn't notice her. *He'd heard them.* All those years ago, Hutch had heard Lonnie's horrible, unforgivable words. For five years he'd sealed them up inside, allowing them to fester. And fester they had…until Ty had lanced the wound. Until he'd taken her son in his arms and given him the one thing she'd never been able to—a father's love and acceptance.

All this time, she'd been resisting any sort of involvement, despite the fact that it was an involvement she wanted every bit as much as Hutch. And why? It didn't take a lot of thought. She'd resisted because she feared being hurt. Because she was afraid to trust, afraid of the lies and half-truths that went along with the death of love. Afraid of being deserted and forced to pick up the shattered pieces of their lives again. Afraid of living day to day on the edge of survival with no hope or relief in sight.

Ty isn't Lonnie. Cassidy covered her face with her hands. No, he wasn't. He was a man who'd offered love and acceptance from the first moment she'd catapulted into his arms. He'd taken her in along with her son and done everything in his power to make them happy. And he'd keep doing it, too. Because love wasn't a one-night stand for him. It wasn't a few meaningless words of passion followed by a quick tumble in the parking lot outside of a high school gym. For Ty it was words backed up by deeds that followed a consistent pattern—the same pattern that would be repeated again tomorrow and the day after and the day after that.

So, what the heck did she do now?

She began by wiping away her tears. Next she'd start pointing her face toward the future instead of constantly looking over her shoulder at the past. No wonder she tripped so often! Then she'd trot on upstairs and pack for her trip to San Antonio. And if Ty asked her to marry him again, this time she'd say yes. This time, she'd allow love to govern her actions instead of fear. This time, she'd open her mouth and tell him what was in her heart, tell him that she loved him with every fiber of her being and had from the moment she'd accidently backhanded him.

Her days of running were over. This time, she'd grab her happiness and hold on tight.

"What do you mean you've never been to the San Antonio Fiesta?" Ty forged a path through the crowd lining the River Walk. To Cassidy's amusement, people gave way with nary a murmur. "Not even to see the River Parade?"

"I've never had the chance." Or the money.

He captured her hand and pulled her close. "Work, I assume?"

"It's a good opportunity to earn some spare cash," she admitted. In fact, she should be staffing one of the booths or waitressing in one of the restaurants right now. People tended to tip well during Fiesta days.

Up ahead at La Villita, a mariachi band blocked the walkway and Ty slipped an arm around her shoulders, pulling her close so they could stand with a crowd of locals and tourists and enjoy the entertainment. Nearby, someone broke a *cascarone*. The colorfully decorated egg shattered, its confetti-filled contents catching on a fragrant breeze and scattering. The bright bits of paper caught in Cassidy's hair, mingling with the flower crown Ty had purchased for her, and she laughed. She couldn't remember when she'd last been so happy.

Ty leaned close so he could be heard above the music. "Hungry?"

"Starving."

He gestured toward a man striding through the crowd gnawing on a huge turkey leg. "Want one?"

She chuckled. "I'll pass, thanks. But I wouldn't say no to one of those fat tortillas."

"Ah. A gordita. You're on."

"So, how long until the floats go by?" She couldn't wait to see the parade of boats that drifted along the San Antonio River. She especially wanted to check out the beauty queens dressed in their magnificent Fiesta gowns—hand-sewn, beaded wonders, some with trains as long as twelve feet. "Do you think we'll be able to see? It's awfully crowded."

"I bought seats. We'll head over in a little while."

"And then what?"

An odd expression crept into his gaze. "We can party until dawn with the rest of San Antonio. Do some dancing. Drink margaritas. Or…"

"Or?" she prompted.

"We can go back to our rooms."

In the middle of the crowd, they were suddenly alone. The music and laughter and raucous chatter faded into silence and Cassidy filled her eyes with the man she loved.

He stood tall and solid, a rock in the middle of a surging river. She slipped closer, and for the first time, took the initiative. She wrapped her arms around him, lifted her face to his and sealed his mouth with the most determined kiss she'd ever pasted on a man. Around her, people cheered.

"You sure as hell pick your times, sweetheart," he growled. "I don't suppose you want to head back to the hotel now?"

"And miss the river parade?" she teased.

Carefully, he adjusted her flower crown, dislodging confetti as he combed the colored ribbons through her hair with his fingers. "I want this night to be special for you."

There wasn't a doubt in her mind. "It'll be special. For both of us."

"Then we'll wait. Tonight..." He smiled tenderly. "Tonight isn't going to be rushed."

No, Ty wasn't the type for a quickie in the back seat of a Chevy, she was willing to bet, not even as a teenager. "Okay. But kiss me again quick, so the wait won't seem so long."

He cupped her face. "My pleasure, sweetheart." When he'd done a thorough job of it, he wrapped an arm around her waist. "Come on. I reserved some seating near the Little Church."

By the time the parade was scheduled to start, he had a five-year-old girl in traditional Mexican dress perched on one knee, while her brother rode the other. Cassidy had managed to snag an infant from the exhausted mother seated next to her and spent almost as much of the next hour cooing at the baby as she did oohing at the entertainment. She hadn't realized how much she'd missed having a baby in her arms, maybe because she'd had so little time and energy to enjoy Hutch at this age. She peeked at Ty from beneath her lashes. Perhaps someday she'd come to the Fiesta holding their—

"Next year we'll bring Hutch," Ty said, interrupting her train of thought.

Startled, she could only stare. "Next year?"

"Yeah. I know he had to be in school this week, but this is too good for him to miss."

"Look!" shrieked the little girl. Her dusky curls spilled over Ty's hand where he held her securely on his knee. "The floats! They're coming."

Cassidy craned to see. Sure enough, the first of the platforms slowly motored down the river toward them. For the next hour, she cheered with the rest of the crowd, waving at the participants and clapping for the bands. But her favorite part was when the beauty queens passed by.

The crowd would shout, "Show us your shoes!" And to deafening cheers and applause, the women on the floats would lift the skirts of their hundred pound, beaded dresses to show off their running shoes. The incongruous sight always provoked a laugh. When the last float had disappeared around the river's bend and the last child had been dropped into his parent's waiting arms, Ty turned to Cassidy.

"Like it?"

"It was fantastic." She smiled up at him. "Thanks for tonight. I'm glad we stayed. I wouldn't have missed it for the world. Especially those fabulous gowns. How did everyone know they were wearing sneakers under their dresses?"

"The beauty queens always do, and it's our job to make them prove it." Nearby, a violin played softly and he reached for her hand. "How about a dance before we go?"

"Here?" She glanced around self-consciously. "Now?"

"Why not?"

He swung her into his arms and she drifted in a leisurely circle, content to be crazy so long as she did it with Ty. To her amusement, other couples joined them in the impromptu dance. With a murmur of pleasure, Cassidy closed her eyes and leaned into him. She fitted so beautifully, her head nestling at precisely the right angle between the crook of his shoulder and his chin. And for once her feet cooperated, allowing her to follow his movements with perfect coordination, responding to the subtle press of thigh and hip. Heaven help her, if they danced this well in bed, she'd be a thrilled—not to mention a thoroughly satisfied—woman.

At long last, the final note slipped into the crowd and vanished and an enthusiastic guitarist took over. With a murmur of regret, Cassidy eased from Ty's embrace. "I guess we should be starting back."

He cupped her face, his thumb stroking the sweeping ridge of her cheekbone. It was as though he needed to touch her and to keep on touching. She more than understood. Standing on tiptoes, she wrapped her arms around his neck. For a long moment, she gazed into his eyes. On the surface they seemed as green and untroubled as a mountain lake. But beneath she caught a glimpse of fiery determination.

He wanted her with a passion that hurt and had since they'd first met. He'd waited patiently while she'd circled, wary and distrustful, deciding whether or not to allow him close. Well, the wait was over. She'd made her decision. She kissed him then—a kiss of promise and faith, of love and commitment. He practically devoured her on the spot. In time, they drew apart and he stared down at her. She'd never seen him so serious before.

"We're getting this straightened out. Tonight."

She didn't pretend to misunderstand. "Yes."

It was all he needed to hear. He caught her hand in his and started off in the direction of their hotel. "You looked as excited during that parade as the little girl I was holding," he commented with amazing calm.

How could he remain so cool? She felt ready to shatter like a darned *cascarone*. "Did I?"

"I get the impression you didn't spend a lot of time being a kid, even when you were one."

"I had a pretty normal childhood." It was only later she got into trouble.

"You were raised by your aunt and uncle?"

"My parents died when I was four and they took me in," she confirmed. "We didn't always see eye to eye."

"Over Lonnie, for instance?"

"Oh, yeah. But they're kind people and they meant well. And as it turns out, they were right about him."

"How do you suppose they'd take to Texas?" he asked casually.

"Texas?" They'd reached the Menger. Across the street she caught a glimpse of the Alamo, a sight that never failed to move her. She hesitated beneath a streetlight and glanced up at Ty. "What are you suggesting?"

He shrugged, opening the door to the hotel. "I have that cabin standing around doing nothing. Now that the skunk stink's been cleared out, it would make a great little apartment for them. They could be as independent as they wanted or come on up to the main house for meals—"

"I can't imagine Gen. Robert E. Lee riding Traveller through the lobby here," she chattered uneasily. "I wonder if anyone gave him a hard time about it. They sure would today if somebody chose to ride a horse right through—"

"You're avoiding my question."

"Don't you think you have enough guests staying at the ranch?" she asked cautiously.

He didn't say anything until they'd reached the Victorian lobby in the older section of the hotel. "You want the truth?"

"Please."

He paused by an old Seth Thomas dial clock. "Honey, if forcing your aunt and uncle onto Texas soil at gunpoint would convince you to stay, I'd load up my shotgun and take off for Georgia tonight."

"I don't think that's necessary," she assured him, starting up the steps toward their rooms.

"I'm relieved to hear it, not that it changes how I feel or what I'm trying to do."

"But it's premature," she explained gently.

He waited until they'd reached their suite and unlocked

the door before saying anything further. "It won't be premature for long," he said, gesturing for her to precede him into the room. "It's that time again."

She tried to hide her smile. "Time for what?"

"Time to ask you to marry me."

"Okay."

"So will you?"

"Yes."

He ran a hand along the back of his neck. "I mean, after tonight, if that doesn't convince you—" His head jerked up. "Did you say yes?"

"I think so." She wrinkled her nose. "Let's see. You said, 'Time to ask you to marry me,' and I said, 'Okay' and then you said, 'So will you?' and I said—" The rest of her words were smothered beneath his mouth. "I shouldn't have teased," she whispered. "I should have just told you. I love you, Ty. I never thought I'd say those words again, but I'd be lying if I pretended I felt otherwise."

His smile was infinitely gentle. "We did promise to be honest with each other, didn't we, sweetheart?"

But she hadn't been. Not about everything. Would it make a difference to him when he found out the truth? Slowly, she slipped from his arms. "Wait here. There's something I need to show you."

Crossing to her bedroom, she retrieved the envelope Hutch had slipped into her suitcase. "This came for you, Mom. Good luck!" he'd scrawled across the bottom. Why it surprised her that he'd figured out her secret, she wasn't sure. That darned kid knew everything. But her son still loved her, she reminded herself fiercely, despite learning the truth. And the fact that he'd put the envelope in her suitcase suggested that he thought Ty would, too. In a few minutes, she'd find out.

Ty was waiting for her when she returned, his long strides eating up the sitting area as he paced. "What is it?

What's wrong?'' he demanded, thrusting a hand through his hair.

She'd worried him, she realized in dismay. ''It's that promise we made. I told you I'd be honest and I haven't been.'' She stood before him, the most vulnerable she'd ever been in her entire life. The envelope crinkled in her hands. ''There's a couple more things on that Yellow Rose application form that we have to change.''

A tight smile touched his mouth. ''Just swear it's not the one that says 'sex' and I can live with it.''

''Oh, no problem,'' she managed to tease. ''I answered yes to that one.''

''Great.'' He started for her. ''That's all I needed to know.''

''No, it's not.'' She fended him off with her hand, backing him into a nearby chair. Then she crawled onto his lap and wrapped her arms around his neck.

A muscle jerked in his jaw. ''That bad, huh?''

''Maybe,'' she whispered against his chest.

''Let me guess. Your real name is Bonnie and Lonnie is actually Clyde and you used to work in the banking industry.''

''Nope.''

''You're a princess in disguise and we're going to have to move to some European capital and raise little dukes and duchesses.''

She shook her head with a husky laugh.

His throat constricted as he swallowed. ''You and Lonnie aren't really divorced,'' he whispered.

Is that what he thought? She gave him a reassuring hug. ''Trust me, we're divorced and I have the papers to prove it.''

''Well, honey, I'm fresh out of ideas. I don't suppose you want to tell me what the problem is?'' When she didn't answer, he gestured toward the envelope clutched in her hand. ''I assume it has something to do with that letter you're busy turning back into pulp. Tell me about it, sweetheart. Tell me what's wrong.''

He was being so patient, so understanding. It wasn't fair to keep him in suspense like this. Not since it was only her pride at stake. ''I told you that when I left home with Lonnie, I was pregnant. But…'' She moistened her lips. ''But there's one more thing I may not have mentioned.''

''And what's that?''

''I…I also hadn't graduated from high school.''

He frowned. ''But you're twenty-nine. How could you not have…?'' A hint of color crawled across his cheekbones. ''Never mind.''

She choked on a laugh. ''I didn't get held back, Ty. The truth is…'' She took a deep breath. ''I'm not twenty-nine, I'm twenty-six.'' She waited while that sank in.

It didn't take long. He shot up in the chair and her head cracked his chin. ''Damn! You were *sixteen* when you got pregnant with Hutch?''

''Well…almost.'' She struggled to escape his lap, but he wrapped his arms around her waist, refusing to let go. Giving up, she subsided against him. ''I'd just completed my sophomore year. Lonnie was a senior. We'd been dating for a couple of months and we went to the prom together.'' It was her turn to blush. ''Suffice it to say it was a memorable night and we didn't spend all of it dancing. Nor did we practice safe sex.'' Her mouth twisted. ''Talk about stupid kids.''

''Then you discovered you were pregnant?''

She nodded. ''It finally dawned on me at some point during the summer. Lonnie had already graduated and offered to take me with him when he left town. As soon as my aunt and uncle realized I was leaving—with or without their permission—they let us get married.''

''And then Lonnie deserted you the month before you gave birth?'' he questioned, disbelief evident in his gaze. ''He deserted a sixteen-year-old *child*.''

She shrugged, fighting to distance herself from the emotions those memories stirred. "He had a better job offer. Or so he said. He promised to send money."

"And did he?"

"Enough to get by." Barely. "He wasn't a total louse. But I wasn't in any position to work. Even if I hadn't been pregnant, it isn't easy for a sixteen-year-old to get full-time employment, as I soon found out. Not the sort that will pay for food and rent and baby-sitting fees. So, as soon as Hutch was born, I got a job by lying about my age. Since I looked older than sixteen and was so tall, I got away with it. Once I'd saved up enough money, I went after Lonnie."

"And that's how you lived for the next five years? Chasing Lonnie?"

She attempted a grin that fell short. "Sounds like a movie title, doesn't it?"

"What ended the chase?" He shook his head. "Never mind. I think I know."

Time for another confession. "I heard Hutch telling you about our breakup."

Ty shot her a telling look. "You should've given that man his walking plate and glass long before you did."

"I realize that now. But I was young and scared and it took a while to figure out that I could make it on my own, that I didn't need Lonnie."

"And now?" He flicked the envelope with his finger. "What's this?"

"This is the answer to a five-year dream." For a long time, she stared at the envelope with the Texas Education Agency's return address in the corner. Carefully, she ripped it open and unfolded the paper.

Progress Report

I'm back in school now. Mom enrolled me at this new place near Ty's ranch. But there's a biiiiig problem. SOMEBODY at my old school squealed about my science project and they want to see it pronto since the kids here are working on science projects, too. Guess it'll really hit the fan now, especially when they find out what I've been doing with all my reports.

CHAPTER NINE

Experiment #9: EXPERIMENTS TERMINATED!

CERTIFICATE *of High School Equivalency*, the diploma read. "Congratulations on the successful completion of the General Education Development Tests." Cassidy's five test scores were listed on a flap folded behind the thick piece of paper. Writing, social studies, science, literature and arts, and the most difficult for her, mathematics. She'd just squeaked by on that one. But she'd passed.

The embossed certificate tumbled from her hands and she buried her face against Ty's chest, soaking his shirt with tears. *She'd done it.* After five long, difficult years, she'd finally done it. She'd accomplished her last goal.

Ty held her tight and let her cry it out. "You're something special, you know that?" It took a moment to register the respect deepening his voice. "That's why you've been fighting me so hard, isn't it?"

She lifted her head, sniffing. "What do you mean?"

"I mean pride, independence and a good dollop of fear have been getting in our way."

"So that's been our problem, huh?" She gave a watery grin. "And here I thought it was my refusing to marry you."

"Well, that, too." He flicked a piece of confetti from her hair before dropping his hands to her shoulders and giving them a gentle squeeze. "My guess is that you've been working toward your GED ever since you got rid of Lonnie." It wasn't really a question. "You wanted to prove you could."

"I decided I had to take charge of my life," she confirmed. "I was twenty-one, working a dead-end job, had a five-year-old genius to support and was about to be divorced. That's not the sort of life I'd planned for myself growing up."

"So you decided what you wanted out of life and went after it." He regarded her with steady, understanding eyes. "Sounds rather overwhelming."

"It was, except…" A look of determination crept across her face. "Except I suddenly realized I was perfectly capable of taking care of myself and my son. Heck, I'd been doing it those five years I'd been chasing after Lonnie. That's when I knew what I had to do. I had to go back to school and earn my diploma so I could get a decent job, and I had to mend fences with Aunt Esther and Uncle Ben."

He shook his head in wry amusement. "But then I came into your life and disrupted all your fine plans. What did you think I was trying to do, Cassidy? Steal your independence?" He cupped her face, admiring the strength of character revealed in every single beautiful line, even though her stubbornness caused him unending frustration. "Don't you understand? I'm not trying to steal anything or hurt you in any way. I'm just trying to make you happy."

"Happy?" Her laugh stirred the air between them, warm and sweet and startled. "That's the first time anyone's ever offered me that."

"I'm sorry to hear it. Because there's not a person on this planet more deserving of happiness than you. All you have to do is reach for it."

She closed her eyes and he feathered a kiss across the lids. "I'm so afraid," she whispered, shivering beneath the tender caress.

"I know you are. You don't like risk and I understand why." His hands slipped deep into her hair. "It's time to take a chance, sweetheart. You're going to have to trust me. What's worse…you're also going to have to trust yourself. Granted, you've made some bad choices in your life. But I swear, this isn't one of them.''

"I just have to believe that we're not making a mistake, huh?'' A shaky laugh escaped her. "You don't ask much, do you?''

"Nah.'' His precious voice rumbled over her. "Not me.''

"But don't you see? I haven't been fighting for my own sake. If something goes wrong with our relationship, Hutch—''

"Hutch needs a father,'' Ty interrupted. "If I was a man who played fair, I wouldn't use that card. But the two of you have become too important to me. You've become a part of my life and I can't imagine you not in it. When I walk into the house, I find myself listening for you or looking around for a noisy squirt with bright yellow hair and mischief in his eyes. I always thought I had a home. Now I know how wrong I was. It's you and Hutch who've turned it into a home.''

By the time he ground to a halt, she was weeping again. "I love you, Ty. I do.''

"And I love you. Would poetry help convince you? How's this? You're the dawn after a long, bad night. You're the rain after the endless drought that's been my life. Don't you get it, sweetheart? You and Hutch are my future. And I'm yours.''

"How can you be so sure?'' she demanded. "How can you be certain it's not going to end?'' *Like Lonnie*. The unspoken words hung between them.

"I can be sure because, unlike the voices you hear, my voices have no doubts and they don't give bad advice.'' He softened his reply with a smile. "The first time I kissed you, remember? I knew. And so did you. The difference is…while it made me more determined to pursue a relationship, it frightened you off.''

The fight drained out of her. "You're right. It did.''

"And you've been running scared ever since.''

She seemed to gather herself as though preparing to leap some insurmountable hurdle. "I'm not running now."

It was all the invitation he was going to get...and all he needed. He lowered his head and captured the sweetness of her sigh. Tasted it, savored it. Drowned in it. She wrapped her arms around his neck. She even did it without half killing him in the process. Not that he'd have cared if she had. What was a broken nose compared to the pleasure of her in his arms?

She was long and lanky and lush and fitted him better than any woman he'd ever taken to bed. He swung her around so she straddled him, groaning at the feel of her so tight against him. Her lips parted, allowing him greater access, and he surged inward. At the same time, he tugged at the drawstring that held her peasant blouse in place. Ripe, firm breasts tumbled into his hands. She groaned, wriggling closer.

"Wait a sec." It almost killed him to stop now, but somehow he found the strength of will. "Maybe we should have discussed this before."

Cassidy stared at him, dazed. "Discussed what?"

"Your intentions."

"Good gravy, Ty." She buried her face in his shoulder with a breathless laugh. "Your timing stinks, you know that? I'm sitting half-naked on your lap. In fact, if we were any closer, I'd be pregnant again. And you're asking me what my intentions are? I'd have thought that was obvious."

"Sorry, sweetheart. But I don't want any morning-after regrets. In a few minutes, I'm tossing you on that bed over there and we're gonna make sweet love until I'm too exhausted to move or until you knock me unconscious, whichever comes first."

A shiver fluttered through her. "Sounds good to me."

"Yeah, well...you mentioned getting pregnant. Don't you think we should discuss that?"

"I'm prepared this time. I...I visited a drugstore earlier

and..." She shrugged. "I figured one of us should take precautions."

His breath escaped in a ragged laugh. "Looks like we were both on top of it. I visited that drugstore, too." Okay, one problem out of the way, one to go. "But I gotta tell you, honey, I'm not taking you to bed until I have a commitment. You can't seduce me tonight and then toss me aside tomorrow."

She feathered a kiss across his mouth. "What if I promised to respect you in the morning?" she teased. "Would that be good enough?"

"Nope. I'm an old-fashioned sort of guy. It's a wedding ring or nothing."

"Okay, you win." She slipped off his lap, drawing her blouse closed over her breasts. Sinking to her knees in front of him, she took his hand in hers. "Will you do me the honor of marrying me, Mr. Merrick? I promise to love and care for you all the rest of my days."

About damned time. "Lady, I thought you'd never ask. I do. I will. And my pleasure." With a growl of satisfaction, he plucked her off the floor and into his arms. Three quick strides brought them to the edge of the bed. Sweeping the comforter off the mattress, he dropped his bride-to-be on the soft white sheets. Her blouse parted, slipping off her shoulders and drooping low over her breasts. The hem of her skirt rode high on her thighs, flirting with the plain cotton of her underpants. She had the longest legs he'd ever seen—the ankles narrow, the calves trim—legs perfectly fashioned to wrap around a man and never let go.

"This would probably be a good time to pick a fight with you," she said.

His brows drew together. "Come again?"

She sat up, wrapping her arms around her knees. "Don't you remember how you promised to end any further disagreements?"

The memory clicked in place and he rapidly thumbed buttons through buttonholes. "I believe it had something to do with stripping off my clothes until you gave in.'' He tossed his shirt to the floor, chuckling at her sigh of satisfaction. ''You should have seen your expression when I changed outside of Freddie's.''

A faint blush touched her cheeks. ''I figured you did it on purpose so you could show off all those ripples.''

''Sorry to disappoint you. I did it because you'd practically ripped the shirt off my back while we were in that café.'' He reclined on the bed next to her, playing with the dangling drawstrings of her blouse. ''I know it was an accident, but—''

''You think so, huh?'' Her smile gave him an idea of what Adam had faced in the Garden of Eden.

He cocked an eyebrow. ''Are you saying it wasn't?''

She shrugged, the rolling movement giving him a glimpse of heaven. ''You ended up with your shirt off, didn't you?''

''And you, sweet liar, ended up with a blush that went from the top of your head all the way down to your tippytoes.'' He tugged at her drawstring, fascinated by the slow downward slide of her blouse. ''Not that that stopped you from staring.''

''Ty...'' Her throat moved convulsively. ''I've never done this before with anyone except Lonnie.''

''I know, and I won't rush you.'' And he didn't. His movements were slow and nonthreatening, clothes sliding first from her body, then from his own. ''What's going to happen tonight won't be anything like what you shared with him.''

She closed her eyes, praying he was right. ''Promise?''

''I promise.'' He gathered her close. ''Honesty and trust, remember?''

Her laughter sounded strained. ''It must have slipped my mind.''

''That's okay. It hasn't slipped mine.'' He smiled down at her. ''Just focus on the ripples and you'll do fine.''

She reached for him, reassured by his solid strength. "There are so many it might take me a while."

"That's what I'm counting on."

Then the long night crept across the room, offering them shadows in which to conceal their intimate whispers and contain their husky laughter. Only the moon dared eavesdrop on the lovers, playing across soft, feminine curves and hard, bronzed angles and turning their bed into a silvered nest. And in those twilight hours, Ty won himself a bride, won her with a love so deep and so profound there was no more room for fear or doubt or independence. Their joining mated them. Completed them. Made them whole.

And Cassidy… That night, Cassidy finally accepted the truth.

Ty really wasn't Lonnie.

The phone rang, dragging Ty from a sound sleep. He rolled over with a groan, knocking the receiver off the hook. By the time he'd found it, he'd succeeded in waking Cassidy.

"What's wrong?" she murmured. "Who is it?"

"I'll tell you in a minute. 'Lo?"

"That Cassidy's voice I'm hearing?" Willie's voice boomed across the line.

"None of your business, old gal."

She chuckled. "I'll take that as a yes. Good on ya, boy. Listen, sorry to interrupt your Fiesta fun, but I'm afraid you'll have to cut it short."

That didn't sound good. Ty slanted a glance in Cassidy's direction. So far, she displayed only mild curiosity. For his own physical well-being, he'd prefer she stay nice and relaxed. "So what's up?"

"The school called."

"And…?" A flailing elbow caught him in the ribs and he hastened to moderate his tone. "Oh, really? Why?"

"Oh, shoot. He's fine, he's fine. Sorry. I worried you for a minute there, didn't I?"

"Just for a minute."

"There's nothing wrong with the boy. Not physically." Laughter drifted across the line. "At least not yet. But he's gotten the teachers in an uproar over something. They've asked Cassidy to come to the school right away."

"This can't wait until tomorrow?"

"Apparently not. And Ty…"

"Yeah?"

"They want you there, too."

Uh-oh. "*Me*? What the hell for?" Cassidy's elbows started flailing again and he threw an arm around her, plastering her to his side. Unfortunately, her knees took up where her elbows had left off.

"You're asking me that? You know the boy. What trouble do you think he's gotten himself into this time?"

The possibilities were endless. "We'll be there in a couple of hours," he said, and hung up.

Now he had a choice. He could either escape the bed and tell her the news from a safe distance, or he could confine her tightly enough to escape serious injury. After the night they'd shared, he knew which he'd choose. He rolled over on top of her, wrapping himself around the most delicious piece of femininity he'd ever had the pleasure of holding.

"I've got something to tell you…." he began.

"I just don't understand," Cassidy fussed. "He's been there less than a week. What could he have done in just a couple of days?"

Wisely, Ty kept his opinion to himself. "Beats me" seemed a safe response.

"I mean, he's only ten. How bad can it be?"

Considering how well his answer had worked last time, he decided to try it again. "Beats me," he repeated.

"And they want to see you, too?"

"Beats me."

"What?"

"Oh. I mean, yeah, they want to see me, too."

"Why?"

He shrugged. "I assume we'll find out when we get there."

The minute they stepped into the office, they were ushered into a conference room. From the amount of gawking going on, Ty had a *really* bad feeling about what had happened. A few minutes later, the principal walked in with a woman he introduced as Mrs. Lopez, the seventh-grade science teacher.

"Thank you for coming so promptly," the principal said, offering his hand first to Cassidy and then to Ty. "I'm Kyle Peters."

"Has Hutch done something wrong?" Cassidy burst out, clearly unable to contain herself a minute longer. The principal and Mrs. Lopez exchanged troubled glances and she groaned. "I know that look. What is it this time? Did he blow up the lab? I'll replace the equipment, I promise. It's just that he's so smart and so curious—"

"The lab's fine, Ms. Lonigan," Mrs. Lopez hastened to assure her.

"And...uh...all the school's computers work? They don't do anything...odd?"

Alarmed, they stared at Cassidy. "Not as far as we're aware."

"Oh, okay, then." She beamed in relief. "Well. I guess that just leaves the snake."

The principal's hands tightened around the folder he was holding. "What snake is that?"

"That coral snake he picked up the other day. I can explain. You see—"

"Er, no." Mr. Peters blanched. "This has nothing to do with snakes."

"Honey, why don't you let them tell us what the problem is instead of scaring these nice people by guessing?" Ty suggested.

"Oh. All right. But if it's about that time he turned everyone blue—"

"*Cassidy!*"

With a weak smile, she subsided. "Sorry."

"It's about his science project," Mrs. Lopez hastened to say. "His former school told us he'd been assigned one, and since it fitted in with our current curriculum, I asked to see it."

Cassidy looked blank. "A science project? That's *it*?" She offered a huge, relieved grin. "What's he want to do this year? Gene splicing? Level five viruses? Cure cancer?"

"Not exactly." Mr. Peters frowned. "I've sent someone to bring Hutch to the office so we can discuss this with him, as well. But first I thought we'd fill you in. I don't quite know how to say this other than to come right out and tell you. He wants to marry you off to Mr. Merrick. It's a…a love experiment, I guess you'd call it."

Ty cursed beneath his breath. Of course. That explained all the cute little stunts. Love…logic-style. "I'm gonna kill that kid."

"I gather you don't approve," Mr. Peters said.

"Actually, I do approve." What he didn't approve of were the looks they were leveling Cassidy's way. Like she'd done something wrong raising the boy.

"Perhaps you don't realize the full scope of what he's attempted," Mrs. Lopez offered. She flipped open the folder in front of her. "According to his notes, he went to Yellow Rose Matchmakers with the express purpose of finding a—"

"A father," Ty interrupted. "Yes, I know. I have from the beginning. My grandmother and I own the Yellow Rose. I was there when Hutch showed up."

Mr. Peters lifted an eyebrow. "And approve of this sort of manipulation?"

Ty leaned across the table so they could get a clear look at his expression. He wanted to be certain they saw just how serious he was. "I'm all for anything that will get Hutch's mother to marry me. Hell, if pasting wings on cows and tying rockets to their backsides so they could be shot over the moon would get Cassidy to marry me, I'd be the first one in the pasture with a bucket of glue.''

In desperation, they turned to Cassidy. ''You realize Hutch set everything up? He caused you to lose your apartment. He disabled your car battery so you'd be at Mr. Merrick's mercy. He…'' Mrs. Lopez blushed. ''He disconnected your bed rails.''

Cassidy waved a hand through the air. Ty ducked. Mrs. Lopez flinched backward. Mr. Peters wasn't so quick or so lucky. ''Oh, sorry. I didn't mean to hit you. You see, I have this false body image and my arms are three inches—''

''Sweetheart? Let's stick to the bed rails.''

''Oh, right. Hutch wanted Ty to come to my rescue. Like a knight in shining armor-type thing.''

''If you say so,'' Mr. Peters said dubiously.

''Hey! He's only ten years old. He wasn't thinking about…he wasn't trying to…'' It was Cassidy's turn to blush. ''It wasn't a bed thing. It was a rescue mission.''

''Let's start with the apartment,'' Mrs. Lopez suggested. ''He caused you to get evicted. Doesn't that concern you in the least?''

''See, you're wrong there. We were evicted because of Miz Mopsey.''

''That's the dog.''

''That's right.'' Cassidy tilted her head to one side, the beginnings of a frown puckering her brow. ''How did you know?''

Mrs. Lopez tapped her notes. ''It's here under Plan B.'' She slipped a pair of glasses on the tip of her nose. ''I quote, 'Walk Miz Mopsey past Mrs. Walters's door and make a racket. Maybe she'll notice for once.''' The teacher glanced up. ''Unfortunately for you, she did.''

''Look…is all this necessary?'' Ty demanded. ''If Cassidy had gone in to talk to the woman, she'd have found out they didn't have to move that night. Doris would have given them time to find a new place.''

''How do you know *that*?'' Cassidy asked, her frown

deepening. "Come to think of it, how do you know her first name?"

He shrugged uneasily, realizing too late that he'd given away more than he should have. "I didn't think it was proper that she throw you out in the middle of the night. So I talked to her about it when I went to pick up your car."

"Ah, yes. The car." Mrs. Lopez shuffled some papers. "It didn't work because of a burned out... Here it is. A caliper switch."

"A caliper switch? No such thing," Mr. Peters interjected.

Ty nodded. "Yeah, I know. It was the battery cables."

Cassidy rounded on him, catching him in the ribs. "You knew? You knew and didn't say anything?"

Damn. "You didn't want my help, remember?" he retorted defensively, clutching his side. "I offered and you said hell no, let the kid do it. If you'd bothered to ask, I'd have told you what was wrong with the rattletrap."

"I did not say hell." She turned to address the school officials. "I did not say hell. I don't swear."

"Yeah, well, you didn't say help, either. And since you didn't, I didn't."

She swiveled again; Ty recoiled again. "Because you wanted to take me home with you. So you lied."

"That's right. No! That's—"

"Moving along..." Mr. Peters interrupted. "Shall we talk about the skunk that got into the cabin?"

"Shall we not?" Ty suggested hopefully.

Cassidy folded her arms across her chest, the first safe move she'd made since they'd gotten there. "Don't try to tell me Hutch is responsible for that, because I won't believe you. He couldn't have found a skunk and then lured him into our cabin in the little bit of time we were at Ty's."

"Knowing your boy, I'm not so sure," the principal observed tartly. "But, in this case, you're right. That's not what he did."

"I didn't think so."

"Instead, he set off some chemicals that smelled like a skunk."

"They didn't do a bit of harm," Ty insisted. "And I had a long talk with him about it and made him scrub the cabin from top to bottom. You'll notice he didn't try anything like that again."

"You *what*?" Cassidy erupted from the chair, practically knocking him to the floor.

He rubbed his sore shoulder. Jeez! That's what he got for defending her son. Next time, the kid could take the heat all by his lonesome. "What? What did I do?"

"You knew about all these things he did and never told me?"

Ty climbed to his feet. "You caught on eventually! Remember when we ran out of gas? I told you then it was Hutch and you said we should ignore him."

Hurt turned her eyes to pewter. "I'm his mother. You should have let me know what he was up to from the start."

"Why? So you'd have an excuse to leave? Damn it, Cassidy. I'd just gotten you there. If I'd ratted on the kid, you'd be in Georgia right now."

"You promised to be honest with me!"

"I think I see what happened," Mr. Peters said. "Hutch contrived all these incidents and Mr. Merrick encouraged him."

"That is *not* what happened." Ty glared at the principal. "You're missing the point here. This ten-year-old boy is desperate for a father. And so, in his own inimitable fashion, he decided to do something about it. Because of the way his mind works, he went about it in a very methodical manner, using logic and intelligence to try to—"

"Manipulate people. Mr. Merrick, I appreciate that you've put up with all this to help out your grandmother and protect your joint business interests, but you must agree it's not appropriate."

Cassidy slowly sank into her chair. "Excuse me? What did you say?"

"I am *not* doing this for my grandmother's sake," Ty interrupted in hardened tones. "I told you why I was doing this. Winged cows with rockets on their butts, remember?"

"Are you sure? With all the bad publicity Yellow Rose Matchmakers has received recently, I can understand why you'd be so accommodating to Ms. Lonigan and her son. I suspect you can't afford any more problems."

"Oh, no," Cassidy whispered.

Mr. Peters shot her a pitying glance. "There's more."

Ty's hands clenched. How he wished he could wrap them around the principal's throat. Everything he'd done could be explained. Though the way the school officials were doing the explaining, it would like as not break Cassidy's heart, not to mention his arms and legs. "I think we've heard all we need to."

"I'm afraid you haven't. Hutch told us about the reporters who were at Yellow Rose when he first showed up. They've been chronicling his adventures. Were you aware he's been sending them progress reports?"

"No," Ty bit out, "I wasn't."

"Wait a minute!" Cassidy's hands started fluttering again—always a bad sign. He shifted a few inches to the left. Mr. Peters and Mrs. Lopez followed suit. "I want to know what you're talking about. What bad publicity? What has any of this got to do with the Yellow Rose?"

Ty gave it one last shot. "I'll tell you later."

"No, you'll tell me right now."

"Okay, fine. It's no big deal. A magazine reporter discovered that one of my grandmother's employees— Wanda—wasn't using the computer to make her matches." He fought to control his fury—with limited success. "It may interest you to know that her success rate outstripped the machines. But because we're billed as a computer dating service, certain individuals suggested fraud was involved. When it all hit the fan, my grandmother ran every last questionable profile through the computer, and whaddaya know? The computer confirmed Wanda's matches. End of story.''

"Well, not quite," Mrs. Lopez retorted. "You fail to mention the follow-up article and its importance to Yellow Rose's future. You need them to give you a positive write-up, don't you?''

For the first time since he'd known Cassidy, Ty saw her look completely devastated. Her arms folded around her waist like a drooping flower blossom. Worst of all, she didn't move. Not a twitch, not a fidget, not a knee or elbow or finger out of place.

"That's why you were so annoyed when the computer matched us," she whispered. "With the reporters watching, you didn't have any choice but to date me.''

Ty thrust a hand through his hair. "Yeah, okay. You're right. I had no choice at that point. But then something happened and you know it.''

She bowed her head. "Hutch started manipulating us.''

"No, damn it all!" he roared. "We kissed. Remember that kiss? I sure do. It had one hell of an impact on me, even if it didn't on you.''

"Mr. Merrick, please! This is a school.''

He fought his frustration. "Where's the kid? Get him now. We're leaving before you screw up my life any further.''

"Yes, please," Cassidy agreed.

"Will wonders never cease?" he muttered. "She finally agrees with me about something. I knew that ninety-nine percent had to kick in eventually.''

"I do agree, Ty. Leaving is a good idea. Actually, it's an excellent idea." A travesty of a smile crept across her mouth. "I'm sorry about the science project, Mrs. Lopez. I'll have Hutch come up with a new one during our move to Georgia.''

She said it so sweetly. So brightly. In fact, everything about her was bright. The hot blush glowing across the full sweep of her cheekbones. Her perky, Southern-syrup voice. The tremulous smile pasted on the mouth he'd kissed with such passion a few short hours ago. But brightest of all were her tear-laden eyes. It took every ounce of self-restraint to keep from sweeping her into his arms and carrying her out of the place.

"You are *not* moving back to Georgia," he informed her through gritted teeth. "We're engaged, in case you've forgotten."

"I hardly think this is the place to discuss—"

"You're right." He turned to the principal again. "But just so you know…just so there's not a single, solitary question in your minds, *I* not only approve of Hutch's experiment, I'm proud of him." He climbed to his feet, sweeping Cassidy up with him. "He wanted a father. What could be a more worthy goal than that? In this crazy world, if that isn't the smartest, most practical scientific endeavor a boy could work toward, I don't know what is. And I'll tell you something else. I'm gonna make sure his experiment succeeds." He slammed his Stetson down on his head. "In fact, I'm gonna make sure he gets a friggin' A+ on it."

If Cassidy had clipped him with a single finger, elbow or knee in protest, he'd have tossed her over his shoulder and been done with it. Perhaps she didn't because she was expending all her energy in keeping her tears from falling. He grimaced. For a woman who never cried, she sure as hell was the cryingest female he'd ever come across.

Just as they exited the conference room, Hutch scurried up. He took one look at their faces and slipped his arms through the straps of his backpack. "I guess we're going, huh?"

"Oh, yeah. We're going." He caught Mr. Peters's eye. "But we'll be back."

Hutch approached the principal and held out a large envelope. "Here."

"What's this?" Mr. Peters asked.

"It's my other science project. You and Mrs. Lopez should like it okay. It's about irrigation and erosion and how to make sure we have enough water to grow all the food we need. It's not the one I wanted to do because right now I don't care about anything but my mom." His mouth curved downward. "I was just trying to make her happy, you know. And maybe get a dad."

"But, Hutch," Mrs. Lopez protested, "someone could have been hurt. What about your seventh experiment? I gather you were going to put that snake in your mother's room. I realize you weren't aware it was a coral, but—"

"Hutch?" Ty growled.

"I wasn't! Honest. I was really just looking at it. Snakes scare Mom. I wouldn't have taken it anywhere near her. I even tried to hide it behind my back until Ty threw a fit."

"Then what was your seventh experiment?" the teacher asked.

Hutch shrugged, a hint of color brightening his cheeks. "I was going to put some of Mom's bubble bath in the pool. I thought it would be romantic."

Mrs. Lopez released a long, drawn-out sigh. "Give us a day to discuss this a little further, Mr. Merrick. There may be some value to what you've said."

A lot of value, he almost retorted, before deciding discretion might be a wiser course of action at the moment. "Thanks. I appreciate it."

Wrapping his arms around Cassidy and Hutch, he ushered them from the building. The minute they hit the parking lot, she pulled free. "Please take us to the nearest motel, if you'd be so kind."

Judging by her expression, he was in it up to his boot tops. "No, I won't be so kind. You've got to listen to me, Cassidy—"

"I most certainly do not. You lied to me."

"I never lied. I didn't tell you what Hutch was up to, but that's because I really *didn't* know what Hutch was up to." He nudged the boy. "Tell her, kid."

"I never told Ty I was working on a science experiment. Honest. He figured out I wanted a dad, but he thought all the pranks were from me being smart."

"Scary smart," Ty added. Cassidy kept walking and he began to feel a hint of desperation. "Granted, I should have told you about the apartment. And the car. And the skunk. I admit that. But I knew the kid didn't mean any harm and it gave me the perfect opportunity to court you."

That slowed her down. "Court me?"

"It's an old-fashioned word, I agree. But it sure fits what I was hoping to do."

"That doesn't change the fact that you were trying to protect your business interests by dating me."

"Damn it, woman. That tears it. There's only one way to win an argument with you." He ripped open his shirt, buttons pinging in every direction. He tore it off his shoulders, balled it up and flung it onto the concrete parking lot. "I did not, I repeat, did *not* date you for my grandmother's sake or for the sake of the agency."

Cassidy rounded on him, wide-eyed. "Ty! What are you doing? Stop that!"

"The hell I will. I'm not stopping until you quit arguing and say you love me. Now where was I? Oh, yeah. I am not marrying you to save Willie's business." He did the unthinkable next, something a cowboy would never do. He yanked off his Stetson and threw it on the ground. "And I'm sure as hell not marrying you because of any magazine article."

She held up her hands. If she'd been any closer, she'd have coldcocked him silly. "All right, all right. I believe you!"

"Sorry, honey. I didn't catch what you said." He hopped up and down on one foot, grabbed the heel of his size fifteens and started yanking. "Don't just stand there. Help me, boy."

Hutch stared at him as though he'd lost his mind. "You want me to pull off your boot?"

"If it wouldn't be too much trouble." Still hopping, he said, "I'm in love with you, you fool woman. I want to marry you because I'm crazy about you, not because of any scientific experiments or because of bad publicity." He planted a sock-covered foot on the ground and held out his other foot to Hutch. "Don't dawdle. Toss that one aside and start on this'un. And then go get in the truck. It might get downright embarrassing from here."

Hutch didn't wait to hear more. The minute he'd yanked Ty's boot free, he scurried across the parking lot and disappeared from sight.

"Okay, woman. We're getting down to the serious stuff now." This better work or he'd light up all of San Antonio with his blush. "Do you believe me or do I bare my assets to the world?"

"Stop it!" Cassidy begged. "I give up. I believe you."

"Well, that's something." He stood in his stocking feet, fists planted on his hips, and faced her down. "But it's still not good enough."

"What else do you want me to say?"

"Not much." He dropped his hand to his belt buckle. "How about, I believe you. I know you wouldn't do anything as unscrupulous as those people said. How about, I love you, Ty. I've always loved you. And I'd trust you with my life. That might make a good start." She flew into his arms and he staggered under the impact. His poor ripples were going to be one mass of bruises by morning. But it would be worth it.

"I love you, Ty. I've always loved you. And I do trust you, not just with my life, but with my son's, too."

"And when are you going to marry me?"

"Right away. As soon as we can get a license."

"And where are you going to live?"

"Wherever you want." She peeked up at him. "But I'm hoping it's on the prettiest ranch in all of Texas."

He lowered his head and branded her with a kiss. He'd have done more, but he had enough sanity left to remember where they were. "Okay, then. Now that you've made me look like a total idiot in front of all Hutch's schoolmates, you can help me pick up my clothes."

She bent down and retrieved his hat, dusting off the brim. "I would have given in sooner, you know."

He scowled. "You would have?"

"Yeah." She grinned. "But I wanted to see how far you'd go."

He slapped his Stetson on top of his head and gave her a wink. "Honey, for you I'd have gone all the way."

It was during the brief drive back to the ranch that Cassidy finally realized the truth. She was going home. A home where she belonged. Where people were waiting for her and would welcome her with open arms.

When they arrived, Willie stood in the yard. Beside her hovered a nervous looking couple. Cassidy inhaled sharply. "Aunt Esther!"

"And your uncle Ben." Ty parked the truck and turned off the engine. He shot her an apologetic shrug. "I guess this is one more thing I should've come clean about. I invited them for a surprise visit. Where it goes from here is up to the three of you. But that cabin's all theirs if you want."

She threw her arms around Ty's neck—only nicking his nose a little bit—and kissed him. Oh, how she loved him. How could she ever have doubted it? She glanced across the yard at the couple who'd raised her, more apprehensive than she cared to admit.

"Go on," Ty encouraged her. "They're as scared spitless as you."

Slowly, Cassidy left the haven of the truck and approached her aunt and uncle. There was a momentary hesitation and then the three were hugging and crying and talking all at once. They were also tripping over each other and knocking elbows a bunch, which explained a lot about Cassidy. Apparently, false body images ran in the family.

At long last, she pulled free. Turning, she gestured to Hutch.

He held back, pointing at the bushes on either side of the porch steps. "Mom, look! Your roses are covered in buds."

She stared in disbelief. They were covered and covered some more. She'd never seen so many blossoms. But then, why should she be surprised? "Seems like they've found the perfect home to put down roots, just like us." She ushered her son forward. "Come and meet your relatives, sweetpea. And then I want you to introduce them to your new dad." Her gaze met Ty's. "I know they're going to love him as much as we do."

EPILOGUE

"OKAY, ladies, stick out your glasses and I'll pour the champagne. No, no, Wanda. Sit and relax," Willie insisted, waiting until the seventy-six-year-old woman had stopped fluttering long enough to find a chair. That's what she got for hiring an escaped fairy godmother from a Disney flick. The woman couldn't move without fluttering. If she wasn't so good at her job... "And, Maria, if you answer the phone again, I'll have one of your relatives tie you to that chair."

She waited until Maria had finished rapping out instructions in Spanish to one of said relatives and was sipping champagne before whipping out the magazine article. "Wait until you hear this update...." She took a quick swallow from her glass and settled into her chair. Plucking a yellow rose from a nearby vase, she waved it at them for emphasis as she began.

"*Ten-year-old boy uses Yellow Rose Matchmakers and science to snag himself a dad,*'" she read. "That's the headline. Then it says, 'Yellow Rose Matchmakers made Hutch Lonigan quite a deal. For just nine dollars and change they gave him the best date ever...a date with destiny. After filling out an application for his mother, Cassidy Lonigan, Yellow Rose's computer spat out the perfect father for young Hutch—the grandson of owner, Willie Eden. But it took a few scientific experiments to convince his mother that Ty Merrick was the perfect husband for her. "I got an A+ on the project at school," Hutch said proudly. "But best of all, I got a dad." It looks like the Yellow Rose's computer matches are back on track!'"

Willie tossed the magazine aside with a sigh and lifted her glass. "Cheers, ladies. I suspect business is going to be

183

booming. Oh! And before I forget, you were right, Wanda. I reran Cassidy's application one last time with her correct age and darned if it didn't come up a one hundred percent fer-sure fire perfect fit, just like you said!''

WILD AT HEART

SUSAN FOX

CHAPTER ONE

"I HEAR B. J. Hastings proposed."

Kane Langtry's voice carried a sarcasm that made Rio stiffen. She glanced his way briefly in the dim stable, then returned her attention to the glossy red hide of the sorrel she was brushing. The secret shame she'd lived with for as long as she could remember welled up. She knew precisely why B.J. wanted to marry her, and his reasons had nothing to do with love or respect—or even the desire he pretended.

It hurt that Kane had decided to corner her on the subject. She knew immediately that he meant to hammer it all home to her as if she were too infatuated with the neighboring rancher to see it for herself.

Her softly challenging, "So?" was much less defiant than she'd meant and she instantly regretted it.

"So, I sure as hell hope you know that B.J. and his daddy see you as a way out of their money troubles."

The low words cut cruelly. The subtle reminder that she was unworthy of being one of Sam Langtry's heirs was another cut.

Rio finished with the sorrel and tossed the brush to a nearby hay bale. She gave Kane a lazy smile to cover her hurt. "You don't think hot sex had anything to do with it, huh?"

Kane's expression grew hard and his eyes wandered down her slim, feminine figure. It was a critical inspection, insolent, lingering and ultimately derisive before his gaze came back up to hers. "If you've been giving it out, then it's even more certain Langtry money is his only reason for proposing marriage."

Kane's animosity toward her was as relentless as it was heartbreaking, but Rio kept her smile in place as she looked up into his harsh features. "Jealous, Kane?" The question was retaliation for his cruel remarks. Rio knew—she'd always known—that Kane considered her little more than white trash. The suggestion that he desired her in any way was exactly the slap she meant it to be.

The arrogant lines of his handsome face became more pronounced and the dark glitter in his blue eyes was cold as he took a step closer. His voice was quiet, its silky tone all the more dangerous because it was so controlled.

"I could have you anytime I decided to, Rio." His hand came up and he caught a wisp of dark hair that had worked loose from her braid. A gentle tug sent an avalanche of sensation through her that made her breath catch. A second later, she realized by the faint twist of his mouth that her shock—and her helpless reaction to his touch—had exposed the hungry longing for him that she'd labored to keep hidden.

Rio had loved Kane Langtry for years. Not for his harshness or indifference toward her, but for the man he was with everyone else. In spite of his refusal to accept her into his family, Rio admired him. She'd looked up to him first as a foster brother, but had rapidly developed a crush on him that had nothing to do with sisterly feelings. By the time she'd turned eighteen, she'd come to the unhappy realization that she was in love with a man who saw her ongoing presence in his life as an irritation.

But irritation wasn't the impression she got in those charged moments as she stared up into his face. There was a fierceness about him now, though his fingers still toyed gently with the wisp of hair. The dark sensuality that suddenly burned in his gaze was so intense that she was seized by a strange paralysis. Her knees went weak and she could barely breathe as the back of his finger grazed the side of her throat. The husky timbre of his voice was hypnotic.

"Tell him no, Rio. Not even B.J. deserves a woman who's lovesick over another man."

It took a moment for Kane's blunt words to penetrate. It was that same moment that Kane lowered his head and his chiseled lips came to within a finger space of her parted ones. His hand slipped around the back of her neck to hold her in place, but Rio was so astonished by Kane's sudden advance that she couldn't move. Kane had never, ever touched her like this. His last-second hesitation merely heightened the sensual confusion that whirled over her.

And then his mouth crashed forcefully against hers. The twisting pressure of his lips opened hers and she gasped as she was crushed against his hard, lean body. The raw pleasure of his lips was devastating, and Rio clung to him, unable to withstand the sensual onslaught.

Kane Langtry had been the subject of every wild dream she'd ever had, however foolish, however futile. But she'd never dreamed this, never suspected that any man anywhere was capable of bestowing such pleasure or demanding such an uninhibited response. Rio had never imagined she could lose control of herself, never pictured recovering from her initial shock and returning his kiss with the fervor she did.

But she was wrapped around him, her long fingers combed tightly into his thick, dark hair as she met and returned what his mouth was doing to hers. Reduced to impulse and instinct, she was slow to realize that Kane ultimately controlled the passion he'd forced upon her. He withdrew from her in measured stages, and Rio couldn't help her whimper of disappointment when his kiss began to ease.

By the time his lips finally moved off hers, her legs could barely support her weight. The few kisses she'd had in the past were nothing like the rough mating Kane had given her. It was horrifying that he'd so thoroughly disoriented her and that she'd been so quickly driven to such abandon. Arousal still throbbed heavily through her and she was alarmed to discover that she was powerless against it.

It was her powerlessness that made Kane's iron-willed control all the more awful for her. She opened her eyes and looked up into his hard features, stricken by the faint twist at one corner of the mouth that had so completely mastered hers.

"Tell him no, Rio," he rasped, the roughness of his voice making it sound harsh and condemning to her. "B.J. would want to have a wife that's all his."

Rio swayed when Kane abruptly released her and

stepped back to retrieve his Stetson. She hated that she had to put out a hand to the stall door to steady herself. Kane watched her intently, his eyes burning with new knowledge. Whatever he'd suspected before about her feelings, there were no mysteries now.

Rio was left with nothing to hide behind. Her usual cool indifference, mild defiance—even the sham of allowing B.J. Hastings to date her, would no longer convince anyone but outsiders that she didn't have feelings for Kane Langtry.

Kane had stripped her of everything in the past few moments. The fact that she'd helped him do it was something she wouldn't get over for a very long time.

There was something edgy and restless about Rio Cory when she came up to the main house late that afternoon. Sam Langtry noticed it the moment she stepped into the kitchen from the back door and tugged off her Stetson to hang it on a wall peg. She hadn't seen him yet, sitting at the table in the breakfast nook off to her right, so he had an opportunity to study her.

The eleven-year-old orphan he'd taken in had grown into a beauty. Her waist-length braid was nearly black, her dark-lashed eyes large and jewel blue, but her delicate features promised an enduring beauty that age would never diminish. Just like her mama.

In many ways, Rio reminded Sam Langtry of the woman he'd loved but had never married. The biggest heartache of his seventy years was the fact that Lenore Cory's frail health had given out two years before her drunken husband had got himself killed. While she'd been alive, Sam had hinted to no one that he'd been in love with her. He'd done everything propriety, and Lenore's pride, allowed to help her and her child. Later, he'd taken in her orphaned daughter after her husband's death. Raising Rio had been a balm for the loss of her mother.

But fourteen years after Lenore's death, Sam had come to the end of his time on the earth. His heart was failing, he could feel it weaken by the hour. It was now, when he made himself take stock of his life and his deeds, that his memories of the past had come so clear. He was surprised sometimes at the depth of his feelings, but it was a soul-deep pleasure that his memories of Lenore had grown even more precious to him.

As her daughter was precious to him. Sam loved his son, loved his stepdaughter, Tracy, but Rio shared equally in his love for the children he considered his. The fact that he felt more tender toward her than he did Kane or Tracy was because Rio had always been the one who'd needed him most. She'd been deprived of the most, had lost the most. She'd also given back the most with her love and unswerving loyalty to him.

His only regret in dying was that he knew Rio would take his death hard. For all she'd become, for all her strengths, she was still that lost, frightened child who ran wild after her mama died, then had run off to hide on Langtry range after her father was killed. The wounds that had been inflicted on her because of her father's drunkenness and the notoriety of the fatal accident he'd caused still undermined her confidence, still kept her from feeling fully the pride she should have had in being a vital part of Langtry.

Perhaps he should have legally adopted her after all. His hope for Rio and Kane to fall in love, marry and together carry on the impressive history of Langtry Ranch now seemed every bit the foolish romanticism of an old man. Kane and Rio had never seemed less likely to forge such a bond. Rio loved Kane deeply, though she'd carefully kept it to herself. Kane appeared to be indifferent to Rio—when he wasn't jumping down her throat about something. He'd never been more critical of her than lately, but then, Sam knew his taciturn son well enough to suspect that his criticisms might be an effort to make sure he kept Rio at a distance. After all, Rio was a beauty, as skilled and capable as either of them in the running of Langtry. And there was a powerful tension between the two of them. Sam hoped his plan would keep them together long enough after his death for the tension to be resolved.

Rio turned her head just then and saw him at the table. Her edginess vanished, and a smile came over her lips. Her feminine stride as she crossed the kitchen to lean down and kiss his cheek was loose and relaxed, but the moment her hand touched his shoulder, he felt the tremor in it.

"I hope that's decaf you're swillin', cowboy," she said, then stepped over to the counter to help herself to the coffeemaker that held the real thing.

"Decaf coffee, no red meat, no liquor, no cigars, no salt, no fat, no fun. If it weren't for sugar, I'd have no vices whatsoever," he grumbled with good humor.

Sam was watching Rio's face closely when she turned back. He noted the slight swelling of her lips before she took a sip of coffee. He hoped B.J. Hastings wasn't responsible for the telltale fullness.

Rio had told him about B.J.'s proposal. She'd also confided that she thought B.J. was really after a Langtry loan. Sam suspected B.J. was after the impressive inheritance he meant to bestow on her. That Rio had called B.J.'s sudden interest in marrying her a bid for a loan reflected her lack of presumption where inheritance was concerned. She'd made it clear to him the first time he'd brought up the subject of her share in his estate that she wanted to inherit nothing from him. He'd given her the most important things in her life, she'd declared, so she wouldn't need his money. The only thing she'd asked was that he put something in his will to compel Kane and his heirs to allow her to return to the ranch from time to time.

Rio's wishes where his will was concerned were worlds different than his second wife's. As if she'd forgotten their prenuptial agreement, Ramona had already gone over every bank balance, investment, stock portfolio and business holding, and had handed him a lengthy list of the ones she wanted for herself. Her wish list had been the most blatantly greedy demand she'd ever made of him. She didn't realize yet that he'd found out about her infidelities. But it was because of her secret mistreatment of Rio that he meant to see that Ramona didn't receive a nickel more than the law assigned a surviving wife. She had a legal right to half of everything he'd earned during their six year marriage, but because the law allowed it and because of the prenuptial agreement, that made Langtry Ranch and the lion's share of Langtry holdings and stocks exempt. Ramona was certain to pitch a world-class tantrum when she found out that he wasn't going to be generous, but Sam believed the purpose of a will was as much to reward or insult heirs as it was to divide the deceased's assets. The idea appealed to his sense of justice.

"You got time for a drive up to the Painted Fence?"

Sam's question sent a ripple of unease through Rio. She set her coffee aside to give herself time to recover. Sam referred to the family cemetery on Langtry as the Painted Fence. That he'd wanted to visit the small, private cemetery with increasing frequency the past few weeks was another reminder to Rio that he believed his life was near the end.

The thought was unbearable. Sam was not just the only real father she'd ever had, he was her dearest friend. It was inconceivable that the tall, strong man whose word was law on Langtry could actually die.

Her quiet, "Give me a moment to wash up," was all she could get out before she turned and forced herself to make a sedate exit from the kitchen. Rio managed a reserved smile for Ardis and Estelle, the cook and the housekeeper, as she passed them in the back hall, but the moment she reached the refuge of the small bath, she closed the door and leaned against it.

The anguish that had disrupted her sleep for weeks was suddenly agonizing. Sam was dying. He refused to consult another heart specialist and had warned both her and Kane that he wanted no heroic efforts to extend his life. That included the wheelchair Kane had bought, which had been banished to a garage. All Sam agreed to was his special diet, his medications and his naps. Rio was powerless to change his mind, powerless against the rapid advance of his illness.

Her mother's death had been long and slow. Rio had been just as powerless against it. In the end, it seemed her mother had just given up, first resisting ongoing treatments, then finally refusing them altogether. She'd died very soon after, leaving her only child to a neglectful, alcoholic father. Those had been black days, with no warmth, no affection in the little house they'd lived in on Langtry for as long as she could remember. By then, her father's drinking binges lasted for days, and Rio was so ashamed and afraid of him that she spent nearly all the time she wasn't in school working odd jobs around the ranch or exploring the land. More often than not, she slept in one of the barn lofts or hay barns, anything to avoid her father's rages and drunken stupors.

And yet, Ned Cory's death two years after her mother's had been anything but a relief. Because he'd caused the highway accident that had also killed two teenage brothers, the notoriety of his drinking had mushroomed, making Rio more an object of scorn than sympathy. His death had also cost her the last of what little she'd had: the right to live on Langtry and have some sort of home.

But she'd lived a long time on her own, keeping out of the way, doing what she could to keep herself fed, clothed and attending school. The social worker who'd showed up hadn't been convinced an eleven-year-old could do such things, and had insisted on placing her with a foster family in the city. The woman's overbearing manner gave Rio no confidence in any family the woman would choose for her, so she'd fled. She'd known all the best places to hide around the ranch headquarters, known several ideal places on the range. She hadn't been able to risk going back to the little house, except for a few things which she'd taken away and carefully hidden. She stopped going to school, too, afraid the social worker would have too much help from the principal and teachers. She'd finally got so hungry that she'd made nightly raids on the cook house, plundering the food store and enjoying the furnace heat for as long as she dared before she climbed back out a window into the chilly fall night.

Until Kane had caught her leaving one night with a pillowcase of food. Until he'd hauled her to the main house to face his father as the fugitive and thief she'd become.

Sam Langtry, as always, had seemed a giant of a man—and never more so than on that night when he'd looked down on the ragged, dusty child who'd stood before him with her pillowcase of stolen food.

"Who owns what's under your feet, girl?" he'd asked in that low, gravelly drawl. Though his tone was soft, it carried the unmistakable authority of a powerful man whose word on any subject was final.

Rio's quiet "You do, sir," was wary. After eleven years of living with a father who yelled and smashed things with his big fists over every minor irritation, she'd been prepared to vault out of harm's way at the smallest sign of anger from Sam Langtry.

"Do you figure I got some say around here?" he'd asked her next, all the while staring so steadily and deeply into her eyes that Rio felt he could see everything bad and wrong in her.

"You're the boss," she'd got out, and realized sickly that no matter how hard she'd tried not to be taken away, no matter how much she feared having to go with the social worker, she would. She'd have to if Sam Langtry decreed it, and she'd mind him fast and with no complaint because she was terrified of him.

"If you know that, how come you didn't think to come talk to me?" It had been a stunning question. Rio never would have risked actually facing this man for any reason for a talk. He'd been nice to her in the past, but her mother had been around then. The foreman let her do odd jobs for money, but for almost two years she'd done her best to stay out of Sam Langtry's sight. Her father had always been in trouble and Rio was ashamed of that. Besides, no one seemed to like her any better than they had her father. Now, she was completely on her own. She had nothing, she was nothing. Trash like her didn't dare pester anyone, especially someone as important as Sam Langtry.

"Are you shy?" The hard line of Sam's mouth bent a little with the question, but his look was just as direct, just as penetrating.

"I'm scared." The horrifying admission slipped out and Rio felt her face go hot.

"No need to be scared, girl," he said, then asked,

"How about somethin' hot to eat, an' maybe a piece of apple pie to top it off?"

The question caught her off guard. Her nervous gaze veered toward the big clock over the door behind the big rancher. "But it's the middle of the night," she said, then caught her breath, suddenly worried that he'd think she was arguing with him.

"Might be, but a meal sounds good." He stepped away from her to the hall from the big kitchen to call out, "Hey, Ardis! If you're up, we could use somethin' hot to eat out here."

To Rio's astonishment, the cook had shuffled into the kitchen in a robe and fuzzy slippers, her dark hair wound over brushy rollers. Her eyebrows climbed high when she saw Rio, but her mouth was a noncommittal line.

"Is this that Cory girl?"

The cook's blunt question embarrassed Rio. She heard herself referred to that way often, and never in a kind way.

"This is Miz Lenore's daughter, Rio," Sam said, his choice of words somehow a correction. "While we were talkin', I got hungry for an early breakfast— steak, eggs, toast and some of them spicy potato chunks. Hot chocolate, if we got some, Ardis. And apple pie. Miz Rio's gonna join me, so you'd better make plenty."

Ardis's brisk "hmm" as she looked over Rio's dusty clothes was disapproving, but she moved off toward the refrigerator to get started.

That night marked the biggest turning point of Rio's young life. It had been more stunning than the death of either of her parents, more unexpected than anything in her eleven years and, because of Sam's kindness, more wonderful than anything a lonely, frightened child could have ever dared hope.

And now the man who'd done that for her, the man who'd taken her in, treated her like his own and given her more love and understanding and stability than she'd ever known, was dying.

The reminder hurt, the daily evidence of his decline filled her with despair. Her life wouldn't be the same without him. She could bear the loss of Langtry, she could bear having to leave and lose her last hope that Kane would ever truly accept her. She couldn't bear to lose Sam.

Rio quickly turned on the cold water tap and splashed her face with water. She resolved then to stay close to the house, close to Sam. There weren't many days left, and certainly not many days until Ramona and Tracy were due home for a short respite from the social whirl of Dallas. Until then, she would spend all the time with Sam that she could. She'd do her best to cater to every whim he had. And if that included a hundred trips to the Painted Fence, she'd make certain she took him on every one.

Sam got his hat and ambled out the back door. The heat from the late-afternoon sun was overpowering now that his heart was so susceptible to the stress of temperature extremes. The big ranch pickup he and Rio normally used for their little excursions had a good air conditioner, so he made his way around the pool and across the huge back patio toward where they'd left it the day before.

His chest hurt and he was out of breath by the time he reached the truck and climbed into the passenger side. He leaned over and twisted the key that had been left in the ignition. It didn't take long before the cool air from the compressor rushed through the vents at him, but it took a little longer to get his breath back and for the ache in his chest to ease.

By then, Kane was walking up the lane from one of the stables. He changed direction when he saw his father in the idling pickup.

"Where's Rio?" The stern line of his son's mouth implied that Rio was remiss for not being close by.

Sam leaned his arm on the bottom of the open truck window and watched his son's expression closely. "She'll be along in a minute. Has B.J. been around today?"

The mention of B. J. Hastings made Kane's frown deepen and Sam was relieved to see it. Kane's terse, "No. Why?" was the opportunity Sam had hoped for.

"Rio came in a while ago, lookin' like someone had kissed the daylights outta her." Sam leveled his gaze on his son's hard expression, then felt a run of satisfaction when Kane didn't remark.

"Whoever it was, oughta take it easy. Rio's worked awful hard around here to earn the men's respect. Wouldn't do for someone to jeopardize that."

Kane's hard expression went black. "Rio can be responsible for her own reputation."

Sam wasn't at all intimidated by his son. "That's right, but Rio's more vulnerable than most to gossip."

"Then she should hurry up and marry B.J., or cut the poor sucker loose."

"Rio's had a lot to live down. She's careful about who she offends. Cuttin' B.J. loose will take some unhurried finesse and a lot of diplomacy. You and I might soften the blow by scraping up a loan to help the Hastings out."

Kane swore. "B.J. is a world-class spendthrift. All a loan's gonna do is give him another few turns around the drain."

"Yeah, he and his daddy would rather get their hands on a meal ticket than a loan anyway, which explains the marriage proposal. Neither one of them sees a value in Rio beyond dollar signs."

Kane's mouth tightened and he glanced away from his father. "Hell, Rio could be in love with him."

Sam gave a hoarse chuckle. "B.J. is too much his daddy's little boy to appeal to Rio. Besides, any man who takes a shine to that girl is already being measured against an impossible standard."

Kane didn't comment directly, but gave an irritable grunt. His father wasn't finished with the subject, however.

"And just in case you didn't take my meaning earlier, Mr. Impossible Standard, you go easy on that girl."

Kane's gaze swung back to his father's and narrowed. He'd assumed Sam was the impossible standard Rio measured other men against. On the other hand, he should have realized his father would never have used such words to describe himself. It would have been conceited. But to hear Sam bluntly remind him of his status as the object of Rio's hero worship angered him. "Rio needs to grow out of her adolescent crush."

Sam tipped his head back slightly to study him for a long moment. "Then don't play kissing games with her, Kane. She doesn't have your experience, and she'll never be as hard bit. You could hurt somethin' real special in her."

Kane felt his anger mount. Rio Cory was as tempting to him as she was an irritant. He wasn't certain anymore that there was any real difference between the two feelings. It was bad enough that at twenty-three she still lived on Langtry Ranch. The eleven-year-old orphan he'd caught stealing food from the cook house had grown into a Texas beauty. Despite the fact that she worked on Langtry as hard as any ranch hand, there was a polish to her now, a feminine allure he wouldn't have imagined from someone with her background. And yet, there was something not quite tame about her, a wariness that made him think of a green-broke mustang more accustomed to following its wild instincts than submitting to a firm hand on the reins.

His father had gained her trust, her loyalty and her love. But then, Sam had taken her in, given her a home and provided her with the chance to be something more than she would have been had her father lived. In return, Rio idolized his father, devoted herself to him like a daughter and lived up to his expectations. It was no secret to Kane that Sam fancied Rio a suitable marriage choice for his only son.

And that made Rio Cory the subject of the only

real argument between father and son. Their other disputes were centered largely in the realm of business. Rio was the lightning rod of their personal disagreements. Kane had opposed Sam's decision to take in the scrawny little thief. She'd had a rough childhood, had run wild for years and the Cory name had made her an outcast in their ranching community. Besides, Kane had known that she was a reminder to his father of things best forgotten. Despite Kane's objections, Sam was almost obsessed on the subject of protecting Rio and compensating her for her dismal childhood. To her credit, she'd rarely allowed Sam to give her much besides food, shelter and basic clothing. She'd worked on Langtry for ranch hand's wages since high school and had been smart enough to win scholarships to put herself through college.

She'd soaked up every bit of the affection and attention Sam had offered, and the bond between the two was unshakable. Nevertheless, Kane didn't want to be Rio's reward or Sam's replacement when he died, so his father's subtle maneuverings to put Rio in his path was something he felt compelled to resist.

His terse, "Then warn her off," was heartfelt.

Sam gave his son a narrow look. "Are you tellin' me Rio's been throwin' herself at you?" The slant that came to his mouth showed his skepticism.

Kane growled a curse and his dark gaze flicked away. "A female doesn't have to throw herself at a man to send the signal that she's his for the taking."

"A lot of red-blooded Texas men would give ten years off their lives if Rio would send them that signal,'' Sam declared, the pride in his voice bringing his son's angry gaze back to his.

''Then she should pick one of them.''

Sam shook his head and gazed out the windshield of the idling pickup to focus into the distance. ''Rio lives by her instincts. She's like a wild mustang filly who's drawn to the biggest, toughest stallion. She's got to survive the elements and the predators. She's too savvy to bother with a weaker, less decisive male. She needs one who's strong enough to take on whatever comes along and survive the longest. She's already lost a lot. When I die, she'll lose again. She'll be lookin' for someone durable.''

Kane chuckled harshly at the mustang analogy that so closely matched his own perceptions of Rio, but there was no amusement in his tone. ''You're gettin' whimsical in your old age, Daddy.''

''Closer I get to the end, the simpler and more clear it's all becoming. Most things between a man and a woman aren't complicated, once they have some care for what each of them needs.'' Sam turned his head and looked at his implacable son. ''Rio wouldn't be such a touchy subject if you'd pay more attention to your own instincts and followed them awhile.''

One corner of Kane's mouth quirked. ''Followed an instinct today...qualified for this lecture.'' With that, Kane took a step away from the pickup and nodded his head in the direction of the back patio. ''The wild child's comin' this way. Don't get yourself tired out.''

Rio didn't let her stride falter when she saw Kane standing beside the pickup. She felt heat rush to her face, then endured the inevitable disappointment and relief when Kane turned away and walked off toward the stable. Her heart sank a little when she saw the grim line of his mouth. She could always tell when Kane and his father were having a disagreement. That she was usually the cause made her heart sink a bit more.

Soon, there wouldn't be any more disagreements. The dismal reminder was suddenly oppressive.

CHAPTER TWO

R<small>IO</small> managed to get through the first few minutes at supper that night by simply not looking Kane's way. It was difficult to do, since he sat across from her. She felt more awkward with him than ever after that torrid kiss in the stable, and wished with all her heart she'd had the good sense to shove him away. Of all the things she'd had to live down, living down her wild response to Kane was made worse by the fact that this was one embarrassment she'd earned all by herself. It helped that he would never tell anyone else about it. It was certain she never would. But the knowledge that Kane was usually unforgiving toward her made the notion of redeeming herself in his eyes a near impossibility.

It was Sam who broke the uneasy silence at the table. "Aren't we gettin' that new bull tomorrow?"

"He's due by nine, but Rio may have to take delivery," Kane answered. "I've got an eight-thirty phone call. If I'm not finished by the time the truck gets here, she can see to it."

Rio accepted the indirect order from Kane as a matter of course. Since Sam's retirement, Kane was the boss. Rio was in charge when Kane was away or unavailable. The foreman took his orders from her in those instances, but she'd learned long ago that he and the ranch hands were competent enough not to need a taskmaster to map out their day. The men deferred to her because Sam's regard for her had ensured it. Rio showed her respect for their experience and competence by issuing few directives. The delivery of the expensive bull required one of them be present to accept it, but because Kane had spent a veritable fortune on the animal, Rio hoped this particular responsibility wouldn't fall to her.

She knew better than to let Kane know how she felt about it, however. Kane tolerated her position in the chain of command because of his father and because she'd managed to never give him an excuse to exclude her. Rio never trifled with Kane's orders and instructions. She'd just have to be especially vigilant to be certain the bull arrived in fit condition and that he was unloaded and settled in with special care.

It was Kane who brought up the next subject. "Ramona called while the two of you were out. She and Tracy will be here by tomorrow afternoon."

Though the news wasn't unexpected, Rio couldn't help the disappointment she felt. Or the tension. Ramona delighted in her petty torments, particularly since she'd learned early on that Rio never reported them to Sam.

Sam's only remark was, "It's about time." Rio didn't remark at all. She knew Sam wasn't happy that Ramona's idea of being a rancher's wife was to live most of the year at her penthouse in Dallas spending Langtry money. Rio usually made herself scarce when Ramona came home, both to avoid the woman and to ensure that Sam had as much time with his wife and stepdaughter as possible. She wouldn't this time, however. Because of Sam's health, Rio meant to remain close to the house.

"I need you to help me with paperwork tonight."

Kane's statement brought her gaze up to meet his briefly before she forced herself to look away. She dared a quiet, "Is this something new?" Kane took care of the lion's share of paperwork, just as he wanted. Rio had barely touched anything to do with papers or book work since Sam had retired. She suspected Kane's mention of paperwork was a ruse in order to speak to her alone, but she still felt shaken by what had happened in the stable that day.

"Come see for yourself."

Rio couldn't help another swift glance at Kane. She'd heard distinctly the challenge in his tone, but nothing on his harsh features confirmed her impression until he reached for his coffee cup and leaned back in his chair. His eyes met hers with a suddenness that sent a tiny shock through her system. The slow lift of one corner of his mouth was pure male arrogance and she felt her cheeks burn. Somehow she managed to keep her gaze steady with his until he broke contact and finished his coffee.

Kane soon excused himself and went off to the den. Rio and Sam headed off to the informal family room at the back of the big ranch house. After a leisurely game of checkers, Sam went to his room for the night. Though he told Rio he planned to watch a movie video before he went to sleep, she secretly doubted he would. He seemed unusually tired tonight, and she was grateful for the small elevator Kane had installed in a storage closet off the back hall. Sam had refused to have his bedroom moved down to the main floor when his doctors had restricted him from using the stairs. When he'd returned home from a hospital stay to find an elevator in operation, he'd taken severe exception. He'd used it grudgingly, but three months ago, he'd stopped disparaging it.

And that was another measure of his declining health, she was reminded, and felt the familiar melancholy descend. A long walk, or better, an evening horseback ride might have lifted her spirits a bit and made it easier to sleep, but she doubted either choice would work any better tonight than they had all the other nights she'd tried them. Besides, Kane expected her to join him and she'd avoided his summons as long as she dared.

Rio made her way to the den, her nerves stretching tight as she was forced to face Kane privately. Why had he kissed her, why had he even touched her? Since it would never happen again, she'd rather not have known precisely what it was like to be in his arms at the mercy of what his mouth could do to hers. And she'd handed him a very painful means to torment her, if he chose. Because of that torrid kiss, she no longer had any secrets from Kane that mattered.

She slowed her step as she reached the den, then knocked softly on the open door before she walked in. Kane sat at his desk, shuffling through a stack of invoices. He didn't look up, didn't offer any pleasantry, but got straight to the point.

"After the bull's delivered in the morning, you can make the circuit of line shacks and cow camps. Take a cell phone and enough clothes to last you a few days."

Rio stiffened. Normally, checking the line shacks and cow camps for repairs and restocking their supplies was a days-long chore she might have welcomed with Ramona coming home. Now that Sam was so ill, she didn't intend to absent herself from the main house for longer than a handful of hours at a time.

Telling Kane that, however, meant she'd be refusing an order. Her presence at the house for the duration of Ramona and Tracy's stay also meant increased tension for them all, but for Kane in particular who usually went out of his way to make their visit as pleasant as possible.

Rio cleared her throat quietly, aware that Kane had yet to look up and that his ongoing perusal of invoices meant she'd been dismissed. Her soft, "I can't do it now," was met with as much surprise as she'd expected.

Kane stilled, his blue eyes rising to hers and going hard. "Why not?"

"Sam's..." Rio hesitated, lifted one shoulder, loathe to put anything pessimistic about Sam into words. "He's a little frail right now. I want to stay close."

Kane tossed the papers aside. "Did it ever occur to you that Ramona might not want to have you hovering? She might want to have Sam to herself."

His criticism stung. But then, most things Kane said to her did. On the other hand, Ramona could seem to do no wrong where Kane was concerned. The years-long frustration of being a target of Kane's disapproval while he turned a blind eye to Ramona's persistent lack of interest in her husband or his health was suddenly sharp.

But Rio knew better than to breathe a word of criticism about Sam's wife. Her chin came up a fraction and her lips thinned into a cynical line. "Ramona can have Sam to herself as much as she likes. Besides, I haven't seen Tracy for a long time."

"And Ramona likes it that way," he stated with brutal candor.

Rio glanced away from his harsh expression, suddenly weary. Maybe she had stayed on Langtry years longer than she should have. It didn't seem to matter to anyone but Sam that she'd spent that time working hard, laboring to repay all his kindnesses. To everyone else, she was still an outsider, an intruder who'd lucked into a fine, rich home that she hadn't deserved.

Bitterness and pride brought her gaze back to meet Kane's as she quietly asserted, "As long as Sam's alive, no one's going to chase me off, Kane. You and Ramona should know that by now."

Kane leaned back in his chair, his blue gaze cutting over her. "I don't want Sam upset."

Rio nodded. "Be sure you tell Ramona the same."

From the flare of annoyance in Kane's eyes, she knew he still considered her the only one responsible for the friction between her and Ramona. Ramona had never had to be particularly clever to achieve that impression, not when Kane was so willing to see Rio as the antagonist.

The reminder sent Rio's spirits lower. Kane would never see the witch beneath Ramona's startling beauty and Southern belle facade. Just as he would never credit Rio with being anything more than Ned Cory's daughter.

She gave him a grim twist of lips that acknowledged the unhappy fact, then turned and left the room with brittle dignity.

Rio whipped off her dark Stetson and ran the back of her wrist sleeve across her damp forehead. She put the hat back on and yanked it down snugly as she watched the back end of the stock trailer roll toward her again.

Her quick, "Slow it down, cowboy!" was loud enough to be heard by the driver, as was her curt, "A little to the left."

The driver of the supercab pickup towing the trailer reacted just as insolently to her directions as he had for the past five minutes. She bit back a swear word as the trailer again went too far to the right to line up with the narrow alley that would channel the bull toward the corral she had selected for him. That the trailer was still moving too fast to stop until it slammed into the far side fence post was just one more aggravation on a hot Texas morning full of aggravations.

The hooves of the startled bull inside the trailer hit the door like a cannon volley. Incensed, Rio started for the driver's side door of the truck.

The wide, fleshy face with a half-burned cigar stuck in its thick lips grinned out at her with more than a hint of mockery. "Sorry there, boss lady. You aren't too good at givin' directions, are ya? Maybe one of yer men could do better."

The enraged bull inside the trailer was rocking both it and the pickup in his effort to break out. If he injured himself, there'd be hell to pay, and Kane would hold her responsible.

Rio reached up and yanked open the door. Her sudden move was enough to startle the grin off the cowboy's sweaty face. "Step out or move aside." She lifted a boot to the running board of the big pickup to indicate not only her preference but her hurry. "One or the other, cowboy, or you'll be hauling that bull back."

"Ain't no one but me drivin' this truck." The sweaty cowboy sounded more like a whiny child than a man.

Rio's brisk, "Suit yourself," and her step off the running board was punctuated by a tight, "Give Mr. Cameron my regards, and tell him Langtry Ranch regrets we couldn't take delivery."

"Now hold on—" the cowboy called out as Rio walked away. She stopped and looked back at him.

"Out or over." Her firm tone brought a petulant frown to the fleshy face, but the cowboy bit down on his cigar and wallowed to the middle of the bench seat.

Rio was behind the wheel in an instant, taking a second to check the side mirrors before she slipped the truck into gear and started it forward a few feet. The bull was too stirred up now to waste another moment. As she stopped the pickup and shifted it smoothly into reverse, she gave every impression of being unaware of the sweaty cowboy who'd moved over only far enough for her to sit. She pretended not to notice that her right arm brushed his as she listened to one of the Langtry ranch hands direct her until she'd backed the stock trailer into position. She switched off the engine and was out the door so quickly that she'd spent a bit more than a minute behind the wheel.

Once out of the truck, she hurried to the back of the trailer. Two Langtry hands were pulling out the trailer ramp. The bull inside bellowed, and the sound seemed to make the trailer shiver. A heavy hoof pawed viciously at the trailer floor.

Rio climbed up the side of the board fence alley next to Boz, one of the older cowhands, and hooked a leg over the top rail.

"You want us to take that dumb sonofabuck out behind the barn and beat some manners into him, Miss Rio?"

Rio let out a tense breath and flashed the old cowhand a grateful smile. "Sounds good to me, but I think we'll let it go by this time. Thanks, anyway." She returned her attention to the back of the trailer.

Once the ramp was out, both cowhands clambered to the top rail of the fence. One gingerly reached down from his high perch. Once he checked to make certain the half dozen cowboys present were atop or behind the fence, he unlatched the heavy door. He'd just given the door a pull that would let it swing open on its own when it suddenly burst wide.

The impact of the bull against the door was like a crack of thunder. Rio started at the sudden boom as

did the other ranch hands. Kirby, the man who'd
opened the door, yelped and recoiled, balancing precariously atop the fence as he tried to cradle his injured hand. One of the men nearby reached over and
grabbed the back of his belt to keep him from falling
forward.

The bull rocketed out of the back of the trailer,
barreling down the narrow alley that angled him toward the gate of an empty corral. The ranch hand at
the corral shoved the gate closed the instant the bull
passed the opening.

Once inside, the outraged bull ran around the corral, charging anything he could see beyond the rails.
Rio jumped down from the fence, but instead of going
directly to the corral to check the bull, she hurried
toward the injured cowhand.

Kirby had climbed off the fence, and was leaning
against it while he cradled his wrist and hand against
his middle. His tanned face was pale and it was clear
to her that he was in pain.

"I'm sure sorry, Miss Rio. I was either a shade too
slow or that bull was three shades too fast."

Rio touched his wrist and hand with gentle fingers
as she carefully examined them. "You did fine,
Kirby. But I think your wrist is broken." She carefully settled his arm back against his middle, then
looked up into the young cowhand's strained features.
"We'll get you some ice and have someone drive you
to the hospital. Hank?" Rio turned her head to look
for the other young cowhand. Hank started quickly
toward them, but Rio redirected him with a brisk,
"Would you go down to the cook house for some

ice? Have Smitty call the hospital and tell them you're bringing Kirby in.''

The cowhand ran toward the cook house and Rio turned Kirby over to one of the other men to escort him to the ranch pickup parked under a shade tree in the drive.

From there, she strode toward the corral where the bull was, unconcerned that the cowhand from the Cameron Ranch hovered impatiently by his pickup. She stopped next to Boz, who was shaking his head and swearing beneath his breath.

''Let's hope that A-bomb on hooves is showing such a sweet disposition because he don't travel good,'' the old cowhand remarked, ''or because Cameron's man stirred him up.''

Rio watched the bull closely, checking for any sign of injury. ''Yeah, let's hope,'' she said quietly. Most bulls were volatile and temperamental, but there was something about this bull that made her uneasy. Boz had apparently sensed it, too. On the other hand, Kirby's injury might be influencing both of them.

Besides, Kane had selected this bull himself. The bull's superior quality and impressive pedigree would make him an ideal addition to Langtry's breeding program. If he could be managed, the animal was invaluable.

As if the bull had sensed her misgivings, he shifted directions in the enclosure. In the next moment, he charged straight for her like a steam engine at full throttle. Rio stiffened on her side of the fence, but didn't move. If the bull was loco enough to challenge the sturdy wood posts and heavy rails of this corral, it was better to know right away.

The last few strides of the huge animal were truly terrifying. Boz stepped aside, as if he didn't trust the fence would hold against the power of the bull. It was at the last second—when Rio was about to give in to the instinct to jump aside herself—that the big bull slid to a dusty halt a mere hand span from the rails. His huge head went down and he pawed so furiously at the dirt that he made furrows in the hard-packed surface.

The hoots and whistles of the cowhands who'd been watching were as much male admiration for the bull's bravado as it was relief that he'd shown he would respect a fence.

It wouldn't have occurred to Rio that the nerve she'd just shown was at least a part of that male admiration. She turned from the fence and walked back to where the cowhand who'd delivered the bull waited.

The cowboy's insolent expression was back, letting her know that he had no intention of showing a female in authority much respect. Either he didn't know or it didn't matter to him that she regularly acted in Kane's stead concerning Langtry business.

Rio's authority had been challenged before by cowboys whose egos were too frail to take orders from a woman. Few of them worked on Langtry, and this cowboy worked for someone else.

She forced her mouth into a polite line that wouldn't be mistaken for a smile. ''If Mr. Langtry buys more stock from your boss, volunteer for some other chore and let him send someone more professional to Langtry. Have a safe trip.''

Rio delivered the advice in a mild tone, then walked past the cowhand to check on Kirby. It was well known that Langtry hospitality always included an invitation for a meal or, at the very least, sandwiches and cold drinks or coffee for anyone who came through the front gate. The fact that Rio hadn't extended that hospitality to the cowboy was a setdown and would be taken as such. Particularly by the cowboy's employer if he found out.

Rio had just rounded the front of the cowboy's truck when she saw Kane standing next to the passenger side of the pickup where Kirby waited for Hank to return with some ice. She continued toward him, then gave Kirby a gentle smile as she stopped by the open truck door next to Kane. ''How're you doin', cowboy?''

''Not bad, Miss Rio,'' he answered, and gave her a tight grin.

Rio nodded past them at Hank who was jogging over from the cook house with two large bags of ice and a pair of folded towels. ''Hank's coming right now.''

When Hank reached the truck, Rio wrapped the ice bags in the towels and positioned them carefully around Kirby's wrist and hand. Kane's ongoing silence, aside from a few words to Kirby, gave Rio the clear impression that he wasn't pleased with her.

But then, he could see for himself that the Cameron cowhand was leaving. As they both stepped back and the Langtry pickup pulled away, Rio steeled herself for Kane's criticism and felt the inevitable dip of her insides when he didn't keep her waiting.

"You didn't offer Langtry hospitality to Ty's man."

Rio turned to him and lifted her chin in subtle defiance. "It was my decision to make. If you disagree…" Rio hesitated, submission to Kane tasting bitter. "I'll chase him down and bring him back."

Kane's harsh expression didn't alter, but his blue eyes burned down into hers. "Like hell you will."

Rio's lips parted in surprise before she swiftly recovered herself.

Kane glanced away from her and growled, "Disrespect toward you is a challenge of my authority to put you in charge."

"I appreciate that, Kane," she said. "Thanks."

Kane's gaze streaked back to impale hers. "It doesn't have a damned thing to do with you."

Rio's breath caught at his sudden hostility, but she forced her mouth into a curve that she hoped concealed her dismay. "I'm sure I could figure that out for myself," she said, then gave him a mock salute as she started to back away. "I'm going up to see if Sam needs anything," she added, then turned to walk to the house, hoping she could escape before Kane could voice any other unpleasantness.

CHAPTER THREE

RAMONA and Tracy arrived on Langtry at four o'clock that afternoon. They'd flown from Dallas that morning with neighboring rancher, Deke Sanderson, in his private plane, but instead of landing at Langtry's airstrip, they'd touched down at the Sanderson ranch.

Though Rio secretly disapproved of Ramona's and Tracy's hours-long visit with the widowed rancher, she kept her thoughts to herself. Their return to Langtry would likely prove difficult enough once Ramona realized that Rio would be at the main house.

Rio allowed them the time between their late afternoon arrival and supper to catch up with Sam and Kane and to get settled in. Because their homecoming was considered an occasion, Rio set aside her usual choice of jeans and a blouse in favor of a blue sundress and sandals before she came down to supper.

She entered the living room where everyone but Sam waited for Ardis to announce supper. Tracy sat at one end of the sofa and Ramona stood with Kane in front of the liquor cabinet. Rio walked toward a wing chair at the edge of the formal furniture grouping in front of the stone fireplace. Ramona was the first to see her arrive.

"Ah, here's Rio now, Kane, just as you said," Ramona announced, and immediately flashed Rio a saccharine smile. ''Kane is mixing drinks,'' she told Rio. ''Would you like him to fix you something?''

''No, thank you,'' Rio murmured, and sat down.

Ramona nodded sagely and gave Rio a sympathetic look. ''A wise choice for you, my dear, considering.''

Rio tensed at the bald reference to her father's alcoholism but sat back in her chair and pretended not to have noticed. She glanced toward Tracy who hadn't acknowledged her yet. Two years younger than Rio's twenty-three, Tracy was a small, delicate blonde like her mother, with huge blue eyes and a flawless complexion. Tracy was usually as sweet as her mother was witchy. When Tracy glanced her way, Rio gave her a soft smile. ''Hello, Tracy.''

Tracy's, ''Hello,'' was plainly obligatory. She immediately turned from Rio, her manner cool and unfriendly.

Taken aback by Tracy's snub, Rio glanced Kane's way as he left the liquor cabinet and came toward the sofa to sit down with his drink. His hard gaze met hers, then moved appraisingly over her sundress and down the smooth length of her legs before it shifted away. It wasn't the kind of look she usually got from Kane, and Rio's self-consciousness escalated.

Sam came into the room shortly after, just before Ardis called them to the meal. Sam offered his arm to Ramona, who cooed with exaggerated pleasure and glided to his side in a cloud of chiffon and perfume. Sam offered his other arm to Tracy and escorted both women into the dining room.

That left Rio with Kane, creating an awkwardness that made her squirm inwardly. Kane usually managed to avoid being paired with her socially, whether it was at some grand occasion or something as simple as escorting her from one room to the next with company present. She couldn't believe Sam had put either of them on the spot, particularly since he knew how Kane felt about her.

Suddenly deciding to spare them both, Rio started to follow Sam and the others. She'd not gone more than two steps past Kane before his hard, strong fingers closed around her arm and brought her to a halt. Rio turned toward him in surprise. His handsome features were as harsh as ever, his blue eyes glinting with irritation.

Meanwhile, the firm grip on her arm was sending a tide of sensation through her. The memory of the kiss in the stable came flooding back, shocking her with the sudden craving to be kissed again.

"Sam expects me to do the gentlemanly thing by you," Kane was saying before his mouth curved with a mixture of amusement and mockery. "And if Ramona could see your face right now, she'd give you a tongue-lashing that would cut you to ribbons."

Rio stiffened and tried to free her arm. Kane tightened his grip and tugged her closer. She braced a hand against his chest to maintain the narrow distance between them. Her defiant, "Leave me alone, Kane," was a bit breathless.

"Then keep those soft, hungry looks to yourself." The low words were brutal.

Her face flushed. She gave him a shove that should have pushed him away, but he stood before her like a granite column. The heat from his shirtfront seared her palm, the steady rhythm of the heart beneath her hand beating once for every two beats of her own. She was suddenly overwhelmed by his maleness, and staggered by the powerful longings of her own body.

What a fool she was! Self-preservation won out over desire and gave her the strength to push away from Kane and step back. She couldn't look him in the eye, but she felt the laser intensity of his gaze as she turned and walked swiftly toward the dining room.

She was so attuned to him that she heard every unhurried boot step as he followed. And though she avoided looking at him during the meal, she sensed every move he made, and felt it like a touch each time he looked at her.

At least Ramona allowed her to eat her meal in peace. Rio began to think the older woman's attitude toward her had mellowed, which put her a little more at ease. It wasn't until later that she realized Ramona hadn't mellowed a bit.

They had all moved back into the living room. Ardis was carrying in a coffee tray. Sam had excused himself for an early night. Ramona barely waited long enough for the elevator at the back hall to reach the upstairs level before she began.

"Sam's been quite charitable toward you all these years, Rio." Ramona's voice was soft and sweetly modulated, but her words were like a slap.

Rio hesitated as she reached for the coffee cup Ardis passed her. The old shame that burst up made her break contact with Ardis's watchful gaze as she took the cup and saucer.

She didn't respond to Ramona's opening salvo. Kane would take a dim view of any verbal retaliation on her part, and perhaps Ardis felt the same way. Ardis had never been particularly friendly toward her, so Rio didn't think of her as an ally.

As if she were flaunting the knowledge that no one in the room would object, Ramona went on. "I'd think you'd have more pride than to keep hanging around, playing up to that poor old man in hopes of getting more out of him."

Rio sipped her coffee as she struggled to conceal her anger. Any sign of upset would please Ramona, and Rio was determined to thwart her. She lowered her cup and calmly met the malicious gleam in Ramona's eyes. "Sam's no fool, Ramona."

Beneath her quiet words was a warning to Ramona about the infidelity Rio suspected her of. She doubted the others in the room would take those words at anything but face value, but Ramona took them exactly as Rio had intended. There was no mistaking the wild flush of outrage that colored her flawless face.

Ramona turned toward Kane who grimly watched them both. "Can't you do something about her, Kane?"

Kane's mouth quirked in faint sarcasm. "What is it you want me to do, Ramona?"

"Fire her, make her leave—" she waved one hand impatiently "—whatever it takes."

Rio set her cup aside, her nerves going painfully tight as she prepared to rise and leave the room. She shouldn't have stayed for coffee, she never should have hung around once Sam had retired for the evening. She'd lived on Langtry long enough to know how things were and how they would always be.

"Finish your coffee, Rio." Kane's rough drawl carried the steely undertone of an order. She glanced up, but Kane's blue gaze was fixed on Ramona.

"Rio earns her keep, Ramona. And since she works for me, I'd appreciate it if you'd let me decide whether she's out of line or not."

Ramona's perfect face was suddenly the picture of dismay. "Kane…" she hesitated, clearly confused. "Surely you aren't—"

"Leave it alone." Kane's icy tone cut her off.

Ramona's mouth rounded in surprise, but she quickly affected a wounded look. Kane appeared oblivious to the act as he turned his attention to Tracy. Rio could only stare, as shocked by Kane's unexpected intervention as Ramona was.

The excitement that stormed over her when she realized that Kane had actually defended her ebbed swiftly. He wasn't really sticking up for her, he was responding to a challenge to his authority. And, as he'd said that morning, it had nothing to do with her.

Rio picked up her cup, but was no longer interested in coffee. She could feel the hostility that radiated from Ramona as Kane made small talk with Tracy. She rose to her feet with unhurried grace to set her cup and saucer on the tray, then slipped out of the room while Kane was distracted by his conversation with his stepsister.

She might have made good the escape to her room, but the doorbell rang. Since she was closer to the front of the house than either Ardis or Estelle, she took a quick detour to answer the door.

B.J. Hastings waited on the doorstep. Peacock handsome, his blond hair and blue eyes made him look almost angelic. Though he was almost as tall as Kane, his lean body didn't carry the hard muscle that Kane's did. But then, even though Kane managed several Langtry business interests, he still did ranch work with surprising regularity. B.J., she knew, enjoyed being the boss when his father left him in charge, but he wouldn't have dreamed of working with his men. He often chided her for working with the Langtry ranch hands, vacillating between horror and careful ridicule depending on the work Rio was doing at the time.

And that was just one of the many reasons Rio found him lacking as a marriage prospect.

"Hello, darlin'," he drawled, his eyes wandering down her slim body with open appreciation. "Any chance we've got the house to ourselves tonight?"

Rio managed a soft smile and a quiet "Hello," secretly unhappy about the question. She ignored it and said, "Come out to the kitchen. It's a little less crowded there." She turned and led the way, quickly passing the wide doorway into the living room. She heard B.J.'s irritable murmur as he tried to keep up.

Ardis and Estelle were in the kitchen, a Scrabble game laid out on the table in the breakfast nook as they watched a network news program. Disappointed that the room wasn't free, she smiled at the two women and continued on out the back door to the patio as if that had been their destination all along.

She went to one of the shadowy areas near the far end of the pool before she stopped. B.J. caught up to her, then took her arm and turned her toward him. In the next second his open mouth swooped down on hers as his arms tightened like bands around her.

Warm and wet, his mouth was not firm but soft, as if he were smearing it over her lips. Coming so soon after Kane's steamy kiss, Rio couldn't help noticing the difference. She also couldn't help that B.J.'s kiss repulsed her.

As quickly as she could, she managed to pull back, privately appalled that B.J. compared so unfavorably to Kane.

"Ah, come on, Rio," B.J. groaned, then tried unsuccessfully to recapture her lips with his. Rio braced her hands against his chest to create some space, but his mouth found the side of her neck. "Girls like you are supposed to be wild and willing," he murmured as he nibbled the delicate flesh. His marauding lips were repellent, but his words were chilling.

Rio gave him a shove that gained her freedom, then took a step back. Something in her rigid posture discouraged him from reaching for her a second time.

"Girls like me?" she asked quietly. "What about girls like me?"

Though his face was heavily shadowed, Rio could see that B.J. was too annoyed with her to realize he was treading on shaky ground. He answered with a foolish lack of caution.

"Yeah, girls like you." Frustration made him give the words a faint sneer. "Beautiful, come-from-nothin' girls who know how to play up to big money. Only in your case, you never try too hard.''

Rio stared, not really surprised by the insult. She'd known much of B.J.'s attention was an act, she'd sensed it from the first. It was because of his sudden attention and her less than exalted status in their community that she'd not immediately rebuffed him. Somehow, things had rapidly escalated, until B.J.'s surprise proposal had left her scrambling for a way to turn him down without offending him. She should have known it was inevitable.

Her soft, ''I think you'd better leave,'' sounded as calm as she could make it, but she was trembling with anger.

B.J. cocked his head as if he hadn't heard correctly. ''What did you say?''

The deep voice that intruded startled them both. ''I heard what she said, Hastings, and I'm standing over here.''

Rio turned and saw Kane standing across the pool from them in the deep shadow of the stone wall. ''Give your daddy our regards.''

It was a blatant invitation to leave. B.J. stood there a moment, his hands clenching and unclenching at his sides, before he spun away and headed toward the patio gate and the sidewalk that would take him to the front driveway.

Rio watched him go, more relieved by Kane's intrusion than she wanted to admit. The problem of how to deal with B.J.'s proposal had just been solved, and she didn't care that she hadn't been the one to solve it. She could not, however, let Kane know she appreciated his intrusion.

She looked toward the deep shadows across the pool at Kane.

"Spying?" she asked, forcing just the right touch of challenge into her tone.

"Looking out for Langtry interests. Saving B.J. a world of sexual frustration." He paused a moment before his voice went rough. "I told you to tell him no."

Rio was grateful for the dimness that concealed the heat in her face. The memory of how Kane had been touching her when he'd first said those words sent a torrent of longing through her. Somehow she made her voice sound strong. "I take your orders where the ranch is concerned, Kane. You don't have any say in my personal business."

"We won't argue about that tonight, Rio. You're done with B.J. I hope you're smart enough to keep it that way."

She stared warily into the darkness that concealed him, as mystified by his sudden intrusion into her personal life as she was by his intervention with Ramona earlier.

On the other hand, he'd said he was looking out for Langtry interests. Only a fool would take that blunt statement at more than face value—particularly since it was Kane who'd said it.

Before she could respond to his autocratic remarks he was gone, striding toward the back door to the kitchen, his brisk manner emphasizing the emotional distance between them.

*   *   *

Rio wasn't eager to leave the house after breakfast that next morning. Sam seemed more tired than usual, weaker. She'd seen him take one of his tiny pills at the table, but a frown from Kane made her conceal her worry.

In a departure from the norm, she and Kane lingered over coffee. Ramona and Tracy weren't awake yet, and it would be hours before either of them came downstairs for breakfast. In the end, it was Sam who sent them on their way, gruffly reminding them that they had responsibilities.

Rio was present when Kane discussed work with the foreman and their men, but as usual, she kept in the background. By the time he dismissed them, she realized that he hadn't assigned her anything in particular.

Kane waited until they stepped out of the cookhouse before he spoke to her. "I'll be in the office this morning. Find something to do until you think Ramona and Tracy have had time to come downstairs and finish breakfast. Come see me after that." His eyes met hers solemnly, and Rio had the startling sense that he was including her as his equal in their vigil over his father's health. "Unless I send for you sooner."

The words made her heart sink, but she nodded. "I'll be close by."

They went their separate ways, Kane to his office, Rio to one of the stables to work with a colt she'd been training. A feeling of foreboding wound around her heart. The minutes crawled along until at last it was time to go to the house.

* * *

Sam Langtry couldn't remember being too young to ride a horse. His daddy had bragged that his fine, strapping son had ridden in front of him in the saddle by the time he was strong enough to hold up his head, taking the reins in his chubby little hands by the time he was nine months old. Since all that was true, it was no wonder that not riding a horse for the past year had seemed so damned unnatural.

The old red roan gelding nudged his arm as if to remind him of the sugar cube he'd promised. Sam dug into his shirt pocket and brought out the treat. His hands were shaking so from weariness that he almost lost the cube before he could hold it out in his palm.

He stepped to the horse's side and checked the cinch with expert hands before he gathered the reins. He got his foot in the stirrup and swung himself upward, alarmed at how much strength was required to mount, but pleased that the movement still felt as natural to him as breathing.

Once he was atop the old horse, the pain in his chest sharpened. Dizziness made him feel sick and his breath came hard. The vial of pills he was never without was in his pocket, and he went for a last dose with weak fingers.

It took so long to feel better that he began to worry that he might pass out before he could get clear of the stable door. He was hurting, but at least he'd got the saddle on Spinner before it had got this bad. Despite the pain and that odd kind of wooziness, he felt better than he had in a long time.

At his signal, the roan stepped forward as if he,

too, were eager to head out like old times. Sam had been hoping Spinner's gait was still as smooth as he remembered, and to his relief, it was. He relaxed as the familiarity of being on horseback gave him a reviving feeling of youth.

He and Spinner moved sedately down one of the alleys that bisected the network of corrals. If anyone had seen him, they sure hadn't tried to stop him. He released a cautious breath when they cleared the headquarters and the only thing before them was the massive, sun-bright Langtry range.

Rio was walking up the path from the shaded corral she left the colt in. Out of habit, she scanned what she could see of the headquarters and the open land beyond. At first, she didn't pay undue attention to the tall cowboy she saw ride through the last gate toward the range. The sight was so familiar to her that what she was seeing didn't fully register until she was about to glance away.

It seemed odd that someone was taking Spinner out. The roan cowpony was Sam's, but Sam had long ago retired him. They'd brought him in from the range a month ago to doctor an infected cut, but some of the kids around the ranch had been as drawn to the old horse as he was to them. Kane had decided to allow them to ride the cowpony for the summer as long as they were easy on him and didn't bother him during the heat of the day.

And that was why it was so strange to see one of the ranch hands riding him out to work. Rio's steps slowed as she continued to stare, struck by the notion

that she was seeing Sam ride away from the headquarters as tall and strong as ever. And when the cowboy reached up to adjust his hat, the familiarity of the
gesture confirmed it.

Panic jolted her into movement, sending her running for the main house and Kane.

Sam and Spinner made it to the tree-scattered rise of
the Painted Fence. Sam's elation at escaping the ranch
headquarters on horseback was probably all that kept
him from folding over with the terrible pain in his
chest.

Lord, it was good to be out in the open, a warm
wind on his face, a solid horse beneath him and all
of Langtry spread around him like a vast kingdom.
He hadn't wanted to die in a hospital, he hadn't
wanted to die indoors. He'd wanted to die like this,
exactly like this, natural, without fuss, beneath the
Texas sky with the sight and sound and smell of the
land around him.

He let Spinner walk up to the hitch rail just outside
the white picket fence that surrounded the family
cemetery. The old horse came to a halt and stood
patiently.

Sam managed to dismount, barely able to hold on
to the saddle long enough for his buckling knees to
steady. The pain that was cleaving his chest made him
feel weak as a baby, but he forced himself forward.
Once he was inside the gate, he made his way past
the assortment of gravestones.

His first wife, Marlie, wasn't buried here. She'd
died of pneumonia the spring Kane had turned two,

and her mama had wanted her buried with the rest of her family in a cemetery near Dallas. Sam had given in out of pity for his mother-in-law of three years.

He was almost glad now that Marlie wasn't resting here, though he'd loved her with the intensity of a newlywed husband. If she were, he would have been obliged to leave instructions that he be buried beside her. As it was, he meant to be buried next to Lenore Cory.

It'd been easy to get Ned Cory's agreement to bury his wife on Langtry, easy because Sam had offered to pay all the costs for the casket, headstone and funeral. But two years later, when Ned Cory had died in the car crash, Sam'd had him interred in the county cemetery ten miles away.

No one had ever questioned Sam about the arrangements for either funeral, and he himself had never remarked upon it to anyone. He'd been in love with another man's wife. The moral torment of that had kept him from taking her away from Cory while she was alive; it hadn't kept him from keeping her away from Cory after her death. Besides, it had seemed right for Lenore to be here, right for little Rio to be able to have her mama's grave near enough to take flowers to.

Sam almost reached the lovely headstone at Lenore's grave before the very last of his strength began to wane. He didn't make it to the shade before he collapsed.

"God, Rio, don't tell me you've come in to hang around the house." Ramona made a face as Rio rushed past her from the back door. Rio was in such a hurry to find Kane that Ramona barely made an impression. She raced down the back hall and charged into Kane's office.

Her breathless, "Where's Sam?" was choked. Kane glanced up, took in her pale face, then returned his attention to the stack of papers before him.

"He's been in bed since after breakfast," he told her. "Doc Kady's coming out for lunch so he can check on him."

Rio shook her head. "I just saw him take Spinner out."

Kane grunted. "He's not well enough to ride, Rio, you know that."

"Then explain how he did it," she blurted.

Ramona stood in the open doorway. "Kane, why do you allow her to speak to you in that tone?"

Kane didn't answer either of them, but fired a question at Ramona. "Is Sam still upstairs?"

Ramona seemed surprised, but shook her head. "No, he said he was going down to the stable. His color wasn't the best, so I thought it would do him good to get some sun."

Rio felt a surge of rage she could barely contain. It was just like Ramona to think in such a superficial way about the seriousness of Sam's illness. Kane was on his feet in an instant, coming quickly around the desk before he suddenly stopped and turned back for the cell phone beside the lamp.

An instant later they were both running through the house to the back door. Kane slowed long enough to order Estelle, "Check the house for Sam. If you find him, call me right away on the cell phone. If you don't, call Doc Kady, tell him we think Dad's gone riding, and have him come out early.''

They both were out the door and halfway across the patio before Estelle could reply.

CHAPTER FOUR

THE heat reminded Sam of that first day. He'd been riding the bad manners out of a green-broke colt and had ended up checking the fence along the south highway. He'd seen the old brown pickup, seen the back end sagging under the weight of mismatched furniture and cowboy tack. One of the front tires was flat.

Then he'd seen the woman. Tall and willowy, she wore her dark hair wound up in a loose knot. The blue flowered dress she'd had on belled and fluttered in the light breeze. She'd been balancing a sleeping baby on one slim hip and she'd lifted a hand to shade her eyes when she caught sight of his approach.

He'd drawn the colt to a halt at the fence. She'd smiled at him then, a sweet, shy, nervous little smile that had got him by the heart. He'd tipped his hat, then dismounted and tied the colt to the fence.

Neither he nor the woman said a word to each other until he'd crossed the shallow ditch. As he got closer, he saw that her lovely eyes were a breathtaking blue. Her face was delicate, her nose and high cheekbones already turning pink from the sun. The one-year-old she balanced on her hip was a rosy-cheeked cherub of a child, her small dark head on her mama's shoulder, sound asleep.

Sam reckoned then that he'd never seen a more

lovely sight. The beauty and her babe. And as he'd looked into her remarkable eyes, he'd seen the sweetness, the tender spirit of her, the loneliness and the lifetime of yearning he'd felt in his own heart...

The pain in his chest almost made him pass out. Sam forced himself to stay conscious, unwilling to let go of the memories until he came to the one he loved most...

Lenore, working in her garden behind the little house her family lived in on Langtry. She'd grown flowers around the neat plot of vegetables. Beautiful flowers. Some she'd dug from a pasture and reset, some she'd grown from dime store seed. More than a dozen different kinds, dozens of colors and hues.

She'd had on a faded housedress with no sleeves. She'd been barefoot, walking among the profusion of blooms without crushing a single stem. Carefully, tenderly, she'd been clipping off a bloom stalk here and there, adding to the rich bouquet she'd been gathering.

She'd looked up to see him, smiled that tender Madonna smile, and started toward where he stood, hat in hand, at the edge of her garden. She'd shyly thanked him, for at least the tenth time, for allowing her to plant a garden. He'd gallantly told her that if he hadn't needed to graze cattle he might have had the whole of Langtry plowed so she could grow flowers.

That's when she told him she'd been picking the bouquet for him. "For some brightness in your day, Sam," she'd said in her quiet, shy way. "The sweet smells and colors always give my heart a lift. I surely hope you might enjoy them, too.''

Oh, God, he had! He could still feel the feather-light brush of her slim fingers as he'd taken the flowers. The lump in his throat had about strangled him, but he'd managed to thank her, even as his heart clenched with love and need and despair.

Because he could never have her. He'd struggled with the agony of the moral dilemma, struggled to contain his feelings, struggled not to beat hell out of her husband for not appreciating how lucky he was.

And he'd kept that bouquet. He'd bought the biggest, heaviest book he could find in Austin, and he'd pressed every blossom in its pages. No bloom had been too frail, no petal too small. He'd left the book for Rio...

''Sam?''

Lenore's voice was barely audible above the pain. ''Sam?''

He could feel her cool palm on his cheek. Only because he thought it was Lenore did he open his eyes. The haze of pain eased enough for him to see that it was Rio, and his emotions rose again as he noted her distress.

''You're her image,'' he managed to tell her.

He felt the tremor in her hand as she stroked his forehead. Her tearful, ''Please, Sam,'' carried an edge of pain that he expected. God, he hated that after everything Rio had meant to him over the years, that he was going to end up hurting her.

He was glad to see Kane with her, relieved that their concern for him was bringing them together.

They each had taken hold of his hands and he wondered if either of them knew how wonderful it was to touch them, to feel the vitality of their youth and the power of their love for him one last time.

The sun must have gone behind a cloud bank. Sam welcomed the dimmer light, welcomed the gust of coolness that swept him. The pain in his chest was still intense, but there was an odd numbness that made it more bearable.

It took so much for him to get the words out. "Love you both. Take care of each other," he whispered. "The letters...say for me..."

The last pain didn't hurt so much as it paralyzed. Sam was looking up into the two faces he loved most when his eyelids grew too heavy. His last breath eased away and took the pain with it.

Rio stared in disbelief as she watched Sam's eyes close and felt his weak grip go slack. Grief settled so heavily in her chest that she thought at first the pressure would crush her.

Tears blurred her eyes, but not so much that she couldn't lean over and place one last kiss on Sam's cheek. She laid his hand reverently across his middle, painfully aware of Kane.

Somehow she made herself turn from Sam and get to her feet so she could take a few steps away. Shock made her feel dazed and sluggish. The reminder that Sam was the only person she could have safely shared this terrible grief with made her feel even more desolate.

She wrapped her arms around herself, and when

the first spasm of sobs came, she couldn't get control
of them for a few moments. She jumped when she
felt Kane's big hand settle on her shoulder. The com-
pulsion to turn to him and fling herself into his arms
was so strong suddenly that she shook with the effort
to control the impulse.

It was a relief when she heard him speak quietly
into the cell phone. His attention wasn't on her, and
his distraction gave her more time to compose herself.

It was the warm weight of Kane's hand, or rather,
the deceptively consoling feel of it, that made Rio
ease away and walk through the gate to where Spinner waited at the hitch rail. She and Kane had brought
the Suburban. Once some of the men arrived, they
would take Sam home in the back of the big vehicle.

Spinner gave her a gentle nudge. Rio stroked the
old cowpony's head, then fought a new flood of tears
when the horse pushed his head against her as if he,
too, were grieving for an old friend. Rio wrapped an
arm around the horse's neck and hugged him.

The sound of a ranch pickup was almost welcome.
Rio turned and glanced over her shoulder toward it.
Kane was standing between her and the oncoming
truck. Her gaze connected with the bleakness in his,
then veered away.

"Come on, Rio," Kane said, his big voice sound-
ing odd, choked. "Someone else can bring Spinner
in."

For a moment, Kane thought she'd refuse. She nodded and he watched as she drew herself up straighter,
tighter. He could see she was still shaking. She looked
as shell-shocked as he felt, and though she managed

to control her tears, he could see the stark grief in the wild shine of her eyes.

Sam was laid gently on a pallet in the back of the Suburban, his black Stetson resting over his face. Kane and Rio rode on either side of his body. By the time they arrived at the headquarters, it was noon. The ambulance had already arrived.

Rio couldn't watch as Doc Kady directed the transfer to the ambulance. She felt chilled, and the restlessness she felt made it almost impossible to stand still. It seemed every ranch hand on the place was there, hat in hand, looking on soberly.

When at last the ambulance pulled slowly away, Kane started for the house. Rio automatically followed, then hesitated. Now that Sam was gone, there wasn't a person at the main house who wanted her around. The desolation she felt was compounded by the worry that Kane might expect her to leave the ranch as soon as possible.

The reminder that she'd not only lost Sam but her home and her place in the world filled her with dread. The anguish she felt overwhelmed her and she turned from the house, so restless and unsettled inside she thought she might fly apart.

Instinct drove her to hide, to vent her grief in private, until the worst of it was over and she found the courage to face what was ahead. She'd done that when her mother died, and later when her father was killed. There were several safe places on the ranch, beautiful solitary places that she might never see again once Sam was laid to rest and she was finally banished from Langtry. She could find them all one last time and say goodbye to them just as she somehow had to say goodbye to Sam.

Indecision made her waver only a moment more before she was rushing toward the stables and the sanctuary of the land.

"Do you know where the will is?"

Ramona's question stunned him. Kane had just told her that her husband had passed away. Ardis and Estelle were already crying, and Tracy was teary-eyed, but Ramona's first response was to ask if he knew where Sam's will was.

He saw the flash of horror in her beautiful eyes when she realized her gaffe, and she scrambled to recover herself. "Won't you need it right away to ensure a smooth transition of ownership? I mean, there must be a million legalities with the ranch and all those holdings and investments. I—I'm certain your father wouldn't want you to be further upset at a time like this."

"That's right, Ramona, he wouldn't," Kane said bluntly, then abruptly turned to leave the room.

But Ramona stepped in front of him and pushed her way into his arms, doing an elegant job of dissolving into the teary show of grief that had been a bit long in coming. Kane automatically put his arms around her, but he tolerated her delicate sniffles only a few moments before he set her away from himself and left the room.

Rio didn't come back to the headquarters until after dark the next evening. The desolation she felt had kept her riding over the Langtry range for hours at a stretch. She'd stopped periodically to water her horse and unsaddle it to graze, but shock and restlessness pushed her to keep moving, keep riding, in an attempt to make it ease.

At last, dazed by exhaustion and hunger, she rode back to the stable. She took care of grooming her horse, then turned him into a stall with fresh water and a generous measure of grain. On the walk to the house, she slowly became aware of the number of cars and pickups that virtually clogged the ranch drive and covered the lawn around the house.

Panicked by the sight that promised a houseful of guests, she changed course and circled the lawn, hoping to slip unnoticed into the kitchen from the patio. She couldn't face so many people in her present state. Besides, Sam wouldn't be there now. Without him to ensure her acceptance, Rio wasn't certain she wanted to put anyone's real feelings toward her to the test.

She made it into the kitchen, relieved that no one was there. Ardis and Estelle were probably waiting on guests, so she hurried to the back hall and the stairs.

She didn't escape unseen, but was forced to give a small wave of acknowledgment to two ladies from church who were carrying empty trays back to the kitchen. The surprise on their faces made her flush self-consciously, but she rushed up the stairs then along the hall to the safety of her room.

Once there, she closed the door. She didn't turn on the lights, but tossed her hat toward a chair and made her way across the room by memory. She entered her bathroom and sat down tiredly on the edge of the tub. The murmur of voices from downstairs was faint, but she could hear them. She leaned forward and braced her elbows on her knees. She combed her fingers into her hair and rested her forehead wearily on the heels of her hands.

The church ladies' surprise was probably fright. After most of two days and a night on the range in the dust and wind and heat, she knew she was a sight. She was just working up the energy to stand and get undressed for a hot bath when a loud pounding started on her bedroom door.

She jerked her head up, but before she could call out, the door swung inward. Kane's tall, broad-shouldered body blocked the light from the hall momentarily before he stepped in and flipped the light switch. Once he looked across into her bathroom and saw her sitting on the edge of the tub, he shut the door with a snap.

"Where the hell have you been?" he demanded.

Rio thought she had her emotions under control—she'd cried until she was numb—but the moment Kane snarled at her, the misery she'd worked so hard to distance herself from came flooding back.

"You look like hell," he went on as he stalked toward her and stepped over the threshold into her bath. He mercilessly switched on the light and Rio winced from the brightness.

"I feel like hell, too, Kane. Leave me alone."

Kane stared down in private horror. Rio was a mess. She was all-over dust, her unbound hair looked like a hip-length tangle of witch's hair, but the desolation in her eyes was frightening. He thought about Ramona downstairs, her hair perfectly coifed, her makeup just so, and wearing an elegant black dress. She was carrying a black lace hankie around as a prop, but as far as he was concerned, her grief was playacting compared to Rio's.

He lowered himself to a crouch before her and Rio instantly turned her head. She'd started shaking again, he noted, and he could tell from her tense profile that she was biting her lower lip hard enough to draw blood.

"Think you could eat something hot if I brought it up to you?"

If Kane's harsh tone upset the frail control she had over her emotions, his gentle drawl blew it to smithereens. The breath she'd been slowly exhaling suddenly jerked back in on a sob. She sprang to her feet and tried to step past him. Kane stood and blocked her way.

"Damn it, Kane—why are you—mean—then nice?" Rio got out around the series of sobs, then covered her face with both hands, mortified that she was crying in front of him.

"Because I worried about you," he growled.

His answer was so unexpected that Rio lowered her hands to look at him, her tear-filled eyes wide. As if he'd been waiting for her complete attention, he went on brutally.

"But I don't want to worry about you, do you understand?" He leaned aggressively toward her and she drew back, dismayed that his wonderful confession had been dashed. He caught her wrists to halt her retreat. "I don't want to worry about you. I don't want to think about you—I don't want to feel the things I feel when I look at you."

Rio stared at the fierceness on his handsome face, cut to her soul by his angry words. She looked away from him and gave a small, stiff nod, her heart so heavy with the added grief Kane's words caused her that she was amazed she didn't die.

Her whispered, "All right, Kane, I get the message," was barely audible.

Kane gave her a small shake that brought her dispirited gaze back to his. "No, you don't, Rio. You don't get it at all."

He let go of her then, but slowly. The turmoil in his eyes riveted her. Either she was too exhausted to break contact, or she was mesmerized by his intensity. His hand came up briefly to her cheek, the tender caress part consolation, part apology.

It was Kane who ended those tense moments for them both. He turned abruptly from her and stormed toward the door, leaving her room just as suddenly and forcefully as he'd entered it.

Rio's appearance at breakfast the next morning was a necessity. Kane had brought a tray of food to her room last night while she was in the tub, but she'd only picked at it. She wasn't certain she could eat much now, but because she'd gone most of the past two days without food, she knew she had to try. Kane was already at the table. He glanced up when she entered the dining room. Rio sat down, quietly thanked him for the tray he'd brought up, but neither of them said anything more to disrupt the pall of silence in the big room.

Ardis maintained the silence as she served breakfast, but to Rio's surprise, the cook gave her shoulder a gentle pat as she set her plate in front of her. The small gesture had been unexpected and, as Rio was finding, kindness made it more difficult for her to keep her emotions in check.

"Did you sleep?" Kane's brusque question disturbed the tense silence.

Rio shook her head, then decided to bring up the subject she'd been mulling over. She couldn't look at him. "I know I haven't been around to do my share the past two days. But since I'll be leaving after the funeral, I thought I might as well use the day to get my things packed. You can dock my pay accordingly." She slid her fork under a fluffy corner of her scrambled eggs and lifted them off her plate.

"Are you quitting?"

Somehow his question made her feel in the wrong, as if she were running out on him, and she resented that. "I suppose you'd rather fire me," she guessed wearily. "Be my guest."

The silence that followed was ominous. She got the forkful of eggs to her mouth, but had to force herself to eat them. Though they tasted wonderful she had a terrible time getting them down. When Kane tossed down his napkin and shoved his chair back, the violence of the action startled her. Rio kept herself from looking his way as he left the room, and sat frozen until she heard the back door slam.

She lowered her fork to her plate, no longer interested in food at all. She laid her napkin aside and rose to begin the sad task of collecting her things and preparing to leave.

Rio worked most of the morning moving the belongings she'd stored in the attic down to her room. About midmorning she went out to the attic space over the huge garage to search for the boxes of her mother's things that she and Sam had stored there.

There weren't many boxes. Lenore Cory had never been rich, never had many belongings. She'd owned only a few pieces of jewelry, none of it expensive. There was a shoe box of photographs, a baby book and a scrapbook of pictures. She found a box of legal and personal papers. There was even an old cookbook crammed with extra recipes her mother had clipped from magazines or written on recipe cards and bits of paper. Rio almost overlooked a box that held the small sewing chest and the hand-stitched quilt top she remembered her mother piecing together. There was also a box of her mother's dresses, one that held a very feminine Western hat and another with two handbags and a pair of black low-heeled pumps.

Something about those few boxes—that contained what remained of her mother's meager possessions—increased the weight of grief she felt. She carried them down from the top of the garage, then moved them into the house and got them up to her room.

By the time she'd gathered everything from both attics, it was time for lunch. She went downstairs, though she dreaded having to deal with anyone. The activity of the morning had given her another focus besides grief, but the full weight of it came back by the time she made it down to the dining room.

Rio hesitated in the doorway when she saw Ramona sitting opposite the head of the big table. Tracy sat midway down the table, and Kane was nowhere to be seen. Though Kane was more antagonist than ally, it surprised Rio to discover how much more at ease she might have felt had he been there.

Ramona glanced toward where Rio stood and gave her a spiteful smile. Tracy looked her way, too, but the indifference on her pretty face before she found a sudden interest in the fresh floral centerpiece on the big table made Rio feel like a nonentity. As usual, Ramona started in.

"You might as well come sit down, Rio," she invited, and made a weary sound as if she were resigned to some awful task. "Ardis and Estelle warned us you'd be in for lunch. They also said you were packing to leave, though I hardly dared hope until I saw you lugging in those boxes from the garage."

There was no reason for Rio to subject herself to a meal with Ramona. Her appetite was poor enough as it was. She shook her head. "Just looking for Kane." With that lie uttered smoothly enough, Rio retreated from the room, then took a circuitous route through the large house to the kitchen where Ardis was putting the finishing touches on the meal she was about to serve. Estelle was taking salads from the refrigerator.

"Do you mind if I eat out on the patio?" Rio asked Ardis.

Her quiet words got both women's attention at

once. It was Estelle who said, "Ain't good for you to keep to yourself so much." Rio glanced away from the faint reproach on the housekeeper's face. The brusque remark landed hard on her tender feelings. Ardis was looking at her as if she was waiting for her to change her mind.

Rio had rarely asked anything of the two women. When she'd first come to the big house, she'd been afraid of the dour sisters. She'd learned quickly that if she took care of her own room, did her own laundry and always carefully cleaned up after herself, the two women tolerated her presence well enough. Friendship was something neither one of them had hinted at, and Rio had never been presumptuous enough to make any overtures. As a result, she didn't know Estelle well enough to decipher the personal comment she'd just made about her behavior. Instead, she backed toward the door to the hall. "On second thought, I need to get into town to pick up a few things. I might as well get something there."

Rio turned and left the room too quickly for either woman to comment further. She dashed upstairs for her car keys and her purse, then hurried back down, exiting the front of the house to avoid everyone else.

CHAPTER FIVE

BY SUPPER that evening, Rio had returned from town and finished sorting the stack of boxes she'd stashed in her walk-in closet. She'd been down to the stable to locate any odds and ends of tack, then packed it in the large trunk in one of the tack rooms that held the rest of her gear. Because of the trunk's size and weight, she needed to leave it and her saddles in the stable until after she went to pick up the small U-Haul trailer she'd reserved for the next day.

The shock of losing Sam and having to leave the only home she'd ever known jarred her emotions every time she slowed in her efforts to gather her things and get them in order. The hour of inactivity she endured before the evening meal left her feeling edgy and emotional by the time she'd showered and changed and gone downstairs.

Ramona and Tracy were in the living room, so Rio waited in the hall. Kane arrived just after she did. His dark hair was still damp as if he, too, had just showered. In his Levi's and white shirt with its sleeves folded back, he looked even more darkly tanned and fit than normal. Despite her grief, Rio had a hard time keeping her eyes off him.

Fortunately, Ardis called them to the dining room before the moment became too awkward. Rio led the way, then silently took her usual chair down from

71

the head of the table. Ramona sat at the other end, but instead of taking his father's place at the head of the table, Kane sat across from Rio as he normally did. Tracy—who usually sat next to Rio—now sat down next to Kane.

It was a departure from the norm, but Rio was careful not to let anyone see that she'd noticed. She was very aware of the sharp tension in the room, which only seemed to emphasize the fact that Sam's place at the table was empty.

After Ardis served, Ramona barely gave anyone a chance to taste their food before she began a fresh campaign against Rio.

"Will we *all* be riding in your car to the visitation tonight, Kane?"

Ramona gave the word "all" just enough emphasis to let everyone know that she not was not only talking about Rio, but hinting that the idea of Rio riding in the same car with the family was unacceptable.

Kane hesitated as he cut into his steak. His dark blue eyes came up and connected with Rio's for a heartbeat of time before he looked over at Ramona. "You and Tracy might as well take your car, Ramona. Andy washed and serviced it the day before you got back. Besides, Rio and I have other business to take care of."

Ramona's mouth rounded in a little *O* of surprise before she recovered. "What kind of business could the two of you possibly have at that time of night?" she scoffed gently. "Honestly, Kane, now that Sam's gone and she's leaving, why would you feel the need to include her in any kind of business, particularly on the night before your father's funeral?''

If Ramona didn't recognize the warning signs, Rio certainly did. Kane had paused after he got the piece of steak cut. His handsome features turned hard, and a dull flush crept along his cheekbones. His eyes were flat with disapproval when he looked toward Ramona.

"Since you've never been privy to the business end of Langtry, Ramona, I'd appreciate it if you wouldn't try to tell me when or with whom I can do business.''

Ramona looked stricken, her beautiful eyes going misty. "Why of course, Kane, dear," she fluttered. "I wasn't trying to tell you what to do, exactly. No—I was merely reminding you that as far as I could see, there's no reason to burden yourself with Rio any longer.''

Kane went utterly still at that, and his blue gaze began to glitter. He didn't say another word, but then, he didn't have to. Ramona grew genuinely fretful under that harsh gaze, then finally bent her head and turned her whole attention to her meal.

Even though Kane had deflected Ramona's attack, Rio's frail confidence had taken a blow. No doubt there were many other people who'd be at the visitation tonight and the funeral tomorrow who would think those same things.

The reminder added nervousness to the grief she already felt, and all but demolished her weak appetite. She forced herself to eat a few bites of steak, then made a try at the chocolate parfait Ardis brought in before she gave up. It was a huge relief to excuse herself from the table and retreat to her room.

The visitation at the funeral chapel in town was just as nerve-racking as Rio feared, but the worst part was bearing up under the ordeal of seeing Sam in his casket. The crushing grief she'd worked so hard to escape that day overwhelmed her, leaving her raw emotions more battered than ever.

Ramona added her touch to the cheerless evening, doing everything she could to ensure that she and Tracy were all but attached to Kane's arms. It looked to Rio as if Kane and Ramona had smoothed over their differences. Certainly no outsider could have detected anything but closeness between the three, because Rio could not.

She stood carefully to the side, a bit away from the threesome so she wouldn't look presumptuous. She lost count of the number of people who eventually got around to her and asked what her plans were now that Sam had passed on.

She did her best to evade the question when she could, until her raw emotions and bad nerves became too much. She was about to slip away when the soft chime of the clock in the foyer of the funeral chapel marked the hour.

It wasn't long after that before the suffocating crowd began to ebb away, taking much of Rio's tension with it. To her vast relief, Ramona and Tracy walked out with the last cluster of people, until only she and Kane remained.

By the time they reached Kane's car, the sun had set and most of the traffic had thinned. Kane opened her door for her, then closed it solidly beside her once she was inside.

The black dress she'd chosen for tonight was less formal than the one she planned to wear for the funeral. Less formal and with a shorter hem, she was reminded as she again tried to adjust the slim skirt so it didn't reveal so much of her legs. She'd just got settled when Kane got behind the wheel and shoved his key into the ignition. The expensive car purred to life, but he didn't immediately put it into gear.

He was wearing one of his best suits, the fine cut and black color emphasizing his size and his very masculine physique. By comparison, with her hair up, the black dress on and the slinky feel of silk stockings and satiny underthings, Rio felt supremely feminine.

Guilt assailed her for the thoughts that had nothing to do with grief. She felt her face pale and turned her head to stare miserably out her window. She jumped when Kane touched her wrist.

"Are you all right?" Kane's voice was a low, warm drawl, and Rio swore she could feel it gust gently across her skin. His strong, calloused fingers slid down her wrist to her hand. Rio turned her head and looked at him before her gaze fled the calm watchfulness in his.

His hand wrapped around hers and the firm flex of his fingers pressed her palm against the hardness of his. Rio cautiously forced her gaze back to his, as fearful as she was amazed that he was touching her like this. The bleakness in his blue eyes matched hers, and she realized that the small gesture was an acknowledgment, however fleeting, of their common grief.

"Are you all right?" she returned quietly. "I don't think I told you that I'm sorry your father—"

She'd been doing so well that her sudden inability to finish what she'd meant to say surprised her. Kane's grip tightened briefly.

"I know."

With that, Kane slowly let go of her hand and faced forward a few moments. She was watching when his expression hardened, when the grimness came back over him. He reached down to put the car into gear, then slowly pulled away from the curb.

The other business that he'd mentioned to Ramona didn't materialize. The long ride home through the dark, star-studded night was slow and silent.

Rio slept poorly that night. She awoke feeling heavy-hearted. The 5:00 a.m. breakfast she was accustomed to had been delayed until seven, so Ramona and Tracy could join them and Ardis would be spared having to prepare two meals. She was so restless by the time she dressed in slacks and a blouse to go downstairs that her insides were in knots.

The moment she got to the hall outside the dining room, she heard Ramona's voice. "All right, Kane, perhaps I *should* explain why I despise Rio Cory."

Rio came to an abrupt halt in the hall. Indecision

made her take a half step back before Ramona's next words froze her.

"I don't think her relationship with your father was healthy at all. Not that Sam, rest his dear soul, ever did anything dishonorable," she hastily added. "But God knows how it's looked to everyone else with her hanging around all these years, fawning over him. I'm ashamed to say that several people have made remarks to me about her."

Kane said something to Ramona then, but his voice was so low that Rio couldn't make out the words.

A second later Ramona blurted, "Dear Lord, that girl came between Sam and I from the beginning! She made me feel as if I didn't belong here, as if I was too citified and frivolous to bother with. And she was so unkind to poor little Tracy—oh, not in front of the two of you, she was too clever for that— but in secret. Tracy came crying to me many times, heartbroken and mystified by Rio's jealousy and spitefulness. If Sam hadn't felt so sorry for her, the four of us might have had a happy little family...Sam and I might have had a different marriage."

Ramona's voice broke tragically on the word before she paused, then continued in a voice sharp with dislike. "But it's too late now, too late because of *her*. And if losing my dear sweet Sam isn't bad enough, then it's the worry that she's still so obsessed with him that she'll cause a huge scene at the funeral. My God, we'll be lucky if she doesn't throw herself on the casket and beg to be buried with him!

Oh, Kane, what can we do? That girl has robbed us all of so much!''

The tide of nausea and outrage that swept Rio made her step back, staggered by the monstrousness of what she'd just heard. She was shaking so badly that as she turned to retreat to her room, her knees almost gave way.

The added shock of suddenly coming face-to-face with Tracy, who must have been standing just behind her, almost accomplished what her mother's cruel words had started. Tiny dark spots swirled before her eyes and she felt her body start to go limp for a terrifying second before she somehow rallied and stayed upright.

Tracy stared at her a moment, then looked away. The aloof set of her delicate profile gave Rio the impression that she'd heard the outlandish things her mother had said. That she didn't intend to get in-volved—even if it meant condoning a pack of lies—was clear by her tight-lipped silence.

Tracy's complete lack of friendliness toward her had been perplexing, but there was no way now to avoid the notion that Tracy had turned against her. Since she and Tracy had gotten along well in the past, she couldn't begin to guess the reason.

Rio stepped around her and retreated to her room in a haze of fresh shock.

For someone who shrank from emotional displays, Rio's worry that the rising tide of grief she felt would overwhelm her self-control added a new tor-ment to the painful business of the day. Of the cruel things Ramona had said that morning, the one that haunted Rio was the remark about throwing herself on the casket.

With the funeral a mere hour away, the volatile mixture of heartbreak and nerves combined with the terror of being completely alone in the world. The knowledge that there was a tiny, sad part of her that almost wished she could be buried with Sam only magnified the horrid possibilities that Ramona's cruel words had conjured up.

Though she would never do anything as dramatic as throw herself on Sam's casket, the notion that she might be capable of making a scene that would shame her—or worse, shame Sam—upset her deeply. Later, when she tried to brush her hair and pin the hip-length tresses into a conservative knot, she was shaking. Again and again, the thick length escaped confinement before she could get it pinned into place.

By the time a knock came at the door, her hair still wasn't tamed and she hadn't even tried to put on her dress. Holding on to the thick swath of dark hair, she hurried to the door, certain it was Ardis or Estelle reminding her of the time.

She pulled the door open, saw it was Kane, then shoved the door closed until it was only open a crack. Her cheeks burned at the knowledge that Kane had seen her in little more than her black slip and stockings.

"Are you about ready?" The gruff words sounded impatient.

Rio glanced over her shoulder, spied the black

dress on the bed, then was suddenly, maddeningly overcome with emotion. The knowledge that she was too upset to get ready in a timely manner undermined her confidence in being able to handle herself at the funeral. Oh, God, she couldn't go disheveled, and she couldn't go if she was going to burst into tears and weep through the service.

She'd lived her whole life under the scrutiny of a community that had more bad expectations of her than good. Because she didn't want to bring scorn on Sam's faith in her, there was no way she could appear before these people and be anything short of perfectly groomed, perfectly behaved. And if she couldn't...

"Go on ahead, Kane," she called softly. "I'll be along later."

His low, "What?" was terse.

"I can drive myself," she offered in a more confident voice, then gasped and jumped back when her door swung sharply inward.

"We go together," he growled.

"But I'm not ready—my hair," she said, feeling again the precariousness of her control.

The sudden realization that Kane's blue gaze was sliding slowly over the curves accentuated by her black slip made her breath catch. Flustered, she let her hair swing loose and she turned from him. The door closed behind her with a quiet click. She glanced back, relieved until she saw that Kane hadn't gone.

"Just run a brush through it," he told her, then nodded toward the dress on the bed. "That what you're wearing?'' He walked over and picked up the dress in one large hand, then turned back to her and held it out.

The sheer forcefulness of the gesture underscored his determination to rush her. It was also a signal to her that the perfect appearance, perfect behavior she was worried sick over meant nothing to him. As she meant nothing to him.

She turned from him suddenly, then hurried to the mirror over her vanity table. A few quick strokes of the brush and her hair was again tidy enough to put up. She managed to gather it and twist it over and over until she'd wound it into a thick knot.

With fingers that had somehow lost their dexterity, she tried to shove enough hairpins into place to hold the knot just so. Seconds after she'd finished, it all began to unravel.

''Go on without me,'' she snapped, so frustrated that she began tearing at the hairpins.

Kane's abrupt move—which sent her dress sailing back onto the bed—drew her attention to his reflection in the vanity mirror. He stalked toward her, then to her complete surprise, he reached past her and grabbed up the brush.

The moment he gathered her hair in his big hand, she felt prickles of sensation strike her scalp like tiny lightning bolts. She tensed, expecting him to yank the brush through the dark tresses as mercilessly as she had earlier, but the brush strokes that began near the ends of her hair were brisk, gentle. As he worked his way up the length to the top of her head, he efficiently banished the tangles, until he was merely brushing her hair, running the brush from the crown of her head to the blunt-cut ends.

Rio stood, nearly paralyzed by surge after surge of pleasure as Kane wielded the brush. Her eyes were riveted to his reflection in the mirror, fascinated by the absorption on his harsh, handsome face.

Everything slowed in those quiet moments. The whisper of the brush marked the time that passed. At last his gaze lifted and met hers in the mirror. The brush made one last pass that was slower than the rest before it reached the end of its path and fell away.

"What's wrong with wearing it loose?" he asked, his voice a quiet rasp.

His question dispelled the peculiar lethargy that had gripped her. The answer brought a swift sting of tears. "Because I need to look conservative," she managed to tell him.

Kane's lips quirked with disbelief. "Conservative? What the hell for?"

She could barely get out the words. "For Sam." Honesty made her add, "And because someone might disapprove."

"Of what? Wearing your hair down?" He looked incredulous.

"You wouldn't understand," she said quietly as she broke eye contact with his reflection. She turned toward him to take her brush.

"Try me." The terse words were a demand. When he didn't release the brush, she glanced up at him momentarily, then away.

"Please, Kane," she whispered, but her small tug

on the brush only made him tighten his grip. She took in an uneven breath. "You know how people feel about me."

"How's that?"

Rio felt such a surge of hurt that she almost couldn't get the words out. "Don't pretend you don't know." She made herself look at him as she said, "No one's more critical of me than you—unless it's Ramona."

Kane's expression went stiff. Rio tried again to take her brush, but Kane glanced past her, saw her handbag on the vanity top and reached for it. Just that quickly, he'd shoved the brush into the purse, hesitated, then pinched a wad of tissues from the nearby dispenser and crammed them in, too. His, "Get the dress on," was low and angry as he fumbled with the zipper and flap on the purse.

Rio stared at his harsh profile as a fresh tide of sadness rose in her heart. Wordlessly, she walked to the bed, picked up the dress, then tugged it over her head and smoothed it down.

Remorse stole over her. Kane's father had died, and she was more worried over how she wore her hair than being ready for the funeral on time. She got out a quiet, "I'm sorry, Kane. I don't mean to cause problems," as she pulled her hair forward, then reached behind her back and tried to slide the zipper up.

To her surprise, Kane's fingers brushed hers aside. He slid the zipper up in no time, and Rio pushed her hair back over her shoulder to let it stream down her back.

The next thing she knew, Kane stepped so close to her that she felt the heat that radiated from his tall, strong body. Her breath stopped as his hands slid around her waist to pull her back against him. Her soft sound of surprise and her self-conscious move to step away made him tighten his arms and lower his head to press his jaw against her cheek.

The heat that scorched through their clothes enveloped her in weakness. She could feel every detail of his unyielding maleness, and something deep and primitive and female in her stirred.

She rested her hands hesitantly on the thick-muscled forearms that were cinched around her. Kane rubbed his jaw against her soft skin, and drew her even closer to him.

Oh, God, it was heaven to stand there like that! Heaven to feel his arms around her, his body against hers, heaven to feel the physical comfort he was lavishing on her, whether he knew it or not. Whether he meant to or not.

The sharp edge of feminine arousal that followed shocked her. She couldn't help that she'd raised her hand to gently place her palm along his strong jaw. The freshly shaved skin was softer than she'd expected and she couldn't resist exploring the smooth texture with her fingertips.

Suddenly she felt ashamed of herself, ashamed to be standing there with Kane, practically trembling with longing and desire. They were burying Sam today. She had no business feeling anything but grief. Misery came roaring back, worse than ever.

She slid her hand from Kane's jaw, then turned

abruptly, stepping neatly out of his arms before she stopped, her face turned slightly away from him. She reached for the handbag Kane had tossed to the bed, rummaged nervously for the brush, then ran it briskly through her hair to smooth it a last time.

When she finished, the room was utterly still. She didn't need to see or hear him to know that Kane was there, silently watching her, because she felt his long, unhurried scrutiny as if he were running his hands over her.

"You're beautiful." The rasped words were an accusation, but his next ones softened it. "Anyone who can criticize the way you look, especially right now, can go straight to hell."

His gruff fervency brought such a sharp sting of tears that a couple spurted down her cheek before she could control them. She dashed them away with her hand, striving to make the gesture look as natural as possible. She couldn't look at him and her soft, "Thanks," was choked. She put the brush away and closed her purse. "I'm ready."

The small declaration was a lie. She wasn't ready for this final goodbye to Sam, but admitted to herself that she might never be. As she started toward the door, her legs seemed to grow more heavy with each step.

She and Kane left her room and went downstairs without speaking. At a quick word from Kane, Rio waited in the front hall near the door while he stepped into the living room to let Ramona and Tracy know they were ready to leave.

She heard Ramona say something then abruptly

cut herself off. Rio pretended not to notice that the older woman was flushed with temper when they all joined her. Kane opened the door, ushering Tracy and Ramona through it before he held his hand out to Rio.

Assuming he was hurrying her along, Rio stepped past him and followed the other two women. Kane caught her arm, then tugged her to a halt while he closed the door behind them. His hand was wrapped around hers as they walked to the waiting limousine. No one was more surprised than Rio when Kane sat next to her, his strong arm on the seat behind her shoulders in a gesture as possessive as it was protective.

CHAPTER SIX

THE funeral took place in the country church Sam had faithfully attended since childhood. The graveside service was held at the Painted Fence just before noon.

Rio was grateful for Kane's constant presence at her side. At first, she'd felt wooden with him, unaccustomed to being touched by him—by anyone—in public. The fact that every eye strayed their way often enough to catch Kane touch her arm or take her hand only compounded her unease. But once the funeral started, the battle to keep her emotions under severe control made her forget everything but getting through the somber service.

The eulogy made her cry, ruining her intention to remain dry-eyed. The service came to a close at last, with the mourners filing quietly out while family remained seated.

When it was time for the four of them to go out to the limousine that would follow the hearse to Langtry and the gravesite, Kane again took her arm, allowing Ramona and Tracy to precede them.

None of them spoke during the ride to the ranch. Ramona sat as still and perfect as cool porcelain, while Tracy tried to powder the redness from around her eyes. Kane sat between Rio and the door, his arm again resting over the back of the seat behind her.

When they turned off the highway onto the ranch road, then finally onto the much rougher twin tracks that led to the private graveyard, Rio's heart grew heavier than ever. The royal blue awning pitched over the open grave was colorful enough to hurt the eyes in the bright sun. Rio couldn't look as the hearse came to a halt and the pallbearers removed the casket to carry it to the grave.

Kane handed Rio out of the car. He hung back to assist Tracy, then Ramona who had spurned the funeral director's effort to help her out the other side. Ramona latched onto Kane's arm, discreetly snapped her fingers in a silent order for Tracy to take his other arm, then stepped forward regally, sweeping them past Rio and leaving her to follow alone. Clearly, Kane had become the prize in the war Ramona seemed intent upon waging.

The huge chain of cars and pickups that had followed in the funeral procession across Langtry range were pulling up. The long line of vehicles broke gradually, parking in shorter rows around the fenced cemetery so no one would have to walk far. Rio followed the other three, surprised when, before Kane had taken another half dozen steps, he had tactfully disengaged himself from both Ramona and Tracy.

Rio could see Ramona fairly vibrate with outrage as Kane gently pressed her and Tracy forward while he hung back. Tracy meekly touched her mother's arm only to find her shy touch thrown off as Ramona marched on indignantly. Kane turned toward Rio and waited until she caught up to him.

Rio couldn't meet Kane's eyes as she joined him

and they walked together toward the cemetery. She couldn't let him see that for one bright exhilarating moment on that dark, sad day, that her foolish heart was thrilled by his attention, and almost giddy with speculation about what it all meant.

Those few seconds of brightness dulled as they walked through the open gate toward the blue awning. Ramona and Tracy had already been seated across from the casket. Funeral attendants were still racing back and forth bringing more flowers, though most of them were already being sent to nursing homes and hospitals in the area. The minister was taking his place next to the casket, leafing through his prayer book.

The Langtry ranch hands had shown up, most in their best finery. Boz was one who stood just outside the whitewashed fence near the head of the casket and Rio walked over to grip the old cowboy's hand. The men next to Boz nodded to her in deference or took her hand for a brief handshake. Kane had followed Rio and was himself shaking hands and receiving quiet words of condolence.

When they finished, Kane escorted her back to the row of chairs across from the casket. He seated her next to Tracy, then ignored the chair set out for him as he stood behind the two of them.

The graveside service was brief. The procession of mourners who filed past them to shake hands or express condolences seemed endless in the noontime heat. In the end, it was the heat that prompted Kane to interrupt the procession early and suggest that they all head to the house where it was cool and lunch would be served.

It was a relief to be able to retreat to the limousine that had been left idling with the air conditioner running. The moment the door was closed behind them and the tinted glass obscured the inside of the limo, Ramona's lovely face turned petulant. Not a hint of tears marred her perfectly made-up features, though Rio noted the woman had a lace hankie at the ready.

With a selfish lack of concern for Kane's grief, Ramona turned toward him, a militant expression on her face. "Why on earth is Sam being buried next to that—that Cory woman?"

After all these years, the shock of hearing anyone refer to her late mother as "that Cory woman" jarred her. A brief flash of memory—the tall dark-haired woman with the musical voice and the gentle touch— burst through her grief for Sam, compounding it somehow and bringing a fresh rush of tears.

The second shock Rio suffered was when she realized that Sam was indeed about to be buried next to her mother. She glanced toward the cemetery in a fog of disbelief as she belatedly acknowledged that she'd been so intent on the service that she'd failed to notice how close Sam's grave was to her mother's. Their graves couldn't have been much closer, particularly in that part of the cemetery where the only graves would be theirs.

"My God, Kane," Ramona was saying, her voice trembling, "you've got to tell them to dig a new grave—away from *there!*"

"My father's instructions were precise." Kane's harsh tone was final.

Rio glanced toward Kane, unable to conceal her surprise. Sam had instructed Kane to bury him that close to her mother? The fact that Sam had wanted it done and that Kane had done it—in the face of his dislike for the Cory's and the speculation and gossip such a thing was sure to cause—astonished her.

"I don't understand..." The words were barely out of her mouth before Kane's eyes shifted and bore down sharply into hers. The impact of his glittering blue gaze silenced her and Rio faced forward, her mind spinning as she searched her memories of her mother—and her memories of Sam—for something that would explain Sam's stunning order.

Rio had known Sam to at times become strangely gruff when they'd talked about Lenore Cory. She'd always suspected he'd had some special feelings for her mother, but to leave instructions that he be buried next to her indicated something much more significant than casual admiration.

The whole idea made her feel strange, as if there was some enormous secret that she'd been too dull-witted to sense. As the limo pulled forward slowly and rolled into a wide turn that would take it back down the twin tracks, Rio glanced toward the blue awning. Again she saw the close proximity of the two graves and felt another little start of surprise.

Fortunately, Ramona said no more, though the silence from her end of the long seat was turbulent. The tension between the four of them was so pronounced that Rio couldn't wait to arrive back at the ranch house. Once there, Kane got out of the limo and turned to hold the door for her. Rio got out hastily and walked quickly to the ranch house.

There had to be two hundred people in the house and on the patio behind, with more people walking from parked cars. Kane had hired caterers to provide a buffet, and they had set up in the formal dining room. A double line of guests was filing through the dining room, then exiting toward the patio or one of the other rooms on the main floor.

To Rio, it was a nightmare. People were everywhere. The strain of the day was telling on her, making her feel light-headed. She'd lost track of where Kane was, and made her way through the front hall, finding herself waylaid several times by ranching neighbors and business associates of Sam's and Kane's.

Suddenly, Ty Cameron, the rancher who'd sold Kane the bull, stepped into her path. Tall and handsome, his blond hair a bright mix of bronze and wheat and white from the sun, Ty was ruggedly handsome and was what Rio thought of as cowboy gallant.

"Hello, Miz Rio," he said, his deep drawl somber. "I'm real sorry about Sam. I know the two of you were close."

Rio managed a tight smile and nodded her thanks.

"I was about to find myself something cool to drink. Can I get you something?" Ty gently took her arm and tugged her a little more out of the current of passing guests before he released her.

"I—I was thinking of that myself," she managed, a faint hint of color seeping into her cheeks. Ty's eyes were a warm, gold-flecked blue, and the intensity in them as they roamed her face made Rio feel self-conscious. His eyes crinkled at the corners when he smiled down at her.

"If you'll allow me, Miz Rio," he said, his voice charmingly formal, "I'd like to escort you someplace where you can sit down awhile. I can get whatever you want to drink on ice and bring it to you quick."

Rio glanced away momentarily, and felt the color in her cheeks rise higher. "That's very nice of you, Mr. Cameron, but you must be hungry. Why don't we get something in the dining room?"

Ty led the way with his hand solicitously around her elbow, keeping her slightly behind him as he made a path through the crowd. It amazed her how quickly he managed to get them to the buffet table. Though Rio had no appetite, she made a few selections, mindful of her increasing light-headedness and the fact that she hadn't eaten since the day before.

They left the dining room carrying their drinks and plates. Every available seat was taken in the house. They walked to the kitchen, and Rio came to a halt as she glanced through the door to the patio and saw that every seat available in the shade outside was occupied, as well.

She turned to Ty. "It looks like it's no better outside. If you don't mind, we might find a place to sit on the stairs."

"The stairs would be fine," he returned, then let her lead the way to the staircase that opened off the back hall. Rio sat down on the third step from the bottom. Ty sat beside her.

Though she was initially stiff with the handsome rancher, she gradually relaxed. They talked about ranching, but Ty didn't ask her what her plans were now, as nearly everyone else had. It seemed he was the only person in Texas who didn't assume Kane would never let her stay on.

On the other hand, there was something speculative in his gaze, something that suggested he had made the same assumptions as everyone else, but was too much a gentleman to let on.

His solicitous, "I'd be happy to get you something more to eat or another glass of tea, Miz Rio," prompted her to shake her head.

"Thank you, no, but go ahead if you'd like something," she told him.

"I'm full enough for a hot day," he said, then reached over to relieve her of her plate and sit it with his on a step behind them. When he turned back, his eyes made a brisk search of her face.

"My ranch manager is buying a ranch of his own, so I'm looking for someone with experience running a place the size of Cameron." He gave her a half smile that was loaded with masculine appeal. "I thought I'd mention it to you in case you ever got the notion to try a new challenge."

As he spoke, he slipped a hand to the inside pocket of his suit jacket. He withdrew a business card and passed it to her. "If I'm not available at that number, my people will have instructions to notify me immediately of your call, and I'll get back to you right away." He shrugged. "Or, if you'd just like to get away sometime, I'd be honored to take you to dinner and show you what we do for excitement down in San Antone.'' The smile he gave her was warm, and there was no mistaking the personal interest in the gaze that was fixed so intently on her face.

Rio glanced down at the card. The possible offer of a job as good as this made her feel less terrified of the future, but the personal offer made her wary. She hoped her soft, ''Thank you, Mr. Cameron, we'll see,'' as she lifted her gaze to meet his would be taken as a more businesslike response than a personal one.

On the other hand, what would it hurt if things did get personal between them? As she considered what she knew of Ty Cameron's character along with his rugged good looks, she realized he was probably the only man she'd ever met who had the potential to make her fall for him and forget her feelings for Kane.

As if the possibility of caring for someone else and forgetting her feelings for Kane was destined to be thwarted, she heard a sound, then turned her head to see Kane standing next to the staircase. His blue gaze shifted from her face to Ty's before it shot back to hers and narrowed.

''There are people asking after you,'' he said gruffly, managing to make her feel in the wrong.

Ty said smoothly, ''That's my fault, I'm afraid. I've been dominating Miz Rio's time.'' Ty got to his feet, then reached out to shake Kane's hand and offer condolences.

Rio stood to her feet while the two men talked briefly, stepping out of the way when a waiter came scurrying down the hall to collect their empty plates and glasses. Kane seemed to relax a bit as he returned the handshake, but by the time Ty had taken his leave of them both, his expression was again stony with disapproval.

"Is there a reason the two of you were hiding out back here?"

Kane's terse question took her aback. She answered before she thought about it. "There was no other place to sit."

"Some rental place called," he went on irritably, as if her answer was too trivial to acknowledge. No doubt he was annoyed at being bothered by the call. "They wanted to let you know the trailer you reserved is ready. I told them to hold it another day."

Rio shook her head slightly. "I need it today."

"Not with a crowd around to watch the little melodrama of Rio Cory packing her things and driving off into the great unknown," he said grimly.

The words stung. It was as if those few moments of closeness they'd experienced that day hadn't happened. Rio turned from him and walked briskly toward the front of the huge home. The grief that had seemed to ease the past half hour settled back into place, bringing with it a fresh sense of loneliness.

Rio made her way through the crowd, stopping to speak briefly here and there, doing her best to be as visible as possible for as long as she could stand before she slipped away to the quiet of her room.

She never had an opportunity to leave the ranch that day after all. Guests came and went at the main house until after seven that evening. Two of Kane's cousins from his mother's side of the family stayed the night, not leaving the ranch until late afternoon the next day.

Too restless to wait around at the house, Rio put in a full day's work so Kane could visit with his cousins. By the time she got to the house that evening, she felt uncommonly tired, and didn't care if she ate supper or not. The fact that Ramona would be at the table was added incentive to forgo the meal.

Rio stopped in the kitchen only long enough to grab a small jar of fruit juice from the refrigerator and tell Ardis not to set a place for her. She went upstairs to her room, her feet so leaden with fatigue that she almost wished she'd taken Sam's elevator.

The emptiness she'd run from that whole day was suddenly so much worse in the silence of the big house. Ardis had given her usual taciturn greeting of ''Evenin','' but Sam wasn't somewhere nearby calling out to her or asking about her day

Rio stepped into her room and closed the door, then walked across the floor to her private bath. It seemed to take forever to get her clothes off, unbraid her hair and step beneath the hot spray of the shower.

When she stepped out later, wound her hair in a huge towel and dried off, she felt more exhausted than ever. Finishing the fruit juice refreshed her a bit, but by the time she'd wrapped up in a robe, brushed her teeth and dried her hair, she was worn out.

She walked into her bedroom, and was about to turn down the comforter and top sheet when she was startled by a knock at the door. She cinched the belt of her robe tighter and was halfway to the door when

the knock came again, louder. Kane called out an irritable, "Where the hell are you, Rio?"

Rio opened the door a few inches and looked out
at Kane's dark expression. "Where do you think?"
she answered in a false show of spirit, secretly hurt
by his impatience.

"We're waiting supper for you," he said gruffly.

"I told Ardis—"

"I know what you told Ardis," he cut in. "Get
dressed and come down anyway."

A flash of temper banished some of Rio's fatigue.
"My workday's over," she told him. "Permanently.
Find someone else to boss around." She gave the
door a smart shove to close it in his arrogant face
when his hand flew up to stop it.

The look in his eyes was dangerously grim. He
walked forward slowly, his hand on the edge of the
door to push it wide. Rio stepped back.

"I'm asking you to get dressed and come down to
supper," he said in a low, rough voice.

Rio's chin came up. "And I'm telling you that I'm
going to bed now. I could care less about eating."

"Are you sick?"

She must have been imagining the hint of concern
in his eyes. She shook her head. "Just tired. I'm not
up to you and Ramona tonight." She gave him a humorless quirk of lips. "No offense."

Kane's stiff smile was just as humorless. He
stepped farther into the room and closed the door.
"What are your plans for tomorrow?"

"To leave Langtry," she answered simply, drawing herself up a bit straighter as she said it. Not for

anything did she want Kane to see how much it hurt to have to leave her home. If things had been different between them, she might have moved out of the main house into the quarters at the end of the bunk house. She loved the ranch, loved the outdoor work, and would have been content to stay on indefinitely as a ranch hand. Because of Kane, she couldn't.

"The lawyer's coming out tomorrow morning. He'll be reading the will," he said. It was clear by his low, rough voice that he wasn't happy to have to tell her anything about it. His brusque, "I understand from him that you need to be present," explained why.

Rio shook her head. "The will doesn't concern me. The only thing I'm interested in is the letter Sam mentioned that day." She'd been unable to forget Sam's weak, *Letters say for me,* as he lay dying. If he really had left a letter for her, it would be like one last talk, a keepsake she could see and touch and take with her.

"The lawyer mentioned he had them. He'll pass them out after the will is read."

Rio turned away, wearily shaking her head. "I'm only interested in Sam's letter." She brushed a wide swath of hair behind her shoulder and walked to her bed to tug the comforter and sheet down. She lifted her hands to the belt on her robe and paused. "Could you please close the door on your way out?"

She stood there for several long moments. There was no sound from Kane, not even a whisper of movement. Finally, she glanced back, saw Kane's dark expression, then felt herself wilt a little more.

"Please take your angry looks someplace else, Kane," she said softly as she faced forward.

The sound of Kane walking up behind her made her stiffen. The big hands that settled over her shoulders were warm and sure, and Rio tried to move away from him. Kane thwarted her with the tight flex of his strong fingers.

"Just stand still," he whispered gruffly. His right hand lifted from her shoulder. "You've got something in your hair. Looks like a pillow feather." She felt him comb his fingers down the length of her hair, sending a shower of bright sensations across her skin from her scalp to her toes. Her legs began to weaken as heat flooded her. Kane lifted his hand to run his fingers down her hair a second time and she twisted abruptly from him.

The grip he had on her other shoulder when she wrenched away pulled her robe open. Kane caught her wrist with an ease that mocked her quick move, and his blue gaze dropped to the shoulder and breast that had been uncovered. Rio grabbed for the edge of her robe to cover herself, but he seized her other wrist.

His eyes fixed on her bare breast and darkened. Her gasp drew his attention to her mouth for a fraction of a second before his gaze fell again to her exposed flesh.

Rio realized dazedly that he was drawing her closer, and tried to pull away from him. Though years of ranch work had made her strong, she was no match for Kane's superior strength. Their brief struggle managed only to loosen the tie belt until the top of the robe gaped open.

She froze, her cheeks flushing a dark red. In the next instant Kane released her wrists and slid his calloused hands around her bare waist. She grabbed for the edges of her robe to close it, but the hot, determined look in his eyes made her fingers sluggish. She stared up at him, mesmerized as his lips descended to hers.

The next thing she knew, she was lying back on her bed, pressed to the mattress by Kane's big body. His denim-clad leg slid between hers and more of his weight shifted atop her until he was lying fully on her, his clothing gently abrading her tender skin. And all the while he was kissing her, dominating her with the skill of his lips and tongue and hands until she wept with frustration at her body's helpless response.

Suddenly his mouth slid off hers and he dropped his forehead to the mattress beside her head. The low growl that rumbled up from his chest was shockingly feral and sent a light shiver of fear through her.

"Damn it," he growled, then turned his head until his lips were touching the shell of her ear. "What is it about you?" he demanded softly. "If I take you here, right now," he said as his hand found the soft mound of her breast and toyed aggressively with its tip, "then maybe you can get the hell off Langtry and I'll never give you another thought."

The words were unbearably cruel, but the tender expertise of his fingers made her move restlessly beneath him. The terrible confusion of cruelty and sharp pleasure tore at her. A silent sob rose painfully in her chest, but she bit her lip until she tasted blood to stifle it.

"I hate wanting you," he growled. "I hate looking at you and knowing that you're not only the one woman I ache to have, but the last one I want."

The breath she'd been holding gusted out on a wave of pure misery. She turned her face away. Her voice was so hoarse that it was barely audible. "Rio Cory, tomboy trash, daddy caused an awful crash. Killed them two boys, killed himself, now he's gone to drunkard's hell."

The silence that descended was thunderous. Rio's blood was pounding in her ears. She'd never repeated to anyone, not even Sam, the malicious little verse she'd been tortured with those years after her father's death. The mayor's daughter was the first to actually say it in her presence, but it had been rapidly picked up by her classmates. It had seemed to take forever for everyone to forget the awful rhyme.

But nobody forgot, not really. She was still "that Cory girl" no matter what she'd done, no matter what Sam had tried to do for her. Wasn't Kane's insulting declaration proof of that?

Heartache and exhaustion took the last of her strength. She let her hands slide from his wide shoulders. She all but wilted beneath the warm crush of his hard body, her face turned away, tears leaking from her eyes.

"I hate wanting you, too, Kane," she whispered. "I'm ashamed that I've loved someone all these years who holds me in such contempt."

At last Kane's fingers stopped toying with her

breast. She shivered when he pulled the soft terry cloth of her robe over it. He slowly shifted himself off her, then quietly drew the facings of her robe together until they overlapped from neck to hem, covering her nakedness.

Rio was too exhausted and too dispirited to even open her eyes as she waited in the harsh silence for Kane to move off the bed and leave the room. She felt him shift, then felt the warm gust of his breath the second before his lips touched her neck. His hand slid around her waist and pulled her tighter against him, but Rio didn't move.

"Oh, God, Rio, I must be losing my mind," he rasped as he nuzzled her neck, then drew back to smooth a few strands of hair from her temple. "Forgive me for being such a bastard."

Rio didn't answer. She couldn't. The weight of grief and disappointment pressed so heavily on her heart that she almost couldn't breathe. Kane eventually rolled away from her and got up. He must have taken her silence for sleep because he gently moved her until her head was on a pillow. He drew her robe more snugly around her and pulled the sheet and comforter over her. The light switched off and she listened to his booted tread as he walked to the door and left the room.

CHAPTER SEVEN

KANE took somber note of Rio's empty chair at the table that next morning. He knew she was awake—he'd heard her moving around in her room. He knew she'd slept the night through, because he'd checked on her several times during the restless night he'd put in.

Just when he was about to give up on her, he heard her quiet footsteps on the front stairs. Rio was probably the only person he knew who could wear boots and walk quiet. Even her spurs, when she wore them, didn't rattle and chime. She had a way of moving that didn't demand attention, but it was that very grace and elegance that made her stand out.

Rio Cory, tomboy trash… The hateful rhyme made another pass through his mind before he ruthlessly silenced it. So many things about Rio suddenly made sense.

"I was wondering if you were going to come down this early."

Kane's voice had a deep, rusty sound at 5:00 a.m. Rio walked toward her place at the long dining room table and slipped onto her usual chair across from him. She didn't look him in the eye and she didn't speak. There was nothing to say. Besides, he'd merely made a comment.

104

All she had to do was get through the next few hours. The last thing she felt like doing was eating the steak and eggs breakfast Ardis was carrying in. The fact that she hadn't eaten since noon the day before was her only incentive to show up for this meal. She'd chosen to have breakfast when Kane did because she knew he'd allow her to eat in peace. Ramona wouldn't be so charitable.

The silence between them was oppressive. Rio ate mechanically, forcing herself to chew her food. The time or two she'd dared a glance at Kane, her gaze had collided with the laser intensity of his. Eventually the self-consciousness she felt made it impossible to eat. She set her fork down and plucked her napkin from her lap to toss it next to her plate.

"Where are you off to?" he asked as she stood.

Rio stepped aside and pushed her chair up to the table. "I have to finish packing," she said quietly, then turned to start for the door.

"There's no need to rush off."

Kane's deep voice made her hesitate. She looked at him, meeting his gaze full-on before she shook her head. "There's every need, Kane. Especially after last night."

Her soft words intensified the stillness of the big room. The deep blue of his eyes flickered a moment, then dulled, but he didn't look away. Instead, his gaze made a lightning tour from her face to her toes before it sped back up to meet her eyes.

"Suit yourself."

Irrational as it was, that was the moment Rio realized that she still hoped Kane would ask her to stay on. She'd helped run Langtry for years, with the authority to act for him on many occasions. She'd done a competent job, but Kane's bad feelings toward her were evidently too strong for him to even suggest it.

After last night, it was probably just as well. She didn't have the strength to deal with too many incidents like that one. She still longed for him to kiss her again, to touch her that aggressively, but those very longings seemed perverse in the light of how much he disliked her.

Rio turned from him then and hurried upstairs to finish getting her things together.

Rio stood just inside the door of the den, as far out of the way as possible as Ramona and Tracy got settled on the sofa. Kane was standing in front of the massive bookcase that took up an entire wall, leaning back against it with his arms crossed over his wide chest.

The lawyer sat at the desk. In front of him was Sam Langtry's will and four copies laid out in a row along the front edge of the desk. He'd set a white envelope on top of each of the four copies. Though Rio couldn't read the words printed on the envelopes from where she stood, the lawyer had indicated there was an envelope addressed to each of them.

Rio tried not to fidget as the lawyer began reading the document. The solemnity of the occasion—the sheer formality of the legal phrases combined with the enormity of Sam Langtry's fortune—filled her with dread. As she listened to everything Sam had built and owned detailed and disbursed, the growing suspicion that Sam's affection for her might have prompted him to leave her something significant made her feel sick.

The first inheritance that meant anything was Ramona's. The clause the lawyer read reminded them all of the prenuptial agreement Sam and Ramona had signed. The fact that Sam had ruthlessly adhered to its limits was soon apparent. Ramona's gasp sounded abnormally loud in the quiet room, but the lawyer continued to read.

Tracy, however, fared spectacularly compared to her mother. From the sound of it, she'd never have to concern herself with money again.

Kane was next, inheriting the lion's share of everything Sam had owned. Aside from his several businesses and the various ranches Sam held title to in Texas, Langtry was the very last holding mentioned. The fact that Kane was due to inherit only half of Langtry gave the clue to what was coming.

As soon as Rio heard the words, "'I leave to my foster daughter, Rhea René Cory, known to all as Rio Cory...'" a wave of dizziness passed so forcefully over her that she felt faint.

"'...The sum of five million dollars...half interest in Langtry Ranch... Must remain a full and equal partner for a minimum of one year... After which time, she is free to do with her share of Langtry as she pleases, and she is entitled to all proceeds and profits thereof... Should she refuse to accept this inheritance, or refuse to adhere to the minimum time requirement of ownership set forth here, her half interest in Langtry Ranch will pass instead to the Texas chapter of Friends for Equal Rights for Animals.'"

Rio sagged back against the wall, too stunned at the enormous bequest—and its bizarre consequence—to listen to the rest of what the lawyer read. When the lawyer finished, Rio glanced toward Kane, her heart falling at his stony expression. The blue gaze he turned her way glittered with an unholy mixture of anger and bitter humor.

"Friends for Equal Rights for Animals, huh?" Kane looked away from her and addressed the lawyer. "And I suppose that particular clause is ironclad."

It wasn't a question, but the lawyer nodded his head. Ramona was suddenly on her feet, shoving her way up the line of copies on the desk until she found the one with the envelope bearing her name. She snatched up both will and envelope, then marched from the room, her eyes fiery with hatred as they fixed on Rio those last seconds.

Tracy sat on the sofa, a dazed look on her face. The lawyer came around the desk and picked up a copy of the will with the envelope addressed to Tracy and handed it to her. He swiftly scooped up both Kane's and Rio's, stepping across to the door to hand Rio hers before he took Kane's to him.

Rio stared down at the envelope with her name on it in Sam's handwriting. She glanced up, her eyes going directly to Kane. Kane's face was more sober and stern than she'd ever seen it, and she felt her heart break a little. What had Sam done?

Too restless to remain in the room, Rio turned and

quickly left, rushing upstairs to the privacy of the bedroom that would remain hers for the next year.

Rio,

Since I don't know exactly how long I have left, I thought it best to put a few things in a letter to you, just in case I don't have the time or opportunity to say them at the end.

First off, one of the highlights of my life was when you came to live with us at the main house. You've been everything a man could want in a daughter: you're beautiful, smart, and you've got a gentle, loving heart. Your love and devotion to me, particularly these last years as my health was waning, is a source of comfort and great pride to me. As you are a source of comfort and great pride.

I'm sorry as I can be that you're hurting now, and that I'm the cause. It's not possible for me to spare you grief. It is possible for me to do what I can to be certain you always have a home and plenty in the way of material things. That's why I left you what I did. Giving you half of Langtry is the thing I most wanted to do for you at the end. I hope that when the year is up, you will retain your share of the ranch. It gives me great peace and satisfaction to know that you will be living on Langtry and that you will raise your children there.

You and Kane will likely have some troubles in the beginning, but I know the two of you will work things out. You're both smart people of good character and common sense, so, if nothing else, remember how much I loved you both and try a little harder to settle your differences. Somehow, I'll know when you do.

I've left a book for you—*Plant and Animal Species of the World.* It's not what the book is, but what it contains. Your beautiful mother once gave me a bouquet of flowers for my table that she'd grown herself. I pressed them in that book and kept them all these years. You'll find a few other keepsakes in those pages that will remind you of her. Forgive me for keeping them to myself all this time, but there never seemed to be a time when I wanted to part with them. They belong to you now.

Remember that I love you, my precious daughter. God bless you. May you have a good, long, healthy life and find more love and happiness than a body has a right to.

                                            Love,
                                            Sam

The letter made her cry. Rio lay on her bed in the silence of her room, in shock about what Sam had left her, and confused by further evidence of his deep affection for her mother.

She stayed in her room a long time, rereading Sam's letter, searching her memories of Sam and her mother as she tried to make sense of it all. Finally, she put the letter in the lacquered box she'd already packed. Since it was almost time for lunch, she stepped into her bath and splashed her face with cool water.

She hadn't expected to still be here for lunch. Normally, this was a workday, and she would have put in six hours of outside work by this time. Now that she wasn't leaving, it would seem even more a privilege to be able to come to the cool of the big house and eat in the quiet of the dining room.

The idea that for the next year she would be an equal partner with Kane in all this was staggering. The fact that she felt like a thief ensured that she would give back his family heritage on the very day the year was up.

Kane's and Ramona's reactions to the reading of the will made her apprehensive about going down for lunch. Only the reminder that she'd have to face them sometime made her start downstairs.

When Rio walked into the dining room, Kane and Tracy were sitting at the table. Tracy glanced at her, then away, but Kane's gaze followed her all the way to the table. Rio sat down at her usual spot and waited in painful suspense for Ardis to finish bringing in their food.

The silence between the three of them was daunting. At least Ramona didn't put in an appearance. Tracy finished her lunch, then excused herself to drive to town. Since this was the first meal in days that Rio had managed to eat most of, she did her best to clear her plate by the time Kane finished eating.

Kane leaned back in his chair, his hard eyes wandering over her face as he sipped his coffee. Rio brushed her lips with her napkin, unsure how to diffuse the anger she sensed in him.

She set the napkin aside and met his blue gaze directly. "There are some things I'd like to talk about," she said quietly.

Kane's mouth slanted. "Same here. Where do we start?" The hint of sarcasm in his voice put her even more on edge.

"I can't keep the money or the half share of Langtry," she began. "I'll find a lawyer and start whatever legal action is needed to have it all transferred back to you—" Kane was shaking his head before she finished, so she asked, "Why not, then?"

"Because of the damned clause about that animal rights group," he said grimly.

"I know the clause makes it difficult, but I thought if I got a lawyer to draw up a private agreement to return it to you when the year is up, you'd know that I don't intend to keep it."

Kane's frown deepened. "Why would you do that?"

"Langtry is rightfully yours. The money shouldn't have gone to me, either. I know Sam meant well—"

Kane cut her off with a terse, "Scared of me?"

"Why would I be?" she asked, careful to hide her surprise at his perception.

"Because you're afraid it's going to be a year-long bronc-busting session between us if you don't." As if disgusted, he tossed his napkin to the table and stood up.

Rio got to her feet, too. "Will it be?"

Kane glared over at her, taking in the worry that ran so deep she couldn't quite conceal it from him. But then, he doubted she'd ever been able to conceal much from him. He'd always seen things in the beautiful blue of her eyes. The cruel rhyme made a lightning pass through his mind.

Suddenly what he saw was the fear of a lonely, tormented child who'd never valued riches or a fine home as much as she'd valued love and acceptance. There was no doubt in his mind that Rio Cory could give up a multimillion dollar inheritance without batting an eyelash if she thought it could buy even a token truce between them.

The whole idea made him angry. It also gave his heart a solid kick.

"We'll just have to see," he grumbled. He saw the quick drop of her gaze and sensed her dismay. His voice went lower. "You're free to go anywhere you want, do anything you want. If you want to turn down the inheritance before the year is up, go ahead. It would be the perfect revenge for you."

Rio's shocked gaze sped up to his and he went on. "I'm not about to promise you a year of peace and sweetness when we both know we're probably in for a choice piece of hell." He couldn't keep his gaze from making a slow, meaningful sweep of her very feminine body. "Stay or go, Rio. It's your choice. But don't stay thinking the two of us will ever be anything more to each other than we've ever been."

Rio couldn't say exactly why it hurt so much for Kane to remind her that her feelings for him were as futile as ever. Perhaps it was because he disliked her so much that he felt he had to pound the message home at every opportunity.

And perhaps he was right. Perhaps she was a fool who needed to be rebuffed and rejected until what she felt for him was crushed and killed. A great tide of exhaustion swept her. *Why had Sam done this?*

Rio somehow kept her voice steady as she pushed her chair up to the table. "I'd rather you ran Langtry. I can fill in when you need me to, as usual."

Kane was shaking his head again. "The will states that you have to stay on as a full and equal partner. Until we find out from the lawyer exactly what that means—"

"And who will guess that I'm not?"

"If you're staying, you're going to do exactly as the will requires. If you aren't, you might as well turn it all down now and get the hell off Langtry."

Rio felt her face flush. "Fine, but I don't want to live at the main house. The empty cottage by the pecan grove will do."

"Like hell it will," he groused. "You'll live in *this* house, just like you've always done, or you can haul your backside down the highway."

Rio was suddenly too furious to speak. Kane had never seemed more brutally domineering than he was at that moment. A secret part of her placed a high value on that dominance, but another part of her burned with the unfamiliar fire of pure rebellion.

Too upset to stay, she turned and stalked from the room.

The next several days were wearing. Rio asked Kane about the book Sam had left her. He didn't recall a book with that title, but he told her he'd keep an eye out for it. They were so busy making up for the time they'd lost to the funeral that it was soon evident that he'd forgotten about it. Rio searched the den herself, but there were no books with the title Sam had given her, not even in one of the cabinets.

Ramona and Tracy stayed on at the ranch, their presence adding to the friction between Rio and Kane. Rio didn't move out of the main house, and they were both forced to endure the discomfort of being nearly inseparable as Kane filled her in on more of the ranch's paperwork, legalities and tax information than she'd ever needed to know before.

He also outlined his short-range and long-range plans for Langtry, then told her gruffly that she had the right to either cooperate with those plans or to suggest others—for at least the next year. Rio had no intention of changing a thing. When she'd told him so, his angry glare had baffled her.

After a few days of having her outside work drastically curtailed, Rio grew restless. She and Kane were in the den one morning. He was showing her the new software he'd bought for their computer, when her gaze once again wandered toward the huge picture window that looked out on a section of the lawn and the ranch buildings beyond the wide driveway.

"Damn it, if you don't pay attention, we aren't going to get through this before nightfall." Kane reached past her, and punched the key he'd just told her to push. His temper had been hair-trigger all morning, sending Rio's downcast emotions into a fresh slide. She'd had trouble concentrating the past week—much to her frustration and to Kane's. She needed to be outside in the fresh air doing something physical to clear her head and lift her spirits, but Kane had been dogged on the subject of teaching her everything he thought she needed to know.

She had tolerated his near tyranny because she understood he might be worried about fulfilling the requirements of Sam's will. But he was wearing her down, and their close proximity to each other did nothing to help ease the painful tension between the two of them.

"I need to get out of the house for a while," she said as she rolled the desk chair back and got to her feet.

"You need to master this program," he grumbled.

Rio shook her head. "Later. I want to work that colt before it gets too hot."

"We've got people to take care of that colt. You're the only one who can take care of this," he said as he tossed the software manual to the corner of the desk.

"I need a break, Kane."

His brusque, "Take it, then," made her feel as if she didn't deserve it.

The soft knock on the open door of the den distracted them. Tracy stood shyly in the doorway dressed in a chic silk shirt and designer jeans.

Kane glanced over at her, the stern set of his rugged features softening as he smiled at his stepsister. "Did you decide to take me up on that offer?"

Tracy's fair cheeks colored delicately. "If you have time now," she said shyly, then cast a quick glance toward Rio. "And if I'm not interrupting something important."

"Nothing that can't wait," Rio offered pleasantly.

She'd been trying to break the ice with Tracy for days in an attempt at friendliness. She started around the desk for the door to leave the other two in private, but Tracy behaved toward Rio as she had all week, virtually ignoring her.

Though it was a relief to make a quick escape, Rio couldn't miss the gentle, affectionate look on Kane's face or the pink-cheeked glow on Tracy's. Her low spirits sunk further as something that felt a whole lot like jealousy pricked her heart.

Kane gradually let up on her, allowing and even encouraging her to work outside as she preferred. He made a series of small business trips that took him away from the ranch for a day at a time, but he was usually home by evening. Rio was grateful he wasn't gone long, particularly since Ramona and Tracy were still around. She couldn't remember a time that their visit had lasted longer than a week, so their continued presence made her uneasy.

Meanwhile, her energy seemed to have deserted her. Since she'd been an early riser all her life, she was baffled by the sudden difficulty she had getting up in the morning. Fatigue made her drag around most of the day, but at night, sleep was long in coming. Her appetite didn't improve, and she couldn't seem to concentrate. Weariness and frustration made her irritable.

She missed Sam terribly. The grief she felt ebbed into a melancholy that seemed to sap what was left of her energy. The morning she overslept, she awoke more groggy and exhausted than ever. It was almost ten o'clock before she got dressed and hurried down the lane to the stables, her stomach twisting with horror and guilt at starting the day so late. She was halfway to the stable when she met Kane.

"I was just coming to get you." The impatience she sensed in him made her feel worse.

"I'm sorry. I must not have set my alarm clock." She couldn't maintain contact with the probing look he was giving her.

"It doesn't look like the extra sleep did much for you," he said bluntly.

The truth was, it hadn't. She still felt tired enough to sleep the day away, but she was too ashamed of this sudden weakness to admit it to Kane. "Gee, thanks," she murmured, then started around him. Kane caught her arm and stopped her.

"Are you feeling all right?" The gentle concern in his voice warmed her, but she steeled herself against it.

She nodded, but didn't look at him. He tugged her closer, the heat from his body penetrating her clothes. The feel of his fingers encircling her upper arm sent a sensual charge through her that was only magnified by his nearness. His grip tightened slightly.

"Did you eat?"

Rio tried not to show her surprise at his question. "All I wanted," she answered, giving her arm a slight tug to free herself. Kane's grip was firm.

"And, as usual, it probably wasn't much," he grumbled. "How long do you think you can go without getting enough food and rest?"

Rio didn't let herself mistake his concern for caring. And because she didn't, his questions irritated her.

"I'll eat when I get hungry and I'll try to go to sleep earlier at night. That enough for you?" Rio lifted her gaze and glared up at him, hating that nothing between them changed for the better, not really.

"It's enough," he said as he released her. "The cabins and cow camps still need to be checked for repairs and supplies. Pick someone to take care of it, unless you'd rather see to it yourself."

Rio edged away, putting a small space between them. "I'll work the colt first, then if you don't mind, I'll pack a bag and a cell phone and take care of it." She didn't need to add that Ramona would be delighted for her to absent herself from the main house for a couple of days. Tracy certainly wouldn't miss her and, truth to tell, Kane himself was probably eager for her to leave for a while. He seemed to be taking her ongoing presence on Langtry remarkably well compared to what she'd expected, but then, it had only been a couple of weeks since the will had been read.

"Handle it however you want." Kane's gaze probed hers a moment more before it wandered over her face. "I'll be at the house until after lunch."

Rio nodded, then turned to head down the path to the stable.

CHAPTER EIGHT

THE sorrel colt was an enthusiastic student, even-tempered, willing and intelligent, but his high-energy exuberance made him a handful. Rio worked him in the round pen the first half hour before she rode him through the gate and along one of the alleys that cut through the corrals toward the range.

The colt fairly pranced with excitement, then responded to her minor scolding and her firm hand on the reins by walking a bit more sedately as they passed through the last gate.

She kept the horse under tight control until she felt his excitement moderate. She rode him to one of the creeks, then into the water. He shuddered beneath her as the water rushed around his ankles, so she urged him to the middle where the creek was knee-high. She stroked his neck and murmured words of praise and encouragement, then had him walk in the water parallel to the bank. They stayed in the creek until the young horse calmed and she felt him relax. After a few moments more, she reined him toward the bank and rode him out of the water.

They rode on for two hours and the colt did well, quickly obeying her signals as she took him from one gait to the next and rode him in a huge zigzag pattern that led them past several hazards. The creek was the first of those, then a couple of windmills, and four oil pumping stations. They practiced going through a gate several times before the colt stood quietly for Rio to reach down to open and close it. The young horse's resistance to allowing her to close and latch the gate once they were through was the biggest problem.

Rio rode him to a pasture with cattle next, and moved a handful of cows and calves a small distance before she turned from that and started working with her rope. The colt shied the first few times she tried to lasso a fence post, but soon tolerated the throw of the rope.

Deciding the colt knew enough to begin doing some real work, she coiled her rope and tied it on her saddle before she started back for the headquarters. They took a different way back, again zigzagging to visit a few other hazards.

Working the colt on the range had lifted some of her gloom and caused her tiredness to ease, but the hollow feeling of sadness was as heavy as ever. Now that the colt was moving along, competently responding to her signals, her mind started to wander.

She thought about the book Sam had left her, and felt a new pang. She hadn't been able to find it in the den or in any of the other bookcases around the huge house. The only place she hadn't checked was Sam's room. She'd reminded Kane about it a couple of days before, but he'd evidently forgotten it again. Perhaps she should suggest that the two of them check in Sam's bedroom later.

She was cantering the colt along a barbed-wire fence when she heard a snort and the pounding of hooves. She glanced back in time to see the new bull charge up behind her and the colt from the other side of the fence. In the next instant, the bull hit the wire, breaking through it with terrifying ease.

There was no time to spur the colt out of harm's way. The moment the bull broke through the taut wire, the impact yanked the top three strands free of their staples. The broken wire recoiled, hissing through the air in Rio's direction.

She had only a moment to throw her arm over her face before the strands of wire whipped around her and the colt. The colt squealed as the wire barbs twisted into the hide of his chest and lashed his legs. His sudden lunge into the air set the barbs deeper, and his drop to earth tangled his front ankles.

The next few moments seemed to move in slow motion as the colt continued to fight the wire. Rio struggled to regain control of the young horse, but it was a lost cause almost instantly. The wire slashed at her, ripping her clothes and her skin. The animal's irrational hop toward the intact section of fence next to them caught him in more wire. He stumbled and fell against the four-strand barbed-wire fence and sent them both crashing to the ground.

She had no more than a second for the horse to realize he was more tangled in wire than ever. Just that quickly, he tried to thrash clear of the wire. It took every bit of strength she had to pull the reins so tight that at last the colt lay still.

Rio gasped for breath, dragging in quick little puffs of air as the sharp barbs of the wire cut painfully through her clothes and into her skin. Her left leg was pinned under the colt, but the placement of the weathered fence post he'd knocked down kept her leg from being crushed.

Wire curled over them both, lashing them to what was left of the fence and to each other. But the most dangerous piece of wire lay tight across Rio's right shoulder and angled snugly against the tender flesh of her throat. She tried to lift her left hand and wedge her fingers between the wire and her throat in hopes of pushing it away, but her arm was caught in the wire.

The only hand she had free was her right hand. The colt started struggling again, and it was all she could do to keep her grip firm on the reins as she tried to keep the frightened animal down. She couldn't risk letting go of the reins to get the wire away from her throat, but if she couldn't hold the horse...

Panic overwhelmed her as she held the reins tight and tried to carefully wiggle her left hand free. The sun pounded down hotly, and it surprised her a little to realize that she was already drenched with sweat. She murmured to the young horse, trying to calm him, though they were both shaking with the tremors that went through his big body.

The bull snorted nearby and she froze. She turned her head as far as she could and caught sight of the huge animal standing not a dozen feet away, his head down as he pawed the sod. The dust he stirred floated toward her like a low cloud.

"Oh, God, please—" She watched in horror as the bull continued to dig at the sod. He paused, then lifted his head and bellowed. The horse started at that, and

Rio felt his muscles bunch for another attempt at escape.

Tears of pain and frustration crowded into her eyes as she fought to hold the horse still. The wire barbs cut into her skin in what felt like dozens of places. Every time the horse moved, the barbs bit deeper, until she was hurting so much she almost couldn't lie still herself.

Just when she thought she couldn't hold the reins any tighter, the bull made a shuffling sound. Terrified, she looked over in time to see the huge beast take a step toward her. He took two lumbering strides then suddenly, amazingly, he turned and ambled off until he was out of the narrow view she had in that direction.

Relief stole her strength and she felt herself fairly melt against the ground. The restless move of the horse as he again tested the tautness of the wire made her go rigid again as she gripped the reins.

She laid there for what seemed like hours, murmuring to the colt, fighting to keep her grip on the reins while she tried to free her left hand and arm. The longer she lay there, the more pain made an impression.

Heat and thirst heightened her torment and dizzying fatigue compounded it. Every so often, she turned her head as far as the wire would allow, hoping she'd see another rider, but no one came.

She laid there for so long that she felt herself start to drift. The cloud that passed between her and the sun sent a small breath of coolness over her.

"Hey there, little girl—what is it you got yourself into?"

Sam's voice, strong and familiar, moved through her and her eyes sprang open to look for his face. The sun was bright behind his head and shoulders as he leaned over her. She couldn't see his face clearly, but the certainty that it was Sam comforted her so deeply that her fear immediately eased.

"Sam..."

"I'm here, baby," he assured her, "just lie still. That little sorrel will stay calm if you will."

How many times had she heard him say that to her when she'd worked a young horse? Just when she realized she was probably dreaming, he said, "Kane's comin'."

The slight move of her head caused her pain. "He doesn't know where I am," she rasped.

Sam's voice was confident. "He doesn't, but the Good Lord knows exactly where you are, honey."

"H-how are you here?" she got out, then swallowed convulsively at the painful dryness of her throat.

"As long as you remember, a part of me never really leaves. I'll always be there in your heart, in your memories—" The colt stirred and Sam told her, "You need to keep that rein tight, Rio, cause you can't come where I am for a good many years. You gotta lot of livin' ahead of you."

Rio's mouth was so dry that she merely moved her lips to say, "Please, Sam, come home." Her eyes were blurred but she could see him shake his head.

"I am home, sweet girl," he said gently. "I had

my time on the earth. Got myself a strong, healthy, young body again and a good baritone voice to sing in that big church choir up yonder. I'm only here now so you don't lose heart.''

Somehow it seemed important to let him know that she would hang on. She tried to tell him, but her mouth was too dry to get the words out.

''I know, Rio. I can tell,'' he said, as if he'd read her thoughts. ''Ain't you named that colt yet?'' he teased, then chuckled. ''Might want to call him Barbie. Boz'll get a kick outta the name, 'specially after this.''

Rio felt a smile pull at her lips, but she was drifting again and could hardly keep hold of the reins.

Sam's soft, ''I'm leaving now, honey. Kane'll be here in a minute,'' made her stir, but she was so weak. She felt herself begin to sink and her fingers went slack. The coolness gusted over her face and, thinking Sam had come back, she forced her eyes open.

''Sam?''

Kane's voice was brisk. ''Take it easy. I'm here.''

Rio tried to focus on him. The sun was not nearly so bright now, and Kane leaned over her, his big body shading her face. ''Sam was here,'' she got out, but her voice was barely a whisper.

Kane was growling at someone, cursing, and the colt began to shift on the ground. Rio tried to hold the reins, but they were no longer in her fingers.

''Get those damned cutters over here.'' Kane's voice sounded strange to her, but she couldn't focus sharply enough on his face to discern the reason. Kane moved, and she felt the tight wire that cut into her shoulder and across her throat go slack. It took her a moment to realize that the quiet snip she was hearing was the sound of a wire cutter.

The colt shifted again, and Kane swore. "If he won't lay quiet, shoot him."

The words penetrated her foggy thoughts and alarmed her. "No, please." She licked her dry lips and tried again. "Don't hurt him, Kane."

Kane grumbled something, then swore softly. Rio felt one wire after another snap loose. Once she could turn her head, she could see that there were three cowhands with Kane. He leaned close, then slid his hand beneath her shoulders to gently lift her.

Kane had never felt fear so strong that it made him gut sick, but seeing Rio on the ground in a bloody tangle of barbed wire with a frightened colt tangled up with her had done it. He hadn't been able to get to her quick enough to ease the terror he felt, the terror he still felt as they worked to free her from the wire.

She was already bleeding from a score of cuts, and he was suddenly terrified that she would bleed to death. When he slipped his hand beneath her shoulders to lift her in preparation for getting the colt off her leg, he felt the sticky wetness that had stiffened the back of her shirt and glued bits of grass and dirt to the fabric.

He glanced over at the cowhand who was getting ready to pull her leg free. Kane carefully lifted her until she was partially sitting up. The other two men had clipped the colt free of the wire and were positioning themselves to help the horse get up. At Kane's signal, the two men pushed the colt to his feet while he and the third ranch hand pulled Rio out of harm's way.

It was over in seconds. The colt was unsteady on his feet at first, then stood trembling as flies swarmed over his wounds. The man at his head coaxed him forward. He moved stiffly, favoring his left front leg.

Rio was limp in his arms, her eyes closed. One of the men brought a canteen and Kane trickled a bit of water onto her dry lips. The water roused her and she reached weakly for the canteen. Kane allowed her only two swallows before he took the water away.

"Sorry, baby," he murmured, "just a little at a time."

From there, it was a race to get Rio to a hospital. Kane carried her to the ranch pickup that Boz roared up in a few minutes later. By then, he'd sacrificed his shirt, tearing the sleeves out, then ripping it in a few strips to bind the wire cuts on her left arm and wrist. He used what was left as crude pads for the other deep cuts on her left side and back. By the time they got to the ranch headquarters, the helicopter from the nearest trauma center was touching down on the front lawn.

The paramedics took only a few minutes to check her vital signs and start an IV before the helicopter took off. Kane's last sight of Rio lying so still and frail and bloodied on the stretcher haunted him all the way to the hospital.

Rio lay uncomfortably in the private hospital room, her left arm and side sporting several inches of stitches. Her ribs, hip and leg were badly bruised, and her face and hands were sunburned. Her body temperature had been brought down, her blood pressure was in a good range, but the doctor had insisted on admitting her.

And she was weak. She'd managed to doze off a couple of times, but those brief naps had done nothing to strengthen her. Because she'd insisted on making her own trek to the bathroom a while ago, she knew precisely how weak she was and it had frightened her.

Kane was in the hospital somewhere, but so far he'd not come to her hospital room. He'd waited outside the trauma room for hours and she'd caught only an occasional glimpse of him as the doctor and nurses worked to lower her body temperature, then to stitch her many cuts. He'd come into the cubicle briefly a couple of times, but finally elected to sit in the hall out of the way.

On the other hand, visiting hours had just ended. Since it was nearly dark, Kane might have already started home. Because they were both early risers, she understood why he might want to spare himself the ninety-mile ride to the ranch at a late hour.

The idea that she was in the hospital alone sent her spirits downward. She was lying on her right side and tried to shift to find a more comfortable spot, but her battered body ached no matter how she tried to lay. In the end, she gave up and closed her eyes.

Booted steps outside her door roused her from the twilight of half-sleep, but when they stopped without coming into the room, she closed her eyes again, unable to help the disappointment she felt. This was a Texas hospital. Boots were common footwear. Kane's confident stride was as familiar to her as his face, but perhaps it was her imagination that had conjured the distinctive sound.

She thought again about Sam. She realized now, of course, that his visit that day had been a dream or maybe a delusion brought on by fear and heat and blood loss. But it had seemed so real. She'd actually heard his voice, or thought she had. Hadn't the way she'd strained to see him been real, either?

In the end, it didn't matter whether it had been a dream or a delusion. Sam hadn't really come back to her but, as he'd said, he would always be there in her heart, in her memories. *I am home, sweet girl,* he'd said. *I had my time on the earth. Got myself a strong, healthy, young body again and a good baritone voice to sing in that big church choir up yonder. I'm only here now so you don't lose heart...*

How comforting those words had been! Even though Sam hadn't really been able to say them himself, they were a balm to her heart and soothed the pain of losing him. His *Ain't you named that colt yet?* made her smile.

Kane hovered outside the door of Rio's room, reluctant to disturb her if she was asleep. It didn't surprise him to realize that the only place he wanted to be was in that room, watching over her. The protectiveness he'd secretly felt toward her for years was suddenly fierce. He'd never forget how helpless and hurt she'd looked lying in that wire. He'd never forget that in one blinding moment of emotional clarity, his turbu-lent feelings toward her had settled neatly into place.

And though his feelings toward her were more stormy and primitive than ever, he now knew exactly what he wanted from Rio Cory.

The wire was so tight, and it hurt so much. The colt was frantic. She tried to keep him calm, to hold the reins so tight he couldn't get up, but the bits of leather were slick, defying her effort to hang on to them. And the bull was charging toward them, faster and faster, closer and closer...

Rio cried out, the horror of the dream making her jerk as she flung up her arm to protect herself. It was several moments before she realized that she was ly-ing in a hospital bed and that the big hands manacling her wrists were trying to help, not hurt.

A huge sob sent pain shooting everywhere. The familiar traces of Kane's after-shave made an im-pression before the low, gruff sound of his voice did. "Kane?"

"It's me, baby. You're safe."

"The bull was—" She belatedly cut herself off. The nightmare lingered, but reality was flooding back. Relief made her wilt against the pillow and Kane's grip on her wrists eased. The dim light coming from behind him made it difficult to see his face.

"What about the bull?" The terse question alerted Rio. She remembered then that she hadn't told anyone exactly how the accident happened. All they knew was that she and the horse she was riding had got caught in barbed wire.

Her concern for the colt made her ignore his question. "What about the colt? Is he all right?"

Now that her eyes were adjusting to the dimness, she saw the harsh lines of his face ease. "I talked to Boz this evening. The colt is about as cut up and battered as you, but he's okay." Kane's expression went grim again. "Though for two cents I feel like selling him, or better, sending him to the meat packer."

Rio was instantly alarmed. "What for?"

"For being enough of a bubble head to tangle you both in several feet of barbed wire. What'd he do, take off in a bucking fit and try to go through the fence?"

Kane's assessment of the circumstances of the accident stunned her, but the consequences he seemed so anxious to carry out upset her.

"No—you can't do that, Kane. He's a good little horse," she told him quickly.

"And you're too softhearted and sentimental," he growled.

Rio shook her head, then winced at the pain. "It wasn't his fault."

Kane's expression was stony. "Then whose fault was it?"

"It was the new bull." The moment she said the words and saw the impact they had on Kane, she wished she'd found a much less blunt way to tell him. Kane not only placed a high value on the animal, he'd spent a fortune for him. The dangerous gleam in his eyes suggested that he was furious suddenly. The fear that Kane was angry with her—again—made her heart sink. Rio pressed her lips together, reluctant to tell him more.

"So what happened?" Kane was brisk with her, all business, and his steely tone made her dread his reaction more than she already did.

"We were riding along the fence. I didn't know the bull was in the next pasture until I heard him coming up behind us from the other side of the fence." Rio told him the rest, quailing inwardly at the dark anger on Kane's face. And because she was anxious to be certain the colt wouldn't somehow be blamed, she added, "The colt probably handled it as well as a more seasoned horse, given his inexperience. He was frightened and he was in pain. I don't know how much time passed, but he stayed on the ground a long time. I either passed out or fell asleep at least once. He could have taken advantage of that."

She went silent. There was no need to say more. Besides, she'd never seen the kind of anger—no, rage—she was seeing in Kane's eyes now. He couldn't be that angry with the colt, so it had to be her he was furious with. He was probably thinking she could have been more alert to the bull's approach, or that she should have been able to keep the colt from panicking and falling into the fence.

Years of not measuring up, of loving Kane and knowing he was forever beyond her reach, brought a suspicious fullness to her eyes. She'd failed again in his sight, and she was so exhausted and uncomfortable and heartsore over losing Sam that this new failure was more than she could bear.

She put up her right hand and covered her eyes,

mortified that she was on the verge of bursting into tears. Her hoarse, "I'm really tired, could you leave now?" ended on a sob that sent sharp pain through her bruised ribs.

Kane plucked her hand from her face the very instant the tears began to seep over her lashes. She glanced up into his harsh face before her eyes shied from the strange dismay in his.

"And I'm sorry. Again," she blurted, then clenched her teeth together to get control of herself. She tried to pull her hand from his, but his firm grip made it impossible. Frustration made the tears come faster. "D-damn it—will you let me go and leave me alone?"

Kane released her hand and Rio quickly used it to brush impatiently at the hot tears cascading down her cheeks. The bed jerked a bit, and she realized that Kane had lowered the side rail. She was about to edge away when he leaned over her and braced his hands on either side of her head to come close, his lips a hand span from hers.

Rio pushed her hand against his chest to force him away, but he was immovable. She read his intent in the hot gleam of his eyes before his lips closed the distance and toyed softly with hers.

"Don't do this, Kane, please," she got out as she tried to turn her face from his. His hand on her cheek kept her from evading him while his lips continued to flirt with hers. She groaned, then slipped her fingers up to press over his mouth to keep it from touching hers.

"I can't take this, Kane," she whispered brokenly.

"I can't make my heart hard like you can, I can't make myself stop—'' She cut herself off before she made another foolish confession of love.

But she dissolved into tears anyway, unable to suppress the weak, wounded sobs that sent stabbing pains into her bruised side for those first few moments. Kane sat on the bed and gathered her carefully into his arms. She was too weak physically and emotionally to fight him any longer, and so she clung to his shirtfront and cried.

It was heaven and hell to be held by him, just as it had always been heaven and hell to be anywhere near him. She was too exhausted to grapple with the insanity, too broken to try to analyze it. Kane knew her most important secrets anyway, so he had surely detected the pleasure/pain of her feelings for him.

By the time the crying jag had spent itself, she was limp in his arms and so weak she could hardly move. Kane laid her back on the pillow, then grabbed a tissue from the side table and blotted her sunburned cheeks.

Rio didn't open her eyes. She lay still for a few moments after he finished, then felt him lean toward her. His minty breath gusted softly over her face before his lips again settled on hers.

The firm caress of his mouth as it moved masterfully over hers sent a reviving heat through her. Rio's eyes came open, then fell shut as his mouth moved demandingly on hers. Her fingers found the hand he'd braced beside her head. She slid her palm beneath his and felt their fingers lace together.

The pressure of his lips eased and he pulled back

slightly to rasp, "I'm going to have you, Rio. Soon. Today changed things between us, and I'm done fighting the urge." He brought a hand up and trailed a finger along her jaw. He let the finger drop to the front of her gown and traced a line to her breast. His eyes were like blue flames. "You get well, Rio Cory. You get strong." His lips descended swiftly to hers and his kiss left her breathless. He withdrew slowly. Rio's eyes opened and clung to the fiery intensity of his. He pulled his fingers from hers and raised the bed rail.

"Sleep tight, baby. I'll be back before breakfast." And then he was gone.

CHAPTER NINE

RAMONA had been frantic to find the book. She'd secretly read about it in Sam's letter to Rio, so she knew what was supposed to be in it. Now that she'd finally found it, she was beside herself with excitement. Quietly, she lifted it from its resting place in the bottom drawer of Sam's dresser.

She'd searched all over for the key to the damned drawer—the last place in the house where the book could possibly be. She must have gone through every pocket, shelf and potential hiding place before she'd found it. It had been hanging by a string among Sam's collection of ties. She never would have noticed it had she not got frustrated with the search and slapped spitefully at the ties to muss them.

The moment she'd discovered the key was the moment that her daring plan was assured of success. Ramona felt good about this, clever, superior. In the past few days she'd become quite good at going through the private papers of others to find what she wanted. Not even the witch sisters, Ardis and Estelle, had been able to catch her at it.

Ramona set the book carefully on the bed. It was stuffed so full of dead flowers and papers and photos that it would never lay flat, and that annoyed her. How could you find one specific thing among such a collection of garbage? Only someone pathetic enough and sentimental enough to examine each page would ever find anything specific.

Fortunately, Rio Cory was pathetic enough and sentimental enough. And because she was, she was certain to find out the ugly truth in the book all by herself. Ramona only had to make sure that the truth was there before Rio got the book.

Kane came back before breakfast that next morning as he'd promised, but the doctor didn't come to examine her until midmorning. By then, the floral delivery man had come by her room and left her a dozen red roses in an expensive Lalique crystal vase. Rio had assumed they were from Kane until she read the card.

Kane's face had been rock-hard when she'd glanced up from reading it. His gruff, "Who's the romantic?" made her hesitate to tell him.

She said nothing, but passed him the card. Kane took it, and to her chagrin, read it aloud. "'Glad you're all right. Will make it up to you. Ty.'" He virtually sneered the name before he glared over at her. "Sounds like I need to make sure everyone knows you've been cut out of the herd."

Rio's gaze fled his. She loved Kane with all her heart, but what he'd proposed the night before shamed her. The thrill of his declaration to "have" her died the moment she realized that no declaration of love or proposal of marriage had followed it. He'd said he was tired of fighting the urge. Urges were more lust than love.

She deliberately ignored his statement and instead

gazed at the roses. "How did he know I was in the hospital?"

"I told him when I offered him the bull back."

Rio glanced over at him, surprised. "What?"

"I offered him the bull. On the hoof for a price, or over a barbecue pit for Labor Day."

Rio was shaking her head before he finished. "That bull is too valuable. You'll never get your investment back if you sell him at a loss—and it will be a loss. It will also be a waste to slaughter him."

Kane's gruff "Money doesn't matter, he could have killed you," gave her heart a pang. She knew Kane was upset that she'd been hurt, but not because he was madly in love with her. Suddenly bitter, she gave him a cynical look, angry at herself for loving him so foolishly and angry at him for not being able to love her.

"You don't have to grandstand," she told him quietly. "You don't need to worry about my health, either. I've already seen a lawyer and made a will. If I should die, my half of Langtry will go directly to you. If I become disabled somehow, and I'm not able to fully participate as your co-owner, I've signed papers that give you the authority to act for me. Sam's will won't have been violated, you won't have an animal rights group on your back, and you can live happily ever after."

Kane's face had gone dark. He was furious. "What the hell's the matter with you?" he growled.

Rio expelled a weary breath, but her gaze didn't waver from his. "Maybe I'm wising up." She'd already considered what she wanted to say. Now was the time to say it. "So you'll need to keep fighting that 'urge' you mentioned last night. Exciting as it might be, I won't have an affair with you. You already have my love, and you might always have that, but I won't give you what's left of my self-respect."

The sadness she felt made her look away from the blue flare of outrage in his eyes. Fortunately, the doctor strode into the room. A nurse shooed Kane to the hall, and the doctor made his examination.

The nurse helped her dress in the clean clothes Kane had brought, gave her two bottles of medications plus prescriptions for more should she need them. She brushed and braided Rio's hair, then helped her into the wheelchair. Rio held the crystal vase of roses on her lap as the nurse wheeled her out.

By the time Kane got her settled in the car, she was worn out. Kane was still furious with her, the air between them was turbulent with it. He only spoke to her when necessary all the way to Langtry.

When they arrived, Rio tried to get out of the car by herself, but she was so stiff and sore she'd barely got the door open before Kane came around to her side of the car. Despite her protest, he carefully slid one hand behind her back and one under her knees before he lifted her out.

Rio couldn't help but notice that his profile was rigid with bad temper. Neither of them spoke as he carried her up the walk, then in the front door that Estelle held open for them. He ignored Ramona and Tracy, who'd come out of the living room as he stalked past, his no-nonsense glare keeping them all silent.

Tension and dread distracted Rio from the discomfort of being moved around as Kane carried her up the stairs. A confrontation was coming, that was certain. More heartache would follow, that was also certain.

When they reached her room, Kane got the door open, then carried her in. He paused to kick the door shut before he walked over to her bed. He sat her gently on the bedspread, then towered over her. Impatiently, he reached up to yank his hat off and toss it toward a chair.

"So you don't want an affair, huh?"

Rio looked up at him. Kane Langtry was a ruggedly handsome, virile man. The longing to have him make love to her was suddenly so sharp that she almost reached for him then. Her body hungered for whatever he could give her for as long as he wanted to give it, but sadly, she knew her heart could never withstand physical intimacy without love. She'd never survive the pain when he tired of her and pushed her out of his life. Her eyes stung. "I love you, Kane, but enough is enough."

He hunkered down in front of her and she had to make herself meet his solemn gaze. He touched her hand and she eased it away.

"I reckon I deserve for you to think that I'm a complete S.O.B.," he growled. "I've acted like one long enough to qualify." He lifted his hand and slid two fingers into his shirt pocket. When he brought them out, something bright sparkled between his fingertips. "But I'm in love with you, Rio Cory. I don't want an affair with you, either. I want you to be my wife.''

It took a moment for her to realize that Kane had proposed marriage. He rolled the band of the ring between his thumb and finger so that the huge diamond winked boldly at her, drawing her attention. The ring was magnificent. What it represented made her breathless, but heartache brought her back to earth and she forced herself to look at him.

''But you hate wanting me,'' she whispered sadly. ''You said yourself that I'm the last woman you want.''

''I've had too much control over my life to appreciate losing my head over a woman. None of the others ever made me feel anything I couldn't walk away from, so I hated it when I realized you had some special power over me.''

Rio glanced away, not certain she could believe what she was hearing. Perhaps the accident had somehow pushed her over the edge and she was imagining this as she'd imagined Sam coming to her. Kane placed a finger under her chin and silently coaxed her to look at him. It took her a moment to find the courage.

''You were nineteen when I started comparing other women to you,'' he said, his voice husky and low. ''But none of them had eyes like sapphires or hair so long and thick that a man aches to wrap his hands in it. None of the others was as beautiful or as loyal and smart as you, none of them made my heart race and made me dream wild dreams.''

Rio was stunned. Oh, God, what he was saying was a miracle, but she was terrified of being disappointed.

Kane ran the back of his knuckle gently along her jaw as his look grew somber. "I almost lost you yesterday, baby. I found out then that there are scarier things than what I feel for you."

Joy burst in her heart but Rio's gaze fell from his as she automatically tried to conceal it from him. Everything he was saying to her was wonderful, but they'd lived at odds for too long for her not to be wary.

Kane's softly spoken, "Rio?" made her look at him again. "If it's not too late for me—for us—then marry me, honey. You'll never regret it."

She looked deep into the dark blue of his eyes, searching for love, searching for the truth. All she could see was the utter sincerity of the man she'd loved for nearly half her life, the man whose heart was too hard won to doubt. She lifted her hand and placed it on his hard jaw, terrified, nonetheless.

"We've both been through a lot lately, what with Sam…" She had to pause a moment because it was still hard to verbally acknowledge his death. "And then the accident shook us both up." She watched Kane's expression grow hard as she went on, "I know you Texas men are loathe to consider it, but maybe our emotions aren't what we think they a—"

The sudden advance of Kane's mouth cut her off. His lips fastened on hers with a fervency that stole her breath. When he finally withdrew, she couldn't think straight.

"You've loved me for a long time and I've loved

you,'' he growled. "It didn't start yesterday or last week or last month. I doubt very much that either one of us will ever wake up one day and decide that what we feel now was some kind of emotional overreaction or a byproduct of grief for my father.''

Kane lifted his hand and held the ring between them. One side of his handsome mouth kicked up in a half grin. "If it's the ring you don't like, you can pick out something else. I can have the jeweler bring a selection to Langtry before supper.''

Rio released a short, surprised breath and shook her head. "It's beautiful, Kane," she whispered.

"Then will you marry me, or do you need to think about it?''

She felt herself melt as she stared into the intensity in his eyes. She recognized the look, the unyielding resolve of a strong, powerful man who decides what he wants and goes after it. It reassured her to see that in Kane and to know that she was the focus of that resolve.

Her quiet, "I'll marry you," was barely audible.

Kane's intense expression relaxed and he reached for her hand. Rio felt a bit dazed as she watched him gently slide the ring on her finger. He lifted her hand and placed a tender kiss on the back of it.

He looked into her eyes then, his gaze hot and sensual. He kissed her hand again, then turned it over and kissed her palm, all the while watching her face to gauge her reaction. Rio leaned toward him and he met her lips with a kiss so tender and profound that it flooded her heart with joy.

*   *   *

The world had shifted on its axis. It was the same sun, the same moon and stars, the same year and month, the same house and ranch, the same people involved who had always been involved—and yet everything had changed. Kane had changed and Rio realized she was changing because he had. The world was new suddenly, and she felt like a child at Christmas.

Kane Langtry loved her at last and though he was not publicly demonstrative, everyone saw instantly the change in their relationship.

Ramona noticed right away and her reaction to the news of their engagement surprised Rio almost as much as Kane's proposal had. The older woman gave every impression of being delighted with the match, even going so far as to volunteer to help with the wedding or to recommend a wedding planner.

Tracy seemed as aloof as ever, though she coolly offered her best wishes and seconded her mother's offer of assistance. Ardis and Estelle reacted reservedly to the news, as they always did, but it pleased Rio when they started making plans for a thorough deep cleaning of the house for the wedding reception and began to pester Kane about making a few decorating changes.

The days following the riding accident passed swiftly for Rio. Though she was still quite sore from the stitches and bruises, she wasn't one to lie around and wait for herself to heal. She couldn't ride yet or do outside ranch work, but paperwork suited her. She did her best to work the soreness from her abused body by walking and doing simple exercises. The removal of the stitches made increased activity a bit easier, and by the end of the second week, she was riding for short periods of time.

Kane was wonderful to her. He took her along on two day-long business trips, one to Austin, the other to Dallas. Both days, he finished business by noon, then took her to lunch and shopping. While Kane had been in his morning meetings, she'd checked on wedding consultants in both cities, selected one, then immediately panicked at the number of things that needed to be done.

"Hell, I've heard for years about the pomp and bother of big-ticket weddings," Kane told her as they flew home from Dallas. "But I figure to be married only one time, and since I aim for you to marry only one time, I'd like our big-ticket wedding to be something along the lines of spectacular."

That said, he smiled over at her doubtful expression, then reached over and caught her hand. "Come on, baby. I'm proud to marry you and I want everyone in Texas to know it. That wedding consultant you hired can take care of the headaches. All you'll have to do is put on the dress, walk down the aisle, then promise to love and obey."

That startled a laugh from Rio. "I thought it was the groom who promised that," she told him.

Kane shook his head adamantly. "No you don't— the traditional vows suit me just fine," he declared, then looked over at her, a gleam of laughter in his eyes. He tugged on her hand and brought it to his lips to kiss the back of her fingers before he returned his full attention to flying.

Rio settled deeper in her seat, marveling at the easy companionship between them, grateful beyond words that they were no longer at odds with each other. She still missed Sam terribly, but her new closeness to Kane eased the hurt.

Sam had told her in the letter that he'd somehow know when they settled their differences. She wasn't certain he'd had in mind a marriage between them when he'd written the letter, but plans to marry certainly signified a level of harmony and cooperation they'd never had while he'd been alive. The reminder gave her a pang. How much better it would have been for them to come to this point while Sam had been around to enjoy it. On the other hand, it had happened at last. Rio hoped Sam really did know about it somehow.

As had become their habit, Kane slipped into her room later that night just before their early bedtime. He was there waiting when she emerged from her shower and the bathroom.

He was lying on her bed with his shoulders braced against the headboard, his hands resting on his lean middle and his legs crossed at the ankles. His blue gaze was smoky with desire as he watched her walk out of the bathroom and cross to the side of the bed. His lips twisted faintly. "That bathrobe ought to wear out one of these days, baby. If it doesn't in time for the wedding, I promise to burn it."

Rio couldn't help the shy, pleased smile on her face. Kane had a difficult time reining in his libido, but he did. He understood her reluctance to preview their wedding night. But although he complied with her wishes, he either made up outrageous stories about how debilitating abstinence was for Texas males, or he came up with new destruction scenarios for her robe.

Rio gave him a look of mock reproof, then pointed at his feet. "Boots off the bed, cowboy."

A slow smile spread across his handsome mouth. "Make me, darlin'." The sultry look he gave her was an enticement to come closer.

When she hesitated, his hand shot out and caught the hem of the terry-cloth robe. She reached down to catch his hand as he pulled on the robe to draw her closer. Suddenly he seized her wrist. Just that quickly he pulled her down on top of him then rolled over, neatly pinning her beneath him.

She answered his gruff, "Am I hurting you?" with a slight shake of her head.

His mouth opened voraciously over hers, urging hers to open and respond before he deepened the kiss and his tongue did a strong imitation of what they both ached for. Rio was breathless before he eased his lips from hers and slid down her body to nibble at her neck. The expertise of his hand beneath her robe made her tremble.

"Oh, please, Kane—it's wonderful," she panted. Then, frustrated with herself, rasped a pained, "S-stop."

Kane complied, but slowly. She could feel the tension and hardness of his body and realized dazedly that this time, they'd almost instantly reached the point of no return. It didn't take much anymore for a kiss or a touch to send them soaring, and she began to have real worries about being able to wait until their wedding night. She had just as many worries about whether she might perish from frustrated desire before they could get to the altar.

Kane growled against her neck and slid his hand from beneath her robe. "Damn, baby, one of us needs to move that wedding date, or we won't have a snowball's chance of making it."

"T-the soonest is four weeks from Saturday," she stammered, absolutely horrified that four weeks wasn't much time to pull off the huge wedding Kane seemed to want.

Kane's groan was so eloquent that it made her giggle. He lifted his head and looked down at her. "That sounds nice. And that smile. Just wraps around my heart, darlin', and makes me feel fine." He lowered his head and feathered a few gentle kisses over her lips. "I love you."

Rio felt her heart burst. Kane told her regularly now that he loved her, and each time he said it was more thrilling than the last. Her soft, "I love you," was almost painful because the words were so inadequate to express what she felt for him. She reached up with both hands and slid her fingers into his thick, dark hair. She lifted her head from the pillow and pressed her lips against his, starved for the taste of him.

Kane kissed her back and Rio melted beneath him until, reluctantly, he pulled away. "This would probably be a good time to give you what I found. Otherwise..."

He rubbed his jaw on her cheek, then eased off her

and rolled to his back. He rested his forearm over his eyes and gave a deep sigh. They both lay quietly, and though they were no longer touching, Rio could feel her body straining toward the male heat of his.

Kane reached for her hand and gave it a squeeze before he sat up and got off the bed. Rio rolled to her side and tried to hold her robe together as she followed. She stood by the bed as Kane walked to her dresser. When she glanced past him and saw the huge book, she sprinted after him.

"Is this the book Sam left for me?" The question was an outburst of surprise and delight because it was plain that it was. Though the title *Plant and Animal Species of the World* was the one Sam had indicated, it was also obvious that the book was so crammed with pressed flowers that its cover would never lie flat.

"Sorry it took so long. I didn't find a key until this evening. I was about to pry the lock on the drawer I thought it might be in, when I remembered a collection of old cabinet keys Estelle keeps in a pantry drawer. One of them worked in the lock."

Rio touched the book then slipped her fingers under the edge of the front cover and carefully opened it. The first thing she saw was a photograph of her mother and five other women at a Langtry barbecue. The other women were each holding up a dessert they'd made. Her mother was holding up a tall chocolate layer cake.

It startled Rio to see the picture. She'd never realized how much she looked like her mother. She'd seen other pictures, so she'd known there was a strong resemblance, but it was even more evident in this photo.

"You and your mama could be taken for twins. She was a beautiful, tenderhearted woman," Kane said quietly as he looked on. "He was in love with her, you know."

Rio looked over at Kane. "I didn't know, exactly. He spoke fondly of her." She paused and glanced down to turn a page. "But until I realized he and my mother were going to be buried next to each other..." She shook her head. "I can't think of a single time that I ever saw them touch or talk about anything other than the weather or her garden or her health, and yet, now I feel the strangest..." She paused and turned another page.

She carefully leafed through the first few pages. The flowers were dry and frail. She suddenly had a mental picture of Sam's big, calloused hands tenderly laying each stem and bloom between the pages. For all his tough, rugged looks, and hard-edged masculinity, Sam Langtry had had a core of gentleness and compassion that you didn't suspect when you looked at him.

Her eyes filled with tears and she blinked them back to turn another page. A small square of blue plaid cotton had been smoothed between these pages. From the look of it, probably taken off the wire barb that had torn it from a dress. Rio touched the fabric. Shapes cut from the same fabric had been pieced into the quilt top in her mother's sewing box.

Kane's voice was low, almost hushed. "How sentimental does a man have to be about a woman to press flowers she's grown in a book and keep them all these years?''

It wasn't really a question he expected an answer to and Rio didn't answer it. "Sam never said anything to me,'' she said quietly.

"He didn't say anything to me, either. I knew he thought she was a fine woman and too good for Ned, but I never would have known he was in love with her if I hadn't overheard them talking.''

Rio turned her head to look at him. "When was this? What did they say?'' She was suddenly hungry to know. She couldn't imagine a more perfect childhood than if Sam and her mother had married. Because her father had been so abusive, the reminder that her mother would have had to divorce him to marry Sam didn't bother her.

"You must have been about seven, because I was seventeen. I knew your mother was going to take you down to one of the hay barns to see a new litter of kittens. My father must have joined her there, because I was walking up from the creek and heard them.''

Rio carefully closed the book and gave Kane her complete attention. "What did they say?''

Kane glanced away a moment as he remembered. "Lenore's voice was shaky, which got my attention, since she was always so cheerful, even when she didn't have much to be cheerful about. She was saying, 'We're both people who honor the Good Book too much to let our emotions lead us, Sam. I know Ned's not much as a husband or provider, but I made vows with him before God.''' Kane's gaze came back to hers. "That's when I heard my father say that he'd never put her in a position to choose. He told her he'd love her till his dying day, but unless she became free, he'd keep his feelings to himself.''

Rio's lips parted in shock at the enormity of what Kane was telling her. She left the book on the dresser, then walked, stunned, toward the bed and sat down on the edge as she tried to recover.

''Then they were in love with each other,'' she whispered as she looked over at Kane.

''For all the good it did either of them,'' he said darkly. ''I think it about killed him when she got sick and died. He got the very best doctors for her, but there was no hope.'' Kane went silent for a long time. Rio glanced away and didn't speak, either.

She was suddenly awash with memories of her father's drunkenness and his terrible temper. She still had dim memories of him backhanding her mother or shoving her around. Most times, it seemed he barely noticed there was even a child in the house, much less that the child was his. ''Why didn't she do something? Why didn't she divorce my father?''

''Too much honor, I reckon,'' he said solemnly. ''She'd made a vow she felt bound to keep. My father apparently couldn't bring himself to steal another man's wife, no matter how bad a husband she had.''

Kane's lips quirked humorlessly. ''Old-fashioned morality at its most noble and most painful. You don't often hear about honor like that these days. I admire their restraint.''

''And that's why they're buried so close now,'' she guessed.

Kane nodded. ''Reckon so.''

Rio's eyes stung as she looked over at the book. "Thanks for finding it for me. If you'd like, you can look through it yourself." She was so overcome with emotion that she had to push the words out.

"I think I'd like to save it for another day, when it's not so late in the evening and Dad's passing isn't quite so fresh." He paused, then walked over to the bed and crouched down before her to take her hand. "And I'd rather you took it in small doses yourself. I don't think he left it for you to make you sad."

Rio reached up and put her hand on Kane's hard jaw, touched by his concern. "I know," she whispered. "I probably can't get through all of it in one sitting anyway. It looks like there're other things besides flowers in it. On top of which," she said, then took a bracing breath, "I'm still a little in shock about finding out that they were in love with each other."

"Are you gonna be all right?" he asked gently, and she nodded. He smiled at her. "All right then, baby, give me a kiss to last till morning."

Rio smiled then and leaned forward to touch his lips with hers.

CHAPTER TEN

Two days later, Kane went to Dallas on business. Since he planned to be there for the next few days, Rio stayed behind to meet with the wedding planner and draw up a guest list.

Their foreman took over for them both while Rio met with the planner and her assistant. To her relief, one of the few tasks left for her to do in preparation for the wedding was to select her gown and those of her bridesmaids. Her two closest friends, whom she'd met at college, had been thrilled to hear she was marrying Kane and that she wanted them to be her bridesmaids.

She made a quick trip to Austin to shop for the dresses, then decided not to choose until she'd seen what else was available in Dallas.

It was while she was packing an overnight bag for a trip to Dallas to shop for a dress and to drop in briefly at Kane's office there, that she glanced over at the book Sam had left for her. Kane had been right about going through the book slowly. She'd already found a couple of notes to Sam from her mother. One was in a sympathy card Lenore had sent when Sam's cousin had died, the second was about the doctor's prognosis of her illness. Both had made her more emotional, and she'd found that giving herself a chance to absorb each new thing was preferable to one long, intense session.

Because she was planning to be gone until late the next day, she finished packing and carefully leafed through the next few pages of pressed flowers, until she came to a page with a single sheet of paper wedged in the seam.

She knew at first glance that it was a birth certificate. The raised stamp of the notary public authenticated the document. She saw her given name, Rhea René Cory, her birth date and the Texas city and county she'd been born in, before her eyes skimmed over the names of her parents.

The name *Samuel Kendall Langtry* jumped out at her. At first, her mind refused the words. A hot, painful pressure began in her chest and shot upward to the top of her head. Her hands started to shake. *Samuel Kendall Langtry.*

No matter how many times she forced her eyes to read the name, it didn't change. Instead of Ned Cory's name in the space where her father's name should be, Sam Langtry's name was neatly typed.

Panicked, she snatched up the document and examined it closely, as if by doing so Sam's name would suddenly become Ned Cory's instead. The name didn't change and the horror she felt made her nauseous.

It took several minutes for her brain to start working again. She remembered the boxes of her mother's things still sitting in her closet. All Lenore's legal papers were there, and Rio felt a glimmer of hope. Of course—her real birth certificate had to be in the small metal box. She'd needed it when she'd got her driver's license and again for college, hadn't she?

She rushed to the closet, yanked the door open and switched on the light. The huge walk-in was more room than closet. It easily held the personal things she hadn't had time to return to the attic, as well as the few boxes of her mother's things.

In moments, she'd found the metal box. She fumbled with the key that had been taped to it, then opened the lid. Her fear and frustration mounted as she flipped through the small selection of papers until she found a folded document at the very bottom of the box.

Rio set the box aside and quickly unfolded the paper. The name Ned Cory was printed neatly in the space where it should have been, and her relief was so profound that she sagged against the wall.

But the movement made the light and shadow cast by the overhead fixture shift over the printed lines. The tiny marks around her father's name caught her attention. She straightened, her heart thumping wildly as a new wave of panic shot through her.

She rushed back into her room for the lamp on the bedside table. She switched on the lamp, then lifted off the lampshade to hold the birth certificate up to the bulb. The series of white marks beneath the dark print were plainly visible. What must have been the white print from correction tape spelled out enough letters on either side of Ned Cory's name for her to read. *Samuel Kendall Langtry.*

Rio lowered the paper. She walked shakily to the dresser and picked up the other birth certificate to take to the lamp for comparison. Both of the notarized documents were identical. Except for the correction tape letters on the one with Ned Cory's name typed over them, the original name in the father space on both documents was Samuel Kendall Langtry.

Rio set the documents down, her head spinning, her body quaking. She barely made it into her bathroom before she became violently ill.

Rio moved through the rest of the morning in a fog, her heart so turbulent with emotion that she was perpetually nauseous. The pain was unbelievable. The horror of realizing she was madly in love with her own half-brother devastated her.

The bitter sense of betrayal added more torment. She'd loved Sam as the father she'd never had, loved and trusted and devoted herself to him. But he'd known all along that he was her real father, or he couldn't have placed a copy of her birth certificate in the book he'd left for her to find. Why had he done that? Why had he allowed her to find out this way?

The letter he'd left for her said, *You've been everything a man could want in a daughter... Remember that I love you, my precious daughter...* The words had been a beautiful compliment when she'd read them. Now they seemed to be a confession of sorts. Perhaps he'd written them to prepare her for what he'd planned for her to find later.

Though she'd never told Sam directly, she'd been certain he'd somehow known that she was in love with Kane. Why hadn't he warned her away from her own brother? The shock of it made her head swim, and yet it was unbelievable that Sam could do such a thing.

She and Kane had marveled at Sam's restraint, she remembered bitterly. The way he and her mother had placed honor and morality above their own desires had been admirable. But the sad truth was that their parents' sense of honor and morality had evidently come late in their relationship. *Too late.*

Rio couldn't imagine telling Kane what she'd discovered. She couldn't bear to put the hellish burden of horror and guilt on Kane that was causing her such agony.

Oh, God, if there was a way to stop the engagement, yet spare him the truth, she had to find it! Anything had to be better for Kane than knowing he'd been planning to marry his own half-sister.

None of the others ever made me feel anything I couldn't walk away from… you had some special power over me, he'd said. Remembering the words increased her agony. He shouldn't love her, he couldn't love her. She'd loved him almost half her life and she was terrified she'd never be able to stop loving him.

Somehow she had to spare him that, she thought wildly. It would be better for Kane, and perhaps some small comfort to her, if he suddenly hated her.

Rio ended up packing a second bag. On her way downstairs with her luggage, she took a stealthy detour to Kane's room and slipped inside. She propped the note she'd written in the middle of the marble tray on his dresser, then set the beautiful engagement ring he'd given her next to it.

Because everyone in the house knew she was driving to Dallas today, she didn't bother to tell anyone goodbye. She carried her bags directly to the big garage, stowed them in the trunk, then got her car out. In seconds she was speeding down the ranch road, heartbroken to have to leave Langtry and everything she'd ever loved.

Kane,

I'm sorry to tell you this way, but I'm afraid I can't go through with our engagement or the wedding. I feel like the spoiled brat who cries for a toy until she gets it, then suddenly loses interest because the toy isn't as wonderful as she thought, or she finds something newer and shinier.

I've left the phone number of my new attorney below in case you need to get in contact with me. Don't worry about my half of the ranch going to the animal rights people. I'm not refusing the inheritance. We can just say that I've taken Sam's death hard and that I need to get away from the ranch for a while.

I think I might go to Colorado. I've hardly been off Langtry my whole life, except for college, and I'd like to see the mountains. Or maybe I'll go to Paris, since I took a year of French. I'll call in a few weeks.

Rio

Kane was brutally tired from his trip and the taxing flight he'd had coming home. One of the engines on the small plane hadn't been running right and air turbulence had been strong. Rio's note hit him like a two-by-four across the chest. He read it again, then growled long and low.

If he hadn't been so tired, he'd have seen past the toy analogy. He'd have realized that everything was even more desperately wrong than it appeared. Particularly when Rio, who craved the massive spaces and distances of Langtry, suddenly wanted to go to Paris. He wouldn't remember for days that she'd never taken a French course in her life.

Rio was numb and she welcomed the lack of feeling.

But if her heart was numb, her mind was roiling with confusion.

Had she been born before or after Ned and Lenore married? Had Ned known all along that she wasn't his child? Why had her mother married Ned instead of Sam?

She knew so little of her parents' backgrounds and families due to their early deaths and lack of information that she had no idea what the answers were.

She couldn't stop thinking about Kane. How was he? Had he found her note? Was he angry? Did he hate her now?

Rio ruthlessly stopped the questions before she could feel the pain they caused her. It had been three weeks since she'd fled Langtry. Though she checked in regularly with her lawyer, Kane had only placed one call to him. As instructed, the attorney had declined to answer Kane's demand to know where she was.

Even if the lawyer had told precisely where she

was, she would have been gone from there by the next morning. She'd rarely spent more than one night anywhere since she'd left the ranch. She'd been driven before by grief and restlessness when she'd roamed Langtry back home. The difference now was that a much greater pain drove her.

Instead of running toward the soothing vistas of the land, she'd fled to the much more complicated vistas of the big city. If there was any way to stop loving Kane, she had to find it.

Rio was sitting in a small, comfortable restaurant in San Antonio one afternoon. Her appetite was even worse in the heat, so she'd only ordered a large iced tea. She was moodily stirring the ice cubes with a straw, her spirits as downcast as ever, when someone stopped by her table.

"Is that you, Miz Rio?"

Ty Cameron's voice was a low, smooth drawl, but it startled Rio to hear her name. She glanced up and forced herself to smile at the handsome rancher.

"May I join you, or are you waiting for someone?" he asked her next.

Rio shook her head and made a tense gesture toward the chair across from her. "Please sit down, Mr. Cameron. I'd be pleased for you to join me."

She felt heat climb her cheeks as Ty sat down and his blue eyes met hers full-on. She should have known better than to come to San Antonio, but she'd felt as if she'd been nearly every place else in Texas these past weeks. Because Ty Cameron was also a businessman who traveled widely, their paths might just as easily have crossed in Dallas or Houston as in San Antonio. On the other hand, being seen by him in San Antonio might project a different message than if she'd met him in another city.

"Did you decide to come down and see what we do for fun in my little part of the country?"

Rio couldn't help noticing how good-looking Ty was. Or that his gaze was intense with male interest.

"I'm taking a sort of vacation," she said awkwardly. "I thought it might be nice to see some of the state."

Ty's gaze gleamed with curiosity the smallest moment before he gave her an easy smile. "I'd be proud to show you around."

Rio gave a tiny shake of her head and a rueful twist of lips. "Thanks, but my feet are already two sizes larger than they were this morning," she told him, then took a nervous sip of her iced tea.

His smile widened as he leaned back in his chair. "What you need is a quiet, comfortable place to put your feet up so you're in a better position to get spoiled. Since hotels and motels tend to lose their novelty quick, I'd like to ask you to come out to the ranch. You can have your pick of guest rooms, and I got a gal who runs my house who's not only the best cook in Texas, but the most dedicated chaperone in the whole southwest."

Rio couldn't help but get the message. Ty was perceptive enough to realize that she'd never consider staying at his ranch unless there were other people around. The mention of a dedicated chaperone was meant to put her at ease and show his respect for her. It also hinted that he might have romantic intentions.

The automatic refusal she wanted to give him suddenly stuck in her throat. She'd been traveling for weeks, lonely and suffering the worst emotional pain of her life. Ty Cameron was a gentleman. She was mildly attracted to him, and he apparently was mildly attracted to her.

It was either common sense or desperation that reminded her that she had little hope of letting go of her love for Kane or loving anyone else, unless she made an attempt to get to know someone new.

She toyed with her straw as she made herself give him a small smile. "Thank you, Mr. Cameron. I think I'd enjoy visiting your ranch."

Cameron Ranch was massive. It took them twenty minutes to drive from the front gate on the highway to the main house. Ty led the way in his car while Rio followed him in hers.

The ranch house was a sprawling one-story adobe with a red tile roof and arches all along the front. The barns, ranch buildings and corrals were set behind the house and to the east. The familiar sights and sounds made Rio homesick suddenly, but she made herself smile as Ty carried her luggage and ushered her into the cool interior of the tiled entry hall.

Ty's housekeeper was a Mexican-American woman with a wide smile and dark eyes that sparkled with good humor. She welcomed Rio effusively, then led the way to a guest room.

At supper that evening, Maria proved to be every

bit the good cook that Ty had boasted, and her happy, gracious presence as she bustled in and out from the kitchen put Rio at ease. Ty was an even better conversationalist than in the past, and his pleasant, easygoing banter lifted her spirits tremendously. Rio ate more at that meal than she had in weeks, but afterward, she became so sleepy that she could barely keep her eyes open.

Ty saw her to her room, then thanked her for accepting his invitation. He asked if she'd like to go for an early ride to see part of the ranch, and seemed pleased when she said yes.

That night, Rio got the best night's sleep she'd gotten in what felt like months. She awoke the next morning less heartsore, and realized that for the first time in a long time, she looked forward to the day.

Before she knew it, Ty had persuaded her to stay at the ranch far longer than the one night she'd meant to. She felt better staying at Cameron than anywhere she'd been these past weeks. She wasn't certain exactly why that was, other than her private speculation that ranch life was far more familiar to her than cities and traveling.

She wished she could credit a romantic attraction to Ty with her improved outlook on life. Though he'd made no secret of his interest in her, Rio could summon no more than a distant appreciation for Ty's sunburnished good looks and a pleasant feeling of friendship toward him.

It was on the fifth morning of her visit that the two of them were down at one of the corrals watching one of the wranglers put a showy two-year-old Arabian gray through her paces on a longe line. They were standing together at the fence when Ty's hand brushed hers.

As if merely touching her had given him the idea, he took her hand and threaded his fingers with hers.

Rio had to force herself not to automatically pull her hand from his. She tried to be patient as he casually rubbed his thumb across her knuckles. The tiny spark of feminine response she felt gave her hope for a mere instant before the sudden memory of Kane's bold touch doused it. Though her heart had felt numb for weeks, the sharp memory pricked it.

"You're as tense as a bronc about to blow, Rio. Are you just skittish, or does my touch put you off?" Ty had been the soul of tact and gentlemanly behavior her whole visit, but his question was to the point.

Rio was overwhelmed by a surge of emotion so strong that she couldn't speak for a moment. She gave his hand a tentative squeeze of apology, then felt his warm, hard grip tighten in silent consolation.

"I'm sorry, Ty," she said softly. She couldn't look him in the eye, she couldn't have looked anyone in the eye while she said, "Your touch doesn't put me off, but it does remind me of someone I'm trying to forget." Her voice broke unexpectedly on the last word.

"Kane Langtry?"

Ty's question had come so quickly that it made her breath catch, but she gave a stiff nod.

He chuckled. "Well, I reckon you came to the right place," he said, then leaned close. His voice went low to drawl out the shameless brag, "I'll have you know,

Rio Cory, that I'm probably one of the few men in Texas who could make you forget all about Kane Langtry…if you're sure you want to forget."

Rio gave another stiff nod. "I have to."

Ty released her hand and slid an arm around her shoulders to pull her against his side. "Then give it time, darlin'."

Rio hesitated, then slid her arm around his lean middle. Neither of them said more as they watched the Arab filly.

Kane stared at the fax the private investigator had just sent. After weeks of waiting for Rio to come home to Langtry or to at least call him, he'd finally given in and hired an investigator. It galled him to have to do such a thing, but he'd done it.

He'd fumed over their broken engagement and the cavalier note she'd left for him. If she'd turned out to be the spoiled brat in her note, then to hell with her. It took all of a day for his fury to burn itself out. The rest of the time since then, he'd carried around an ache that rarely eased. He blamed himself for Rio's flight.

She had taken his father's death hard. The riding accident had to have been traumatic for her, though she'd taken her share of spills before. His sudden proposal, his insistence on a large wedding and his impatience to have it soon might have been too much.

Rio was strong, but she felt things deeply. She was a reserved woman, shy and sometimes self-conscious. Her aversion to drawing attention to herself might have made the prospect of a huge wedding frightening.

He'd concluded all this from what he thought he knew about her. He'd hired the investigator to find her so he'd have a chance to get her back. He'd been so determined to be understanding and forgiving. He'd forgo the big wedding, he'd let her have or do whatever she wanted, as long as she came home with him. He'd meant to do everything in his power to make her happy—until he'd read the last entry of her itinerary.

According to the information that was staring him in the face, Rio might just have caught up with the newer, shinier toy she'd mentioned in her damned note.

"Would you like me to fix you a drink?" Ty asked as he joined Rio in the spacious family room at the back of the huge ranch house after supper.

Rio smiled, more and more at ease with him, but secretly troubled that she couldn't summon anything more than feelings of friendship for him. Her soft, "Nothing for me, thanks," made him nod with clear approval.

"To my knowledge, my mother never touched a drop of alcohol in her life," he said as he crossed the room. "But we've got plenty of soft drinks over here," he added as he reached the liquor cabinet and got down two crystal tumblers. "You could either choose a soft drink, ice water, or I can get you some iced tea."

He glanced back at her and she smiled. "Then pick any soft drink, lots of ice."

"Comin' up," he replied, then turned away to open the small refrigerator and select one.

Rio watched him use tongs to put ice in her glass, then pour the cola. The confidence in his every move fascinated her. Kane bore the same confidence, though his was tinged with a natural arrogance that managed to be more appealing than conceited.

The shaft of pain that speared her heart made her look away from Ty. The moment she'd first caught herself comparing Ty to Kane, she'd been horrified. From then on, her mind had been flooded with scores of examples of parallels and contrasts. She could barely notice anything about Ty anymore that her mind didn't automatically compare to Kane.

The frustration she felt suddenly made her eyes sting. She'd thought her numb emotions would somehow help her get over loving Kane. She'd thought that Ty had potential to help her forget. The bitter irony was that Ty and Kane were as disturbingly alike as they were different. She could barely look at Ty now without thinking about Kane, without longing for Kane.

"Something wrong?"

Rio started at Ty's voice so close, then realized belatedly that he'd walked over to where she sat on the sofa and was holding a tumbler of cola over ice out to her. Her soft "Sorry," and her haste to take the drink covered her lapse.

Or so she thought. Ty sat down next to her so they were touching from shoulder to hip to knee as he stretched his long legs out. He gave a deep sigh, then turned his head to look at her.

"You know, the more I'm around you, the more I realize that old saying, 'Still waters run deep,' must have been written with you in mind." He smiled at her as he reached over and slipped his hand around hers. "You've loved Kane Langtry a lot of years, haven't you?"

Rio faced forward, dismayed at the question. She made a tiny move to pull her hand away from Ty's, but his grip tightened gently. "I don't mean that as a criticism or to hurt you in any way, Rio," he said softly. "I reckon I can live with the agony if I don't thrill the daylights outta you, but I would count it a misfortune if I couldn't be your friend."

The smile she heard in his voice made her turn her head and look at him. He was smiling, a rueful, sexy, masculine smile that communicated his sincerity.

"And because I'd like to be your friend," he went on, "I'm offerin' myself as someone who'll keep your confidence to the grave, should you ever need someone to talk to."

Rio glanced away and looked down at their clasped hands. She put her other hand on top of his and rubbed it fondly. Her soft, "Thanks," was muddled by the emotion clogging her throat. How she'd love to unburden herself to Ty! He was everything she could want in a man, everything she should want in a man, but the fact that he wasn't Kane Langtry was a tragedy for her.

Suddenly she'd carried the pain and the horror long enough. She heard herself make a faltering start, "I loved Kane almost from the moment Sam moved me to the main house. At first, I looked up to him as a sort of brother..."

It took a while for Rio to get the whole story out. By the time she finished, she sat with her head back against the sofa, staring into space, almost too emotionally wrung out to move.

CHAPTER ELEVEN

"PLEASE, Kane, let me go with you," Tracy pleaded. "You're still so angry with Rio—you might need someone there to be a buffer."

Tracy trailed anxiously after him as he got ready to leave the house for the airstrip. Tracy with her large eyes and delicate, aloof ways was clearly upset and more emotional than he could ever recall her being.

On the other hand, in spite of Ramona's efforts, he didn't really know his meek little stepsister. Hell, she'd barely spent any significant time on Langtry after the first six months of his father's and Ramona's marriage, and she'd been a shy, fragile fifteen-year-old then. This weeks-long visit was turning out to be the second longest time she'd ever been around.

Kane paused and gave her a steady look. "Why should you care? I thought you and Rio didn't get along." He watched as Tracy quailed beneath his harsh gaze. She looked too fragile to be a buffer for anything tougher than a carton of eggshells, and she certainly couldn't withstand the verbal brawl he meant to have with Rio.

Tracy looked desperate for a moment before she blurted, "Rio's always been misunderstood. I—I think that's what's going on now."

Kane gave her a cynical smile. "Rio's been a lot more than misunderstood. What makes you suddenly think you're an expert on someone you can barely bring yourself to speak to?''

Tracy blushed heavily, but she was surprisingly dogged on the subject. ''Please, Kane, let me go with you. I think I can help.'' She hesitantly touched his arm, but he politely moved it away.

Ramona had been throwing Tracy at him every day since Rio had gone. He hadn't appreciated his father's attempts to matchmake, but Sam's efforts were nothing compared to Ramona's absolute determination to see the two of them wed. Tracy had seemed embarrassed by her mother's machinations, but she went along with anything Ramona wanted like a trained pet. This could be another ploy engineered by Ramona, and Kane wanted no part of it.

''This is between Rio and me. There's no need for a third party, Tracy, however good their intentions are,'' he told her, then turned away to finish throwing a few things into an overnight bag.

Once he'd zipped it shut and picked it up to turn around, he noticed that Tracy had vanished. He had other things on his mind, so he didn't give her another thought.

He stopped by the office at the bunkhouse to speak to his foreman. The veterinarian arrived and delayed him for another hour. By the time he had one of the ranch hands drive him to the airstrip, his mood was darker and more volatile than ever.

The fact that he then had to deal with Tracy, who was already waiting in the plane and refused to get out, made him so surly that neither of them spoke the whole flight to Cameron Ranch.

*   *   *

Ty was watching a video of cattle from an upcoming cattle sale, so Rio had come down to the stables in search of something to do.

The wrangler she'd watched work the gray filly the other day had offered to let her put the young horse through her paces and Rio had been delighted to do it. She'd finished with the filly and gave her a brisk grooming. It wasn't until she turned the horse into one of the small, shaded corrals that she let herself think of the colt she'd been working with at Langtry. Barbie, as she'd named him after all, had been healing nicely before she'd left the ranch.

All it took was thinking about the young horse to make the melancholy that never seemed to leave her settle more heavily on her heart.

Oh, Kane, how are you? Do you hate me now? She couldn't silence the questions. She'd worked so hard to keep her thoughts away from Kane, but she felt as if she'd been staggering through a mine field, stepping on one trigger after another. Was she doomed to love him the rest of her days? Why couldn't she make herself stop?

Because it can't be true.

For a moment, hope swelled her heart and lifted her spirits until the stark memory of Sam's name on her birth certificate brought her crashing back to earth. Rio reached up and gripped the wood rails of the gate as she struggled to contain her roiling emotions.

Only a coward would have kept silent all those years, she thought bitterly. Only a coward would have allowed her to find that birth certificate and suffer the terrible shock that she had. The part of her heart that was still loyal to Sam reminded her that perhaps he *had* meant to tell her, but time had run out for him before he could.

Tears of heartache and frustration made her eyes smart, but she stubbornly blinked them back. The confused thoughts raced around and around in her head until she was gripping the wood rail of the gate so hard that her fingers stung. When she let go of the rail to look for the cause of the pain, she saw the series of splinters across her fingers. She started to flex her hands, winced, then stopped.

"Damn it," she whispered through gritted teeth, then swung around and stalked toward the main house.

She heard the small airplane circle just as she got to the house. She glanced to the west, and shaded her eyes against the afternoon sun. Ty wasn't expecting anyone until early tomorrow when a buyer was flying in. Her heart thumped oddly when she saw the small plane, but she sternly reminded herself that Kane wasn't the only person in Texas who owned a Cesna. There had to be dozens exactly like his.

Determined not to speculate, she rushed into the house.

"Looks like two more, darlin'," Ty murmured as he used the fine points of the tweezers to catch the tip of the next splinter. Once it was out, he angled her hand differently under the lamp he'd placed on the corner of the desk and went after the last one. When he finished with the delicate job, he let go of her hand and gave a gusty sigh.

Rio inspected her fingers beneath the light while Ty opened the bottle of peroxide and pulled a handful of cotton balls out of the bag to toss into a bowl. He had rounded everything up for her to take care of the splinters herself, then had taken over. Still upset by thoughts of Kane, she'd allowed him to, selfishly hoping...

"All right, comes the hard part," he announced, then liberally poured peroxide over the cotton balls in the small stainless steel bowl.

She looked on when he held first one hand, then the other over the bowl while he swabbed the stinging antiseptic over the tiny spots where the splinters had been.

Rio couldn't help but smile when he took a deep breath and blew strongly across her fingers to soothe the sting of the peroxide. He took another breath and repeated the process, only this time, he glanced over at her face as he did so.

One moment, Rio was looking over into the bright sparkle in his eyes. The next, Ty leaned over and kissed her gently on the lips. He pulled back slightly to whisper, "A kiss to make it better," before he was kissing her again. She felt his hand come up to the back of her head to hold her for a firmer kiss.

The low drawl that intruded was almost a growl.

"Is he the newer, shiner toy?"

Startled, Rio's eyes flew open, but Ty's firm grip kept her from pulling away until he slowly ended the kiss. He drew back, his blue eyes gleaming into hers before he turned his head to look over at Kane.

"What brings you by, Kane?" he asked, the sound of his voice somehow challenging.

Rio stared over at Kane in disbelief, the very sight of his broad-shouldered, lean-hipped body sending a longing through her that was so sharp and went so deep that she could barely breathe.

"I came to see your houseguest. She and I have some unfinished business." The smile Kane gave Ty was anything but civil.

Clearly untroubled by the aggression in Kane's stance, Ty leaned back in his chair and gave Kane a measuring look. "Miz Rio's a guest in my house. And as long as she's on Cameron Ranch, her safety and her happiness are my top priorities."

Kane's expression hardened. "You think I'd hurt her?"

Ty's expression went just as hard. "She came here hurt, Langtry. I'd say she's had enough."

Distressed, Rio suddenly came to her feet. "Please—don't." Both men gave her their complete attention and it flustered her. She looked from Kane to Ty. "Maybe it's best for me to talk to him."

"You don't have to, Rio," Ty told her gently. "I'll abide by whatever you decide, and I'll see that Kane does, too."

Though Rio wasn't looking at Kane, she felt his outrage like a sudden shock wave. She gave a nervous little shake of her head and made herself look over at him. His face was like stone, and his blue eyes blazed at her. It was difficult to tell him, "I'll talk to you, but I need to get something first." Kane started to disagree, so she quickly added, "It will explain better than I can."

Kane glared at her mistrustfully, but didn't object when she started toward the door and left the room. She reached back to close the door behind her, then turned and came to a surprised halt.

"Hello, Rio." Tracy was standing in the hall, squeezing the life out of the small handbag she had in her delicate hands. "I—I've come to tell you something."

Despite her upset at Kane's sudden appearance on Cameron Ranch, Rio couldn't help but be astonished. Not only because Tracy had come, too, but because Tracy was actually speaking to her. Her cold, aloof manner had faded to a nervous, clearly miserable one.

Rio watched, a bit amazed as delicate, perfectly turned out Tracy LeDeux, who'd always been grace personified, fumbled awkwardly with her handbag, nearly managing to drop it before she got out a folded paper.

"Here," she said as she shoved the paper toward Rio. "I'm so sorry."

Rio raised her hand to take it, then saw the backside of the notary imprint on the paper and froze.

Tracy anxiously pushed it against her fingers. "Please—look at it. It's your birth certificate."

Rio pushed it back and shook her head. "No thanks. I already know."

"No, you don't," Tracy insisted, and Rio saw the definite sparkle of tears in her eyes. "Please read it." Tracy's face was anguished, and Rio's own anguish rose.

Again she shook her head and started to step around Tracy. Tracy caught her arm urgently. "S-Sam Langtry isn't your father," she blurted, then flinched as Rio abruptly turned toward her.

"The birth certificates in that book and in your mother's papers are forged," Tracy said tearfully.

Stunned, Rio stared at her a moment, then demanded, "How? The book Sam left me was locked in a drawer and no one but Sam knew about my mother's papers." Oh, God, how miraculous it would be if the birth certificates had been forged, but she couldn't let herself hope.

Tracy was losing the battle not to cry. "My mother found the book and the papers," she got out. "She'd gone into your room when no one knew and she found the letter Sam left you. That was when she found out about the book with your mother's flowers and pictures and keepsakes. S-she went through everything of yours and found your real birth certificate. Then she hired a forger—I don't know who—then found Sam's book and put one fake birth certificate there, then put the other one in with your mother's papers."

The tremor that quaked through Rio made her feel faint. She put out a hand to the wall for support.

"I'm so sorry. I should have done something, I should have said something before now. But I c-couldn't—I know my mother h-has a problem, but I hoped she'd—" Tracy's breath caught as Rio looked at her. "I'm sorry, Rio, so sorry!" Tracy suddenly broke down but she was still trying to push the birth certificate into Rio's hand.

Rio was in shock. Hopeful, yet terrified, she took the paper and unfolded it. The forgeries were so imprinted on her mind that she could see right away that this paper had the slight off-white color of age.

"A-and here," Tracy sniffed. "I s-sent for a copy of your birth certificate. It came two days ago, but I never opened the envelope, in case you needed more proof." Tracy was pawing awkwardly through the handbag, her eyes so blurred by the tears that were spilling down her flushed cheeks that she was having a hard time seeing. She finally got the envelope and passed it to Rio.

A fresh wave of terror gripped Rio's heart. She couldn't bring herself to open the envelope and see for herself, but this was too important for her not to make certain. She hadn't let herself read the name in the father space on the other one, because she couldn't bear to see Sam Langtry's name in the space again.

"So you've known from the day Rio left."

Kane's voice was chilling. It startled both Tracy and Rio, and they turned their heads to look at him. Ty stood beside and just a bit behind Kane, his expression just as forbidding. Either man in a mood as dark would have been formidable. Both standing together, with Tracy the sole focus of their attention, was downright horrifying.

"N-not from the first day. Not until a few days later, but I've known for a long time," Tracy admitted shakily. "I was hoping Rio was going to that county to check the birth records herself. W-when she didn't come back, then I knew I had to do something right away." Tracy sucked in a huge sob, then choked on it a bit. "But I couldn't," she got out.

"You left because of a forged birth certificate?" Kane asked grimly.

Rio nodded. "I'll get them." On legs that shook so badly she could barely walk straight, she rushed toward the guest wing of the sprawling home. Once there, she found what she was after in seconds, then hurried back to the den.

The other three had gone into the den and Rio hesitated in the doorway before she walked toward Kane and handed him the birth certificates Tracy said were forged. Kane took them quickly, then glanced at them a moment before he stepped over to the lamp that was still sitting on the corner of Ty's big desk.

"The one with Ned Cory's name has little correction tape marks beneath it. If you hold it closer to the light, you can see that they spell out Sam's name," she told him, then gripped the envelope and the folded document Tracy had given her.

When she couldn't bear the suspense another second, she made herself unfold the paper. Ned Cory's name was clearly printed exactly where it should have been. Rio walked over to the lamp and used the bright light to inspect it closer.

Relief unlike any she'd ever felt started deep in her heart and spread in slow, repeated waves through her mind, body and emotions until she felt limp with calm. It didn't trouble her now to slip a finger beneath the flap of the envelope and tear it open. The duplicate birth certificate inside also bore Ned Cory's name.

Kane's voice was low. "I could have told you we weren't related, Rio. My father wouldn't have had so many romantic plans for us, and he never would have left me a letter that told me how much a fool I'd be if I let some other lucky bastard marry you."

Rio looked up into the dark fire in his eyes. "He never said anything to me. In my letter, he called me his precious daughter. So, when I found the birth certificate in the book he'd left for me that had been locked up in a drawer you had trouble finding a key for—" She had to stop and look down. She bit her lip a moment while she waited for the surge of emotion to ease.

"I wanted you to hate me," she whispered, then looked up at him. "I didn't want you to know you were planning to marry your own half-sister." She offered him a faint smile that trembled precariously.

"So does this mean..." Kane let his voice trail off. The vulnerability she saw in him just then shook her. Kane had never in his life been vulnerable. "I love you, Rio. Please come home."

Rio's soft "I love you," was the catalyst.

Kane suddenly took the step that separated them and caught her up, crushing her against himself as he buried his face in her hair. Her feet no longer on the floor, Rio wrapped her arms around his neck and dropped the documents as she held on to him and cried.

Moments later, he was kissing her, hard, desperate, hungry kisses that made her wild with passion. Neither of them knew it when Ty took Tracy's arm and quietly escorted her from the room.

"Never leave me, never leave me," Kane chanted gruffly when they paused to catch their breaths. "Oh, baby, anything you ever want, anything you ever want me to do, it's yours. As long as there's breath in my body, I'll get it for you, I'll do it for you, only don't leave me again."

Rio flexed the fingers she'd combed into his thick black hair, ignoring the slight sting as she angled his head so she could kiss him again. The edge of pain in his low voice compelled her to reassure him, but she was too overwhelmed to speak. She couldn't get enough of the feel and taste and male strength of him. She'd been starving...

The warm breeze blew lightly at the Painted Fence, riffling their shirts and toying with Rio's hip-length hair until it danced in the air around her like a sable aura.

Kane watched as she bent down and tenderly placed half of the red sweetheart roses in the bronze vase on her mother's grave. She straightened, then walked around the headstone to the vase on his father's grave and placed the rest of the small, perfect roses there.

When she finished, she straightened again, then glanced his way and smiled a soft, sad smile. He held out his hand, and she walked toward him, bypassing his hand to instead step into his arms to hug him and press her cheek against his chest.

"I love you more than my life, Rio Langtry," he whispered as he tightened his arms around her. His voice was rough with the emotion that still surprised him with its fervency.

"I love you more than mine," she whispered back as she rubbed her cheek against the soft cotton of his shirtfront and snuggled closer.

"Are you feeling all right?" he asked gently, then drew back and slid a finger under her chin to coax her to look at him. Rio complied and smiled up at him, the light sheen of sentimental tears clearing slowly from her beautiful blue eyes.

"Never better. Pregnancy must agree with me. So far, at least," she added, then reached behind her for his hand and brought it around to press it against the slight swell of her belly.

Kane's face went stern. "I still think you ought to stay off horses and stop working with the men."

"I will soon," she told him, then pulled his hand from between them so she could hug him tighter.

She heard the frown in his voice when he grumbled, "That's what you said a week ago. How soon is soon?"

"Soon," she said as if soon was a definite date on the calendar.

As much as she'd loved Kane, as long as she'd loved him, she'd never suspected how wonderful it would be to be loved by him and to love him openly, fully, with all her heart. In the year since their wedding, love had been a revelation for them both. Kane's love and devotion had steadied her, given her confidence and soothed old wounds. Her love for him had gentled him and made him tenderhearted, though he was just as stern and fierce a man as he'd ever been.

"Don't wait too long," he said gruffly. "My nerves are raggedy enough."

Rio laughed and drew back. "You haven't had a nervous minute in your life."

"Not until lately," he groused, but she could see the faint twitch that told her he was trying not to smile.

"I love you, Rio. Somehow I can never say it to you often enough." He brought a hand up to her cheek.

Rio smiled, then pulled her arms from around his lean middle and went up on tiptoe to wrap her arms around his neck.

"Go ahead and say it as often as you like. I'm never going to get tired of hearing it." She pulled his head down to hers and kissed him, deeply, passionately.

Kane suddenly loosened his hold to bend and catch her behind the knees to lift her in his arms. He ended the kiss and pressed his forehead against hers. A rare, boyish smile came over his lips.

"When I was getting the roses for them, I got a couple of armloads for you, Mrs. Langtry. The problem is, every one of them is up in our room. Now the whole bedroom smells like that bath oil you use sometimes when you think you've got to do something extra to get my attention." He paused to place a brief, tender kiss on her lips. "I don't think I can wait till tonight to...show 'em to you."

Rio smiled. "I don't think I can wait until tonight to…see them," she said softly, then held on tight as Kane turned and strode toward the pickup that was parked just outside the gate.

Modern Romance™
...seduction and
passion guaranteed

Tender Romance™
...love affairs that
last a lifetime

Sensual Romance™
...sassy, sexy and
seductive

Blaze.
...sultry days and
steamy nights

Medical Romance™
...medical drama on
the pulse

Historical Romance™
...rich, vivid and
passionate

29 new titles every month.

*With all kinds of Romance for
every kind of mood...*

MILLS & BOON®

Makes any time special™

MAT4

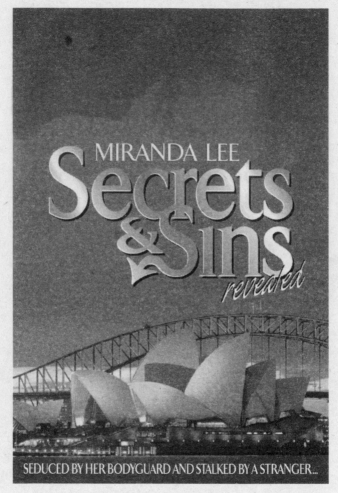

Available from 15th March 2002

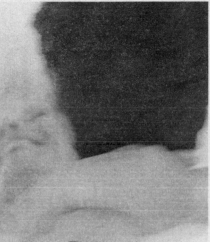

SANDRA MARTON

raising the stakes

When passion is a gamble...

Available from 19th April 2002